EDGE OF
DARKNESS

CHRISTINE FEEHAN
MAGGIE SHAYNE
LORI HERTER

JOVE BOOKS, NEW YORK

JOVE

An imprint of Penguin Random House LLC
375 Hudson Street, New York, New York 10014

EDGE OF DARKNESS

A Jove Book / published by arrangement with the authors

ISBN: 978-0-515-15621-8

PUBLISHING HISTORY
Jove mass-market edition / August 2015

PRINTED IN THE UNITED STATES OF AMERICA

10   9   8   7   6   5   4   3   2

Cover art by Dan O'Leary.
Cover design by George Long.
Text design by Kelly Lipovich.

Penguin
Random
House

CONTENTS

Great

Should be read
before "Dark Carasel
5/17/17

DARK CRIME

CHRISTINE FEEHAN

For Joyia and Pat McGuire.
Much love to you, my friends.

FOR MY READERS

Be sure to go to christinefeehan.com/members/ to sign up for my *private* book announcement list and download the *free* ebook of *Dark Desserts*. Join my community and get firsthand news, enter the book discussions, ask your questions and chat with me. Please feel free to email me at Christine@christinefeehan.com. I would love to hear from you! Each year, the last weekend of February, I would love for you to join me at my annual FAN event, an exclusive weekend with an intimate number of readers, for lots of fun, fabulous gifts and a wonderful time. Look for more information at fanconvention.net.

ACKNOWLEDGMENTS

With any book there are many people to thank. Thanks to Slavica Ostojic for help with the terms of endearment Maksim uses for Blaze. I really appreciate your help.

In this case, the usual suspects: Domini, for her research and help; my power hours group, who always make certain I'm up at the crack of dawn working; and of course Brian Feehan, whom I can call anytime and brainstorm so I don't lose a single hour.

ONE

BLAZE MCGUIRE PULLED her waist-length red hair into a high ponytail at the back of her head and contemplated the fact that she was going to die tonight—and it was of her own choosing. She was going to war with the Hallahan brothers and their mobster boss. They didn't know it yet, but they would be walking right into hell. They thought they were going to have everything their own way, but they were wrong. *Very* wrong. She was a woman. She was young. They dismissed her as no threat to them. And in that they were making a *very*, *very* big mistake.

Her hair wasn't just red hair, it was *red*. Her hair had been that vivid, insane color of red since the day she was born. Hence the name her father had given her, staring down at his newborn daughter who was already giving the doctors hell for dragging her out of her safe little world, kicking and screaming into the cold light, her hair blazing along with her lungs—and that should have given them a clue what they were buying when they murdered her father.

Most people didn't know when they were going to die,

she mused as she rigged the explosives on the door to blow, the charge precise, sending anyone in front of it outward with little blowback into her beloved bar, hopefully leaving it intact. Still, if the charge didn't kill them all before they got inside, she would give up the bar's interior in order to take the battle to them. Tonight, the four Hallahan brothers were going to come for her, and she would take as many of them with her as possible.

Sean McGuire had been a good man. A good neighbor. An even better father. The bar was successful because he had a reputation for being honest and was a good listener, because he genuinely cared about his customers, his neighbors and especially his daughter.

He knew everyone by name. He laughed with them. He attended funerals when they lost someone. He got them home safely at night if they drank too much. He cut off the ones that were spending too much and needed to be home with their families. He was just a good man. A good man some mobsters had pulled out of the bar and beat to death because he wouldn't sign his establishment—the one that had been in the family for two—now three—generations over to them.

Sean had also served in the U.S. Marines and he knew his way around weapons, especially the making of bombs. He was a specialist in the field, so much so that he actually had helped out the local bomb squad the three times they'd gotten calls, because what he knew about explosives, few others did—and what he knew, he taught his daughter.

Blaze had been given an unusual education and she'd loved every minute of it. Her father made it clear he loved her and was always proud of her, and he'd always been patient with her, but he believed in teaching his daughter everything he would have taught his son. He was patient, but he didn't make it easy because she was a girl. She was required to do everything—and learn everything—he knew about defense and offense. She'd soaked up the training.

It had always been the two of them, Sean and Blaze, after her mother left. Truthfully, she remembered her mother as a disconnected woman who was never happy—when she could remember her, and that wasn't often. Her mother left when she was four. They'd never done one single thing together. Not one. She couldn't even recall her mother holding her. It had always been her father.

Sean had been a boxer, a mixed martial arts cage fighter, and he enjoyed the lifestyle. He had always insisted his daughter work out with him. She had—since the time she was two. She grew up boxing her father. Learning martial arts. Street fighting. She learned to fall properly, and she knew all about joints and pressure points. More, Sean hadn't neglected teaching her how to shoot or to use a knife. He certainly hadn't neglected her training when it came to explosives.

Later, when she was ten, Emeline Sanchez came into their lives. Emeline lived mostly on the street, shuffled from one home to another, but mostly on the street. Emeline became a family member and spent a great deal of time crawling in Blaze's bedroom window from the fire escape and sleeping inside with her. Sean pretended he didn't know. Emeline, thankfully, was away from all of this and in Europe, where Sean had sent her to protect her. Blaze had called her, of course, but told her to stay where no one could harm her.

Blaze smiled grimly to herself as she laid out a grid pattern on the floor of the bar and then paused to glance out the window, looking down the street. This had once been a good, decent neighborhood, a place she had called home for twenty-four years. She'd grown up in the apartment over the bar. It was a big building, right on the corner, prime property. The building and three others on either side had been in their family for generations. Her family had taken good care of them and never sold, not even when property values had soared.

Her eyes narrowed as she returned her attention to the delicate job of setting wires throughout the bar. Low. Mid-calf. Thigh. Hip. She crisscrossed them, building a web. Yeah. They should have known all about that redheaded baby when they dragged her father out of his own bar and beat him to death. They'd broken nearly every bone in his body before they killed him. She knew, because the ME had told her.

Rage welled up. Swirled in her belly. Deep. So deep she knew she'd never get it out. She knew why they'd broken his bones. She'd heard about the "persuading" technique from a few of the other business owners. The mobsters wanted properties signed over to them. Her father had already signed his property over to her. *She* owned the bar. They'd gone after the wrong person. And now they were coming for her because she'd sent them an invitation. Not to buy her out, but to war.

She would have signed over the bar in a heartbeat to them if they'd called her and told her they had her father. They thought it was important to teach the neighborhood businesses a lesson: what they wanted—they got. They weren't going to get what they wanted, not even after they killed her. She'd made certain of that. They wouldn't touch Emeline, either. They wouldn't get to harm the last person in the world she loved.

Blaze pressed her fingers to her eyes to stop the burning. She hadn't slept, not in days, not since she'd come home to find her father gone, the door to the bar open and blood on the floor. She'd been frantic, running through the streets like a maniac, calling the cops repeatedly only to be told they couldn't do anything for twenty-four hours, but they'd send someone by. They hadn't. She'd sat alone in the apartment over the bar, arms around her knees, rocking herself, trying to tell herself that her father was strong and he knew how to take care of himself, but there was so much blood.

She taped a knife under the table closest to the stairs. If

she lived through the initial attack, she would have to have an exit plan. She needed to rig the stairs. If she got to the apartment—and she knew the chances were slim to none—she could go out the fire escape and up to the roof. She did that often. She'd been doing that with Emmy since she was ten years old. Once on the roof, she could choose any direction. She would stash a couple of weapons up there as well.

Two factions of mobsters had moved into the neighborhood, the first and the most brutal one, a year and a half earlier. Four brothers—Irish, by the look of them, but Sean hadn't known them and he knew every Irishman in the city—who went by the name of Hallahan. The four were always the front men for one of the crime lords, with their grim faces and their ugly demands, and all four were quick to dirty, extreme violence. And they owned the cops. The police, who had always spent evenings and sometimes days in the bar playing pool, had stopped coming around. She knew they worked for a man by the name of Reginald Coonan. Their boss always stayed in the shadows, but he liked blood, and his men liked violence.

A few weeks earlier, a tall, extremely good-looking man in a business suit came by the bar and handed a business card to her father. It had a number printed on it, nothing else. The man was soft spoken and simply told them if they needed protection, to call that number and someone would come. She found it significant that her father hadn't thrown the card away, even though they both thought this was another crime lord intending to take Coonan's territory from him. Sean had never discussed the incident with her, but he kept the business card safe, right by the phone.

Blaze had never moved the card. But she'd looked at it numerous times. She'd done a little investigating, and it hadn't been easy to uncover the identities of any of the mobsters. She knew now the four Irish brothers. Each of them had grown up in Chicago and had moved to her city. The Hallahans were all short, muscular and very scary. They had come here because it had gotten a little too hot for them where they'd grown up and, she suspected, because Reginald Coonan, their boss, had moved from Chicago as well.

She had very little on the other mob faction. The man that had come so silently into the bar was named Tariq Asenguard. He owned a dance club—an extremely popular one in the neighborhood. He was quiet, only came out at night and owned a very kick-ass estate edging the water. The entire place was fenced—and he had multiple acres, a gatehouse and a boat. She didn't know where he'd come from, and every avenue she'd tried to find out more had been shut down.

Everyone knew he had money—lots of it. He was also a very scary man. He could take over a room just by walking into it. She had heard mixed reviews about him. Half the people who had encounters with him thought he was the devil. The other half was certain he was a saint.

He had a partner. A man by the name of Maksim Volkov, whom no one knew anything about. He was the silent partner. He owned the property bordering Tariq Asenguard's estate, but few ever saw him. He was partners with Asenguard in the dance club. Asenguard, who was there often, was clearly the face of the club, but few actually ever saw Volkov. There was something about his name that made Blaze shiver—and she wasn't given to flights of fantasy. Tariq Asenguard was definitely a badass, but he was cool about it. Maksim Volkov was a question mark. She knew others worked for them, but it didn't matter now. She didn't care. *They* hadn't murdered her father, so therefore, she was throwing in with them. After she was dead.

Methodically, Blaze positioned weapons throughout the room and around the bar, and then practiced getting to them. She didn't want to hesitate. She'd need every second she could get. If nothing else, she wanted to take the Hallahans with her when she went. She felt calm. Nerves would come later. And then the kick of adrenaline.

She glanced at her watch. Outside, light was beginning to fade. The streetlights wouldn't come on. Someone had shattered the old-fashioned gas-looking lights that lent character to the streets. The four brothers almost always came at night. She knew they didn't care if anyone saw their faces and knew who they were. Everyone was far too intimidated by them to come forward.

She just plain wasn't the come-forward-and-testify type, not when she didn't believe for one moment that there would be a conviction. These men had killed her father. They'd tortured him first and then they'd killed him and thrown his broken body out of a moving car, in front of the bar like trash, right at her feet. She hadn't seen them torture or kill Sean, only throw his body at her.

The brothers had timed it just right, coming into the bar at closing when Sean was standing just inside the door. The ME said he found Taser marks, puncture wounds where her father had been taken down, not by one Taser, but by four. The moment they had incapacitated him, they had struck brutally, leaving behind a good amount of blood. It had been Blaze who came home to find the bar unlocked, blood on the floor and her father missing. Even with the blood, the police had done nothing. They promised to send someone around to take a report, but no one showed up. That hadn't surprised her. The cops had all but abandoned her neighborhood and everyone in it.

Blaze looked around the bar. The building—and the bar—was over a hundred years old. She didn't understand why the mobsters spared some of the properties and went after others. Their takeovers seemed random. She'd tried to put together a pattern, but she couldn't find one. It wasn't the businesses they wanted, because after they acquired property, they never opened the business again. The dry cleaner's six doors down was closed. The lovely little grocery store on the opposite corner remained closed, forcing all the residents to go out of their neighborhood to get food.

She made her way up the stairs, leaving a trail of weapons. She didn't believe she would ever get to them, but still, she had been taught to plan for every contingency, and living was one of them. The apartment where she'd grown up was large. She loved it. It had been home all her life.

Home. Her father had done that. Given that to her. He laughed a lot. His eyes lit up when he laughed. So many times he'd whirled her around the living room floor, singing at the top of his lungs, making her laugh with him. He lived life large and he'd wanted her to do the same.

She knew her father dated women, but he never brought them home. She asked him a million times why he didn't remarry, because she was always afraid if she found someone he would be lonely, and she didn't want her father ever to be lonely. Sean simply told her there was no point in settling. It was either the right one or no one. He'd learned that lesson the hard way and he hadn't found the right one, but he was still looking.

She had always wanted that for him. Wanted someone else to love him the way she did, but he'd never let anyone other than Emeline fully into their lives, and maybe that was what made her the same way. She dated, but she never gave herself to anyone, because she knew it wasn't *the* one. Maybe there wasn't really the perfect one. The right one. She'd never know now because she was going to die tonight.

She stashed a go bag with clothes and money on the roof by the fire escape, tucked out of sight. Two more guns and that was it. She was more than ready for war. She stood on the roof for a few minutes just looking out over her neighborhood, remembering the sound of laughter. There had always been the murmur of voices and the sound of laughter. Now there was just . . . silence.

Blaze sighed and made her way back down the stairs to the bar. It was a beautiful bar, all curved mahogany. Gleaming dark wood. The long mirrors and bottles and glasses stacked neatly. She was a good bartender. Fast. Efficient. Flashy. She could flip the bottles and do tricks with the best of them, and some nights her customers called for that. Her father would stand back, shaking his head and laughing, but his eyes were always alive with pride in her.

She'd nudge him out of the way with her hip, tell him, "Let me show you how it's done, old man," and perform a few outrageous tricks, getting the customers fired up. When she did that, they always had a spectacular night. It brought in crowds outside of their neighborhood, so the bar was nearly always full. They didn't lack for money. Still, the mobsters who had murdered her father weren't after the money. They wanted her home. The property. And they were never going to get it, not even after she was dead.

She caught up the phone and dialed the number on the business card, and then idly tapped the edge of the card on the surface of the bar while she waited as the phone rang. Two rings only.

"Talk to me." The voice was soft. Male. Scary beautiful. Just plain scary. Definitely *not* the same man who had come by the bar and left his card. This man had an accent she couldn't place. He sounded dangerous, like a man who didn't have to raise his voice to command a room. Like a man you never—*ever*—wanted to cross.

"I'm Blaze McGuire. Someone with this number came by a couple of weeks ago. The Hallahan brothers killed my father and they're coming for me. An envelope containing the deeds to the properties will be sent to you on my death. Tariq Asenguard and Maksim Volkov will inherit. You can deal with what's left of the Hallahans after tonight."

There was a small silence, and then that voice whispered into her ear. Low. Commanding. "Get. The. *Hell*. Out. Of. There. *Now*."

She froze, her fingers curling around the phone. She felt every single word resonate right through her body. He was good with that voice. Even through the phone she wanted to obey him, and she wasn't all that good at obeying anyone—not even Sean sometimes.

"Can't do that," she said softly. "I'm going to die tonight and they're going to pay. If they don't get inside, and I'm gone, be careful. The entire bar is rigged to blow. One wrong step and you're dead. In the envelope you'll receive instructions for disarming everything. Where you can safely step and what to avoid. How to get through the maze."

"Blaze. Get. *Out*."

He said her name as if he knew her. Intimately. As if he had the right to be worried about her. Protect her. As if she belonged to him. Blaze was a name that, to her, didn't sound feminine. He made it that way, his accent caressing the name, making it something altogether different.

Her tongue touched her upper lip. Her breath caught in her lungs. She had to fight the pull of his voice.

"You don't understand," she said. "And you don't need to. I have to do this. They aren't going to get away with this."

"No, sweetheart, they are not, but this is not the way to do it. Get out of there and wait for us. We are on the way."

The way his voice moved over her body, stroking like a caress, rasping like a tongue, yet still commanded, sent a chill down her spine. More than anything she wanted to obey. Not because she was afraid of dying, but because the note of command in his voice was affecting her in ways she didn't understand.

"Not going to happen," she whispered, her heart pounding. She had the feeling that he was on the move and that he was moving fast. "They killed my father."

"I know, *draga mea*." His voice was even softer. More persuasive. Sliding into her mind so she felt warmth where there was darkness and cold. Where there was rage. Where she had to keep a hold of that rage and not allow whatever was in his voice to warm that cold. "We will handle this for you, and these men will pay. Get to safety. We are on our way."

She pressed her hand hard to her heart. It was beating far too fast. Pounding. Her mouth had gone dry. Even her head hurt, as if by defying him, her physical body protested. It didn't make sense to her. She'd always been her own person, able to stand up to anyone. She didn't want to talk to him anymore, but she couldn't pry her fingers loose from the phone. She just stood there, one hip to the bar because it was holding her up. Her body trembled when she hadn't been trembling faced with certain death.

"I-I . . ." She found herself stammering. All she had to do was put the phone down, but she couldn't. Her fingers were locked around it.

"You do not want your beautiful bar blown all to hell," his voice continued to whisper in her ear. "Our way is so much better. You will continue to have your property. Your home. The neighborhood will be rid of a couple more of the monsters."

So soft. So intimate. As if they were in bed together. Tangled up. Arms and legs. She could almost feel him moving in her. That intimate. And she couldn't drop the phone. She should. But she couldn't. She was mesmerized by his voice. She stared out the large window that took up nearly one entire wall. On the other side of the window were thick iron bars. She'd cried when they'd had to install them. She'd lived there most of her life in complete freedom, and then someone somewhere made the decision to ruin their neighborhood.

"People are dying."

"I know, *draga mea*. We will stop them, but giving them your life is giving them another victory."

"They killed my *father*." The words broke from her. She hadn't cried. She'd refused to cry, not even when she'd told Emeline. Not until after. Not until the men who killed him were dead. "They broke him into pieces and then they killed him."

"I know, *inimă mea*," he whispered.

She had no idea what language he spoke, only that he spoke it with the most intimate accent possible. She didn't dare look away from the window or she would have closed her eyes. To hold his voice to her. Wishing she had known him before she was a stone inside. Before her smoldering fire had grown into a wildfire burning out of control, for vengeance.

"Let us handle this. It is what we do."

"After." She tilted her chin. Straightened her shoulders. "You handle them after." She forced her fingers to loosen their death grip on the phone. His voice was so mesmerizing, so hypnotic, she could almost believe he was a dark sorcerer bent on controlling her through his voice alone. But she wasn't given to flights of fantasy. She had been raised to deal with any issue, and the murder of her father was personal. "After," she whispered again. "You deal with them after."

"Wait. Blaze. Wait for me."

His voice. That voice. It seemed to be inside her. Inside her head. Stroking her from the inside out. She had always relied on herself or her father. Sean had taught her that. Given her that confidence. But his voice and the way it seemed to be inside her head made her feel as if without him, she wasn't Blaze anymore. She was adrift.

"At least do that for me. Go up into the apartment. I'm about four minutes out. We can deal with them together. You go upstairs. I will come to you from the roof after we get rid of them, and we will make a plan. Together."

Blaze closed her eyes and forced her numb fingers to work. She hung up. The moment she did, she felt sick. More, her head hurt. Not a little bit, but pounding, as if by hanging up, something inside her got left behind and set off little jackhammers tripping in her skull. She pressed a hand to her knotted belly and picked up one of the guns lying on the bar. Her hand shook and that shocked her.

She had absolute resolve when it came to bringing justice to her father's murderers. Of course she was afraid. No one wanted to die. But she was confident. And utterly committed to her cause. Still, her hand shook when it never had before. That was how much his voice had shaken her.

A slow heat curled in the pit of her stomach, and a small shiver went down her spine. She would have liked to have met the owner of that voice. Then again, maybe not. She talked with men all the time, the bar separating them. She could laugh and flirt and know there was that boundary no one crossed. His voice had crossed it.

She slammed the magazine into her weapon and turned her attention toward the bar-covered window. She saw the flash of headlights as the car raced down the street toward her property, and she knew instantly it was them—the Hallahans. They had come. Her stomach settled. Adrenaline began to pump. She took a few deep breaths as the big SUV slammed into the sidewalk and screeched to a halt. All four doors popped open and the men spilled out.

She could see them all clearly, even in the waning light, because she'd changed the lightbulbs outside the bar to illuminate the sidewalk. She'd used a high-wattage bulb, uncaring of what the electricity would cost. She wasn't going to be around to pay it. She studied them, these men—no, monsters—who had beat her father to death. They'd broken his bones on purpose to torture him. They could have called her, but they hadn't. They'd enjoyed hurting him.

She didn't take her eyes from the window, watching them come up the sidewalk, moving with confidence, their beefy frames rolling side to side as they moved together to approach the bar.

Everything went silent. Time tunneled, as it often did when a fight was close. Her attention focused on the door. She became aware of her heart beating. Each separate beat.

Each pulse. The ebb and flow of her blood as it rushed through her veins. Everything around her went still. Utterly still. She didn't hear insects. She didn't hear traffic. There were no solid footsteps as the men with their steel-toed boots came closer. There was only Blaze and the gun in her hand.

Her hand was rock steady now, and she took a slow breath, watching the window, keeping an eye on the door handle of the bar. If they touched that, if they opened the door, it would set off the charge.

Without warning, the Hallahans backed up, moving toward their car, all four of them. Blaze took a step forward, her body hitting the bar. She shook her head. They couldn't leave. She moved quickly around the bar and stopped dead, looking at the web of wiring. The entire room was a trap. She would have to spend an hour dismantling everything. What had tipped them off? They hadn't even gotten close to the entrance. Damn. Damn. *Damn.*

TWO

CURSING, BLAZE RUSHED up the stairs, automatic cradled in her arms. She raced through the apartment for the fire escape. Slinging the weapon across her back, she climbed fast and made it to the roof before the SUV with the Hallahans in it was all the way down the street. It was moving fast, but still, as she leaned out over the thick cement wall that formed the railing, she counted all four of them inside the vehicle.

She closed her eyes briefly. She was going to have to take the fight to them, on *their* turf. Never a good idea. In the meantime, she couldn't leave her bar rigged with explosives. If somehow, someone innocently found an entry point, it could be very bad. She sagged against the low wall and slowly pulled the gun from around her neck.

All that preparation and now she would have to start all over. She knew where the Hallahans holed up. They owned a strip joint just a few blocks over. Well, *they* didn't own it. Their boss owned it. The faceless man who called himself Reginald Coonan. There were no pictures of Coonan. None at all. He owned a significant amount of property in her neighborhood as well as a few buildings between her neighborhood and the one where the strip club was located.

There were no properties in residential areas listed as belonging to either the Hallahans or Reginald Coonan, which meant she was going to have to work a lot harder to get to them. She'd start with the club Coonan owned, but she had no idea where they actually lived. She bit out a few more curses and kept staring down the empty street. Nothing moved. "Damn it," she said aloud as she turned back toward the fire escape to climb back down to her apartment entrance. "Just damn it."

Going to the mobsters' lair would be really dangerous and would call for completely different tactics. She didn't want anyone innocent to get hurt, especially the dancers and employees at the club. She couldn't imagine that the Hallahans treated the strippers with respect and would mind if the dancers were caught in a cross fire.

She removed the magazine from her weapon and tossed it on the kitchen table. She had the blueprints for the club. It hadn't even been that difficult to get them. There was an apartment over it, like she had over the bar, but they didn't stay there. They only used it to take their women. So where did the Hallahans actually reside? She would have to do a little surveillance and follow them, find a way to take the war to them without endangering innocents.

With resignation, Blaze started down the stairs to the bar. She had a *lot* of work to do to remove all the traps and explosives she had rigged. She gathered up the weapons she had placed on the curved stairway and made her way to the bar. She'd taken two steps in when arms came around her, large male hands removing the guns.

Blaze whirled around, hands up, ready to defend herself, heart beating wildly, shocked that anyone could have penetrated the bar without blowing themselves up. Shocked that she hadn't heard a sound, or sensed a presence. The man facing her was already a distance away, and she hadn't seen or heard him move. He was utterly still, his arms relaxed at his sides, the guns loosely in his hands.

She drew in a breath, knowing, without him speaking, exactly who he was. This man had to be Tariq Asenguard's silent partner. She'd never seen a more handsome man, not in the traditional sense of handsome. He was too rough for that. But he was undoubtedly sexy and all masculine. His shoulders were set wide. His hair was as black as night and long. He had it pulled back and secured behind his head. That wasn't why she took a step back. Away from him. She wasn't a coward. She really wasn't. But this man wasn't just dangerous. He was terrifying. His eyes were absolutely the blackest—and the coldest—eyes she'd ever seen in her life. There was no expression on his face at all. He was remote. Removed. Ice-cold.

His gaze moved over her and left behind a chill. He didn't miss anything. He took his time, still, not moving a muscle, yet conveying a readiness to deal with anything. All with no expression.

She knew he wasn't in the least bit like the Hallahans. They enjoyed violence. This man didn't enjoy anything at all. He was too removed from it. Too removed from humanity. He didn't seem capable of emotions. He would explode into violence, but he would do it all without even the slightest hint of feeling.

Time slowed down. Tunneled. Blaze couldn't breathe for a moment, taking another step back—toward the bar. She let her gaze shift, just for a moment, to the room. The grid was gone. Something that would take her an hour or so to unravel, this man had done in minutes. How he had gotten in, she had no idea.

She had made a terrible mistake choosing Maksim Volkov and Tariq Asenguard to be allies. She'd told them about the envelope giving them the property when she died. The Hallahans had turned and gone away without so much as pulling a gun. Were the two factions of mobsters really allies, working the neighborhood?

She knew his partner was close, right there in the room. She could feel him, but he was somewhere behind her. She hoped not close. The gun was taped under the edge of the bar. She just had to get to it. They couldn't have cleared out every weapon, not when they had to dismantle the explosives she'd rigged throughout the room.

"Do not try it," he said softly just as she moved.

She ignored the compulsion to allow his words to rule her, already, thankfully in motion, diving over the bar in an aikido roll, tearing the gun from the tape beneath the edge of the bar. She felt the solid slap of the stock in her palm; her fingers closed around it, and then her wrist was caught in a fist so tight she couldn't release the weapon, but she couldn't use it, either. He pinned her arm across his chest, the barrel of the gun directed away from him.

She smelled him. All man. He smelled good. Too good. He felt like a rock, hard and unyielding, as if instead of skin he wore armor. Instinctively she held her breath, afraid to take anything of him into her body.

"I do not want to hurt you, Blaze," he said, his mouth against her ear. "You clearly know what you are doing and I cannot take any chances. Release the weapon to me."

There it was again—that need to obey him. She barely obeyed her own father. Why she felt such a need to do what this man told her—simply from the low, very soft sound of his voice, she didn't know, but she couldn't let him stop her. If she stopped, even for a moment, she'd have to face the sight of her father's body, bloody and broken, thrown out of a moving car to roll onto the sidewalk and come to rest there beside the door of the bar, right at her feet.

Reflexively her fingers tightened on the stock, and she tried to shift her body weight in order to use his weight against him. There was no getting him off-center. He didn't shift, not even when she did. His fingers didn't move. Didn't waver. He didn't seem to even take a breath. She wasn't altogether certain he was human. He was too still. Too confident. Too easily anticipating her every move, and she was very well trained.

"Blaze."

A million butterflies took wing in her stomach. That had never happened to her before. Never. She didn't have butterflies. She didn't react physically to men. She especially didn't react when the man was an enemy and her father's body had barely been put in the ground. Still, she nodded slowly because she had no other choice. One arm, feeling like an iron bar, was around her belly, and he held her there, immobile.

She nodded again. Swallowing. Trying to get her brain to think past feeling like a captive, an immobile one, and come up with a plan of action. Trying not to feel what his body felt like against hers. Not to be aware of herself as a woman—and him as a man.

"Let go of me," she hissed. She kept her voice low as well, but it didn't come out commanding the way his did. She sounded shaky. She felt shaky.

"Release the weapon to me and I will step back. I am not going to harm you. Neither is Tariq. We came to help you. You asked us, remember?"

She relaxed her fingers, allowing him to take the gun from her hand. The iron bar disappeared from around her belly and he was gone, moving so silently she didn't hear him, but she knew he was no longer pressed up against her. He'd taken all the warmth with him.

"I don't remember asking you to come here until *after*," she reminded. She turned, allowing her gaze to sweep the bar. She caught sight of the other one. Tariq Asenguard. Her heart accelerated even more, if that was at all possible. He looked as remote as his partner. She thought a nightclub owner would be all about fun and passion. These two men were ice-cold. "In fact, I've totally changed my mind and would like both of you to leave."

"I am Tariq Asenguard," the one to her left introduced himself. He waved a hand toward the other one—the one with the mesmerizing voice. "This is Maksim Volkov. We were very sorry to hear about your father. He was a good man."

She winced. She couldn't talk about her father. She couldn't think about him. If she did, she would totally go to pieces, and the men who had murdered him would get away with it, just like they got away with murdering others.

"Mr.—er—Asenguard—I appreciate you both getting here so fast, but the Hallahans turned tail and ran. Now I'm going to have to take the fight to them . . ."

Maksim shifted his position, and her gaze jumped to his face. His expression hadn't changed, but emotion flared in his eyes. Something dangerous moved there and was gone. He was back to ice-cold. No, glacier-cold. But his shift, as minute as it was, had moved him closer to her.

She could feel his heat again. Not in a good way. He was absolutely expressionless, but she felt fury radiating off of him. It sucked the air from the room and replaced it with something heavy and oppressive. She took a step back and bumped the bar. He took a step toward her and his step was a *lot* longer than hers. He was in her space. Both arms extended so that he gripped the bar on either side of her, effectively caging her in.

"Are you *trying* to get yourself killed? Is that your ultimate goal here?"

He bit the words out between very white teeth. *Very* white. She found herself staring at his mouth. At those teeth. Strong. Straight. But not perfect, not when two of them came almost to a point and looked—sharp. Her heart jumped at the sight of his mouth. Sensual. Hot. Defined lips. Straight nose. Aristocratic. Still, those eyes, so cold. So black. A dense glacier that had never been touched.

"Of course not." She managed not to stammer, but he was too close. His body heat seeped into her pores. His scent swirled in her lungs. She held her breath, desperately trying to keep from inhaling him. He was invading. Taking her over.

"You. Are." He bit the words out around his beautiful, *clenched* teeth.

She opened her mouth to protest and then closed it. Light dawning. Was she? She felt guilt that she hadn't been home. She felt guilt that her father had signed the properties over to her. Her name had been on the deeds ever since she was born, but he'd quitclaimed them on her twenty-first birthday.

"I was out that night. It was my shift, but there was a class I wanted to take on bar tricks. Jimmy Mason was teaching the class and he's the acknowledged master. I thought it was a once-in-a-lifetime opportunity . . ." She trailed off, realizing she was blurting out private information to total strangers. Worse, something inside her was shifting. Breaking apart. She couldn't let that happen.

She couldn't think about the terrible night of waiting. Of knowing. Of trying to hope. Of utter despair. She'd been so desperate, she'd driven to the strip club, but the Hallahans weren't there. Or if they were, no one was saying.

"Inimă mea," Maksim said softly. His hand came up to slide along her cheek. "I am sorry about your father. He was a good man. We were out of town. The moment you called, we were on the move." The pads of his fingers, whisper soft, traced over her high cheekbone and then swept down to the curve of her jaw as if he was memorizing her. "These men will be taken down. But not by you. Let us handle this."

His voice slipped inside her mind. So gently. So softly. Almost not there, but still she felt it—the compulsion to obey him. To give him what he wanted. Still, she shook her head resolutely.

"It's too late for that. They murdered him and then they threw him out of a moving car like so much garbage right at my feet. *I* have to do this. You don't have to understand. I don't expect you to understand." Nice girls didn't plot revenge. They didn't rig a bar full of explosives and hide weapons from one end of the bar to the next. Nice girls did what they were told. She hadn't been born nice. She hadn't been raised nice. She didn't *feel* nice.

Blaze didn't like the fact that she was showing this beautiful man just who she was inside. She knew he saw—saw the need for vengeance and her resolve that she would bring the fight to the Hallahans. She closed down all reaction to this man. She wouldn't think about him or dream about him or fantasize. She didn't care if he thought her the worst person on the face of the earth. And she didn't care if he didn't understand. It only mattered that she did.

"Then we do it together. You cannot take them down alone, and I think you know that." The pad of his thumb moved to her lower lip. "We do it smart and we do it right. Blowing up your bar is not the right way to go about it, Blaze."

If she wasn't going to survive, it was. But living . . . that meant she kept the bar and her home. That meant she faced the fact that her father was dead and she was guilty because she'd insisted on going to take Jimmy Mason's "cool" class on doing tricks while fixing drinks. Her father was old-fashioned, but he'd gone along with her learning because she'd had fun flipping the bottles in the air and juggling them back and forth with him. He'd done that—for her. He'd taken her shift—for her.

"Blaze."

There it was again. Only her name. But the way he said it, as if he knew what she was thinking and he was comforting her.

"You have to know they would have found a way to take your father regardless of where or when they did it. The attack was not in any way random."

She couldn't think about that yet. His broken, bloody

body. She turned her head away from his cold, black eyes. Eyes so black she felt she could see all the way into the very depths, and she didn't dare look. She didn't understand why she was so drawn to him. The man or the voice. Especially now.

"I know. They want the property, but I don't understand why. They shut down the businesses the moment they acquire the buildings. What's the point? They aren't making any money from the businesses," Blaze said.

Tariq moved closer and when he did, Maksim dropped his hands to his sides, but he didn't get out of Blaze's space. If anything, he took a step closer so that his body brushed hers, turning as he did so to face his partner. Blaze thought it might be the opportune time to try to slide away from him and the bar, but he wrapped an arm around her belly and tucked her front against his side.

Possessively. Protectively. There was no mistaking the gesture. Not even for her when she knew nothing about men. He was claiming her. No man had ever done that before. No man had *dared* to. She didn't put up with it. She didn't respond to it. At least not until she'd heard his voice on the phone. Not until he was so close to her that with every breath she drew, she pulled him deep into her lungs.

Not only was she aware of Maksim Volkov as all male, but she was suddenly aware of herself as a female. Her body, instead of being the body she'd trained for combat from her second birthday, was soft and pliant. Needy. Hungry. *Aching*. Her breasts hurt. There was a throbbing between her legs, and she felt every single pulse beat in her most sensitive core. Right there.

"I am going to do another sweep of the bar," Tariq said, ignoring Maksim's body language. "Get her upstairs and settled. We still have to track the Hallahans tonight."

She sent the man a scowl. "I'm going after them, not you. No one else is taking out the men who killed my father. Not unless I'm dead. That was the point of the phone call, to tell you about the deeds, so hopefully if I fail you would take over."

"Your plans are going to have to change, Blaze."

It was Maksim who answered, not Tariq, and his voice was that soft command she recognized from her phone call. There was no doubt it had been Maksim who answered the phone. She found herself shivering, icy fingers traveling down her spine. He was not a man to cross. She got that. She got that neither of them wanted her to kill the Hallahans. She straightened her shoulders and lifted her gaze to Maksim's. Forced herself to stare into the twin glaciers.

"Is there a reason you don't want me to kill them? Are you allies or something in this takeover of the neighborhood?" She didn't care if she sounded melodramatic or like she was quoting a line from a bad mobster movie. She needed to know.

Tariq ignored her. He turned his back to her and began a slow perusal of the bar. She had the feeling he'd lost interest in her and the conversation. He was wholly focused on what he was doing—and she couldn't see that he was doing much.

Maksim's fingers settled around her biceps. Gentle. Barely there. Still, she felt shackled, and the wild part of her wanted to fight.

"Do not," he said softly. "If you fight me, you will not win and then you will be afraid of me." He tugged gently and took a step toward the stairs.

"Do you read minds?" She was joking, of course. Clearly she didn't have a poker face, and he could read everything she was thinking. She went with him because it was the least line of resistance. If he thought she was cooperating with him, then he'd go away and she could do whatever she wanted to do.

"Yes."

She glanced at him as they moved up the staircase toward the apartment. His expression hadn't changed, not even when he joked. She didn't think he was human enough to joke and that surprised her. He still looked as remote and as cold as he had when she'd first laid eyes on him.

"I bet you can play poker," she muttered, annoyed.

"I enjoy the game once in a while."

"Do you win?" Distracting him.

She bent to retrieve a gun she'd slipped between the ornate dowels of the railing. The moment her fingers closed over the stock, his hand wrapped tightly around hers. His body covered hers, pressed her down so she couldn't straighten.

She hadn't realized he was a big man. He was so well proportioned, she hadn't been able to tell he was so tall, or that he was so enormously strong. Wrapped around her like he was, she felt the muscles in his body. The sensation was like being enveloped in steel. There was no budging him.

"Relax," she said, forcing the tension from her body. "I was just getting the gun so it wasn't lying out in the open."

His arm locked around her belly like a vise. He dragged her upright as he removed the gun from her hand. "Not only do I read minds, I hear lies. You do not know me yet, so there is no trust between us, but know I do not like lies. Especially coming from you."

He was telling her something important, but she wasn't certain what it was. His statement wasn't just about lying. She let her breath out and tried not to feel his body. Willed herself not to react. She didn't understand why her body had chosen him. Why her muscles went soft and her blood went hot when she was so close to him.

"I can hear your heartbeat," he said softly. "I can see it, right here." He touched her pulse on the side of her neck.

It was all Blaze could do not to jerk away from his touch. The pad of his thumb felt like a brand against her skin. She was aware that her heart pounded, raced even. Her breath felt ragged and labored, caught in her lungs in spite of her determination to remain impassive to him.

She went very still. "Please don't touch me."

"I am not hurting you."

She steadfastly refused to look at him. She didn't want to be alone with him in her apartment. "I know."

"I will not hurt you. I give you my word that I will protect you with my life."

She closed her eyes briefly; her heart jerked hard in her chest. Her stomach performed a slow roll, and deep inside where she shouldn't even acknowledge him, she felt him and there was a reaction, a hot seep of liquid, a clenching that reminded her she was a woman and he was a very, very attractive man.

He meant that promise. She tried to tell herself this stranger was playing her for some agenda of his own, but she knew better. She didn't understand what was happening, or why she was so drawn to him, but she had the terrible urge to turn her body fully into his and wrap her arms around him.

Intellectually, she knew the situation was intense. She had expected to die. She'd planned to die. She'd just buried her father. Only a few days before, his broken, dead body had been tossed at her feet. She could understand why she would be feeling raw and vulnerable—even needy, when she wasn't a needy person.

Maksim's hand transferred to the small of her back and he urged her to continue climbing the stairs to the apartment. "I realize that it's difficult to wait, *inimă mea*. The Hallahans have a master. One who sends them on his errands and decides who will live and who will die. And how. They are his puppets. We have to find the man behind them."

She stumbled at the doorway, and his hands steadied her. "I have to go after them." She sounded as desperate as she felt. She knew she did. But if she stopped, if she had time to sit down and process, she'd have to face her father's death. She couldn't do that. She just couldn't.

Maksim reached around her and opened the door for her,

waving her into the apartment. "We will get them. We will. But you need to be on your game, not grieving and ready to die. Willing to die." He pulled the door shut behind them, closing them together inside her home. It felt—intimate.

The moment the door closed, Maksim shifted position. He glided. Or the floor moved. However it was done, she didn't actually see him move. Suddenly he was standing in front of her. Close. The fingers of his hand curled around the nape of her neck and he leaned even closer.

"You are not going to die, Blaze. I will see to that. If you intend to be a part of this hunt, make up your mind to that. Because. You. Are. *Not.* Going. To. Die."

THREE

WHEN A HUMAN male waited for years to find the right woman—and he found her—he guarded her as best he could and treated her right. When a Carpathian male had waited for *centuries* to find the *only* woman who could save him, he didn't just guard her. He surrounded her with every protection possible. Maksim Volkov stared down at the woman who held the other half of his soul.

Carpathians rarely saw the outer shell of a person. For him, his lifemate was the only and the most beautiful. Always. He could see, though, even by human standards, that his woman was truly beautiful. She was also a warrior, trained to fight, and she had every intention of bringing that fight to the men who had killed her father.

Blaze stared back up at him with her amazing green eyes. She thought she was good at hiding her emotions, but he had been around for centuries, and even without the ability to read her mind, he was more than adept at reading expressions. There was defiance in the set of her mouth. That beautiful mouth kept his attention riveted to it. Defiance was in the set of her chin—the chin he wanted to taste. Her rebellion showed in the glitter of her green eyes.

There was something wild in her. Something untamed that matched the wildness in him. He was predatory. As high up on the food chain as it got. He didn't know anyone who defied him. Or disobeyed him. Or looked at him with feigned innocence, all the while plotting to do *exactly* what she wanted—but Blaze was doing just that.

For his species, there was only one woman to complete a male. She didn't have to be born a Carpathian. She could be a human psychic, they'd learned, and she could be born in any century, in any part of the world. It was a big world and there were many centuries to hunt in. Finding his life-mate was truly like looking for a needle in a haystack—but with even worse odds.

"Did you hear me?" he asked, keeping his voice pitched low. She was susceptible to his voice, although compulsions didn't seem to work very well on her.

He had spent over a thousand years in a gray world. Without any emotion whatsoever. It was a void that few could stand and remain honorable. After the first few centuries, it was impossible to believe one would find a lifemate. He had lived a life of honor, changing as much as possible to fit into each century, but he lived in a bleak world where only his ability as a warrior was important—as a hunter of the vampire. The vampires were those of his own kind who had chosen to give up their souls. Every second he remained alive during those endless, bleak centuries, he was at risk to become the very thing he hunted—until he had picked up the phone and heard her voice.

"I heard you," she replied, just as soft.

He crowded her body, but she didn't move away from him. Blaze McGuire was no shrinking violet. She was afraid of him, but not because she thought he might harm her. She was too smart for that. She was afraid of him for all the right reasons. He was going to change her world and she knew it. She just didn't know how or to what extent.

"I can get the information we need on Reginald Coonan," Blaze volunteered and made a subtle movement to escape.

Maksim stepped into her, forcing her to take a step back. He did it again and she retreated a second time. That was as far as she could go. The door was at her back. "Reginald Coonan does not exist," he informed her, still keeping his voice pitched low.

For the first time that he could remember since he was a child, he was uncertain how to proceed. She belonged to him. There was no denying that. The moment he heard her voice, he saw in color. Vivid, brilliant, overwhelming color. So bright he'd had to close his eyes against the blinding beauty.

Taming Blaze was not going to be easy, and one wrong move would set him back. He didn't have time to make mistakes with her.

"Of course that isn't his real name," Blaze said. "I know that. I know he made up his entire history, but he's still collecting properties in that name." She looked him directly in the eye. "What exactly is going on here?"

He felt the impact of her gaze hitting him right in the gut. Green gems weren't as beautiful as her eyes. He hadn't realized he'd be so susceptible to a woman—even his own lifemate. He hesitated, unsure what to say. How much to say.

"Maksim," she said quietly, "I don't like surprises. You're a huge surprise. I'm not going to pretend I don't feel your pull, because I do, in a big way. But something is happening here I don't understand, and if you're feeling anything at all for me, like I am for you, it's best if you're just honest with me. If you're not, this is going nowhere."

He heard the ring of truth in her voice. He couldn't help but admire her. She laid it out for him, just like that.

"A lot of people say they want honesty, Blaze, but they

really cannot handle the truth. If I give you reality, the absolute truth, you could have a difficult time accepting it—and me. And you will accept me. That much I will tell you straight. You are not walking away from me, not when I spent lifetimes searching for you."

She didn't so much as raise an eyebrow at his carefully worded answer. She didn't look away. She continued to look him straight in the eye, something most humans found uncomfortable. He moved in her mind. She'd heard the word *lifetimes*. She hadn't even flinched. Not physically and not in her mind—almost as if she knew.

"Reginald Coonan is not human. The Hallahans are, but he isn't. He's using them because he cannot go out during the day and he has learned, over the centuries, if he wants to remain alive, it is better to stay in the background and have his pawns take the heat. That is one of the many reasons we interfered tonight. Aside from the fact that I do not want you dead, we need to find him. The Hallahans can lead us to him."

She reached behind her for the wall. This time, her lashes fluttered and he felt her inhale. He felt it, because he'd moved that close. So close he could feel her breathing.

"You probably think I am crazy. Most humans who hear something like this would, but you asked, so I am giving you the truth." But she didn't think he was crazy. She had gone still inside. He stayed in her mind. She was waiting. So still. Knowing, not wanting to know, but knowing all the same.

"If he isn't human," Blaze said carefully, "what is he?"

"Have you been following the murders in the city? Mostly homeless and prostitutes, but a few have been business owners from this neighborhood. Not the ones the Hallahans beat to death for show, but the ones torn to shreds, as if a wild animal has killed and partially eaten them? The ones with very little blood left in their bodies?"

She put a hand on his chest and exerted pressure. "You

can stop right there. We've already been approached and we said no. My father wasn't about to be recruited by fanatics believing in vampires and hunting just about anyone they didn't like. That kind of witch hunt belongs in another century, not this one."

There was a bite of contempt in her answer. He didn't flinch. He'd expected it, although he was a little shocked that she and her father had been approached. Although he shouldn't have been, he realized. Sean McGuire and his daughter were both highly skilled—and Blaze was psychic. If that was common knowledge or if she had ever been tested, she would be on the society's radar. He knew she had to be psychic because she was his lifemate.

"The ones who call themselves the Society for the Preservation of Mankind. I am not affiliated with them, and they wouldn't know an honest-to-God vampire if the monster came up and bit them on the neck."

"Move back," she cautioned when he didn't budge.

There was a threat in her voice. In a strange, perverse way, he liked that she felt confident enough to threaten him. He liked that she was a warrior and she didn't hesitate to defend herself.

"Blaze, you wanted the truth. At least hear me out. Did you think I would tell you this and expect you to take it on faith alone? I have proof of the things I am telling you. But you need to understand, attacking me is not going to work. I have stated repeatedly that I do not want to hurt you. I have no intention of harming you. You asked for this and against my better judgment, I am giving you the stark truth."

He studied her face. She was scared, but she wasn't exactly *not* believing him. She didn't want to know the truth. Somewhere, deep inside her, she was already prepared to hear this, but she didn't want it.

"Please will you step back?" This time she asked. "I can't think straight when you're so close to me."

Even as she softly made the request, her foot came down

hard on his, and her open palm rushed toward his nose. At least that was her intent. Maksim shifted before she could complete the maneuver. Her foot came down where his had been and her hand shot out hard and fast, but he dissolved right in front of her eyes. Was gone. Blaze gasped and took two steps forward, frantically looking around her living room trying to find him.

Maksim locked one arm around her belly from behind and caught her head in a firm grip with the other. He sank his teeth deep, part in need and part to teach her a lesson. The instant he did, he knew it was a mistake. He had fed thousands of times and he had never felt anything when he did, not that he had memory of. This time, everything was different. So different, and he hadn't counted on that.

He was vaguely aware of her gasp, the soft cry of pain when his teeth bit into her soft, exquisite flesh, her body struggling against his tight hold. He was enormously strong, and rather than aggression or fear on her part, he felt each movement of her body as erotic. The smoldering burn he'd felt, from the moment he heard her voice, flared into a bright, hot fire.

Feel me, sufletul meu. My soul. The very air I breathe. He didn't give her the translation in her mind, but he meant every word. She was the other half of his soul. He had no time to court her properly. They were in a war and he needed to get her on his side, but more than that, he needed her to know he would protect her from anyone and anything—even herself. *Feel us. You belong to me.*

He didn't try to soothe her. He didn't need to. She felt the strength of the pull between them all on her own, without compulsion. A need that went so deep, that was so strong, Maksim couldn't possibly resist—so how could she? He let himself feel everything. The beat of her heart matching the rhythm of his. The taste of her, bursting in his mouth like a fine wine, like the blaze of her hair, fiery and passionate, wild and untamed. It was all there in her blood. So rich.

Perfection. He was instantly addicted and knew he'd never get enough of that taste.

Te avio päläfertiilam. You are my lifemate. *Éntölam kuulua, avio päläfertiilam.* I claim you as my lifemate. *Ted kuuluak, kacad, kojed.* I belong to you.

He whispered the vows that would tie their souls back together for all time, meaning every single word. The ritual binding words were imprinted upon him before his birth and he had thought, through the long centuries of gray, bleak, endless nothing, that he would never have the opportunity to say them to his woman.

Essentially, in the Carpathian world, they would be married, but so much more. They were tied for all time, one life to the next. Always together. Bound by their souls. Once bound, never able to be torn apart. He hoped to bind their hearts together as well.

Élidamet andam. I offer my life for you. *Pesämet andam.* I give you my protection. *Uskolfertiilamet andam.* I give you my allegiance. *Sívamet andam.* I give you my heart.

She began to struggle. Her body was on fire, just as his was. He felt the way her soft sank into his hard. She molded herself to him, but she heard the vows he pushed into her mind, and she felt the tiny unbreakable threads tying them together. He felt them, and joy burst through him. She felt them and panicked. Still, he couldn't stop, even knowing her just from the exquisite taste of her blood.

The knowledge was there on his palate, in his body, soaking into every cell and organ. She was more than wild. She was feral, a woman who went her own way and made her own decisions but could ignite with the right man, turn into a storm of passion that would threaten to consume them both. And she was his.

He tightened his hold on her. *Be still, Blaze. You have no need to panic. I could never hurt you.*

What are you doing? You're scaring me.

He was shocked at how strong the psychic connection

between them was. She had no problem speaking to him, mind to mind. She was frightened, but not because he was taking her blood. She was frightened at the words he pushed into her mind and the way he made her feel. The bond that was already growing so strong between them. She didn't understand the ancient Carpathian language, but he interpreted for her in English—in her language, so there was no mistaking what he was doing.

Maksim was determined that he didn't deceive her. She had asked for honesty and he was being honest. This was the truth between them. She was his lifemate and there was no escape. None. No out. She had to learn to live with him and he with her. He needed her to survive. His soul needed her to redeem him. Without her, he had nothing and he never would. Everything that had gone before, his very honor, would be in jeopardy. And that was not going to happen.

Sielamet andam. I give you my soul. *Ainamet andam.* I give you my body. *Sívumet kuuluak kaik että a ted.* I take into my keeping the same that is yours.

"Stop. Stop right now." She whispered the plea. "Maksim, you have to stop."

He felt her slump against him and instantly swept his tongue across the twin pinpricks in her neck, his arms sliding behind her back and knees. He lifted her and carried her to her bedroom, to lay her gently on the thick comforter there. He didn't know if she was pleading with him to stop because she felt the vows every bit as strong as he did, or if she felt weak and that frightened her.

She hadn't lost consciousness, but she was very vulnerable. Her green eyes had gone from burning to glittering. That defiance was there, the need to struggle, to fight, but she had too much control. She knew she was helpless. He'd allowed her to feel his strength and he'd shown his ability to shift. He had begun the binding ritual and she felt that as well. She was dealing with shock and her mind trying to tell her that what she saw with her own eyes couldn't be true.

What she heard in her mind and what she felt, had to be impossible. But all along she had known the truth. She hadn't wanted to accept it—however she'd first learned it—but she had known of his kind or at least of the undead.

Maksim had taken her blood and he hadn't put a compulsion on her. He hadn't calmed her. She had remained calm. He sensed the moment the pain was gone and erotic pleasure took its place. She felt that. He felt it with her.

"I am not a vampire, Blaze," he reassured her. "Vampires kill their prey. They enjoy the rush they feel, like a drug addict's high. The more they terrorize their victims, the more adrenaline is pumped into the blood and the higher they get. I am Carpathian. Without finding our lifemates, we are in danger of becoming the undead."

As he gave her the explanation, he slowly unbuttoned his immaculate black silk shirt to expose his chest. Her eyes followed his movements, mesmerized by his actions, but she heard him. She was listening to him. Her tongue touched her bottom lip and he groaned. Need was on him—a need he had never experienced.

Like all Carpathian males, he had centuries to study every subject, to learn and acquire knowledge. He knew virtually everything there was to know about sex and how to please a woman—and how to teach his woman to please her man. Over the centuries he had had plenty of time to be familiar with the things that intrigued him and he knew he would want.

"You wanted honesty between us, Blaze," he reminded gently. "I tried to tell you. You could not hear the truth, so showing you seemed a much better idea."

He gathered her into his arms, ignoring the hand that fluttered against his chest as if she might find the strength to push him away. His fingers sifted through the fiery red silk at the top of her head, the feel of it against his skin pushing his hunger higher. Blood raced through his veins and centered in his groin. Hot. Full. Aching enough to be painful. He loved the feeling just because he *could* feel it. That was almost as addicting as her taste.

Her green eyes remained steady on his. "What are you doing? Tell me."

"Claiming you. You cannot pretend you do not feel it, too. You know you belong to me. I am exchanging blood with you in the way of my people."

She shook her head, and her tongue touched her lower lip again. "Maksim. I'm not one of your people. I can't take your blood."

"You are my lifemate. This is what lifemates do."

Her eyes widened when he lifted his hand and showed her as he allowed his fingernail to grow into a longer, razor-sharp nail. She gasped as he drew it across his chest, a line over the heavy muscles there. At once beads of ruby red appeared. She shook her head again, her gaze clinging to his in a plea, and then dropping to the red line. Already, because she was his lifemate and there was no denying that fact, she felt the pull between them.

His palm fitted to the back of her head and he gently pressed her against him. She strained back, but there was no way to stop his insistence. The moment her lips touched his chest, fire shot through his veins. The rush was incredible. Her mouth moved, trying to avoid the ruby red line. He kept pressure on the back of her head, refusing to allow her to turn, so she had no option—her mouth remained against him.

Ainaak olenszal sívambin. Your life will be cherished by me for all my time. *Te élidet ainaak pide minan.* Your life will be placed above my own for all time.

She gasped and her tongue touched the line. He knew the instant his taste burst through her mouth like champagne bubbles. His blood was for her. *He* was hers. All of him, and his taste was just as addicting to her as her taste had been for him. There was no way she could resist, and she didn't try to.

Blaze was tentative at first, using her tongue to lick delicately at his offering. Then her mouth was on him and she suckled, drawing his essence—his lifeblood—into her body. Taking him in. Accepting him. Taking what belonged to her. His body was on fire. She was in his lap, and he shifted her in his arms so that she fit more closely into him. His cock, full and throbbing with life, snuggled against her buttocks, and that brush, even through her jeans and his trousers, sent hot flames licking across his body.

"*Te avio päläfertiilam.* You are my lifemate. *Ainaak sívamet jutta oleny.* You are bound to me for all eternity. *Ainaak terád vigyázak.* You are always in my care." He whispered the words aloud, finishing the ritual binding. He brushed a kiss on top of her head, looked around the little apartment and then down at her as she completed the first blood exchange between them. "*Susu,* I am home."

When he knew she had taken enough from him, he gently slid his finger against her lips, between his chest and her mouth. He did so reluctantly because her mouth on his body felt like heaven. "Enough, Blaze." He tipped her head up and brought his mouth down on hers.

He thought to be gentle, but the taste of blood was there, and then he passed that and into the sweet haven of her mouth. Her own taste was there. Just as wild, just as passionate as her blood. The promise of her body was there. Just as wild. Just as passionate. He wanted that. He even needed it.

His mouth was brutal and still she opened for him. Kissed him back just as savagely. Just as ravenous. As if she was just as starved for him as he was for her. He took her mouth over and over. Hunger swept through him. Shook him. His control slipped even more as her hands moved up his bare chest, taking in as much skin as possible. He felt her touch like a brand.

Maksim yanked at her blouse, ripping the material down the front. She didn't so much as flinch as she glanced down at her breasts, cupped in a navy demi-bra. He saw the flare of heat in her eyes right before she slammed her mouth back on his. His hand went to the tie in her hair, and he dragged it off so all that fiery red silk cascaded down around them. Instantly he buried both hands in it, running his fingers through the fiery strands over and over, feeling the sensation vibrate right through his cock.

He needed to be free of the material stretching across his fierce erection. He shifted her again, still kissing her, setting her on her feet so he could stand. He was tall. Much taller than she was, and she had to tilt her head up to keep the connection with his mouth.

He walked her backward across the floor until he could trap her between the wall and his body, the heated, throbbing bulge in his trousers pressed tight against her stomach. He lifted his head, looking down at her, at the emerald of her eyes, and saw stark need. Intense hunger. That fiery passion she couldn't hide from him.

He bent his head to scrape his teeth back and forth over her pounding pulse, that sweet, sweet invitation in her neck. His lips followed, soothing the tiny bites with a sweep of his tongue. Her body shuddered against his. Her lashes fluttered and then swept down, but not before he saw the heat filling her. He massaged her hips, light at first as he pulled her even closer, his mouth continuing a slow assault. Each time his teeth nipped her, she moaned softly and pressed into him, her hips rubbing against his thigh.

His hand came up and cupped her breast, thumb stroking over the lace-covered nipple. She gasped.

"Take your bra off, Blaze," he whispered.

Her hands obeyed before her mind caught up. She reached behind her and unhooked it, letting it fall with the remnants of her shirt to the floor. His breath left his lungs in a shocked rush.

"Beautiful," he murmured, his hands cupping the soft weight. He bent his head, eyes feasting on her body, so perfect. Lust rose, hot and fierce. So sharp he actually felt the slide of his teeth and he had to fight it back. She brought out the savage in him, the primitive. He bent his head, his teeth scraping over her left nipple.

She cried out, the sound heightening his pleasure. He drew her breast deep into his mouth. Hard. Rough. Suckling strongly, using the flat of his tongue to forcefully press her nipple to the roof of his mouth while his fingers tugged and rolled the other one. Her breasts were obviously as sensitive as her neck. She squirmed against him, her cries soft as she reached up to drive her fingers deep into his hair.

He kept at her breasts with his mouth and hands while he removed the rest of her clothes with his mind, leaving her completely naked. She didn't seem to notice, or care. A surge of hunger tore through him, so powerful, so fierce, he could barely think with the blood thundering in his ears and his mind consumed with her. He hadn't known, even with all his studies, that passion could be so strong, so intense, destroying all control so that there was only pleasure, only pure feeling.

Electricity arced between them, sparks he knew weren't real, but still, they were there, like streaks of lightning sinking into his pores to whip through his body, taking every vestige of discipline with it. He lifted his head and she gasped at the look in his eyes. He knew she saw the darkened, lust-filled predator, and yet she didn't back away; she reached for him, matched his uncontrolled hunger with her own.

He kissed her again, lifting her in his arms, his mouth rough, tasting her passion. It was the best thing he'd ever tasted. As her nipples dragged over the hard muscles of his chest, she gasped and let out a little keening cry. He drank it down his throat, kissing her over and over. Her tongue dueled with his.

"More," she pleaded softly. Fiercely. "I need more."

FOUR

ELECTRICITY SURGED THROUGH Blaze. Forks of lightning whipped through her bloodstream, lashing at her most sensitive of nerve endings until there wasn't a square inch of her that wasn't hypersensitive. She squirmed against him, her hips bucking. Hungry. Needy. Demanding. She couldn't stop herself. She was going up in flames and only he could stop it.

She needed his hands and mouth to be rough. She needed the bite in her scalp when he tugged her head back to take her mouth again and again. She needed the way his teeth scraped over her nipples and he suckled so strongly. She heard her own mewling cries, and she didn't care if she had to beg to get what she wanted. What she needed.

"Are you wet for me, Blaze?" he whispered.

He sounded like sin to her. Temptation. Wicked and forbidden. The wild in her rose until only need and hunger controlled her. Only pleasure. Every sharp tug of her hair, the feel of his fingers clenching her buttocks so hard, so demanding, even the graze of his teeth drove her higher.

He didn't wait for her answer. He lowered her feet back to the floor and left a trail of kisses from her mouth to her throat, and then down to her breasts. Every tug of his teeth or fingers sent fire racing straight to her core. She felt the burn, so hot, scorching, between her legs, so she couldn't stay still. Her feminine channel spasmed, clenched, wept with need.

"I want to see for myself," he said softly, licking under her breast and then down along her ribs. "I need the taste of you on my tongue, *sufletul meu.*"

His whispered words shook her. Went straight to her core so that she felt another powerful spasm. She wasn't certain she could survive. She wasn't even positive she could stand up. His marauding mouth didn't stay very long, but continued to journey down her belly, his tongue dipping into her belly button, his teeth tugging at the little gold hoop there. He went down on his knees, pushing her thighs apart.

"Put your foot up on the table for me," he ordered, his voice a velvet rasp. Filled with dark command.

His voice sent a sharp glittering thrill through her, another pulse of hunger inside. There was no disobeying the edge in his tone. She tried not to whimper as she forced herself to look around. She hardly recognized her own bedroom. She hadn't even noticed they were beside the small end table next to her bed. She did what he said without hesitation, even though it made her feel even more sinful and wicked and even decadent.

She would do anything for him right then. She had never felt so desperate or needy in her life. The feeling was so strong, so intense, her body shook with it. Her heart raced, blood pounding out a demand through her veins to center in her deepest core. His face was carved with a dark, erotic sensuality. Harsh. Brutal even. Wild and untamed and it called to something deep inside of her, something she hadn't even known was there—until the moment she'd laid eyes on Maksim.

She was so hungry for him she could feel the hot liquid spilling down her thighs in anticipation. A small whimper escaped and she anchored herself with one hand in his hair, her breath ragged. She was completely open to him and she should have been embarrassed, but instead, she was all the more desperate for him to do something—anything.

"Yes, *sufletul meu*, you are so ready for me. So wet. So sweet." He stared at the fiery curls, damp with heat, his eyes hooded and hungry. His voice was almost a growl.

He blew cool air straight into her heated center and she cried out, gripping his shoulder to steady herself, needing an anchor when she was already spinning out of control.

"All mine," he whispered. "So long, Blaze. I searched so long to find you."

She didn't have time to process his words because he lowered his head to the feast between her shaking thighs. Her cry was shattered. Broken. Keening. He didn't just give a tentative lick. Maksim took what he wanted like a starved man. He consumed her with a ravenous appetite. He devoured her. His tongue plunged deep to draw out the fiery taste of her. He suckled, he used the edge of his teeth. He took her over using just his mouth and nothing else.

Helpless to do anything but hold on, Blaze clung to both shoulders, obeying his hard grip on her thighs, keeping her wide open to his marauding mouth. It was good. So good. Better than anything she could have imagined. Her mind refused to work, centering on the absolute pleasure building like a tidal wave. The sensations were carnal, erotic, the intensity building the wanton need in her higher and higher.

He unleashed such a hunger on her, his tongue flicking, plunging deep over and over, stroking and caressing, she felt an answering hunger rising in her. His deep growls only added to the sensations whipping through her. Lightning was back, forking through her veins, a crack of electricity across her breasts and down her thighs, along her spine and deep, deep in her feminine channel.

She was close, so close, the tension coiled so tight she screamed with need when his mouth covered her most sensitive button, licking just enough for the sensations to overwhelm her, but not release her.

"Maksim," she hissed his name on a plea. Begging. Needing. Knowing he would give her what she needed in his own time. Her body was his. He'd claimed it and he was making certain she knew it. "Please," she whispered, her fingers digging into his shoulders.

He looked up at her and she felt the added intensity of his glittering eyes, so dark with desire, so intensely sensual her body shuddered and shook with need. Her hips bucked, pressing at him, so hungry for the sensations rushing her toward something just out of reach.

His mouth covered her sensitive bud once again, his tongue flicking, licking, pressing with broad, flat strokes and caresses, driving her up higher than she thought possible, until she was sobbing for release. The rapid strokes sent her over the edge, shattering her, fragmenting her with a kind of blinding frenzy.

She pulled him even closer. The wave after wave of excruciating pleasure only built her need, not assuaging it in the least.

"Maksim." She sobbed his name.

He licked up the inside of her thigh and then down the other one, the gesture erotic, feeding that desperate, agonizing desire deep in her womb.

"What do you need, *sufletul meu*? I will give you the world, Blaze. Just ask for it. Just tell me."

"You. I need you."

"I belong to you," he reminded, standing, his body bare. All his defined, flowing muscles sliding up her skin because he was so close.

She took a breath, carefully put her foot back on the floor and looked at him. Took him in. Drank in the sight of him.

He was tall and very muscular. His hair was long and caught back from his face with a loose cord. His shoulders were wide and his hips narrow. His thighs were powerful columns, but her gaze centered on his pulsing, jerking cock. He was bigger than she imagined a man was.

Her mouth watered. Her hand slid down his chest to his belly and then wrapped around that thick bulge just to feel the heat of him. That only made the destructive sensations whipping through her worse. She needed. She couldn't stop herself. She leaned into him, her tongue tasting his skin right over the thin mark on his muscle. She licked and then sucked. Then she bit down.

She actually *felt* the lightning whipping through him. Through her. He was violently aroused. His cock jerked hard. Pulsed in her hand. She used her thumb to slide through the pearl drops, coated the sensitive crown, eliciting a satisfying groan from him.

Maksim growled, his hand coming up to cup the back of her head, the other hand on her shoulder, pressing. A subtle command. She sent him a dark look. He was hers. His body. *Hers.* She could barely breathe, the need and hunger in her so sharp and terrible.

"More, Blaze. Give me everything."

His voice was rough with command. With a hunger that matched or exceeded her own. She wanted that. Wanted him out of control, burning like she was burning. She bit him again and used her tongue to soothe the ache, leaving a trail of kisses down his chest and belly, her free hand stroking caresses while her fist slid up and down in a lazy pump. She was playing with fire. She could sense his predatory nature, the dark hunger that rose sharp and terrible in him.

His needs were not going to be met easily, but she wasn't afraid. He would take what he wanted from her, but she knew the rewards would be great. She had the same well of darker passion in her, and she needed him to give her what she needed. She loved his taste. Loved the hard muscles rippling beneath his skin as she kissed and touched, memorizing his body, imprinting it in her mind.

She looked up at him, loving the look on his face. The dark stamp of sensuality carved so deep into the lines of his face. The hooded eyes, burning into her. The possession deep in his black eyes. True black. Unusual they were so black, but intense and very sexual. Her heart beat harder and she wrapped both hands around his cock and slowly began to lower her head.

His control was definitely fraying. She loved that most of all. That she put that look on his face. That she could shred his iron control. She felt him in her mind. Knew he had never really looked at another woman. Only her. That was power. *This* was heady power. Giving him this. She licked at the pearly crest, and his entire body shuddered under that light touch.

His hands gripped her hair tightly, stopping her, holding her absolutely still. She might think she was the one in control, but at the sharp bite of pain in her scalp, a thrill raced down her spine. Her gaze jumped to his. Her breath caught in her lungs at the absolute carnal lust she saw there.

"Maksim," she whispered, knowing she sounded exactly as she felt. Hot. Needy. His voice was so rich, so commanding and dark with hunger. He touched her with his voice alone, stroking over her skin like a velvet rasp. Her feminine channel spasmed, and she thought she might have another orgasm just from the way he held her, looked at her and spoke with that absolute command.

"Draga mea," he said. "Sweetheart. Kneel down right there."

He didn't loosen the grip on her hair and he didn't move, giving her little room. She had to slide down his body to comply, and his hands moved a scant few inches to allow her to kneel in front of him. Her mouth watered. He was a temptation, and she'd already had a taste of him. Exotic. Dark forests. Masculine. Perfect. She wanted more.

"Put your hands on my thighs," he said softly, his gaze burning into hers.

She took a breath. Shook her head. "I've never done this before."

"I know."

Those two words slipped inside her. Made her shiver. Made more hot liquid spill between her legs, to glisten in her fiery curls. He was so sexy. Everything about him.

"Give me this."

She slid her hands up his thighs because right then, she would have given him the world. He wrapped his fingers around the base of his cock, guiding it toward her mouth, and it was the sexiest thing she'd ever seen. She knew her own hunger was growing out of control, but it didn't matter. She was lost in his dark spell, wrapped up in his hunger, tangled in her own.

He pressed the velvety crown against her lips. The sensation sent another spasm through her channel and she opened her mouth, licked at the drops there, taking the offering and savoring his flavor. His taste was addicting. So sexy.

"Keep looking at me, Blaze. I need to see you, to make certain you want this."

In answer she licked at the drops spilling from his cock in anticipation. She wanted this. She wanted him. There was nothing else in the world but this man and his body and the pure sensual pleasure he had wrapped her in. She loved the husky groan that rumbled in his throat when he pressed the head of his cock into her heated mouth.

"Feel what I am feeling." He whispered the temptation. "Come into my mind, Blaze. Feel all of me."

She knew what he meant. A gift she had. She had always had. She took a breath and let go of all her sanity, reaching for him. Giving him that. Afraid of what she might find.

But when she touched his mind, there was only pleasure there. Pleasure she was giving him.

The electrical current ran from her mouth, through his cock, lashing his spine and whipping through his head.

"Feel that, *draga mea*? Feel what you do to me? It's so good. So very hot."

She tried to draw him deep into her mouth, suckling strongly, her tongue working him, all around the flared head and underneath. Licking. Stroking. Hungry for more. Hungry to keep the devastating sensations whipping through his body. Whipping through hers, because, mind to mind like this, she felt everything he was feeling. It was thrilling. Decadent. Sexy.

He pulled back and she gave a cry of protest, but then he was sinking into her mouth, giving her what she wanted, and she gave him back. He moved slow and easy, each stroke taking him deeper until he was nearly at her throat, careful of her, but she felt the way his body reacted as she sucked hard. It was beautiful, the violent way his muscles contracted from the searing pleasure. Giving that to him made her feel more empowered than ever. Greedy for more. And her own body was going up in flames. Needing him. So hungry for him.

She felt wild inside. Needing so much more. She worked him, wanting to drive him over the edge, feeling her own body giving up control. Tension building. Coiling tighter and tighter.

He watched with those hooded, black eyes, watched as his cock moved in and out between her lips, the crown and shaft wet now from her mouth, glistening with the moisture. She loved that he watched. That his cock was so swollen and engorged. She could feel the heat of him, scorching her tongue, tasting sexy and exotic. Her hunger grew until she couldn't think straight. Until her brain short-circuited. Until she was a flame burning out of control.

She couldn't keep her hands still, couldn't keep from the

wild need as she tightened her mouth around him and used her tongue to lash and caress as he slid in and out of her mouth, shallow and deep, controlling the moves until she thought she would go insane from the desperate hunger threatening to destroy her.

She needed more and, determined to take back control, she slid her palms up his thighs, feeling the heated muscles contract and pulse as she moved her hands inside his thighs, between his legs, cupping his heavy sac, feeling the velvet there, the tightness coiling.

Maksim pulled back, sliding from between her lips, watching her mouth follow, his eyes smoldering as his hands tightened in her hair, and the bite at her scalp sent an electrical current whipping from her breasts to her core. He reached down to capture her wrists and pin them together with one hand, holding them above her head as he guided his cock to her mouth. She parted her lips and took him again.

He thrust deeper, feeling the tight suction, the vibrations surrounding his cock and sending spikes of pleasure torturing him as she made small, desperate sounds around him. Sweat beaded and ran down his back as he tried to stay in control. She was beautiful with her silken lips wrapped around him and her green eyes dazed with pleasure. Wild for him. Frantic for him. So ready. So in need. It was the most beautiful sight he'd ever seen, and the pleasure was almost too much. He knew he wasn't going to last more than another stroke or two. Still, he couldn't stop, pushing his control as his cock sought another perfect moment in the moist heat and tight suction of her mouth.

"Enough, *sufletul meu*," he murmured. The soft velvet of his voice had turned more of a rasping growl. She was destroying him with her wild, uninhibited gift to him. He would never get enough of her wild. Never.

Down through the long centuries he knew he would be so addicted to her taste, to her body, that he would never want to be anywhere else than right where he was. "Come to me, Blaze." A demand. Rough. Harsh. He couldn't help himself. He had to have her. The plea in her eyes, the pure fire burning in her, was too much to resist.

He used her wrists to pull her to her feet, catching her at her hips and lifting her to him with one arm. He used the other to wrap her leg around him. She wrapped the other instantly. He walked them to the bed as she circled his neck with her arms. Putting one knee on the bed, Maksim took them both down, keeping her under him. Her thighs were parted for him and he took advantage, lodging the wide head of his cock into that scorching-hot haven.

He growled at the feeling as her body took just that much of him, squeezing down, molten lava surrounding him, so tight he thought he'd explode right then. He began to exert pressure, little short surges that forced his way through those tight muscles. So hot. So perfect. Too tight. Strangling him in paradise. The sensation was pure ecstasy as around him, her body stretched and burned, slowly, reluctantly accepting his invasion.

He reached that thin barrier and held himself still with an effort, the sweat beading on his forehead as he fought to stay in control. To give her body the time it needed to adjust to his invasion. He wasn't nearly in deep enough. It was a strain to stay motionless.

"Are you all right, *sufletul meu*, look at me." He had to see her eyes. She had them closed and he needed to know he wasn't hurting her.

Her lashes fluttered and then lifted. His stomach muscles contracted violently. His body shuddered and his cock impossibly thickened, throbbed, desperate for more. She looked so sexy.

"I need more," she whispered. "Please, hurry. Please. I'm burning up. I need . . ."

"I know what you need." His arm tightened around her hips, lifting her. Instantly her legs wrapped tighter around him, her ankles hooking at his waist, her fingers locking at the nape of his neck, eyes pleading. He took a breath because the sight of her was killing him, destroying all control. He surged forward. Hard. Taking her body. Claiming her as his. Driving past her innocence and powering through her tight folds, the scorching fire taking his sanity as her tight channel had no choice but to accept all of him.

She cried out at the lash of pain, but he felt liquid flames wrapping his cock tightly, dragging him deeper until he was lodged all the way. Her tight channel rippled around him, squeezing and milking like the tightest fist, or a hundred fingers, gripped and moved around him. He clenched his teeth, fighting for control again, trying to give her body time to adjust.

Her hips bucked. Her head thrashed. A small whimper of need slipped from her throat and stroked a flame over his cock. The need to thrust hard and deep over and over nearly drove him insane, but he breathed through it, holding on for her.

"Are you ready, Blaze? Breathe for me, sweetheart."

Her green eyes met his. Wild. So wild his breath caught in his throat. He held her still while she kept trying to buck against him, desperate to move.

"Please," she whispered again.

Her voice sent him over the edge. Raw. Arousal making the sweet fire hotter than ever. He moved then, drawing back and then plunging deep into her fiery channel. Her inner muscles, so much scorching silk, gripped his cock like the tightest fist imaginable. He felt the last of his control shred and he began to power into her. He was rough. Too rough for her innocence, but there was no regaining control once it was lost. The pleasure enveloped him, was so intense it actually bordered on pain.

His mind was in hers and he could feel her rising toward her orgasm. Rushing toward it. The sensation of a tidal wave threatening to engulf her. He gripped her hips hard, flexing his fingers and then digging in deep, holding her, for a moment, savoring the tight, silken, wet channel, and then he surged into her over and over with hard, deep strokes, letting the fire streak through his body. Feeling his balls tighten. Feeling the sudden, overwhelming convulsion in her sheath. The ripples surrounding him. Her cries filling his ears—his mind. Pleasure swamped him, took him. Took her. Each hard jerk of his cock spilling into her was a punch of pure pleasure.

Maksim buried his face in her neck, that soft, sweet neck, listening to the pounding of her pulse, the ebb and flow of her blood. Her body was soft under his, his cock still gliding and hard, but that dark lust that drove him so hard, so brutally since the moment he'd heard her voice, knew she was going to defy him and fight her battles alone, eased enough to allow him to be sated.

She was unlike most humans in that she had been able to resist compulsion, but they'd exchanged blood. She'd allowed him into her mind. She wouldn't defy him so easily a second time.

He lifted his head and looked down at her, at the helpless, dazed pleasure on her face. Her lashes fluttered and before she could open her eyes all the way, he took her mouth. Gently. Tenderly. Completely at odds with his roughness earlier.

Sufletul meu, sweetheart, you need to let yourself grieve. She stiffened and her hands went to his shoulders to push him away. *You are safe here with me.* He slid the words softly into her mind.

All along he'd felt her grief. She had refused to face the reality of her father's death. Her only living blood relative other than a mother who had left years earlier and never returned or bothered to find out if her daughter was even alive. Sean McGuire had meant everything to his daughter. He had been brutally murdered.

You need to allow yourself to fall apart. Just this once,

when I am holding you close. Tomorrow night you can be strong again, but right now, holding me, me inside you, give that to me, too.

He tried not to use a compulsion, but he knew she needed to grieve. To finally let go. The hard knot inside her was never going to go away until she allowed herself to acknowledge he was gone. She would never accept her father's death until she faced it and forced herself to realize he wasn't coming back. She needed to begin that process. She would never look at the future, and the last thing Maksim wanted was for Blaze to be thinking about giving up her life for revenge. She was far too accepting of dying.

Their lovemaking had been wild. Rough. Intense. It was an intense situation, and he stayed there in her mind, waiting for her to give him that last gift. Her sorrow. Her tears. Her absolute grief. He was her lifemate and, although she didn't yet know what that meant, she still felt their deep connection.

FIVE

THE HEADACHE POUNDING through her head made it difficult to emerge from a heavy sleep. Normally, Blaze woke quickly no matter the time. She didn't linger in bed, or have to have three cups of coffee to clear her head, but the headache made it difficult to think. She felt disoriented and a little nauseated. Her body ached everywhere. *Everywhere.*

Heart pounding, her eyes flew open and she turned her head to see if someone else was in her bed. Clearly alone, she drew in a long, shuddering breath, the events of the night becoming much clearer in her head. She preferred the fog to reality. Groaning, because even the light hurt her eyes, she flung one hand over her face to protect herself from the bright light of day.

She had cried for hours last night. For hours. In his arms. Maksim. Virtually a total stranger. She groaned again, her face flaming. She'd done more than cry in his arms; she'd let him have her body. Not once. But again and again. In between her crying jags. She'd lost her mind last night. Totally lost it.

She couldn't pretend Maksim Volkov away or the things she'd done with him. There was no denying awesome sex, and the sex was both intense and incredibly awesome. She wanted to regret it. The man was a total stranger and she'd all but torn his clothes off of him, but then the entire night had been intense. That was the only excuse, the only explanation she had. She had expected to die. She'd been prepared for it and truthfully, a part of her had been wishing for it, which would have made her father very, very angry with her.

She groaned a third time and rolled over onto her stomach, burying her face in the pillow. She was fairly certain everything had happened just as she'd remembered it, with the exception of the blood part. That couldn't have happened, because blood didn't taste like that. Addicting and hot and totally masculine. Her mouth watered at the remembrance. If blood actually was so good that she couldn't even get the taste out of her mind and she craved more, people would be selling it on the black market and making a fortune.

As for vampires—she winced a little at the word—she didn't want to go there. She knew about vampires. She'd known since she was ten years old and Emeline had come into her life. Of course, in the beginning, neither girl had believed. Whenever they were together, they had the nightmare. The same nightmare. It was powerful and ugly and scary. They were together a lot. The more they had the nightmare, the more it unfolded and became longer and more detailed.

She groaned again, trying to shut down her brain, not wanting to think about vampires or monsters she couldn't control. Since she wasn't going to see Maksim *ever* again, for as long as she lived, she could pretend, like she'd been doing for years, that she didn't believe in any of it. In the meantime, she didn't have the luxury of lying around her apartment feeling sorry for herself. She had work to do.

Her cell buzzed along the end table, vibrating across the

wood surface. She snagged it quickly, trying not to remember how she'd put her foot up on it and what had happened after. Still, her body remembered, even if her brain tried to shut the memory down. She felt an answering twinge deep inside. At once a smoldering burn started.

"You got Blaze," she answered.

"Where have you *been*? I've called you thirty times," Emeline Sanchez, her best friend, burst out without even saying hello. "You turned me into crazy stalker woman. I've been *worried* sick. Thank God you waited for me. I totally have your back on this, honey. I got a job at the strip club. You know, The In Place. Seriously. They hired me right away."

Blaze sat up straighter, shoving at the fall of hair cascading everywhere. "Em, are you insane? This isn't a game. These men killed my father. You cannot go undercover at the strip joint." She lowered her voice almost to a whisper. "You know why."

"I may not be a badass like you, Blaze, but I can get information. I'm good at it. You know I am. I have always had that knack and I'm not letting you do this alone. I'm not. You and your father . . ." Her voice wavered and she trailed off. She cleared her throat. "If it wasn't for the two of you, I wouldn't be here. You know that. I'm not letting you do this alone."

Blaze closed her eyes briefly. Emeline wasn't a fighter in the sense that Blaze was. Sean had tried to teach her, and she was capable, but it wasn't in her nature, in the way it was in Blaze's. Emeline was quieter. She was gorgeous. Truly drop-dead gorgeous. Of course the strip club would hire her. She also appeared mysterious, elusive and, just walking down the street, she was sexy as all get-out. She rarely argued, although she had strong opinions, she just quietly went her own way. When she made up her mind to do something, no one could stop her. No one. Blaze had learned that early.

"Emmy, listen to me. It isn't safe for you to be in this city. It isn't safe for you to be in the country. It certainly isn't safe for you to be in that strip club. *Especially that* strip club. What did you do? Go straight from the airport to the bar and apply for a job?"

"Well . . . yeah."

As if that was perfectly reasonable. Blaze wanted to tear out her hair. Her life was out of control. Completely out of control. She should have known the moment she sent word to Emeline that Sean was dead and she was going after the killers, that Emmy would get on a plane, regardless of the danger to herself, and come back to help.

"Do you know who owns that club?" Blaze inquired softly. She glanced down at her body. She was naked. Completely naked. She never slept naked. There were smudge marks on her breasts. Like fingerprints. And a mark above her left one that looked suspiciously like a bite. She closed her eyes, remembering the way it felt when he sank his teeth into her. Her sex spasmed. Clenched. She felt the rush of liquid heat at the memory.

"No. And I don't care."

"Have you ever been in it before?"

"Of course not. I've never stripped before if that's what you're asking, but I took pole dancing to stay in shape and I've danced all my life. I have no doubt I can pull this off."

Blaze sucked in her breath. "Wait. Wait. They hired you as a stripper? I thought you meant they hired you as a waitress."

"Honey, how can I get close to the girls to get information if I'm not one of them?" Emeline sounded as if she was losing a little of her patience.

Blaze wanted to scream.

"Blaze." Emeline's voice softened. "I'm not walking into this with my eyes closed. I didn't come back on impulse. I know the risk and, just like you, I accept it. You and Sean are the closest thing I have to a family. I don't have anyone else, and living on the run doesn't exactly give me the incentive—or time—to make friends. They murdered him. They took him from us. I'm not going to let them get away with it any more than you are. I can't go into combat with you, but I can feed you intel."

Blaze rubbed her hand down her face. She didn't have an argument for that one. It was all true and she knew exactly how Emeline felt about Sean. Emeline had no real family to speak of. Her mother had died when she was three. Her father disappeared and Emeline had been shifted from home to home with apathetic relatives. Blaze met her by chance in an alley behind the bar, and they became fast friends. Emeline had been working in stores since she was thirteen for her various relatives, and she easily got a job and an apartment with Sean as her reference when she turned sixteen. Mostly, before that, she lived on the streets during the day and slept in Blaze's room at night.

Sean had paid for her dance classes and anything extra she'd wanted to take as she was growing up. She went to school as if she had an adult watching over her. When Emeline came to them eight months back and told them she'd witnessed a murder and she was scared, afraid she was being followed, Sean had helped her leave the country.

"Em, you described the murder to the police . . ."

Emeline groaned. "I wish I'd never used the term 'vampire.' I said vampire-like and they didn't believe me. I know there aren't vampires. I even tried to backtrack and say that maybe he had that disease where he believes he's a vampire and murders people and drinks their blood. He had receding gum lines, was pale, his hair was in strings, and all that is explained by the disease. Once I said 'vampire' no one believed a thing I said."

"We both know it was a vampire," Blaze said quietly. "We didn't want to believe it, but that nightmare . . ." She sighed and pressed her fingertips to her pounding temple.

"Emmy, hon, that nightmare is getting closer. You cannot go to work at that club. Some of the things in the nightmare are too real. We both know what happens if it all becomes true. You're safer out of the country. I need you safe, Emmy. Please, go back to France." Her throat closed. She knew Emeline wouldn't go. Not if their nightmare was going to become reality.

There was a small silence. "Honey, you know I love you. You're my only family. Sean was my father, too. I *have* to do this. I couldn't live with myself if I wasn't here helping you. I can't give you that. And you know why. If only I hadn't used the word *vampire* to describe him, the cops wouldn't have dismissed me like I was a lunatic."

"Emmy, listen to me. The cops believed you. They were dirty. Sean knew it and he got you out of here. Some of them work for this guy and his mob. His name is Reginald Coonan and he owns that club. Sean believed you and so did I. There are others who think . . ." She trailed off, reluctant to reveal anything about Maksim. It felt like betrayal, even with Emeline.

"Think what?" Emeline insisted.

"Think he kills like a vampire does. Whatever he is, we know the man calling himself Reginald Coonan murders and drinks the blood of his victims. You saw him."

"Two of them," Emeline reminded in a whisper. "I still have the nightmares every night. I'm afraid to go to sleep."

"I know, honey," Blaze said. "That's why you shouldn't go back to that club. If he sees you there . . ."

"I was hired under the name Sean gave me when he sent me to Europe. I'm doing this, Blaze. For Sean. For you. But most of all for myself. I'm tired of running and I want to come home. You're all I've got."

Blaze closed her eyes and threw herself backward across the bed. There was no stopping Emeline once she made up her mind to something any more than there was Blaze. "Okay, but we have to be smart," she capitulated. "It's really dangerous."

"I practically lived on the streets, Blaze, I'm good at this. I've got mad skills in manipulating people into talking to me about things they'd rather not."

Blaze took a deep breath, her lashes still firmly down. For some reason, the light seeping in from around the blinds bothered her eyes. Her headache was worse when she sat up. "A couple of months ago, a man came into the bar and handed Dad a card with a number on it. They offered to help with the Hallahan problem. I was shocked when Dad saved the card, because we both thought there was a rival mob who wanted to claim our neighborhood."

Emeline remained silent, waiting.

Blaze sighed. "I called the number last night because I put the bar in their names in case of my death. I thought if I died, and the Hallahans were still alive, I wanted someone to kill them. What better way than a mobster, right?"

"You *told* them you did this? Now you've got two different mob families wanting you dead?" Emeline sounded shocked.

"Well. No. Not exactly. I slept with one of them. Accidentally. Well." Blaze sat up again and looked down at her body. "Not slept. He had a lot of stamina. We went at it and then I cried over Dad. In front of him, Emmy. I couldn't believe it. And then again, but slower and sweeter. And then again. And again . . ."

Emeline groaned. "I get the picture. Holy cow, Blaze."

"I know. Right? He was unbelievable. I mean that. One kiss and I melted. Actually I think I melted long before that. Seriously, just hearing his voice. He has this way of talking. Very low. Soft. But totally commanding. He's . . ."

Emeline continued for her. "Domineering? Arrogant? Bossy? Oh no, Blaze. And you slept with him? Honey. You just look at men like him. You don't actually sleep with them."

"Well, actually, Emmy, there wasn't any actual sleeping going on. One look, just his voice, and I totally melted."

"Um, honey, let me just tell you that dominating, super-sexy men are great to fantasize about, but you never, never actually try to have a relationship with one. It doesn't work in real life. Now at least you know the kind of man you're attracted to and you can watch yourself. I fall for the bad boy every time. The real deal. The more tats, muscle and motorcycles they have, the more I'm falling at their feet. But I don't touch that. Why? Because no matter how good the sex, I know myself. My heart would be involved and I'd get kicked in the teeth. So I don't."

"Bad boys?" Blaze echoed faintly.

"One hundred percent. I like macho. Bossy. Arrogant. I don't even feel a twinge without that, but I'm not dumb, Blaze. I'm not going there. You have to pull it together no matter how good this guy was in bed. You were vulnerable and he took advantage."

Blaze cleared her throat. "Not really. I'm pretty certain I jumped him."

"You were vulnerable, honey," Emeline said softly.

Blaze ran her hand over her thigh. There was a bite mark on the inside, a strawberry up high. Her stomach somersaulted and she felt an instant reaction deep in her body. "Maybe, but I definitely participated."

"Where is he now?"

"I don't know. I woke up and he was gone."

There was a telling silence.

"I'm not looking for a relationship, Emmy," Blaze said. "It happened and I can't say I'm not glad. It was amazing. I had no idea sex was that amazing, but I have things to do, and a relationship isn't one of them. It happened. I'm moving on."

"He's one of these mobsters?"

"I'm not certain they are mobsters," Blaze mused. "More like hunters." Her heart pounded when she said it, and her hand crept up to cover her neck right where her pulse jumped and pounded. "But whatever you saw that night, Emeline, they've seen. We aren't crazy. There's someone . . ."

"There were two of them," Emeline reiterated. "Not just one. Two."

"Okay, two of them. But someone else has seen at least one of them. And they saw them kill. They are going after them."

"Good. Let them. We'll go after the Hallahans because I did some research on them. They can go out in the sunlight. We can get them, Blaze."

"Just be careful. I'll come into the club in a couple of hours and watch your back."

"That red hair of yours is impossible to miss," Emeline pointed out. "You can't take any chances, and if you blow it and talk to me, then my cover is blown. As it is, I was lucky I never ran into one of them before Sean got me out of here."

Blaze sighed *very* loud. Loud enough for Emeline to hear. "We aren't in a spy movie, Em. Don't get caught up in the drama."

Emeline laughed. "Very funny, Blaze. I'm about the drama. That's why you love me. I'm the girlie girl and always being dramatic. You're the steady, no-nonsense, mess-with-me-I'll-kick-your-ass girl. That's why we're friends. We both can't be a drama queen." She paused, and then lowered her voice. "I love you, Blaze. You're my only family. I can't lose you. I can't. I wouldn't survive. Don't throw your life away."

Blaze clutched the phone tighter, so tight her knuckles turned white. She *had* been doing that. She was so grief stricken, so determined not to allow herself to even think about those hours before her father had died, that she was willing to put herself in harm's way. She would have— unfairly—left Emeline with no one.

She would be forever grateful to Maksim Volkov and

Tariq Asenguard for saving her life. She knew she would have died. She was fairly certain she would have taken at least a couple of the Hallahan brothers with her, but Emeline was right. She had wanted to die rather than face the nightmare of what Sean had gone through.

"I wish I hadn't gone out. I took a class on bartending tricks. Dad took my shift so I could attend the class. Now, it seems so silly."

"It wasn't silly, Blaze," Emeline said. "It's life. We live our life and things happen and we have to deal. We're dealing. Between the two of us, we'll find the best way to take out the Hallahan brothers, one by one. Hell, I'll seduce them if I have to."

"Emeline." Blaze breathed her name. "Don't you dare."

"Just saying. Gotta go, hon. I'm staying at the Mark Charles Hotel. It's kind of run-down, but I thought a down-and out-stripper might live there."

Blaze clenched her teeth. "Emmy, you have to be safe. Are there good locks on the doors? A peephole? Are you protected there?"

"Sean taught me a thing or two, Blaze," Emeline said, her voice serious. "I know how to be safe. I traveled Europe on my own. Just because I can't kick butt like you do, doesn't mean I wasn't paying attention to the things you both taught me. I can do this. I think I'm safer than you are. If you come into the club, hide that hair of yours."

"Yes, mama," Blaze said. "I know a little something about being safe as well. I'll see you in a couple of hours. But Emmy, if you're dancing, I'm closing my eyes so I won't go blind."

Emeline laughed. Blaze forgot how beautiful her laughter was. Emeline had a beautiful voice. She had a beautiful body. Everything about her was gorgeous. She'd been blessed by the beauty gods, but cursed by the gods for that beauty.

"You do that, honey. Be safe."

"Be safe," Blaze echoed and snapped her phone shut. She threw it on the nightstand and covered her face. She'd come so close to dying last night. She couldn't say she regretted a single thing that happened. She *wanted* Maksim Volkov and truthfully, she wanted him again. But she *so* wasn't going there. She wasn't the type of woman to mesh with someone like Maksim, nor did she think for one moment that she was his only in spite of the things he'd told her.

For one thing, her hand crept up to her neck again, and a slow flush spread through her body. There was the blood thing. Her face burned. His mouth on her had been erotic and her mouth on him . . . His taste was addicting. She wanted more. Blood didn't taste like that. She knew. She was one of those weird people who, when they cut themselves, sucked at the wound. Blood didn't taste *at all* like that.

Still, she'd seen him move. Or more precisely, she hadn't seen him move. He was that fast. If his blood could make her that fast, she would be perfectly fine with being a little more like him because *she* was avenging her father's torture and murder. She wasn't leaving that in a stranger's hands.

Blaze pushed herself off the bed. Instantly she felt dizzy and disoriented. The pounding in her head grew. If heads could explode, she was fairly certain hers would. It was far worse than any hangover she'd ever experienced. She pressed her hand to her rolling stomach and staggered to the bathroom. Every step was difficult. Her feet felt leaden, caught in quicksand.

She had the urge to lie back down and pull the covers over her head to block out all light. Instead, she turned on the shower and stepped under the cascading water, letting it run on her face and body in an effort to clear away the cobwebs. If her problems had only been physical, she would have been okay with it, but her thoughts refused to leave Maksim Volkov alone. No matter what she did, she couldn't stop thinking about him.

She fantasized in the shower as she washed her hair, running her fingers through it, remembering the feel of his hands in her hair, the erotic bite of pain on her scalp. So good. So good that even the memory caused a spasm. She remembered the way his skin felt when she touched him. Hot. Hard. So beautiful, if a man could be described as beautiful. Her hands, as she washed her skin, followed the path of his. Her breasts, her belly, her waist, lower still. She heard herself moan and was shocked.

She wasn't a sensual person. Really. She wasn't. She had looked at a few men, but seriously, she just hadn't been interested. It was weird to think she could go from being semi-frigid, to nearly ripping a man's clothes off. There was no doubt she'd done that—and she wouldn't take a single second back.

She also didn't fool herself into believing everything he said to her. Men said things to get a woman in bed. She wasn't naïve. Even if he was everything he'd told her—another species altogether and not a vampire—there couldn't be only one woman for a man. It sounded awesome to be a man's only one, but a man as hot as Maksim could have any number of women. And he had to have, or he wouldn't have been so awesome in bed. No one could get that good without tons of experience. Not that she had done so bad herself.

Smirking, she rinsed the soap from her body, wishing the water running over her didn't feel so sensual on her sensitive skin. Maksim had opened the floodgates on her sexuality. There was no doubt about that. She was craving him all over again. His taste. His body. His cock. Every single inch of him. She wanted to hear his voice. See his smile.

"Obsession," she whispered aloud. She was doing *exactly* what Emeline warned her against. She wanted a relationship with Maksim, not a one-night stand. "I'll settle for sex," she told the hot spray of water. "Lots of great sex with him. And if he really is that fast, maybe a little of that as well."

She rinsed her hair one last time and turned off the shower, reaching for a towel to dry herself off. Touching her body with the velvet softness of the material was a mistake. The moment the towel slid across her nipples, she felt the arc of electricity rushing to her core. Her sheath spasmed. Deep inside she throbbed with need. She clenched her teeth against the flames sweeping through her bloodstream and kept rubbing.

By the time she got the material between her legs where she was sore—deliciously sore—she was on fire. Just touching the towel to her pulsing button sent a shocking orgasm surging through her. She leaned against the sink, breathing hard, wishing Maksim was there with her. He'd given her this gift. She'd never had an orgasm—self-induced—so strong. Imagining his mouth on her, or his heavy erection in her mouth or in her body, sent another wave crashing through her.

Breathing heavily, she tossed the towel aside and caught up another to wrap her hair in before standing in front of the full-length mirror. The sight made her breath catch in her throat. She'd looked at herself hundreds of times, usually a cursory look to make certain her clothes weren't on inside out or something equally as dorky.

Her skin håd never glowed so much. Her eyes seemed larger, the green more brilliant, almost dazzling. Her lashes seemed thicker and longer. Her body looked . . . lush. She was cut. She worked out and she was used to her muscles being very defined—and they were—but somehow she noticed her curves. Mostly, she noticed the smudges on her body—the marks of Maksim's possession. There were a lot of them, as if he had branded her, stamped his mark so deep it was in her very bones.

She let out her breath slowly. She looked beautiful. She'd never felt beautiful in her life. She knew she wasn't plain, but still, not like this. Never like this. Maksim transformed her in some way, or at least made her aware of her femininity—

something she'd never acknowledged. She dressed slowly, choosing her outfit with care. She dressed for combat. Jeans that stretched easily. Boots that were lightweight enough to allow her to move fast but would take someone down if she delivered a kick to them. A shirt that emphasized her curves, a vest that allowed her to hide a few weapons. She didn't take a purse, but zipped ID and money in her vest pocket. She slipped a knife in one boot and a gun into the other.

Her hair took some time. She braided it and then donned one of several wigs she kept just for such purposes. Sean had taught her how to keep from being noticed, and the color of her hair had always been a detriment. When she'd shadowed him, he'd spotted her every time, so she'd purchased wigs. With the cheaper ones, he'd made her immediately, but when she paid good money for real hair, she'd managed to tail him a few times without getting caught. She put on a short, black wig, made certain it was secure and looked real before sliding on a pair of sunglasses, because the light was *killing* her eyes. She hurried out of the apartment. Surveillance first and then she would go into the club when there were tons of people.

SIX

BLAZE DIDN'T EXPECT it to be so difficult to be out in the light. Even behind her dark glasses, her eyes watered and burned. She parked her motorcycle in an alley behind the building opposite the club. It wasn't difficult to leap up and catch the fire escape ladder, pull it down and begin the climb to the roof. Once there, staying low so in case anyone was watching they wouldn't see her, she made her way across the roof to the four-foot-high wall surrounding the rooftop across from The In Place.

She made a face as her binoculars took in the flashing neon sign over the door of the building. The club was popular. The dancers were good. Rumor was, you had to be gorgeous and a great dancer to get a job there. The pay was good and the tips were even better. She could understand why they would hire Emeline on the spot. Emmy was both.

Blaze moved the glasses along the rooftop first, just to make certain the Hallahan brothers hadn't posted guards up there. She quartered the area meticulously, just as Sean had taught her, and there was no one. Clearly the Hallahans didn't suspect that she would come after them. She knew they had dismissed her because she was a woman. They hadn't entered her bar because they clearly didn't want to tangle with Tariq Asenguard, Maksim or any of their men— if they had brought some with them. She had the feeling they had. It had taken more than the two men to clean out the bar in that time frame, even if they could move at warp speed. The thought that there had been others she hadn't seen didn't sit well with her, but now that she thought about it, of course they had probably brought others. Men like them? Different? How many men like them were there?

She continued to sweep the building. It was two stories and took up a third of the block. The top story was mostly offices, but like her building, there was a large apartment above the bar. She was fairly certain the Hallahans didn't live in the apartment, but they used it. She knew that because after they were threatened, both she and her father had done some surveillance. The Hallahan brothers didn't bother to cover the windows; in fact, she was pretty certain they were exhibitionists, or they just liked people to see and maybe fear them.

More than one woman had been brought up to that apartment and shared if the rumors were true, and she was fairly certain they were. They had also brought men here to beat. And they had beat them right out in the open—in front of that window.

Sean told her that Reginald Coonan owned a company that made porn films, so maybe the women auditioned with the Hallahans first before making the films. According to what Sean had found out, Coonan's company was extremely successful. No one knew where his studios were, and it was reputed that he made fetish films as well. She didn't want to know what those were and Sean hadn't told her. Still, she worried that Emeline would catch the Hallahans' eyes. She was truly that gorgeous.

No one appeared to be in the apartment, and she swept

the street and parking lot. The parking lot was filling up. The sun had begun to set, turning the sky all different shades of red and orange, bringing relief to her burning eyes. She was surprised that her skin felt burned as well. She was Irish, so she didn't exactly tan, but when she went outside in the early evening she never had a problem.

She didn't see any of the Hallahans' vehicles. They normally parked their very fancy cars in the four spots clearly marked for their use. No one ever dared to park in their places, at least not in the last few months. Rumors of baseball bats taken to the owners and total destruction of vehicles that had crossed them before their reputations had spread kept anyone from taking chances now.

Where are you?

The velvet voice slid into her mind easily. Clearly. That edge to it only made her stomach plunge and then somersault. There was no denying the voice was real and it was Maksim.

You are not where I left you.

She took a breath and decided it was better to answer him. Not the smartest thing maybe, not if she didn't want to continue fantasizing about a relationship with him, but still, a slow burn was starting, the tension coiling deep inside her—a burn only he could sate. No, it wasn't smart, but she didn't want to cut ties—yet.

I have a few things to do. She tried to act nonchalant, as if she were talking telepathically every day of her life to a man she had wild, rough, uninhibited sex with. To a man she wanted to have more wild, rough, uninhibited sex with. He might be the sexiest man in the world and drop-dead gorgeous, but he wasn't going to dictate to her. And she sure wasn't staying in her apartment waiting for him to come calling after he left her bed.

I looked for my woman in her bed where I wanted to put my mouth between her legs until she was screaming my name and then have her ride me wild like she does until she screamed it again. Then I wanted to ride her rough, hard and deep until both of us were exhausted. The bed was empty.

A shiver went through her body. It wasn't just his voice. He talked sexy. No one talked like that, did they? She wanted his mouth between her legs. She wanted to ride him wild. And she really wanted him to ride her rough, wild and deep. Screaming would be optional, but good. She moistened her suddenly dry lips and tried not to fog up her binoculars with heavy breathing.

You didn't leave me a note. I had no idea you were planning to come back.

There was a silence. In that silence, she felt a glacier pouring into her mind. She shivered, trying not to let his disapproval matter to her.

You had no idea I was planning to come back? What does that mean? You thought I used you and walked away?

Okay. That was *exactly* what she thought and clearly she was wrong. She caught a flicker of fire-engine red in the parking lot and turned the binoculars on the convertible that drove fast into one of the sacred Hallahans' spaces. Jimmy Hallahan. The oldest of the brothers. He jumped over the door of his convertible and walked with long strides to the side door of the club that no one but management used, disappearing inside.

Well. Yes, she admitted, because there wasn't much else she could do. *I went to sleep with you and woke up without you. I don't have tons of experience with men, so I thought maybe that was your MO.*

The chill factor went to subzero. *My MO?*

Clearly she was not getting the better of the conversation. It was time to retreat. *I can't talk about this right now. I'm really into something here and it's demanding my entire attention.*

"'Here' would not be The In Place, would it?"

His voice sounded soft and silky. In her ear, not her mind.

She was so certain she was alone she didn't react at first, and then she felt his warm breath in her ear. Instantly a thrill went down her spine. She drew in her breath sharply and turned her head to look over her shoulder.

Maksim was close. Too close. He was beautiful. Gorgeous. Dressed casually in vintage blue jeans that clung to his body, and a tight black tee that stretched across his thick chest, showing the multitude of muscle, he was even hotter than she remembered—and her memory was really good. Her mouth went dry and she had to swallow a lump that had formed in her throat.

Her heart began to pound—*hard*. He looked more remote and ice-cold than he had when she'd first met him. His black hair spilled down around his face. It was thick. Luxurious. Her fingers itched to run through all that wild hair and tame it just as a part of her wanted to ignite the fire in him and melt all that ice away.

"I left you sleeping in your bed. What are you doing here?" he persisted.

The velvet rasp of his voice slid over her, both a demand and a caress. She had no idea how he managed it, but the tone was very effective. She shivered and sat back on her heels. Every breath she drew took him deeper into her lungs until she felt surrounded by him. She had no idea why, but she was relieved to see him alive and breathing. A part of her, from the moment she had awakened and found him gone, had been tense and worried. She put it down to secretly wanting a relationship she'd told Emeline she wasn't looking for.

"Blaze." He said her name softly. A warning.

"Was there a question in there?" She fell back on her attitude because, really, who could think when he was looming over her, looking so . . . yummy.

He reached down and took her wrist, forcing her to her feet with casual strength. Not stopping there, pulling her up against his body. He might look ice-cold, but the heat emanating from his body was anything but. He pulled her wrist around his neck, took the binoculars out of her hand, floated them—yes, *floated* them—down to the floor and wrapped her other arm around his neck.

"What are you doing here?"

He murmured the question against the side of her mouth, his lips skimming hers, sending a series of little quakes ricocheting through her pussy. Instant liquid heat dampened her panties. In reflex she threaded her fingers together at the nape of his neck, her body melting into his.

"Working," she answered, turning her head just enough so that her lips brushed his. Seeking his kiss. Needing the feel of his mouth on hers. Right there out in the waning light on the roof of the building across from the nightclub she was reconning. She wasn't a woman who went for public displays of affection, but she needed his mouth more than she needed air—and she had no idea why. Only that he was necessary to her.

His hand slid up her back, her neck, to cup the back of her hair. "I see. You were supposed to wait for me. We were going to work together. Right?"

She tried hard to search her brain, which because she was in such close proximity to him, was fast turning to mush. Had they had a conversation about working together? It was possible. "I woke up first, you weren't there to talk things over with and, at the moment, I'm taking someone's back. I couldn't wait."

His thumb stroked her bottom lip. "You have someone inside?"

She nodded. "I need information. She'll get it."

"You trust her?"

"With my life."

His black, black eyes moved over her face. Brooding. Moody. "That is exactly what you are doing, Blaze. You had better be able to trust her, because I can read your mind. I know who she is to you and if she betrays you, I will kill her."

He delivered the statement matter-of-factly, and she knew it wasn't an empty threat. He meant every word. He didn't raise his voice. He spoke very softly, just as he usually did, but she *felt* his words in her belly. Deep. Branded into her bones. She tipped her head back, searching his remote, icy eyes, looking for an expression.

"Why are you helping me?"

"You belong to me. I take care of what is mine. I searched centuries for you. No one is going to take you away from me."

Again it was a calm statement of fact. She found herself shivering. She believed him. She believed he'd been alive for centuries and that he hunted vampires. She believed him because she'd been having detailed nightmares since she was ten years old and Emeline *saw* a vampire. Emeline didn't lie and she didn't exaggerate. And Maksim had shown her what and who he was. There was something very old world and courtly about him. At the same time when he moved into a space, the air around him electrified with danger, as if he was an extremely dangerous predator.

"Maksim, we barely know each other," she pointed out, still pressed into him, too weak to move even when she knew she should. That predatory air was very much in evidence.

"You know me. You are in my mind. You know I speak the truth. You do not want to know, but you do. We are hunting something monstrous. You need to understand if I allow you to do this thing . . ."

That stiffened her spine and she jerked back, or tried to. His arms immediately locked around her like iron bars. "Allow?" She felt tiny sparks snapping over her skin and in her mind. "No one *allows* me to do anything, Maksim. If that's the kind of woman you believe me to be, you have the wrong woman. You need to keep searching."

His arms remained tight even though she bent backward to try to put space between them. His smile was anything but humorous. "I am not a human, Blaze, and I have immense power. The undead hides from me, and there are few things on this earth more powerful than he is, yet he hides and trembles when I am close. Do you really believe that I would search centuries, *hundreds* of years for the other half of my soul, find her and then risk losing her because she is strong willed and stubborn? You need to look deeper into my mind and really see me."

She didn't want to do that. She already had far too much to process. She realized there was logic to what he said. She knew little about vampires, other than what she saw in the movies and in her nightmares, and who knew how close to the truth that was. If she believed he hunted vampires through the centuries, and he lived that long, he had far more experience than she did. If there was one thing Sean had drilled into her over and over again, it was that her brain was her greatest weapon. Her greatest asset. He had taught her that she always needed to know her own capabilities and limitations. So maybe she could fight the Hallahans and have absolute faith she would be on equal footing, but vampires . . . no way.

"You may have a point, Maksim, but please don't use words like 'allow.' I'm not going to kick you in the shins when you try to dictate to me; I'll walk away."

"We are past walking away. We talk things out. But first, kiss me. You have not kissed me and I think I woke up starving for your kiss."

His mouth was close again. Tempting. He had nice lips. An invitation, and she knew exactly how he kissed.

"When I kiss you, I forget everything. I told you, I have a friend inside and I want to get in there and watch out for her."

"Only Jimmy Hallahan is inside. His other brothers are working, doing what they do, being Reginald Coonan's muscle. At the moment I also have a friend in there. Picture this woman and I will send him a message to keep an eye on her until we get inside."

She took a breath. "It's one thing to trust you with my life. It's something else to trust you with hers." She wasn't being defiant, but really, things were moving altogether too fast.

"*Draga mea*, you know I will defend you with my last breath, and that means your friends are under my protection as well. I see you love this woman. That she is a sister to you. Look into my mind. There is no need to be afraid."

But she was. Not because she feared he would hurt her. Or betray her. She was already far enough into his mind to know that much. She knew he was being honest, but still, he was taking her down a path there was no returning from. She knew that instinctively. Already she craved him. Craved his taste. Craved his body moving in hers. She was becoming lost in him very fast and there was no real explanation for him. She didn't trust anything she couldn't explain.

She felt him move in her mind and she should have protested, but she'd already given him that, sharing herself with him. She was open to him. Vulnerable. He took the information on Emeline out of her head. He didn't pull away from her, allowing her to see him instructing his friend, sending him Emeline's information, including the pictures of her Blaze stored close.

Guard her well, but do not approach unless she is in trouble.

That isn't Asenguard, she protested.

She could tell he was Carpathian like Maksim and Tariq. She sensed his power, just as she felt Maksim's when he was near.

"His name is Tomas. Tomas and his brothers arrived a few days ago and have offered to help hunt Reginald Coonan. We have known each other a very long time, and a few times, when we were on the same continent, in the same vicinity, we have hunted together. He is very good at what he does, as are his brothers. They are triplets. Where one is, the others are close by. Your friend is in good hands."

"Emeline." She cleared her throat. "She saw him. Or someone like him. Two someones."

"She saw Tomas?" Maksim asked.

Blaze shook her head. "Coonan. I suspect it was Coonan. Emeline witnessed a murder. Two men, pale faces, gums receding, sharp teeth biting into a man and his wife. They killed the couple, nearly draining all the blood from both of them. It was messy and horrible to witness. She must have made a sound because one turned his head and saw her, but suddenly others came, men who approached the murderers, and they fled."

"How long ago was this?" Maksim asked gently.

"You believe what she saw?"

He nodded.

"It was about eight months ago, right around the time the cops claimed there was a serial killer loose going after the homeless. They called him 'Strike Twice,' because he always struck twice in one night. He always took two victims. Because there are two of them," Blaze said. "Emeline saw them, but the police wouldn't believe her."

"I was there. Tariq and I were there that night. We just missed them. We have been trying to find their lair ever since. It is a big city. When we realized that the Hallahans were doing Coonan's bidding, we began to concentrate our efforts on protecting the remaining businesses."

She took a deep breath, still leaning into him. Still circling his neck with her arms. She fit there against him. One of his hands slid up to her neck, fingers gently massaging as if he could ease the tension out of her.

"Do you know why they target certain properties?" Her eyes searched his. He knew. "You don't want to tell me, but you know," she whispered. Disappointed. She slid her arms to his shoulders to push away from him.

Before she could, he tightened his grip on her nape, fingers curling deep. "I do not want to frighten you with too much information at once about what it is we are. We acquire fortunes and properties and leave them to ourselves every so often so as not to raise suspicion. All Carpathians do this. I am Carpathian, a species that is older than you can imagine. We have certain gifts and one is longevity. Some say we are immortal, but truthfully, we can be killed. The male loses his ability to feel emotion or to see in color until he finds his lifemate, that one woman who holds the other half of his soul."

He'd said as much before and she figured perhaps it was an ancient belief that still persisted. She nodded her head for him to continue.

"Vampires are Carpathian males who have chosen to give up their souls so they can feel the rush a kill provides them when they feed. Having been Carpathian, they have also acquired property and wealth. Most are too vain and too addicted to the adrenaline in their victim's blood to think or plan, and that makes them easier to track. But some are extremely intelligent and they have learned through experiences, just like the hunter, how to recruit newly turned vampires and use them as pawns. Still others have gone further and created an army of humans by infiltrating their ranks. They are the most difficult because they have patience and the cunning to plot for centuries to get what they want."

She frowned. "So you're saying that these vampires could already own some of the properties in the neighborhood and are looking for the ones they don't own?"

"It stands to reason. They would leave the businesses intact because it doesn't matter to them one way or the other about the business itself, just the building."

"Why?"

"I do not yet have an answer to that. But we are getting closer. Reginald Coonan is the name the Carpathian used to leave his property to, perhaps before he turned vampire.

Tariq is right now researching to see who owns the other buildings, the ones they have not yet touched. If any of the families still own the buildings such as you do, we will also know who they will target next. Still, with all that, your friend should not be anywhere near a property owned by the vampires she witnessed killing that night. If they were able to catch her scent, they can hunt her. They cannot do so during the day, but they can send their human puppets after her, the way they sent them after your father."

"Emeline isn't going to give up any more than I am, not until they're stopped," Blaze said. "She loved my father. She won't let this go. Even if I did, which I won't"—she narrowed her eyes at him to make certain he knew she was giving him the truth—"she wouldn't stop. She's already got a job dancing."

"Blaze. You do not know me very well," Maksim said. "But know this. When a man finds a woman after hunting for so long, he has a jealous streak. A possessive streak. Dancing is out for you, unless you wish to dance for me."

In spite of everything, she found herself laughing softly. Relaxing into him. "You don't have to worry. I couldn't dance even if I wanted to."

He leaned closer, his teeth nipping at her chin, and then he kissed his way up to the corner of her mouth. She felt the soft brush of his lips like a brand, a trail of flames dancing over her skin. His mouth settled on hers. Gentle. Unlike any of the kisses the night before. Gentle scared her. Gentle terrified her. Gentle was about emotion, not chemistry. She couldn't give this man more of herself than she already had, because he could destroy her.

He deepened the kiss as if he knew exactly what she was thinking and wanted to short-circuit her brain. He did so easily. She tasted hunger. Wild. Possession. She tasted need. His kiss went from gentle to hard. Wet. Demanding. She gave herself up without a fight, moving into him, tightening her hands at the nape of his neck, curling her fingers into his hair, her mouth as aggressive as his. Her need as wild and possessive, every bit as hungry as his.

He kissed her over and over until she was on fire. The world dropped away, the danger, the fear, the sorrow, everything, until there was nothing left but pleasure, passion and heat rushing through her veins. She forgot she was on a rooftop. She forgot what she was doing and what her name was, there was only Maksim and his fantastic mouth, his strong arms and hard body pressed so tightly against hers.

SEVEN

MAKSIM'S MOUTH TRAVELED from Blaze's lips to her throat. To the side of her neck. Her heart began to pound in anticipation. Her sheath clenched and deep inside she felt a spasm of pure pleasure. She felt as if she'd waited a lifetime just to see him again, to feel his touch. To feel his teeth scrape gently over her pounding pulse.

Who knew that such a small gesture could feel so intimate? So erotic? Her fingers tunneled deep into his hair. Anchored there. She turned her head to give him better access. The wig was short, the dark hair brushing her chin as his tongue swirled over her skin, sending tiny streaks of fire rushing through her blood.

"Blaze."

He whispered her name over her thundering pulse. Just that. His voice was sinful. Wicked. Stroking over her like fingers. Caressing. Tempting. She closed her eyes, drawing in her breath, taking the scent of him deep in her lungs as his teeth slid into her neck. The bite was painful. She heard her own gasp, and his arms tightened, enfolding her, his heart beating against her body so that her own beat found and followed the steady rhythm.

At once the pain slipped away to be replaced by something altogether different. Pleasure burst through her. Every cell in her body came alive, was aware of him. Of her. Of them. She closed her eyes and gave herself up to him. To the dark passion that ensnared her completely. She should have run screaming from him. Or used one of the many weapons she had on her. Instead she burrowed closer and gave herself to him.

There was no denying him. She didn't want to. She knew exactly what he was doing, and deep inside excitement spread, right along with the flames building and the tension coiling.

Open your mind. Feel what I am feeling.

She didn't stop to think. She obeyed his whispered temptation, letting him inside. Completely. He poured into her. Warm. Strong. Sensual. The feeling of him filling her was so beautiful her eyes burned with tears. She felt alone most of her life, different from others. She had never thought she might want to belong to someone. She felt complete and confident in herself, until the moment she laid eyes on Maksim.

Her legs suddenly felt weak and it was only his arms holding her up. She tasted herself as he drew her blood into his body, as he took her essence, that wild, exquisite *addicting* taste. So good. He would never tire of it. Never get enough of it. Without thinking, without effort, she poured herself into his mind, filling every one of those lonely places. Giving him—her.

She wanted him. She couldn't have told Emeline why, but she knew. She was a strong woman, raised by Sean to be confident and take care of herself—and she liked that. But she was also a woman. She wanted a man to be strong and confident as well, a man who was every bit the warrior she was. Matching her strength for strength. She hadn't believed there was such a man, not until she laid eyes on Maksim Volkov.

Blaze knew it was even more than that. He had incredible gifts—gifts that would allow him to take down men like the Hallahans, and killers like Reginald Coonan. She was warrior enough to want those gifts. She knew that first time with Maksim, when he had given her his blood, had changed her somehow. Her hearing was more acute. Her vision far better in spite of her sensitivity to the sun. She felt the way her body moved, so much more coordinated when she'd always had fast reflexes and extraordinary coordination.

Most of all, she didn't feel alone. Even with her father— and she'd adored him—often she felt very alone. She knew that came from feeling different. She *was* different. The only close friend she'd ever had was Emeline. Emeline never had the family life Blaze did, but still, they worked somehow, filling those empty spots for one another. But all her adult life, Blaze was aware of loneliness spreading slowly through her.

She wanted a man of her own. A family of her own. She just didn't relate that well to the men she met and as a rule dismissed them totally from her mind after she walked away. She thought about Maksim from the moment she'd opened her eyes—even when she was talking to Emeline and had come up to the roof for surveillance.

She felt a pull toward him that she had to admit—but only to herself—was more than sexual. She wanted to know him. To see beyond his cold eyes, and remote expression. She needed to be that person that could have all of him. She might tell herself and Emeline that she only wanted a sexual relationship, but she knew better.

You are going to join me in my world, draga mea, he whispered softly into her mind as if reading her thoughts easily.

She had forgotten she had allowed him in. That she was also just as deep in his mind. His tongue slid across her pounding pulse, a delicious, soothing, *intimate* gesture that stole her breath and maybe a little piece of her heart.

You will be strong. And fast. Far faster than you are now.

He was tempting her. Luring her to take a step further into his world, and he knew it. They both knew it. She held her breath as he opened his shirt. She couldn't look away from his dark eyes. Eyes so black she could see shadows in them. Hunger was there. Dark and terrible. Beckoning.

She knew he was the devil tempting her, but she couldn't resist. Already the taste of him was in her mouth. She dropped her gaze to watch as one fingernail slid across the heavy muscle of his chest, just above his heart. At once ruby beads welled up. She inhaled, taking the scent of him into her lungs. He smelled every bit as good as she remembered.

Maksim's hand cupped the back of her head, urging her mouth toward those drops of tantalizing spice. She glanced up at his face. "If I do this, can I go back?"

He shook his head slowly, his body utterly still. "But I will always be with you. Always. You will never be alone again, Blaze."

She knew she shouldn't. She didn't know exactly what she was getting into, but his body was hard and strong, and he smelled like a gift. And that thin line drew her like a magnet. She was mesmerized by it, unable to do anything but look at the sinful temptation.

She was lost and she knew it. Perhaps this wasn't the way to find herself again, but there was no resisting, not when her body had already melted into his and the hand cupping the back of her head pressed her closer. Especially not when she licked at those ruby drops, brought them into her mouth where the taste of him swallowed her whole. Took her to another place. Sent fire rushing through her veins.

She had been so certain she could just take a small taste, just to see if the memory was real. The moment her tongue touched his chest, brought those ruby drops into her mouth, the craving became overwhelming. Not just for the exquisite, unique taste, but for him. For the hardness of his body. His strength. His scent. The sweep of his long hair and the feel of his hands moving over her, claiming her. Most of all because his mind was in hers, filling her, taking away fear and loneliness.

She drank when she knew it was something forbidden. She took everything he offered because there was no stopping. In that moment, everything he offered was real. What she had searched for. Waited for. Dreamt of.

Take off your shirt.

They were outside. She knew enough to know that much, even though she was lost in the rising tide of passion. The persistent throb between her legs became an urgent demand, and at his whispered command, she felt the growing dampness there.

Someone could see us. She used the more intimate whisper of telepathy. The need for him began to dance down her spine. The lure of the forbidden. He always gave her that, and for some reason she responded with a rush of heat surging through her veins, pounding through her clit, causing a spasm deep inside.

No one will see. Do this for me. I do not think I can go much longer without being inside of you. Carpathians do not dream, Blaze, but all through the day, I dreamt of you. Your soft skin. Your hair like silk. The taste of you. The way you surround me with fire when I am inside you. That mouth of yours. Sweet. Hot. I craved the feel of your hands on me.

She had dreamt of him. She had woken up with the taste of him in her mouth. With his name on her lips. Looking for him. Disappointed and hurt that he wasn't right there in bed with her.

You left me. Her voice betrayed her. Shook. Just a little, but it was enough. He heard. He knew. He felt her hurt.

Very gently he tugged on her hair of her wig. Let his fingers caress the nape of her neck.

Carpathians must sleep during the day, sufletul meu.

We are very vulnerable at this time. The soil rejuvenates us. I expected that you would stay asleep and I would be back before you woke. His hand moved over her shoulder in a caress and he deepened the kiss. Gentled it. Made her ache with need. *Take off your shirt for me. I will keep all eyes away from you.*

Before she could stop herself, her hands went to the hem of her tee and she dragged it off, hating to lift her head and stop taking what she needed from him. Still, she dropped the T-shirt on the rooftop and put her mouth on his chest once again.

His hands moved up her back, along her spine, found the catch of her bra and slipped it off. The night air teased her breasts. She shivered as fingers of desire danced down her spine. The moment he touched her she was lost. He swept his hands down her body, along her spine, over her rib cage, down to her bottom. His fingers dug deep, claiming her. Pressing her tight into him.

Give me your mouth.

Reluctantly she swept her tongue across the thin line on his chest and lifted her face to his. His mouth came down on hers, crushing hers under his. Hot. Hard. Delicious. His tongue teased along her teeth, the roof of her mouth, dueled with hers. Insistent. Making her light-headed. Turning her into a living flame. He trailed kisses from her lips to her chin. His teeth bit gently, causing an instant reaction. Tension coiled and the burn between her legs grew. She moistened her lips. There it was again. The forbidden. Undressing in the open with his hands caressing her body. The night breeze on her. Stirring her senses further. She found the idea aroused her even more.

He pulled back to look at her, his eyes burning over her body. Everywhere his gaze touched felt like the caress of his hands. He cupped her breasts, lifting them toward his mouth as his head lowered. "So beautiful," he murmured aloud.

She felt the sweep of his silky hair against her bare skin. Her breath left her lungs in a long rush, and then his mouth was on her. His teeth scraped back and forth along her nipple, sending shards of desire pounding through her bloodstream. She couldn't stop the excitement, the anticipation rushing through her like the strongest wave imaginable, sweeping her up into a vortex of need.

His mouth closed over her breast, suckling hard. Rough. Demanding. His hands bit into her, massaged, tugged and rolled, never stopping while she gasped for breath, clinging to him because her legs went weak. Anchoring both hands in his hair, she held him to her, needing his mouth, needing the hard suction and the brutal demands.

His hand slid over her hip and she felt the cool air on her bare thighs—between them as he inserted his leg between hers and pushed her thighs apart. The cool air fanned the smoldering fire until she thought she might burst into flames. Her breath came in ragged gasps, and lust rose sharp and terrible.

He kissed his way back up to her throat. Found her mouth. Took it. Over and over. Long, deep kisses while his hands moved possessively over her body. He lifted his head to look down at her, his gaze feral. A dark predator. Another shiver of excitement went through her, arousal burning high. Her need urgent. Before she could say anything, he kissed his way down her body. Over her throat. Her breasts. Her ribs.

Her breath left her lungs when she realized his intentions. She looked around her. Night had fallen. Stars were out. There was no building hiding her. No shadows out there on the rooftop. He crouched in front of her, his hands pushing her thighs farther apart, causing another spasm of pure hunger.

Someone can see us, she whispered into his mind. She should stop him but she couldn't. She needed this. His mouth pushing the terrible, *brutal* burn into crackling flames that would consume her.

I would never allow that. I can shield our presence. No man sees you but me. Ever.

She knew he meant it. She had no idea how he could shield them from sight should someone from another rooftop or window happen to look over at them, but she didn't doubt that he could. Still, even with that knowledge, she still felt the thrill of the illicit.

I want your legs farther apart, Blaze. His voice was a rough command, the sexy rasp and the hot breath directly against her wet, sensitive entrance.

She clutched his shoulder with one hand, his hair with the other, not knowing if she had the strength to drag him away from her. She could feel the warm spill of liquid in response. The bright, desperate hunger shooting through her like an arrow. Her fingers tightened in his hair.

He lifted her leg, pushing her calf over his shoulder, exposing her even more to him, to the night. A sob of need escaped her. He leaned into her and his tongue swiped through the wet, curling, jabbing, sending that burn into violent flames.

Slide your hand down your body. Slow. Feel the way your fingers touch your skin. Let me feel it.

There was no resisting the temptation of his voice. That wicked hunger. The dark promise of passion and beauty. At once she opened her mind further to him, letting him inside her where he could feel everything she felt, every emotion, every spectacular sensation his mouth was giving to her. With one hand she clung to his hair to keep herself anchored; with the other, she found her breast, cupping the soft weight, thumb sliding across her nipple. A streak of fire burst through her, raced straight to her pulsing clit. She threw her head back.

Harder, Blaze. You like it rough.

She did. She so did. Her fingers rolled and tugged her nipple, sending a series of white-hot arrows rushing through her body to find her deepest core. His mouth worked her, licking, sucking, even his teeth scraping. The world seemed to explode around her, fiery sparks raining down behind her eyes.

That is exactly what I want, he said. *So beautiful. Bring your hand down to me, draga mea, slide it down your body. Feel how beautiful you are. Your skin so soft. The way your body is firm but soft. Exquisite. Perfect.*

His mouth never stopped, not even through the wildfire storming through her. Blaze looked down at him, that sensual, predatory face, carved so deep with lust. His eyes were twin glaciers, but beneath all that ice, she could see that flames burned blue and white, consuming her just as his mouth was.

She had no idea arousal could be this brutal, or her body so on fire. The pads of her fingers glided over her satiny skin, and the flames streaked over her nerve endings with every touch. Her fingers dipped inside her belly button, moved lower still until she felt the brush of his hair. His hand reached up and caught hers, drawing it down farther, curling her fingers in, so that she stroked her own inflamed clit, while his tongue lashed deep. It was sexy. It was crazy sensual. It fueled her lust, drove up her passion and with his hand over hers, pushing her finger deep and then drawing it back so that she stroked that tight little bud repeatedly, she felt the wash of another strong orgasm devouring her.

His mouth kept moving, his hand continued to force her finger deep and then stroking. The sensations rolled through her. Danced down her thighs. Up into her belly, spreading like wildfire through her. It was unbelievable, so good. So perfect. She tipped her hips to give him better access, her breath catching on a little sob as he licked and sucked at her strongly, carrying her away on a tide of pure passion.

Her third orgasm hit strong and he pulled his mouth away, waving his hand to strip his body of all clothes as he stood. He wrapped his arm around her, starting to lift her and she shook her head, biting at his shoulder, licking down his chest.

"It's my turn. You taste so good, Maksim. Let me."

He closed his eyes, and she loved that look of sheer carnal pleasure on his face. The lines carved deep. The hunger in him. All for her. When he opened his eyes and looked down at her, the flames behind the ice burned brighter than ever.

"Get your mouth on me, *draga mea*." His hand went to her shoulder. "But my famous control is slipping."

She couldn't stand anyway, so it was a relief to sink to her knees in front of him. The cushion under her hadn't been there and she knew, even in the heat of the moment, he was seeing to her comfort. Her mouth watered, remembering the taste of him. She slid her hands up his thighs, watching the muscles bunch. Cupping his heavy sac, she leaned close to stroke the velvet balls with her tongue. She knew he wouldn't give her much time; already he was thick and long and very hard. Very hot.

Blaze stroked her tongue from the base, up his shaft to the crown. She wasted no time, drawing him into her mouth, suckling strongly, pulling at that spicy, rich taste of him. She loved that he was rough and wild and it was there in his addicting taste. There in the way his fingers dug into the nape of her neck, biting into her flesh so that more damp honey spilled down her thighs.

She took as much as she could as fast as she could, driving him to the very brink of his control, loving that she could. Loving that she knew she did. She lavished attention on him, watching him, keeping her gaze glued to his, seeing the intensity of his pleasure—pleasure *she* gave him. She lashed him with her tongue, curled it around the underside of his shaft, suckled, teased, took him deep and then shallow.

He caught her under her arms. *Enough. I need to be inside you.*

She needed that as well. She let go of him, although she hated losing the feel and taste of him, but he lifted her high, her body rubbing along his so that her nipples felt the scrape of their joined bodies. She wrapped him up, arms and legs, nearly crying as she felt him right there, at her burning entrance.

There was no hesitation. He surged up as he slammed her down over him. All the way until she was seated fully on him and he had pushed through those tight, inflamed folds. She bit his shoulder to keep from crying out with the sheer pleasure of it. It was too much. Too good.

"Maksim."

His name came out a husky whisper with far more emotion in it than she wanted, but she couldn't control her body let alone her voice. Already she was breaking apart inside, fragmenting around his hammering shaft. The burn was different this time, even more intense, and she feared she knew why. She had dreamt too often of this kind of man, and now she was putting all of her hopes, all of her emotions that she'd held back for so long into him. On him.

I love when you say my name. When you know I belong to you. That you are mine. The things you do to my body, Blaze. Sheer paradise.

The things he did to her body were pure sin. She couldn't stop moving through the powerful quake because his hands refused to allow it. He kept her gliding up and down his shaft while he powered into her. She had no idea if her orgasm continued or she just rolled right into another, but she felt him swell, the hard strokes driving deep, and then his face was in her neck and he was rocketing with her into that place they could only find together.

He held her for a long time while their hearts raced and their lungs burned. It was Maksim who lifted his head first, brushing kisses over her cheek and the side of her nose.

"Good evening, my beautiful soul."

She didn't lift her head from his shoulder but smiled at

him. Physically, he was the most good-looking man she'd ever seen—not in the model kind of way. He was too rough for that—too masculine. "Good evening back. That was amazing. Hot and amazing."

"I am very pleased you thought so."

She felt the wind in her face and it cleared some of the fog, some of the daze of the aftermath of having wild, rooftop sex with him. She lifted her head, shocked at herself. At once he set her feet on the ground. She looked helplessly around for her clothes. She had no idea what she'd done with them.

He waved his hands and just like that both of them were fully clothed. Her breath hitched in her throat. She was clean as well. Absolutely clean and completely dressed—as if nothing at all had happened.

"How do you do that?"

"I will teach you one day soon. In the meantime, to relieve your anxiety, we should get moving."

Blaze stared up at him, still shocked at his display of power. There was no explanation, not one she could think of, so she shut down her need for answers and pulled out of his arms abruptly. "I can't believe I'm standing up here on the roof with you, doing whatever it is we're doing and Emeline is in the club without backup."

"She has backup." His voice was a soft growl. "I told you, Tomas is in the club. He will not allow anything to happen to her."

"Still, I don't know him. I barely know you." And that was just a teensy bit humiliating when she'd just had wild sex on the rooftop with him.

"You know me. We will walk in together, you on my arm. Will your girl recognize you in your wig?"

"You can't walk in with me. Jimmy Hallahan is in there. He'd recognize you in a heartbeat."

"He will not recognize me. I can certainly disguise my features." There was a hint of humor in his voice. He bent down to brush his mouth over hers. "I will be your much older lecherous sugar daddy. Why else would a good girl like you go into such a club? Your sugar daddy has a lot of money to throw around and he likes women."

She stared up at his face. "You're going to draw attention to yourself."

"Of course. It will give you a chance to slip off and talk to your girl."

She could still feel him inside her. Deep down in her most private, feminine core. He was there. In her mind. Filling her. He was there. She could taste him in her mouth. He was there as well. In her. On her. Surrounding her. She wanted to move into him, into his heat and strength, but she stepped back.

Emeline was counting on her. So was her father. She had a mission to accomplish and as much as Maksim drew her to him, she knew she was getting lost in him. She pressed trembling fingers to her mouth.

"Why doesn't your blood make me sick? Repulse me?"

He reached for her hand. There was unexpected gentleness in his touch, disarming her completely.

"You are the other half of my soul, Blaze," he said simply. Complicating an already difficult situation. "I have tied us together using the ritual binding words, and we've had two blood exchanges. You are entering my world."

"What does that mean?" She didn't pull her hand away, but went with him when he tugged her toward the thick railing running the length of the roof.

"I will show you." He brought her hand up to his mouth and kissed her knuckles before wrapping her arm around his neck. "Give me your other hand."

She did so hesitantly, uncertain what she was getting herself into. They were right on the edge, so looking down, the ground was a long distance away.

"Lock your fingers behind my neck and hold on tight."

She had barely managed to thread her fingers together

when his arms came around her rib cage and he stepped off the edge. She cried out, but the sound was muffled by his shirt because she'd buried her face against his shoulder. When she didn't have the sensation of falling, she opened her eyes and forced her head to turn just enough to see around her.

They were in midair. Floating. Not falling. Floating. In a controlled float. She looked up at Maksim's face to catch him looking down at hers. His eyes were as black as night, as cold as ever, but very slowly, she saw the grin start. Mischievous. Playful. Full of fun. Something deep inside her responded. She found an answering grin starting. Once it did, she couldn't hold it back, because truthfully, she could either faint—and that didn't feel forthcoming—or she could embrace the moment. She was all about embracing.

EIGHT

THE MOMENT HER feet touched the ground, Blaze lifted her face and went up on her toes to capture Maksim's mouth. He was incredible. A miracle. In the midst of terrible sorrow, he had made her smile. Made her forget for one tiny moment that inside she had broken apart and that she'd been left with nothing but her friendship and love for Emeline. Or that Emeline had once again been left alone just as she had been.

Maksim was extraordinary and even if something happened and nothing was really between them, she would be forever grateful that he had made her forget. That he had made her smile. He might be bossy and some weird species she'd never heard of, but that didn't make him something to be frightened of. That made him all the more intriguing and as far as she was concerned, totally kick-ass.

He was offering her the things he could do. She knew he wasn't making it up, because she was already evolving. Already her hearing was more acute, as was her vision. She felt the strength in her body and the fluid way she moved. She trained every single day. She studied anatomy. She kickboxed and boxed. She practiced falls and rolling. She drilled with weapons and ran daily. She had never felt quite as strong and as empowered as she did in that moment.

Her body melted into his as she kissed him. His arms locked around her tightly, holding her close to him, his mouth moving on hers, meeting fire with fire. Sweetness with more sweetness. He tasted hot and masculine and passionate, but there was something else now, something underlying she couldn't quite put her finger on. The more they were in each other's head, the more she felt she knew him. The closer she felt to him.

Still, she'd been careful not to look too deep. He wasn't human. She knew that. She even accepted it, but that didn't mean she wanted to know too much too fast. By going slow, she could accept the things she learned about him and not be afraid.

"Please be real," she murmured against his mouth. His beautiful, fabulous mouth that could kiss like a dream. "I need you to be real."

"I am real," he assured, nuzzling the top of her head with his chin.

She continued to cling to him. "If you aren't, I need to thank you." She felt the instant tension coiling in his body, the rejection of what she needed to say. Her fingers bunched his hair in a tight fist. "No. I have to say this to you. You have to hear me, Maksim."

She couldn't look at him when she confessed. She was too ashamed. Her father would have been angry with her. Emeline knew her well enough to know what had been in her head or she wouldn't have accepted Blaze having wild sex with a stranger so readily.

"I wanted to die last night. I intended to die." She made the confession in a little rush. "I was supposed to work that shift and Dad took it for me. The police wouldn't help me find him, and I looked everywhere I could think that they might take him, but I couldn't find him. I was outside the bar in the early-morning hours, and they threw him out of a moving car at my feet. He was already dead. It was . . . unimaginable." Pain broke through her voice. "I know I told you this, but you have to understand where my head was, what I would have done had you not saved me from myself."

"Sufletul meu," he whispered softly. Gently. His arms tightened around her, but the way he held her felt like comfort. Like shelter. "I am sorry I was not there to help you when you needed me."

The hint of tenderness was nearly her undoing. She had to choke back a sob. "You saved my life." He had to know. Whatever was between them, he had to know that if he hadn't come along, if he hadn't been so intense and passionate, making her feel alive again when she'd felt dead inside . . . "You were there when I needed you most."

"You saved not only my life, Blaze," he said, feathering kisses down the side of her cheek to her chin. "You saved my honor, and to a Carpathian, honor is everything. I would say we were more than even." His fingers smoothed over her cheek.

Again there was a hint of tenderness in his touch that sent her stomach into a series of somersaults. She smiled up at him. "I just wanted you to know. In case. You know."

He frowned. "In case, I know what? Clearly I don't know."

"Um." Uh-oh. She didn't like that look on his face. He could go from sweet to arrogant in the blink of an eye. Not just arrogant, but scary dangerous, don't-mess-with-me gorgeous. "Just in case," she persisted. But her voice stumbled. "Things don't work out."

His eyebrow shot up. "Things do not work out? What things? We will get those responsible for your father's death. I already have men working on it. They are hunters. They have been hunting for centuries. Coonan will not escape and neither will his human killers."

She really needed to leave it there. Honesty was only

good when a man wasn't looking down at you with predatory, glittering eyes, warning you to stop while you were ahead. So she stopped. But his arms didn't loosen.

"I am not going anywhere. You are my lifemate. I realize we have not had the time to get to know one another or even to talk about what this really means, but know this . . . I. Am. *Not*. Going. Anywhere."

She was getting that. Her stomach fluttered right before the somersaults started. He could do that to her without even trying. She cleared her throat. "I need to get inside. The club is filling up and Emeline is inside. If Jimmy Hallahan spots her before she dances, he'll make a move on her. She's that striking. Dancing, she'll probably start a riot." She wasn't kidding about that, either. Emeline wasn't merely beautiful. There was no way for Blaze to describe her adequately to Maksim. He had to see for himself.

"I am going to allow you to get away with that," he said, his voice low as always. Still, she knew he was annoyed with her. There was the bite of a lash underlying his tone, making her shiver. "Remember I am your sugar daddy. Play your part."

She felt the subtle difference in him immediately and she looked up, gasping at the change in his features. He looked much older, a good twenty or more years older than she was. His hair was short and definitely salt and pepper. His face had changed to that of a man who was definitely a powerhouse, but not so much in a physical way. He was corporate. His suit was worth upwards of a thousand dollars or more. His shoes were Italian.

She glanced down at her own clothes. Her jeans were gone. She wore a halter minidress. The front was two strips of material that barely covered her breasts, plunging below her waist with a bow and ruffle draping gracefully over the tiny skirt. There was virtually no back. The material clung to her body, showing off her figure. Her shoes were four-inch stiletto heels with dozens of straps going up her ankle. The dress was shorter than any she had ever worn before and far more expensive.

"You ever wear something like this without me right next to you, and we are going to have problems," he said, taking her hand and leading her across the street to the club.

"Just pointing out, I don't own anything like this," she said, smoothing her hand down the silky material. It draped beautifully, but she could feel the breeze on her body as she took each step. "I think the thong is a little much," she added. "The skirt barely covers my butt."

"You have a great butt," he pointed out. "We own a dance club and this attire is fairly tame in comparison to what quite a lot of the women wear. Besides, your sugar daddy is a total letch. Otherwise why would he bring his woman to a place like this? He will be touching you every chance he gets. The thong is something he probably wouldn't want you wearing. I gave you that as a concession so I wouldn't have to kill anyone tonight. You will not be leaving my side."

A little shiver of anticipation went through her. The dress was beautiful and it fit like a glove. She wasn't wearing a bra because it was impossible with the back and front, both nonexistent, totally bordering on indecency. She felt the material draping low, just above the curve of her butt, and with every step she took, it brushed over her skin like fingers.

Maksim's hand was a brand on her back, low, right above the material, but sliding down every now and then to stroke the curve of her bottom. In her high heels, her body swayed with a subtle invitation so that the silk dragged across her nipples, sending little darts of fire straight to her core. The feeling was just plain sexy.

They turned heads as they walked in together. Maksim immediately leaned into the bouncer and spoke authoritatively in his ear. The bouncer nodded, signaled for a waitress and pushed the hundred-dollar bill into his pocket. It was done smoothly and Maksim's hand never stopped stroking her bare skin and dipping lower to caress her buttocks.

They were led to a small, intimate booth raised so they could easily see the dancers onstage, but the lighting was low. "Perfect," Maksim said, sliding another hundred toward the waitress. "Just what I asked for. See, honey, the table is draped. You need to slide under there and take care of me; no one can see a thing." He said it loud enough for the waitress to hear. As he spoke, Maksim's hand slid up her thigh, straight under the short hem of her dress to go up her hip.

Blaze stayed perfectly still, trying to control the heat in her body and the blush rising. The lights were low, and Maksim's body was between her and everyone else, but still, it was a highly embarrassing moment. She was an object, there to serve him, and he was making that clear. The waitress flashed him a flirty smile, pushing the money down into her ample cleavage. She didn't even look at Blaze, because clearly Maksim's toy didn't count, instead batting her lashes at Maksim and smiling huge for him.

He winked at the waitress and slid into the booth, pulling Blaze in after him. He ordered bourbon for himself and a blow job for Blaze. It was all she could do not to roll her eyes.

You don't need to be so obvious.

Sure I do. The waitress will report the high roller obsessed with sex to her boss. I want his attention on me. They like high rollers here. They have a back room where the girls take customers for special shows.

They do? What had Emeline gotten herself into?

His hand dropped below the table to slide up her thigh, taking her skirt with it. All the while he smiled at the waitress. "Keep them coming, sweetheart. I heard the shows were great here and I think my girl is going to need to do a lot of work tonight, right, baby?"

Blaze leaned into him and licked up the side of his neck. "I'll keep you happy, handsome. You know I always do."

"Sometimes with a little help from your friends," he said, and laughed coarsely.

The hand on her thigh traced patterns in her skin. His fingers were hot, branding those patterns into her skin. She didn't want to be aware of him in such a sleazy place, but it was impossible. She knew he was playing a part and helping her to do the same, but she was already so aware of him, just the slightest touch sent little sparks of electricity surging through her bloodstream.

The waitress leaned close, giving him more of a view of her large breasts and just a hint of darker nipples barely hidden beneath her bustier. "We are *very* friendly here," she assured in a purring voice.

Do you see Emeline anywhere? he asked.

There was a little note of worry in his voice, and that both pleased and worried her. She liked that he was anxious for Emeline's safety but concerned that he felt the need to be anxious. She'd scanned the room the moment she'd walked in, but there were so many people. The room was dark so that she couldn't see much but the raised stage where the dancers performed and the elevated cages where several dancers swayed, bumped and ground to the music.

She had thought of the club as a strip joint, but she could see it had been made into so much more than that. On the surface, the atmosphere would appeal to many young people as well as the men who came to see the strippers. Knowing there was a back room where other services could be bought explained the extreme popularity.

Emeline wasn't near the stage, and even from their raised dais, Blaze couldn't spot her anywhere. She searched the room for Jimmy Hallahan. He was near the bar, leaning down talking to their waitress. Twice he glanced toward their booth, and Blaze made certain her face was tipped up to stare at Maksim adoringly.

There was a shadow across her face, and she knew Maksim kept it there. No matter which direction she moved, her features were impossible to really see in the darkened room.

Hallahan is over by the bar with our waitress. He keeps looking this way. I don't think he's seen Em yet or he'd be all over her. She must be in the back with the other dancers getting ready for the show.

Just the sight of Jimmy Hallahan sickened her. She wanted to go to him, right there, press a gun to his chin and pull the trigger. When he'd thrown her father's body from the car, he'd leaned out, laughing.

"Not yet," he said softly, bending his head to put his lips against her ear. His hand rubbed along her thigh. The gesture wasn't in the least sexual. He was comforting her. "We want information. Once you kill Hallahan, this place will go crazy. Especially if you do it out in the open. Have patience."

That settled her stomach. She hadn't even known until that moment her stomach was churning and bile was rising. Not until his soft, mesmerizing voice and the stroking caress of his hand calmed her.

"No one can really see my body, either, can they?" she asked with sudden insight. She turned her head and looked up at him. His jaw hardened, and it was already pretty hard. His black eyes burned, almost glowing in the dark.

"Do you really think I would expose your body to other men's eyes? They do not see *you*. They see a woman with short black hair, in a white, not very decent dress, revealing what they believe is her body. It is not. Not even close."

She should have known. He had created an illusion for himself; of course he would do the same for her. She saw herself, but no one else would. No one else could. Whatever body he had chosen, whatever face, definitely didn't look a thing like her.

"I can feel your hands on my skin."

"Because I can touch *you*. No matter what form either of us takes, we can always feel and see each other. If you look close enough, you will see past the form I created for me."

"So do you see me in the dress, or do you see the form

you created?" She was curious, because she could see her own body in the dress, the material teasing her nipples. She could feel his hand stroking up her thigh and over her bottom, sending a series of flames dancing through her core.

"Of course I see only you. I touch only you. You are beautiful, and in that dress—which should only be worn in a bedroom, not a club—I can feel a physical response. I do not have a physical response to other women. I am playing the part of a letch who cannot keep his hands off a woman. I have to make it look somewhat believable, and the only way I can do that is to see you and touch you."

She liked that. She liked that a *lot*. She wasn't certain, once the dancing started, that his assessment would hold true, but she liked that he thought it.

"I like that no one in the club can see me in this dress. More, I like that you don't want them to," she admitted.

"As long as I am close to you the illusion will hold. That is one of the many reasons you do not leave my side in this dress."

"I will have to leave it in order to take care of Hallahan." She looked right into his eyes. "It will be me taking care of him, not you. And not your friend." She made it a firm statement, watching him the entire time. She wasn't going to allow anyone else to avenge her father, and she wanted Jimmy Hallahan to know it was Sean's daughter who took him down.

Maksim leaned into her, his body shifting slightly. At once she felt protected. Sheltered by him. His hand cupped her face gently, his thumb tracing the line of her jaw. "I know you now, lifemate. I see your need and as your lifemate, it is my duty to provide for you. I will not have you in danger, but when you can safely get to this man, I will shield you from the rest of the world and you can do what you have to in order to rid the world of a monster. Make no mistake, Blaze, Jimmy Hallahan was a monster long before Reginald Coonan got a hold of him, and now that he is under the influence of a vampire, he is worse than you can imagine. If your girl Emeline catches his eye, she will be in great danger."

Blaze took a breath. "She'll catch his eye. She'll catch everyone's eye." Including his. Emeline was beyond beautiful and if she was dancing . . . Blaze had seen her moves on the dance floor of clubs and in the privacy of her home when Em and Blaze were having fun, drinking and showing off dance moves. No one moved like Emeline. She had always been super proud of Emeline, but now, she suddenly realized Maksim's eyes would also be on her friend. He might believe he wouldn't have a physical reaction to another woman, but once he saw Emeline, dancing or not, he would know he was wrong.

Maksim caught her chin in a firm grip, tilting her head, forcing her gaze to meet his. His eyes, so black she caught her breath at the emptiness she saw there, the endless black void. Cool. Remote. And then they blazed with life, with emotion, only for her. Only hers. Her breath caught deep in her lungs and she felt him there, inside of her. Moving in her mind. Deep in her body. Surrounding her.

"There is only you, Blaze. I realize it is a difficult concept to imagine that a man could be dead to all feeling, to all color, to everything but hunting until you walked into his life. Until I heard your voice and you brought me to life. That is the way our species is. You hold the other half of my soul. I cannot see other women. Not in the way that you fear. It is an impossibility."

Her heart skipped a beat. He was telling the strict truth. She knew it by his voice. She knew it by the flaring of life in his eyes. She was in his mind and the truth was there as well. She moistened her lips. He was right. It was difficult to grasp the concept, even when he laid it out in front of her. She couldn't imagine a man like him, a powerful, gorgeous all-male man going to a club and not reacting to the women and their bodies on display.

"Tell me your plan," Maksim said. "I know you and your girl have got one. I have waited patiently for you to tell me."

"You might not like it, but it makes sense." Blaze found it strange and a bit thrilling to be sitting in a nightclub, seeing him, yet not seeing him, hearing his velvet hypnotic voice sliding over her skin—skin that wasn't hers yet still was. She liked him sitting next to her. More, she felt safe. They were in the lion's den and she felt safe.

"Tell me."

She could give him that because already she knew his mind. She knew he kept his word, and she was beginning to know if something was important to her, it was important to him. "The Hallahan brothers have a reputation with women. They like to force their dancers to submit to them. The more high class the dancer, they more they're determined to break her. Emeline is going to get Jimmy Hallahan's attention, and he's going to invite her upstairs to the apartment where they bring their women."

"I figured that part out."

His hand dropped to her thigh. Fingers splayed wide to take in as much bare skin as possible. He had big hands, and she felt he could almost wrap them around her leg right there. Her heart jumped and then began pounding like crazy, so hard she felt the rhythm of the pounding music surrounding them pulse in time to the beat of her heart.

"Jimmy will take her upstairs. I'll find my way up there and he'll get his chance to make peace with whatever god he believes in."

"His god is a vampire, Blaze," he said. "He has no mercy left in him. No goodness. He lives for others' pain and for his own depravity. He has to hurt others because it is the only way the man can get off."

She knew he was giving her a warning. He didn't have to tell her that, though; she'd seen her father's broken, torn body. The Hallahan brothers had taken their time torturing him. They'd kept him alive a really long time, and they

hadn't needed to. That meant they had prolonged his life—
and his pain—for their own enjoyment. She felt that monster
inside of her, opening. Blossoming. Needing. It was all she
could do to force her body to sit in the booth and not walk
right up to Jimmy Hallahan, shove a gun in his throat and
pull the trigger.

"My man Tomas is watching your friend. I let him know
to allow her to go up the stairs with Hallahan. I can cloak
you so you can follow. But, Blaze." His fingers bit deep into
her thigh. "I am going to be right there as well. You will not
see me, but if you get into trouble—either one of you—I
take over and kill him myself. Do you understand?"

She knew he was asking more than the simple question.
He was telling her she'd better stand down when he told her
to, or there would be consequences. She wasn't a woman
who feared much but still, the steel underlying that velvet
tone sent a shiver through her.

"I understand, Maksim. There are four of them. I want
all four. And I don't want Emeline hurt, so yes, if everything
goes south, I welcome you bailing me out." She looked up
into his eyes to see if he got it. If he got her. She was giving
him her trust. Walking another step into his world. Giving
him something she hadn't given any other man other than
her father.

His eyes went hot. From cold to hot. For her. She leaned
into him, put a hand on his chest and kissed his mouth. Hard.
Wet. Delicious. Meaning it. His hand cupped the back of
her head and his mouth took over hers. Harder. Wetter. More
delicious than ever. Meaning it as well. So much so that she
felt that meaning in every cell in her body.

Abruptly he lifted his head and pressed his forehead to
hers. *He is heading this way. Time for a show, Blaze. Are
you up for it? Can you take it? Play the part? I do not want
him close enough to see any detail of the real you.*

She felt him moving in her mind, reassuring her. Filling
her. Holding her in strong arms. She swallowed, nodded.

Maksim applied pressure to the back of her head, and she let him ease her down so she was pressed with her mouth against his lower abdomen. She knew what to do, sliding her hands under his shirt, to lift it enough to press her lips to bare skin, effectively hiding her face.

"Jimmy Hallahan," Jimmy said, his accent very thick. He slid into the booth on the other side of Blaze, his thigh touching hers. "The show's about to start and I wanted to offer you anything you might need or want. Everything here can be yours if you want it. See you got your little skank in the right place. You're going to need some relief after seeing what I got to offer for you."

"Max," Maksim stated. "And she's a toy, not a skank. There is a difference, and if you do not know what it is, I feel sorry for you." His hand stroked caresses over Blaze's hair, calming her when the close proximity to the oldest Hallahan made her tense, sick and wanting to kill him all mixed together.

NINE

THE LIGHTS CAME up on the stage, and a small hush settled over the club. The dance music faded away, and men and women shifted eagerly in their seats for a better look in anticipation of what was to come. The oldest Hallahan brother leaned across Blaze's body as if she wasn't there, his concentration on Maksim.

"You're going to love this," he said. "And man, anything you want is on the menu."

His hand dropped casually toward Blaze. Maksim caught his wrist. Showing teeth in a semblance of a smile, but his eyes were ice-cold. "Nothing here is on the menu." The voice said it all.

I can't stand it if he touches me. He's so close I want to vomit. Or kill him. Blaze felt naked without her weapons. A knife. Anything. She could break his neck, but the scuffle— and there would be one—would attract the bouncers, and it was doubtful if she could snap it in time before help got to him. She had to be realistic, and it was getting nearly impossible to breathe. She'd been holding her breath since he'd slipped into the booth next to her.

Hallahan sent Maksim a toothy grin. His gaze dropped to the woman who had to mean something to the perverted man who had come to his club for playtime. A toy he'd said, but still, a treasured one or he wouldn't care if Jimmy shoved her on the floor and used her mouth while he watched the show the other worthless skanks put on for the men. Teasing them. Showing off their bodies for money. He turned his dancers into what they were—whores. Worthless whores who were required to do whatever he or his brothers demanded. And they demanded anything they wanted. Anytime they wanted.

He glanced down at the woman again. Her face was pressed to the wealthy man's bare belly. He couldn't see her face, but her body was prime. He wasn't used to being denied, but he smiled anyway. He would have the woman when he wanted her—right in front of the rich man. He'd make the old man watch for that insult.

He cannot put his hands on you, Blaze. Take a breath. All you will pull into your lungs is me, Maksim assured. *The illusion of you is real enough that if he touches your thigh or your back or any part of you, he doesn't actually feel you, but what I created. You think you feel him, but he is not touching you. I would never allow that.*

Blaze took a moment more, her lungs burning. Raw. Needing air. She believed Maksim, but she couldn't bear it if he was wrong and she allowed Jimmy Hallahan into her, even if it was just the same air. She had no choice but to breathe. She pressed her face—her mouth—hard against Maksim's belly, down low, into the waistband of his trousers, and she took a shallow breath.

She drew Maksim deep. So deep she was almost dizzy. Her next inhale was anything but shallow because his scent, that perfect, wonderful masculine scent, obliterated everything that was Hallahan. She closed her eyes and took herself out of the club. She couldn't be there with the man who had murdered her father pressed next to her, illusion or not. Her tongue slipped over Maksim's defined muscles. She traced them with her tongue just to get his taste. To push Hallahan further away.

I can't watch over Emeline in this position, Blaze said. Worried. She hadn't expected Hallahan to approach Maksim and actually sit at his booth.

Maksim's hand stroked a caress in her hair. *Tomas is up close to the stage just in case your girl gets in trouble. One of his brothers arrived a few minutes ago. Lojos. He is standing beside the stairs leading to the apartment. Leaning against the wall, eyes on the stage. Both are like me. Carpathian. Nothing will happen to her.*

The first dancer came out of the shadows into the spotlight, crawling like a jungle cat, her body in nothing but leopard paint. The paint was clever, hiding everything and nothing at the same time. It was her dancing that revealed her body to them, slow, teasing glimpses as she sensuously shimmied around the stage to the pounding music.

The entire atmosphere in the club changed. The sexual tension ramping up along with the music. Maksim's hand tightened in Blaze's hair.

They are pumping something through the ventilation system, Blaze. Some kind of pheromone that is subtle but with every breath these men and women take, it is affecting them just as a drug would.

Blaze kept her mouth pressed to Maksim's bare skin. *I understand now why they're so successful. They don't need the actual drugs to get the people stirred up to purchase the extras. The sex would be better than ever; at least they all think it is.*

They are selling drugs as well, Maksim said, allowing his breathing to change so Hallahan would believe he was just as affected as everyone else in the club. Just as affected as Hallahan was becoming. It was there on his face, stark depravity. His hand had already dropped to his crotch.

"See what I mean, Maksim?" Jimmy said, all friendly, his voice tinged with need. "When you're through with your woman, I could use a little relief myself." Jimmy's grin was full of confidence, now that the drug was being pumped into the club.

Maksim flashed him a quick, answering smirk, but didn't reply out loud. He had to pretend the drug was affecting him as it was all the others in the club.

The music ended and the crowd went wild. The lights came down and the dancer rushed offstage. A woman dressed in the scanty uniform of a server picked up the money thrown on the stage and shoved it into a separate pocket on her apron.

"A thousand can buy you that dancer for an hour. She'll do anything you want, and your girl can join in or watch or just stay and wait for you," Hallahan offered. "I've had her myself and she's a wildcat, just like her dance shows her."

Maksim's eyebrows shot up. "A thousand?"

"For an hour, and believe me, that's cheap for what you'll get. You want her all night, that's ten large, but you'd better be able to keep up," Hallahan said.

In between the dancers, the strippers in the cages were grinding and slowly taking off their clothes, as the music pumped adrenaline through the club. More and more, the audience was becoming as affected, and as uninhibited.

They have quite the racket going here. The drug everyone is inhaling is already affecting everyone, even without the strippers and dancers. Men are touching their partners openly. Women are beginning to respond by allowing more open public displays. Blouses open, hands on their men's crotches. Two have already knelt down right on the floor and no one's stopping them from what they're doing. It is just adding to the already open, sexual atmosphere. Two uniformed cops are being serviced in the corner by two of the women serving drinks. Blaze, they have cameras in here. This place is a trap for anyone coming in. They drop hundreds on the strippers, then thousands for the extra time in the back room and the way they have everyone worked up, including the strippers and dancers, there is going to be a lot of action in that back room. They will certainly have cameras there as well. That means blackmail. Now we know how they own the police so quickly.

Blaze nuzzled his body. *Emeline,* she whispered into his mind. *I can feel the effects and I'm not watching the show, but she'll be dancing. She's naturally sensual, Maksim. I don't want anything to happen to her.*

She was becoming affected. She could feel the compulsion to slide under the table with every breath she took. Her breasts ached, and a smoldering fire began between her legs. She was very grateful Hallahan could only see an illusion, the image Maksim allowed him to see, not her.

Three more dancers performed before the music changed altogether into a pounding beat—a beat everyone in the room could feel right through their already primed bodies. Men were kissing, touching, pushing partners to their knees, reaching under tables to put their hands up skirts.

They keep changing the angle of the cameras, Blaze. Zooming in. This place is all about blackmail. Hallahan is getting suspicious. Slide under the table and stay low, directly in front of me. I will do the rest. You do not move. Keep your hand on my leg so I know you are safe while I give him the illusion he is expecting. As the wealthy pervert in the room, I should be far more affected by the drug and the sights surrounding me. I am not in the least aroused.

She knew what that meant. She closed her eyes and let her hand slide over his lap, feeling the length of him. He wasn't hard or even semi-hard, a state he had been in when he was alone with her. Her stomach churned. She knew Hallahan couldn't see her, the real her, or even the real Maksim, but this was so insane. Trapped by the drug pumping through the air vents, Maksim had no choice but to respond like everyone else. He was shielding her, and taking the brunt of the disgusting close proximity of Hallahan. Laughing crudely with him. Assessing the dancers and strippers. Rating them. Being a sleaze—for her. She had forced him to come here with her, protecting her. Protecting Emeline. Not just him, but two other of his friends.

I'm sorry, Maksim. I didn't know what it was like inside. I've scouted the place, but never saw it this way. I really didn't know. Em didn't know, either.

It is all right. I do not care about this man. He is already dead. He is letting little things slip while we talk. I am able to see the scope of this operation, and Blaze, it is large.

Hallahan suddenly hitched forward, his hand stilling on his crotch. The room went silent other than the heavy breathing. There were no more shouts of encouragement to the dancers, only enthrallment.

Keeping her hand on Maksim's calf, Blaze lifted the corner of the tablecloth draped so conveniently, so she could see the stage. She knew the moment the hush fell over the crowd that Emeline Sanchez had stepped into the spotlight. There she was and she was gorgeous. Spectacular. Her hair was long and thick, shiny as a raven's wing and a true blue black. The thick mass fell below her waist, caressing her body, a body that was all curves. Narrow waist. Tight belly with just the hint of a womanly curve, soft and inviting. Her body was covered in glitter, gold and silver. Glitter that picked up the lights and threw what appeared to be little sparks as she moved onstage to the music. She wore a tiny thong of gold, and two golden stars over her nipples, a thin gold chain running from one star to the other. Around her hips, low, was a second double golden chain, with small bells that added to the music as she became lost in the pounding beat.

She looked like a woman desperate, hungry, in so much need of a man, her hands moving down her body suggestively as her hips undulated and her breasts swayed. As she danced, she hypnotized her audience. She was sex personified. The kind of dangerous woman a man might kill for. Once he was under her spell, once he had a taste of her, he could never be the same.

Every single male in the room, and many of the women, followed the path of her hands as they moved over her body, so graceful, so sensual, the epitome of perfection.

Hallahan began to swear under his breath, and to her horror, he unzipped his trousers and pulled out his cock. At once Maksim slammed a barrier between Blaze and the man. She couldn't see him or smell him. She huddled closer to Maksim's protection, eternally grateful for him. Had she come into that club alone, she would have fallen under the spell of the drug as well. She had no idea what would have happened to her. She wasn't as far gone as the others in the room, but she knew Maksim was somehow giving her as much clean air as he could, acting like a filter for her.

This has to end, Blaze said desperately. *I don't want Em to regret helping me.*

That dancing is all your girl, sufletul meu; Tomas and Lojos are filtering the air for her. She is very aware something is wrong. They do not know how she is so aware. As a rule, we can read humans easily when we want, but there is something different about her. I have tried as well, but it is impossible.

"Her," Maksim said aloud to Hallahan. "I want that girl."

"No fucking way," Hallahan said. Choking on his own desperate hunger. "That one is all mine. She isn't up for sale."

Blaze heard his breathing change, become labored, and she knew the exact moment when he relieved himself, but she didn't smell it or see it. Still, her stomach lurched again. She detested that he could see Emeline's body. That he thought he could touch her, have her, force her to do whatever he wanted.

Hallahan abruptly stood. "I'll send your waitress over." He kept his eyes on the stage. "She'll take your order." He strode away, straight for the stage.

Blaze immediately slid back to the seat and leaned in to kiss Maksim. She had to get rid of the terrible taste in her mouth. The feeling of having come too close to real depravity. Maksim didn't deny her. He kissed her gently. Tenderly. Blocking out everything but the way he made her feel. Safe. Secure. Comforted. Close to him.

He pulled back, his gaze moving over her face, clearly checking to see if she was okay. "We are going to get up and walk over toward the stairs. The women's restroom is located just beyond them. It will look as if you are heading there and that you disappear inside. You and I will follow Hallahan and your girl up to the apartment. We will have to stay close. He has guards on the stairway. Do not make the mistake of brushing against them as we go up. They will feel a presence, perhaps even the air moving, although all of them are jacked up on the drug, so they will have their eyes on your girl. Do you understand?"

She nodded. "I take him down."

"He will not see me, but again, if something goes wrong, it will be me taking him down. Tomas and Lojos will remain downstairs in case anyone is alerted to something happening and they try to rescue their boss. It is important to remember, his brothers will turn up sometime this evening. Tariq and Mataias have interrupted one of their jobs, and they already blew it by not killing or acquiring you."

"Acquiring me?" She was already up and sliding out of the booth, her eyes on the oldest Hallahan brother, who remained beside the stage on the side where the dancers exited on the way back to the dressing room. He hadn't taken his eyes from Emeline. In truth, no one else had, either, other than Blaze and the three Carpathian males.

"They had no idea you were bringing the war to them."

"I issued an invitation."

He took her hand and pulled her tight against his side, moving her easily through the crowd toward their goal. He didn't speak to or shove anyone, but they moved when they saw him coming. Even in his disguise, he had presence.

"Neither Tariq nor I believed they came to kill you. They came for you. Once we realized you have a psychic ability, we were fairly certain they were there to acquire you for their boss."

They had made their way to the stairway. Maksim took them into the shadows just outside the women's restroom and to the left of the stairs. Instantly, she found herself wearing her normal attire, dark jeans and shirt, and her soft-soled boots. Her weapons were all there, in her belt, in her boots, strapped against her back between her shoulder blades. The weight felt familiar, and she found herself breathing easier.

"How could they possibly know I have a psychic ability?"

"Did you ever go to a place that tested your abilities?"

The music was louder, leading to a crescendo. The mesmerized crowd seemed to be collectively breathing in time to the music, ragged and labored, very sexual, so that tension permeated the room. Blaze switched her gaze from Emeline to the crowd. Emeline seemed to be in her own world, a part of that music, a living flame of pure sensuality. She moved on the stage as if she was alone, calling a secret lover to her. Wanting. Needing. Her body undulating, hands moving over her curves as she danced. The crowd seemed just as hungry now, as if every movement Emeline made onstage, they felt in their own bodies. At last, because she had to, Blaze let her gaze rest on Jimmy Hallahan.

His face was flushed, eyes bright. He looked under the influence of drugs, and he probably was, but it was more than that. She knew it was. Something else drove him, and his sights were set on Emeline.

"My father, Em and I all went to this psychic testing center. We did it for fun. We all had these strange things we could do. Em tested the strongest. She was kind of off the charts. Somewhere along the line, all of us got these bad vibes, so we walked out without really completing the tests. Emeline especially was really upset, and for a few weeks she was always looking over her shoulder. She said she thought the tests were for something else. I just felt the bad vibe and Dad, well, Dad could be paranoid."

"There is a database of women who took those tests. Vampires were after them. Carpathians recently got a hold of the database and we are sending out hunters to protect them. We just have to make certain we get there before the vampires do."

Blaze still wasn't comfortable with the term *vampire*. She believed him. She believed him because she had always believed Emeline. Emeline had described in detail exactly what she'd witnessed, and there was no doubt that two men with rotting flesh had sunk teeth into their victim and drained blood. She could see it smeared on their mouths and on their jagged, stained teeth. And of course, there was the nightmare . . .

For a short while, both women had tried to explain the vampirish-looking males as having a disease, but *two* with the disease? And there were killings of the homeless, of prostitutes, bodies torn and drained of blood. No one believed in vampires but secretly, she and Em, when they were young and Em lived mostly in the streets, creeping up to Blaze's room at night through the fire escape, had believed in another world.

They had the same nightmare and in that nightmare, there were vampires, monstrous creatures chasing them through a long, dark tunnel. They would wake, both shivering, sweating, scared out of their minds. Emeline was always quiet and she stayed awake, curled into a protective ball, her knees up tight into her chest, her head resting on them, arms around her legs as she rocked herself back and forth.

Over the years, the nightmare became more vivid, the tunnel even more real. They could see the gaslights up high on the wall of the tunnels, throwing a strange, yellowish glow through the darkness. The tunnel walls were of brick. Old brick. The tunnel itself was musty and smelled evil, as if it had been used for a long time by malevolent beings for foul purposes.

There were smears of blood on the walls as they ran down them. On the bricks and on the floor. Dark and ugly. They raced through a room with ancient tools of torture and kept going. Neither spoke, but they touched hands occasionally to give each other strength and courage.

Below ground seemed to be a maze of tunnels, of dark, hideous rooms, none good, most empty, but the echo of screams had been left behind. There was a room that was all modern. Totally modern. Computers everywhere. Screens everywhere. They both knew this was the center of the maze, and they had to get out before they were seen. If they didn't . . . They ran faster. Hearts beating wildly. Terrified. Terror grew beyond imagination as the tunnel they rushed through began to contort, the walls closing together, the ceiling lowering and the floor pitching. At that moment, as if by mutual agreement, they woke.

She didn't know if Em still dreamt that terrible dream, but once Emeline had stopped slipping into her room through the fire escape and Sean had sent her out of the country, the nightmares had stopped.

"When this is over, we will have to protect your friend. They will keep coming after her."

"Emeline won't accept protection. She has major trust issues. Her life hasn't been pleasant. She takes care of herself and she's loyal to Dad and me . . ." Blaze trailed off. There was no more Dad. There was only Blaze. Now Blaze and Emeline.

"She will not have a choice."

The music ended with a crashing of drums. The stage went dark. The crowd went wild. Blaze saw Emeline running toward the exit and Hallahan coming out of the shadows, shackling her wrist and jerking her toward him. Emeline struggled and Hallahan leaned in close and whispered something in her ear. She stopped struggling, but her gaze slipped passed Jimmy to scan the room.

"She can't see me," Blaze said, trying not to panic.

"No. If I allow her to see you, someone else might as well. Tomas and Lojos are sticking close. If we cannot get to her, if he takes her somewhere else, they will stop him."

The Hallahan brothers were predictable. They used the upstairs apartment where they had their video equipment set up to record their perverse, depraved acts. They enjoyed hurting the women they brought there, humiliating them and forcing compliance. Still, Blaze didn't like that Emeline might feel abandoned. Scared. She detested that Em might be frightened and afraid that Blaze hadn't come to the club to protect her.

There were too many nights Em had climbed up to the roof and down to the fire escape, running from someone in the streets. Hiding from men who would hurt her. She'd had a shit life, even after Sean had tried to get involved. No one would consider him as a foster parent because he owned a bar, lived over it and was a single parent. A man. That left Emeline to her crazy relatives. Junkies and alcoholics. The worst. They used her as a slave in the store they collectively owned, although she preferred working there to being at home.

She was held at gunpoint four times. Shot once. Was back in the store working the night shift even when she was underage and they mostly sold liquor late at night. Sean kept an eye out, but he had a business of his own to run, so more than once she was in trouble. A young girl alone, men coming in drunk or jacked up on drugs.

Emeline, she whispered softly, trying to connect mind to mind. *Don't be afraid. I'm here for you.*

Jimmy Hallahan gripped Emeline by her arm, and if anyone looked close, he had it locked high behind her back as he dragged her through the crowd to the stairs. Beside her, Maksim radiated heat. Energy. None of it was good. The power was so strong that she touched his arm to calm him, afraid Hallahan and his guards would feel the Carpathian's buried rage.

Jimmy was so far gone, in the throes of the drug, he didn't look right or left, but continued dragging Emeline up the stairs. He had a phone in one hand now, flipping it open, talking into it.

"Answer your damn phone once in a while. I've got a hot one. So hot, man. Get back here when you're finished with your job. This whore is going to make the three of you happy." He snapped the phone closed and thrust open the door to the apartment.

Blaze followed them up the stairs, right behind them, so close she could practically breathe on Emeline. She didn't dare touch her, but she wanted to. Right behind her, Maksim followed. They slipped through the door as Hallahan shoved Emeline, sending her flying across the room. She stumbled, lost her balance in her crystal stiletto heels and sprawled out on the floor.

Jimmy slammed the door, locked it and turned back to her with a vicious, hungry smile.

TEN

JIMMY HALLAHAN STALKED across the room, reached down and hauled Emeline up by her hair. "You stupid little whore. I tell you to come, you come. You got that? You capable of understanding that when a man tells you to do something, you fucking do it?" He slapped her hard.

Emeline didn't answer. She didn't resist. She didn't cry or make a sound. She simply looked at him. Right in the eye. That was Em. She didn't back down. She wasn't trained in warfare like Blaze, but she had courage. She'd grown up on the streets and she wasn't afraid to die. She had never been afraid to die. Sometimes Blaze thought she was more afraid of living.

"I feel you in here, Blaze," Emeline said. "You here?"

Can you muffle sound? Blaze asked Maksim.

Of course. He can yell all he wants, but no one will hear him.

"Yeah, babe, I'm here," Blaze said as she moved into position behind Hallahan and kicked him hard with the toe of her boot right behind his knee. At the same time she fisted his hair and yanked him over backward, stepping to the side so that he toppled hard. The moment he was on the floor, she stomped his throat.

I want him to see me.

He will see you.

Jimmy rolled, swearing, his gaze jumping to her face. She stepped back and watched him stand up, his hand going to his boot to extract a knife. She smiled at him. "Welcome to the party, Jimmy."

"Welcome to *my* party, bitch." He brought the knife low, blade up, and circled her.

"Emmy, why is it that men always call a woman a bitch when she does the exact same thing as the man?"

"I think it's a lack of vocab, Blaze," Emeline said, stepping well back, giving Blaze room. "It isn't like Jimmy Hallahan has much of an education. He dropped out of school to build bombs, and he wasn't very good at it. He got caught *three* times and went to prison all three times. Didn't learn much there, either." She didn't touch her swelling face, cover up or in any way act afraid. That was Em.

"Maybe he learned how to be a bitch, a prison bitch," Blaze said. "That's why he likes to use that word. He's kind of describing himself."

Jimmy roared with rage and stepped into her, using his size, expecting to intimidate her, thrusting upward toward her belly as he came. She slapped his wrist down hard, as she glided to the side, her speed taking her out of his path, her foot slamming hard into the side of his knee, driving it in so that he stumbled. She kicked his kneecap viciously, putting her weight behind it. She didn't weigh all that much, but it only took eighty pounds of pressure to break the kneecap, and she used every ounce she had.

He went down screaming. Swearing. His face twisted in fury. He spat on the floor, eyes wild, as he tried to drag himself up, the knife still clenched in his fist.

"Your father screamed like a girl. Like a fucking pig."

She raised her eyebrows, staying just out of reach. "Like you just did? Because that was you screaming, Jimmy, and a girl did that. Sean's daughter. *She* took you out. No one can hear you. No one is coming to save you. Not your guards. Not your brothers. You're going to die here, and you'll die knowing a girl took your worthless, sorry ass down."

She kept her voice even, although inside she was crying for her father. This man had tortured him. Even enjoyed it. She knew if he got his hands on her or Emeline, he would do the same to them. She half turned away from him, her gaze jumping to her friend's, checking to see that she was all right.

Jimmy shrieked his fury again, trying to rise. At the last moment, he threw his knife straight at her. Blaze moved with blinding speed—speed she didn't even know she had. She was out of the way of the poorly spinning blade. The four throwing knives she had concealed in the loops of her belt didn't miss. She was deadly accurate with them, she had been since she was six years old. That was the last time she could ever remember missing, even by an eighth of an inch. Four silver hilts protruded, one from his throat, one from his heart, one from his groin and one from his belly.

"Overkill much?" Emeline asked.

"He tortured Dad; there is no such thing as overkill," Blaze said, unrepentant. "I gave him his chance. He lost."

Emeline pressed back against the wall, her eyes showing shock, staring down at Jimmy Hallahan. His head was turned toward Emeline, eyes wide open. "You should have heard the things that scumbag said he was going to do to me."

Maksim materialized out of the corner, and Emeline gasped but said nothing at all as he crouched beside the body. Her gaze jumped to Blaze for reassurance.

"He's with me," Blaze said.

"I think I got that. What is he doing?"

Maksim put a hand on either side of Hallahan's head. "I am going to read his memories, before all activity in his brain ceases."

"No." Emeline took a step forward, but carefully avoided touching Maksim. "You can't. There's something—some-one—else in him. I don't care if you believe me. I saw him. I think he was using Jimmy as some kind of conduit. He looked right at me. As he was dying, he turned his head and looked right at me."

Maksim let Hallahan's head fall back to the floor and he slowly stood. Blaze immediately went to Emeline and put her arm around her. Em had all the courage in the world, but she looked pale and shaky.

"It was him. The one I saw before, Blaze," Emeline said, looking into Blaze's eyes, willing her to believe. "I know it was and he recognized me." She shuddered. "Just like in my dream."

"We have to get out of here," Maksim said. "Right now." He waved his hand at the knives on the body and they were instantly gone, returned clean to the loops in Blaze's belt. He removed all evidence of their presence in the room. "I need to take your girl's blood."

"No way," Emeline clapped both hands over her neck and slipped behind Blaze.

Blaze felt her heart twist in a funny way. No one could resist Emeline. No one. Not, it appeared, even Maksim. She stepped away from him, her body protective of Emeline, feeling her trembling. Inside, her own body was shiver-ing, and something precious was crumbling away, but she stood, ready to defend Em against the man she knew she was already irrevocably tied to. She had let that happen. She had gone into the relationship—if you could call it that—with her eyes wide open.

"Sufletul meu." He whispered it.

Blaze knew it was an endearment. It was in the tone. In the way he said it. The way he looked at her. She shook her head, resisting his lure.

"Do you know what that means?" he asked softly. "It means you are my soul. The air that I breathe. And, Blaze, you are. You are both those things to me. Never doubt, not even for a moment, that the only woman I see is you."

Blaze's heart shifted. Melted. Her stomach did a slow somersault. He said the most ridiculous things to her, but they worked. He always sounded sincere. She knew he was capable of great violence. He might be very soft spoken, but he was dangerous. There was no doubt in her mind, but still, he said things like that and she was a puddle on the floor.

"We do not want anyone to see us leave. We want Jimmy Hallahan found in this apartment dead and no one to say we were ever here," Maksim explained gently.

"Everyone saw Jimmy drag me up the stairs," Emeline pointed out. "And there are cameras everywhere."

"Tomas and Lojos took care of the cameras, and the woman Hallahan dragged up the stairs didn't look anything at all like you," Maksim said. "I am not going to hurt you. I need to see what you saw. I need to know you will not ever betray us. If I do not have your blood when I step out of this room, I cannot guarantee your safety."

"I can," Blaze said, anger creeping into her voice. "Don't threaten her."

"I am not making threats," Maksim said, impatience beginning to edge his unflappable calm. "I am stating facts. Think about it, Blaze. I am Carpathian. We are hunted already by humans who believe we are vampires. We hunt the vampires they cannot. If the world knew of us, imagine the persecution of our people."

Emeline kept her hand wrapped around her throat. "I am not going to say a word. I had to leave the country and the only two people in the world I loved because I used the word *vampire* in my statement to the police."

"You knew for certain it was a vampire," Blaze said with sudden insight. "Emmy, you knew. How?"

"We have to leave now," Maksim said. "I have to shield you. Two of the Hallahan brothers just entered the club.

Tomas says we have to move." He gently moved Blaze out of his way. "I swear to you, I will not hurt your friend."

Emeline kept her hands pressed to her neck. "I know what could happen. I know."

"If you know the difference between a Carpathian and a vampire, you know I will not harm you. Let me keep Blaze safe. She will not leave you here to face them alone."

"I want them to come in," Blaze said. "It is my chance to get two more of his brothers."

"We need them to lead us to their master," Maksim said. "Cutting off the soldiers will not get us the head."

Blaze looked into Emeline's eyes. "You call it, honey."

Emeline took a deep breath and slowly allowed her hands to drop, her eyes on Blaze. "Stay with me."

"I'm with you."

"Just like this." She kept staring into Blaze's eyes with trust.

Blaze knew there wasn't a single soul in the world Emeline trusted other than Blaze. "Just like this."

"If he kills me, you'll kill him, right?" Emeline persisted. Her body shook.

"Yes, honey. He wouldn't be the man I believe him to be. You're my sister now. My family. There is just the two of us."

"Three," Maksim corrected. "I belong to you, Blaze, and you to me. She's your girl, so that makes her mine as well. I would protect both of you with my life. My friends will do the same."

"If you're for real," Emeline said, "you'll need a lot of friends to keep us safe, because the vampire is going to come after me."

"Any moment he will be here," Maksim said softly. "We have to get you out."

Emeline didn't touch Blaze, leaving both her hands free in case Maksim was lying and was going to kill her. Blaze didn't understand why Emeline was so certain she was going to die. Em didn't move, but her entire body shuddered when he touched her. He blinked. Startled. Stepped back.

"Your mind is shielded. I cannot help you by calming you. You have to let me in."

Emeline shook her head. "Just do it. I want to know."

"I will be as gentle as possible," Maksim said, not arguing. "You will feel a bite of pain and then it will not hurt. It will not feel the same as it does to Blaze, or if your lifemate were to take your blood, but it will not hurt."

He bent his head and without further preamble sank his teeth into her neck. She gasped, but she didn't move. Blaze stared into her eyes, giving her reassurance. Taking her trust. Maksim opened her mind to his so she could feel what he was feeling. So she could hear.

Get. Out. Of. There. A man's voice whispering in Maksim's ear. Lojos. Blaze knew because Maksim identified him for her.

If you cannot get them out, we will have to kill these two. Mataias already killed one of them. We have only these two to lead us to Reginald. That was a different voice. That was Tomas.

So two Hallahans were dead. Blaze would have killed the other two as they came into the room, but with the vampire after Emeline, she was going to have to have patience and allow them to live so they could lead the Carpathian hunters back to their master. She'd strike then and allow the hunters to kill their prey.

Maksim swept his tongue across the pinpricks at Emeline's neck and waved the women to the side of the door as he lifted his head. "I will mask our presence. The moment the door opens and they are through, Blaze, lead her out. I will bring up the rear. They will not see you, but do not brush up against them or anyone on the stairs."

Blaze nodded and gripped Emeline's elbow. "We'll be all right, Em. We're just going to go straight through the club and out the door."

Emeline's face was stark white. "We have to hurry. Oh, God, Blaze. He's close. I can feel him close now. Do you feel that? Like in the dream." Her voice was a panicked whisper. Emeline didn't panic. She was a street rat and she could disappear when she needed, slipping away through cracks in walls and over rooftops. She had mad skills in the streets, and she never lost her ability to think. Her brain worked at all times, solving puzzles and figuring out the next thing to do. Blaze knew she must be terrified to sound so close to panic.

Before Blaze could reassure Emeline, the door bounced open and Terry and Carrick Hallahan burst into the room. Before Carrick thought to close the door, Blaze hurried through, dragging Emeline after her, trusting Maksim to keep them cloaked from view. She didn't look back, but she heard the shocked curses as she made her way down the stairs, right past the Hallahans' guards. She kept one hand on Emeline's shoulder, but Em didn't hesitate; she moved through the crowd quickly, not even looking at the two men closing in on either side of them.

Tomas and Lojos? Blaze wanted their identity confirmed. She was certain she was right. Both men had the same dangerous look to them that Maksim did. They were tall with that long, dark, gorgeous hair. Clearly they were twins. Still . . .

Hurry, Blaze, Maksim insisted, telling her without answering that the two men were his friends.

She could feel it now, the swelling danger. The feeling of evil slowly invading the club. The air felt poisonous. She held her breath and knew Emeline was doing the same thing.

Around them, the crowd began to shift restlessly. A fight broke out near the front door. A shot rang out. A woman screamed. Two men rushed the cages and dragged a stripper out, throwing her to the floor. More fights broke out between them and the nearest exit. The smell of blood was strong.

Tomas moved up in front of Emeline.

Stay close to him, Maksim warned the two women, startling Emeline with telepathic communication. *Do not speak aloud or even attempt an answer in your head. He is seeking you.*

Something dark and oily slid by, jerked to a halt, and for the first time, Blaze saw him. Her heart nearly stopped beating in her chest. She could see why Emeline had been so terrified from the moment she had escaped this monstrous beast. At first glance, he looked to be a handsome, courtly man in a dark business suit. She stared at him intently and saw through the illusion. It took everything she had in her, every ounce of courage, not to scream.

This was her first real look at the undead. He was far worse than anything Hollywood could ever have conceived. His skin was white, pasty white. His gums had receded, leaving jagged teeth clearly stained with blood. His flesh appeared to be falling off his skull, with small tears where tiny parasites wiggled. His hair hung long in tufts and dank, dirty strands. Bald spots showed through the thin, frizzy threads, and she could see the same wiggling parasites boring through unsightly holes.

His eyes glowed red and his teeth snapped together. "I smell you," he hissed as he reached long arms with bony fingers toward Emeline.

Tomas, the Carpathian guard closest to her, leapt to protect her, to insert himself between them as Blaze threw her body against Emeline's, pushing her forward and out of the vampire's reach. The terrible talons settled around her wrist, jerking her toward the undead. Tomas's body blocked hers from Reginald Coonan.

Blaze screamed as the razor-sharp nails cut her wrist, burning her skin with an acid-like substance. Blood sprayed into the air. Tomas hit Reginald hard, driving him backward into the crowd. The vampire kept possession of Blaze's wrist, his talon sawing deeper, opening the laceration wider. Maksim slammed his fist deep into the master vampire's chest, seeking the heart.

Reginald screamed, still dragging Blaze backward,

falling toward the crowd. The crowd could see his monstrous appearance as he leaned down and drove his teeth deep into Blaze's shoulder, just missing her neck. Chaos erupted; people stampeded for the exits, knocking one another down and trampling the fallen.

Blaze felt the vampire elevating their fear. He twisted and raked Maksim's face and throat with his claws. Swarms of parasites raced up Maksim's fist and arm, eating the flesh, as he tried to burrow deeper into the vampire's chest. It was impossible with the undead twisting and ripping at Blaze's shoulder with his teeth as he did so. Maksim had no choice but to protect her. He withdrew his fist and used both hands to knock the vampire off of her, sending him flying across the room.

Behind them, Emeline screamed. The sound was chilling, filled with sheer terror. Blaze turned her head, trying to spot Emeline through the stampeding crowd. She caught glimpses of Lojos fighting with something every bit as evil as Reginald. The thing, once Carpathian, was now as monstrous as the master vampire, maybe more so, and it had Emeline locked in front of it, holding her as a shield by driving four talons from each hand into the flesh and bone of her rib cage.

Emeline hung suspended in the air, the razor-sharp stiletto knives embedded deep. She thrashed and fought, but the vampire backpedaled through the crowd, holding her off the ground by the blades as he deliberately stomped and kicked men and women lying on the floor like so much litter.

Reginald flew through the air, a dark shadowy figure above the crowd, descending straight toward Blaze, his arms lengthening as Maksim leapt to intercept him. Blaze's wrist continued to spray blood. She felt burns right down to her bones, as if, when the vampire ripped her wrist open, he'd dumped acid into the wound. She could see the arm snaking around Maksim, although the two bodies collided in midair. Hastily she drew a knife from her belt loop, heedless of the blood loss. As the arm approached, the bony fingers stretching to reach her, she sliced down and across, putting every ounce of strength she had into the attack.

Reginald couldn't actually see her because Maksim and he fought viciously, tearing at each other's chests. She leapt back the moment the blade went through flesh and bone, severing the hand. Reginald screamed horribly. Black blood sprayed the room, bubbling on the floor and fallen bodies, burning right through everything. She hadn't expected the hand to fall, but she had a newfound strength she couldn't explain.

The hand didn't remain stationary, but began to roll in an attempt to get back to its owner. She stumbled, terrified at what these creatures were capable of. Emeline's screams drew her attention away from the fear. Her heart nearly stopped when she saw Emmy still suspended in the air by the razor-sharp talons driven into her ribs.

Trusting Maksim to deal with the vampire, Blaze ran toward Emeline, leaping over fallen bodies, ignoring the cries of those being sprayed by acid-like blood, and whipped out a gun. She was a crack shot even on the move. She'd been practicing since she was three years old. She fired five shots in rapid succession at the vampire suspending Emeline in the air. She hit both eyes, his nose, and drilled two more bullets into his gaping mouth.

Instantly the knives dissolved, and Emeline dropped to the club floor, Lojos cushioning her fall. He clamped both hands hard to the sides of her body and lifted her into his arms. Now that Emeline was safe, the adrenaline left Blaze's body and she found herself sitting abruptly. Right there in the middle of the floor. A chill swept through her body. She felt numb, and cold. So cold.

"I am going to lift you," a man's voice said.

She could barely lift her head. He reached over her shoulder and removed the gun from her hand. She couldn't keep a grip on the stock, even if she could summon the will to do so. The gun slipped from her nerveless fingers, and then he clamped his hand around her wrist. Hard. Like a vise. It hurt. Burned.

"I am Tomas." *Maksim, we have to go now if your lifemate will live. Let him go. Mataias will track them. She's lost too much blood. Far too much.*

Blaze found her head too heavy to keep upright and she let it fall against his chest. Emeline was gone, carried out by the man called Lojos that Maksim trusted. She had no choice but to trust him as well. Tomas hurried out with her, and she felt Maksim pouring into her mind. Strong. So strong.

Do not leave me, Blaze.

Tomas rushed through the door, leaving the club behind, and she must have been dreaming because she swore they were moving through the air, the wind rushing past her head. Still, the cool breeze didn't clear the fog from her mind. She remained confused. She clung to Maksim's mind, although it was Tomas holding her, keeping her from tumbling back to earth.

I am with you, sufletul meu. I will always be with you. I have no choice but to bring you fully into my world, or I will lose you, Blaze. Give me your consent. You have lost too much blood. You already are walking mostly in my world with me. Come wholly to me. Give yourself to me. You will be like me, and together we will find the undead who ordered your father's death.

He didn't need to entice her into his world. She'd already made up her mind. Only Emeline held her where she was, and Emeline seemed to know and accept the Carpathian world of the undead far more than she did. In any case, it was Maksim fading in and out, not her.

She tried to reassure him, but the effort seemed too much and she was cold. They shouldn't be rushing through the clouds, so far from earth, because she just couldn't get warm.

ELEVEN

MAKSIM CAUGHT UP with Tomas, slid his arms around Blaze and took her from the ancient Carpathian, making the switch right in the air. *Make certain her friend is safe and attended to.* Blaze definitely needed blood and she needed it fast. He could feel her slipping, but Tomas had stopped the blood loss and sealed the tear so she wasn't losing any more.

Maksim used one nail, even in flight, to open a line for her. He pressed her mouth to the ruby beads. She didn't need to be prompted or pushed. Blaze fed. She took his blood and she did it without hesitation.

Lojos says her friend has also lost a lot of blood, Tomas informed him.

Maksim was grateful Tomas stayed on his flank, protecting his lifemate. The vampires in the bar had acted out of character. Their focus had been to acquire the two women. Emeline, for certain.

Give her blood if she needs it. Keep her alive. Lojos, do not let her out of your sight until we figure out what is going on and why they want her.

This one is a powerful psychic. I can feel the energy pouring off of her, Lojos interjected. *She does not like my touch and wants away from me. I do not feel her fear so much as her distaste.*

Keep her alive, Maksim reiterated, although if she were psychic, each of the men would be very aware of the fact that she could be a lifemate to another Carpathian, and they would guard her with their lives.

He poured himself into Blaze's mind while she fed, filling her with his warmth, reassurance and strength. She stirred, letting Maksim know she was aware of him, but she didn't speak. She let him fill her, not trying to hold barriers between them, accepting him in her mind, allowing him to take control. He knew the things that drove her. He knew the good things about her as well as the bad. He knew the strengths and weaknesses of her character.

She took his blood, knowing full well she was taking that last step into his world. He only had to take her blood for the exchange, and the conversion would begin. He hoped to finish that quickly—as soon as he got her to his home.

He loved that he knew her far more intimately than anyone else on the planet. Her father had shaped her character very early on. She was a fighter. A warrior. She was soft inside, but she had a core of strength that was unbelievable. She was skilled and already she was moving through his mind each time they shared telepathy, in order to acquire his skills as a hunter of the undead.

Enough, Blaze. He couldn't be too weak when he converted her. He would have to help her through what he'd heard was an extremely rough ordeal. His lifemate would die as a human and be reborn a Carpathian.

She obeyed him, again without hesitation, as if she knew how important this night was, and that he had to be at the top of his strength. Her tongue slid across the opening over his heart, and his body shuddered with the pleasure the tiny gesture brought.

He took her toward the river, where Tariq Asenguard had a huge compound. Maksim's home lay behind the larger estate. He had less acreage because he didn't need it, not so close to Tariq. They were neighbors, and few trespassed on their properties. The Asenguard property was set well back from the tall, iron fence, with its scrolls and sharp spear-like points at the top. Climbing over the fence was nearly impossible, and with the safeguards, humans avoided the place.

He tightened his hold on Blaze. She had agreed to come into his world completely. He searched carefully in her mind for any hesitation, and he found none. She believed in him. She could read his mind in the same way he could read hers. She didn't understand their connection, not like he understood it, but she accepted it. He began the descent at the back fence of Tariq's property. The forest was thickest there, a dark grove of trees, unexpected on the edge of the city.

Something came out of the sky just to his left, entering his vision from the south, over the river. It dropped from the clouds, plummeting fast and streaking right toward them. Tomas put on a surge of speed to intercept. The missile went through him with such force it continued on to strike Maksim in the calf. Fire burned white-hot through him, and instantly thousands of needles pierced his flesh and entered his bloodstream.

Tomas grunted and began to drop, forcing Maksim to get beneath him to stop his descent. He managed to wrap one arm around Tomas. To his shock, Blaze stirred, seemed to comprehend the danger, and she reached out and took hold of the Carpathian hunter with her one good arm.

Tariq, we are under attack. Where are you and Mataias?

Maksim's voice was as calm as ever, but he knew the situation was dire. Tomas was in bad shape. The spear of fire had cauterized the wound, but it had also injected both of them with something poisonous. Blaze needed blood. A lot of it.

I have your blood in me, she reminded. *I can feel it working to keep me alive. Tell me what to do for both of you.*

They were close to the ground. Even if he burrowed deep, he knew they wouldn't have been attacked in the air if there weren't something worse waiting on the ground. He had no choice with Tomas so injured.

They will come at us, Blaze. Tomas has put himself to sleep. He will be unprotected and very vulnerable. I do not know what poison has been used, but I can already feel the effects.

Who are "they"?

Two master vampires attacked in the club. They will have lesser vampires and human puppets serving them.

Any special way to kill a human puppet?

They are hard to kill and once you have, you have to burn them. The heart of the vampire must be removed and incinerated for him to die.

He felt the steel in her. Yes, his blood was bringing her back but she was already a warrior, prepared to take on whatever came at them and protect both Tomas and Maksim should it be necessary.

I don't have the strength to punch through their chest to get at the heart.

If you find yourself that close, Blaze, use a knife, go in fast and use a circular motion to cut out a path. Get back, dart in a second time and keep at it. They cannot get their hands or teeth on you. Their blood will burn like acid.

She nodded, taking a grip on Tomas with renewed strength. He felt it now, the Carpathian blood moving through her to continue the change it had already begun. He didn't have time to worry that the conversion might start before the actual third blood exchange, but it stood to reason that the first-time exchanges had already prepared her body's organs.

Maksim floated them to the ground, waving his hand to open the earth beneath them so he could fit Tomas's body in the healing soil. He needed more than the earth might give him, but they didn't have time.

Two of them, he warned Blaze.

She nodded, stepping out of his arms, turning her back on him, hands moving up into position with her weapons.

There is another in the tree just beyond the fence, she said.

That one is vampire, he informed her. *I will see to him. The others are human, yet not human. They live on human flesh now. They seek blood. They will be ravenous and try to come at you with teeth to tear through your body to get at the blood.*

Blaze laughed aloud, the sound unexpected in the circumstances. "Lovely," she said, facing the two puppets as they came out of the trees close to them.

She studied the two creatures shuffling their way toward her. They were like most puppets Maksim had seen. A vampire had promised immortality and had taken their blood numerous times, feeding on them, bringing them to the point of death over and over. Sometimes they fed them a little of the burning blood they desired, but mostly, they corrupted the mind until it was rotting and so far gone they could only follow their master's orders and hunt desperately for blood and human flesh to consume.

The burning obsession for blood and flesh was so strong in puppets, they salivated constantly. Long strings of saliva fell from the corners of their mouths as they shuffled forward, growling and snarling, red-rimmed eyes focused on Blaze. Hair hung in matted messes. Both had stains of old blood on their faces and clothing. They smelled like rotting flesh.

Blaze didn't move. She kept her body solidly between the two puppets and Tomas, who lay as if dead in a shallow grave. Maksim had poured as much soil over him as possible in the short amount of time they had, but even with that, without blood and the necessary healing saliva and the removal of the poison in his system, he wouldn't survive for long. The soil, at least, would give him a fighting chance.

I am ten minutes away from you, Tariq informed them.

I am about the same, Mataias added.

Maksim touched Blaze's hip. *Stay in my mind. If I go down, get out of here.*

That will never happen, she stated firmly, glancing at him over her shoulder.

He caught just the flash of her green eyes, but she meant what she said, and there would be no arguing with her. His woman would stand. Even if the odds were totally against her.

We should get this done fast then.

She didn't hesitate. She launched herself at the two puppets, streaking toward the lumbering humans, a knife in either hand. She was fast. She'd been fast before Maksim had given her blood, but with each exchange, she got faster and stronger. She moved so fast the vegetation under her feet whirled into the air and nearly covered her passing. She was between them, the blades flashing, sinking deep into their throats, twisting and turning and back out as she ran on past and stopped just behind them.

Maksim launched himself into the air, going for the lesser vampire who thought himself hidden from view. The vampire hit him, twisting at the last moment out of the tree, so they collided in the air. He drove the vampire back against the trunk, impaling him on a broken branch. The vampire tore at his neck and chest with sharp talons and teeth, desperate to pull his body off the wooden stake.

The vampire tore a chunk of flesh from his body and gulped at the blood. Instantly he spat, snarling, pulling back, recognizing the poison in Maksim's system. His expression turned sly.

"You're already dead," he hissed.

"So are you," Maksim said and plunged his fist deep into the vampire's chest, driving a hole deep. The acid burned through his arm right down to the bone. He straightened his fingers, staring into the hideous red eyes, unflinching as his sharp nails dug deep to find the rotting heart.

The undead thrashed harder, trying to free himself. There was no way to shift with Maksim's body pinning him against the broken branch and his arm buried deep. Slowly, Maksim extracted the heart, the sucking sound terrible, matching the shrieking protests of the vampire.

Maksim tossed the heart into the air and drew down the lightning, hitting the shriveled organ as it raced toward the ground. He threw himself backward, away from the flailing undead. He landed unsteadily, his legs unexpectedly giving out. Still, he had the presence of mind to send a fork of lightning straight to the vampire where he hung from the stake in his back. The body was instantly incinerated.

Maksim tried to rise to go to Blaze's aid. The two puppets were bleeding profusely from a half dozen places, each cut so deep that the slashes should have been a kill, but the vampire's wishes prevailed at all times. They moved like zombies already dead. Still, their bodies continued to work in spite of the blood loss.

"They aren't going down," Blaze stated unnecessarily.

Maksim hit the ground hard and dragged himself to where Tomas lay. He covered the other Carpathian's body with his own.

Try fire.

She nodded, lifted her gun, fired two shots into the closest puppet, taking his vision and then doing the same with the second.

Slow your heartbeat, Maksim, so they can't hear it. They'll have to use sound and smell to find you. You can mask that.

He wasn't certain if that was the truth. The poison was fast acting. He could slow his heart, or stop it altogether, slowing the spread of the poison, but that would leave Blaze without even the aid of his mind.

Reinforcements will be here in a couple more minutes, Maksim. Do it.

Blaze moved quickly to the right and then sprinted, running in circles around the two puppets to disorient them so they wouldn't know the position of the two Carpathian hunters. She kept an eye on Maksim, willing him to do as she'd asked. She needed him to slow his heart and the poison until the two other hunters arrived and helped.

Hurry, she whispered. Maksim had been moving fast, expending energy. The poison had plenty of time to do damage.

She ripped at her shirt and wrapped it around a very dry fallen branch, forming a makeshift torch. It took two strikes of the match to get the thing burning. The two puppets had homed in on the sound of her heart beating. She let them come in close to her, and then moved back a few steps in order to draw them farther away from Maksim and Tomas.

They followed her one step at a time, their growls deep and constant. Blood ran down their faces from the holes where their eyes used to be. The sight turned her stomach. Bile churned and filled her throat, but she held her ground and let them shuffle closer. The first puppet stretched out his arms toward her. The flames weren't burning enough and she slashed with her knife, cutting deep. The creature didn't howl. His mouth opened wide in a silent scream, but the deep cut didn't deter him in the least from continuing to come at her.

It was all she could do not to throw the torch before it was truly burning. The creatures seemed unstoppable. No matter what she did, they kept coming. Taking a deep breath, her hand burning, she counted slowly in her mind and then moved in fast, touching the flames to the puppet's shirt, his matted hair and his jeans.

The hair and shirt caught fire and she jumped back. The creature continued to shuffle forward, straight toward her, on fire. She needed wind. Something to fan the flames. Her own torch burned hot, almost too hot to keep a hold of. As if hearing her desperate thoughts, the wind shifted, fanning the fire so that flames leapt high, engulfing the puppet.

He kept coming toward her, but now he was a wall of flame. The stench was horrible. She stared in horror, unable to think of anything else to do to kill the mad-driven creature desperate to carry out his master's orders. She stumbled backward, keeping an eye on the other puppet that had shuffled dangerously close. Maksim and Tomas lay just beyond her, and she couldn't leave them exposed. She couldn't give much more ground, or the flaming torch of a puppet would be right on them.

Blaze took a deep breath, threw her small torch at the other creature. It hit his shirt, and the wind followed, fanning flames. She didn't have time to see if she'd accomplished her goal. The fiery flames were close enough to her now that she felt the heat. She ran straight at the puppet engulfed completely in fire. Launching herself into the air, she kicked out with both feet, hitting him squarely in the chest.

The heat was intense, so intense, she knew her jeans had melted in a couple of spots right into her shins and calves, but the puppet fell back and writhed on the ground. Hideous noises escaped. He began to drag himself across the ground toward the two Carpathian hunters lying motionless. The other puppet seemed to have homed in on them as well. His chest and hair were on fire, but only smaller flames crackled, the fire just beginning.

Blaze did the only thing she could think of. She used the knife on herself, slicing across her palm and flinging the blood at the two desperate puppets. The droplets of blood spun in the air between them, as if they had a life of their own. Blaze took a cautious step to the right of the Carpathians. Both puppets turned toward her. Elated, she took a second step, and both turned completely toward her.

Step by step she led them away from the poisoned

Carpathians. She kept breathing deep, deliberately slowing her heart so she wouldn't panic. The one dragging himself on the ground repulsed her, even terrified her. She couldn't stand the sight of the living torches following the blood trail she continuously flung into the air.

Fortunately they didn't move fast, and that gave her time to consider her next move. The one on the ground suddenly let out a shriek as if he finally felt the flames consuming his body. He stared at her through the orange and red tower of conflagration. She froze. The eyes were black holes, no intelligence. Vacant. Gone. Not even red. Suddenly they were alive again, menacing, staring at her with malevolence. There was intelligence there and promise of retribution.

She blinked and the fire consumed the puppet, engulfing him completely so that there was nothing left but black ash. Still, she shivered and deep inside, for the first time, she felt absolute terror. The other puppet was close. His smell sent her stomach churning, and the heat told her the fire was building.

"Step back," a voice said, and she whirled to face a tall man with long, streaming black hair and a grim, weathered face. He looked just like Tomas, only maybe a little scarier, although Tomas had the same look to him that warned others not to cross him.

She did what he said instantly. He moved fast, so fast she couldn't really see the blur. He was like Maksim, one moment there, the next he tossed a blackened heart of the dying puppet to the ground. Lightning forked in the sky. Thunder rolled.

"I have to learn to do that," she murmured aloud as she hurried around the big man to the two Carpathians lying on the ground. Crouching, she ran her hand over Maksim's face, trailing her fingers down to his pulse.

"It kills them faster," he explained.

Maksim's pulse was slow. So slow she almost missed it, but she was patient. He'd trusted her to keep them safe and that meant the world to her. Lightning sizzled and slashed across the sky, jumped down in a long ropy whip and hit, first the heart with deadly accuracy, and then the remaining puppet. To her astonishment, the lightning whip hit dead center in the middle of the pile of black ashes from the other puppet. The ashes went gray and scattered with the wind.

"They both have some kind of poison in their system," Blaze explained as the other Carpathian came up beside her and crouched low. He put a hand on his brother's leg, but remained silent, his eyes on her face, as if expecting something from her. She did her best. "I don't know what to do. Tomas shut down his heart immediately. He took the worst of the hit, but the spear or arrow went through him and hit Maksim in the calf. Maksim took out the vampire waiting here for us, and then he had to shut down his heart as well to slow the spread of the poison."

"I am Mataias." He motioned her to move out of the way. "Stay back. I need to analyze the poison and remove it from their bodies. In some cases, the poison used is a parasite that can jump from one body to another."

Blaze nodded and gave him room, but she remained close enough to help Maksim if needed. She touched his mind. He was there. Alive, but far from her. She swallowed hard. It had taken all of the ten minutes to keep the puppets from the two Carpathians. She wasn't certain if the poison had continued to spread through Maksim's body while he lay motionless, covering the other hunter, still protective even in his hibernation.

A second hunter strode toward them. The first glanced up, blinking as if coming back from being asleep or a long way off. "Tariq," he greeted. "You take my brother. I am already working on Maksim."

He hadn't *touched* Maksim. Blaze nearly protested, but then she realized Mataias was no longer there beside her. His body was. But he wasn't. She held herself very still listening. Feeling. Waiting. Then he was there. *Inside*

Maksim's body. She was connected to Maksim and she felt Mataias's presence. He was pure light. A white-hot light, all spirit. No ego. No sense of self. Only healing energy.

She didn't move. Didn't startle. But she watched and she followed the light through Maksim's body. It didn't seem possible, but she knew she was there with the hunter as he pushed the poison ruthlessly toward Maksim's pores, forcing it out of his bloodstream. Out of every organ and muscle. He was meticulous, slow, taking time to check and double-check that not one single drop of the dark, thin streaks of sludge remained hidden.

She was shocked. Moved. She felt as though she witnessed a miracle. More than the ability to do such a thing, it was the sheer selflessness of the act. Mataias wasn't there at all. He gave himself to his fellow Carpathian, turning himself into a tool to heal, without thought for himself. It was so beautiful, Blaze found tears in her eyes.

"I think we got it all," Mataias said softly.

She blinked and found herself staring into his dark eyes. Mataias was back in his body. Maksim was already stirring beside them.

"I don't think there was a 'we' doing that, but thank you. That was amazing. I wish I could do that."

"You will be able to," Mataias assured. "He needs blood." He brought his wrist to his mouth.

"I have to give it to him," she said softly. "I know I have to."

He hesitated. "He needs strength and Carpathian blood . . ."

"I *feel* that I have to. Strongly."

He held her gaze for a moment and then he nodded. Her palm was still dripping blood and she opened it and placed it over Maksim's mouth, allowing the ruby drops to drip inside. His lips moved against her skin and unexpectedly, little butterflies took off, wings fluttering against the inside wall, traveling down to her sex. She felt him there. In her pulse. In the hot blood suddenly surging through her veins.

Maksim stirred in her mind. Filling her with his warmth. He took the aching hurt of her father's death that she hadn't been able to face and allowed her to grieve when she hadn't. She felt his arms circle her body, and then one hand slid under her wrist, holding it gently to his mouth. The tears streamed down her face. He gave her his love, surrounding her with it, a wall to keep her safe and protected.

He was so gentle with her, yet he could erupt into violence so quickly. Mostly she loved that he gave her license to be who she was, who she needed to be.

Mine, he whispered into her mind. *My lifemate. A warrior woman. You kept them off of us.*

You believed in me. That meant the world. Not just trusting her with his life, but with the life of his friend. He had put himself to sleep, trusting she would keep both Carpathians safe.

I see you, Blaze, the core of steel running through you. You are already Carpathian. You just have not crossed to us fully. Giving me this blood will complete the third exchange.

She didn't know if he was warning her or praising her, but she took it as praise. She had known all along she needed to be the one to give him her blood—that to be reborn as a Carpathian, wholly into his world, she would have to take this last step. She wanted this. Only Emeline held her to the human world. She loved Emmy. She would always love Emmy, but she could better protect her from her enemies as a Carpathian.

Maksim drank deeply and then slid his tongue across the wound, closing it. He sat up and took her into his arms.

"She held them off," Mataias said. "Using her own blood to draw them away from you. No doubt she would have tried to cut out their hearts next."

She knew that was high praise from a hunter because she

knew Maksim was startled by the compliment to her—startled and proud.

"I knew she would do it," Maksim said. "I have to get her to safety before the conversion starts."

"I will take Tomas as soon as Tariq is finished healing him," Mataias said. "Lojos reported he has healed the other woman. She is safe for the moment."

"It will take some time for that wound to heal in Tomas," Maksim observed.

Mataias nodded. "We will watch over him."

There was something in the way Mataias made the statement that set off a series of chills throughout Blaze's body.

TWELVE

MAKSIM LIFTED BLAZE in his arms and carried her to the large, sprawling two-story house set back on the property. The house was old, very old, but it had been carefully reconstructed, preserving the glory of the time while modernizing the windows, plumbing and wiring. The wood had been restored to a golden hue on the floors, and the walls were a light mauve. High ceilings, crystal chandeliers and ornate wainscoting added to the beauty of the old mansion.

"Is this your home?" Blaze looked around with awe. The floor had beautiful patterns of the night sky all in inlaid wood. "I've never seen anything like this."

"I came here some centuries ago and found this spot. Later, I came back and purchased the land, had the house built, and from any of the windows, depending on where the moon is, you can see it and the stars. Upstairs there are moon windows in the ceiling. The open sky is always close."

Blaze paced across the floor. There wasn't a single creak. The house had a feel to it, one of peace and security. Home. She liked that. Still, she pressed a hand to her stomach. She felt hot, her temperature rising. "What can I expect, Maksim?"

His gaze met hers without flinching. "I have never actually witnessed a conversion, Blaze, but I have heard they can be brutal."

Her eyebrows shot up. "Brutal?" She repeated the word and waited for his slow nod. She was very aware he was watching her closely. Expectantly. She took a deep breath. "I suppose it's too late to back out? 'Brutal' doesn't sound good."

"Back out?"

She nodded. "Seeing as how there wasn't full disclosure," she added. "Had you used the term *brutal*, I might have rethought my decision." She was teasing, but then again she wasn't. She didn't like that word and all it implied. *Brutal*. What did that even mean?

He slipped his arm around her waist and pulled her to his side. Tight. That felt nice. Safe. Protected. But the heat moving through her body wasn't the usual heat she felt for him. She swallowed down fear and tilted her head to look up at him.

"Even if you haven't seen someone go through a conversion, can you at least tell me what to expect? I do better if I know what to do and what is going to happen ahead of time." She kept her eyes glued to his.

Maksim didn't look away from her, but there was wariness in his gaze—in his mind. She clung to his strength.

"This is going to be bad, isn't it?"

He nodded slowly. "Your body's organs have to be reshaped. It will rid itself of all toxins. I think it best if we go to ground and neither of us has clothes on."

She swallowed hard and nodded. The first wave of pain was severe. Hard. Abrupt. No warning. Sweeping through her like a tsunami. The pain took her breath, and both hands flew to her stomach, where it felt as if shards of glass and hundreds of razor blades cut through her insides.

Her eyes widened, but she didn't drop her gaze from his. There was sorrow there. Compassion. Fear even. He was afraid for her. Blaze forced air through her lungs and tried to relax her body, to put her mind far away where she couldn't feel the pain. There was no stopping it as the wave took her, but she managed to ride it, stay on top of it, and the moment she felt it ease, she acknowledged it to herself so she would always know it came and went. One could endure anything for a length of time—her father taught her that.

"We'd better hurry, Maksim," she whispered. "It's starting."

"*Dragostea mea*, my love, you are very strong. A warrior unsurpassed."

She realized he felt the pain through the connection of their minds. She pressed her hand against his chest over his heart. "Don't do that, Maksim. Don't stay connected to me. I want you to remember this—I *chose* this. You didn't force me. I *wanted* to come into your world, and I knew it wouldn't be easy. This was *my* decision."

He shook his head. "It is impossible not to love you, Blaze, but if we are being strictly honest, which all lifemates must be with one another, I didn't give you a choice. I bound us together, soul to soul. I needed you in my world to survive. I have lived centuries, and the moment I met you, the temptation was far too much to resist. The ritual binding words are imprinted on the male before birth. I *had* to bind us."

If his confession was supposed to make her think less of him, it didn't succeed. She went up on her toes, pulled his head down and kissed him. "I like that you need me, Maksim, because I need you. Now take me to the ground, or wherever we need to be, because I can feel the heat inside growing and I'm uncomfortable."

Maksim swept his arms around, pulling her wholly into his body. Tight. His hand slid along her jaw and he tipped her face up to his. "I love you, Blaze, more than I can possibly express to you. Whatever happens tonight, know I am with you."

He kissed her, and the man could kiss. He kissed hard, and deep, pouring himself into her. She tasted the essence of him, that addicting flavor she'd never get her fill of, but more, she tasted love. Tears burned behind her eyes. Her father had died and practically a day later, she found a man to love forever.

Dad missed knowing you by a day.

He knew me. We talked. I had no idea his daughter was my lifemate, but he made it his business to know who was in his neighborhood. He was an exceptional man. It stands to reason he has an exceptional daughter.

He lifted her into his arms and took her through the house fast, heading toward the kitchen. The door to the basement was tucked in a corner. He waved his hand and it opened for them. They floated down the stairs in the dark. She could see everything, but it didn't matter. Nothing mattered but concentrating on the wave of pain, much worse than the first one, that shook her entire body.

She convulsed right there in his arms. Her teeth bit down so hard into her lip she drew blood. Her breath slammed out of her lungs. There was no way to control it.

Do not fight it, his voice whispered softly in her mind.

He was there. She wasn't alone with the agony. It was hard to concentrate, not when her body twisted and jerked and the knives and razors slashed through every organ and muscle. Her head felt as if it might explode. Her spine curved, straightened, slamming her up and then down so Maksim had to work to hold on to her.

You have to give yourself to the pain. Let it take you. Let it consume you. Like in battle, Blaze. When you are hurt, you have to let it just have you so you can continue. Let this pain have you. I will not leave you.

She wanted to reassure him she knew he wouldn't leave her alone. He was there with her even when she'd told him not to be. She knew. She relied on his strength and he would see her through this. She hadn't expected such a physical battle, but he was right, if she were going to survive, she would have to give herself to the pain. And it was excruciating.

Her body stopped convulsing, but she felt sick. Her stomach protested the human toxins. She didn't want to vomit there in his arms. She wanted her hair out of the way and him gone so she could do this in private where he couldn't *see*.

You have to go and let me do this. Stay in my mind, but don't watch. I can't bear for you to see me this way.

Maksim opened the earth deep. The soil was cool as he laid her naked into the loam rich with minerals. *I will be right here.* His hands moved through her hair, loosening the thick mass and then sweeping it up on top of her head to secure it in a loose knot. There was finality in his tone, and she knew instinctively that Maksim wasn't a man to argue. He wasn't leaving her.

When you make up your mind, you're every bit as stubborn as I am.

She tried to inject humor into her tone, but her stomach was churning. Heaving. She turned on her side. As fast as she emptied the contents, Maksim cleaned the dirt around them, keeping the air smelling rich and earthy. The scent eased her, as if somehow the loam, dark and sparkling with natural deposits, reached out to aid her. She felt the soil moving around and beneath her and that was soothing as well.

I guess there are a few good reasons for keeping you around.

His hand rubbed her back, down low, just in the curve of her spine above her buttocks. *A few*, he acknowledged.

If both of us are stubborn, we might have a few arguments.

I do not argue.

He confirmed what she already knew about him. Laughter bubbled up in spite of the situation. Of *course* he didn't argue. They were in for some interesting times.

The pain hit again, coming out of nowhere. This time her body seized. Was picked up and slammed down. She curled into a ball, was straightened and thrown backward. There was no control. No breathing through the agony. No way to stop the humiliating shedding of the toxins. They poured out of every pore. Her mouth and nose. Her stomach and every other place as well.

In her mind, when she started to panic, she felt him there. Maksim. Her anchor. He calmly disposed of every drop of the poisonous toxins the Carpathian blood was pushing from her system. He didn't shirk away from her. He kept one hand on her back, or moving up into the knot at the top of her head, his fingers sliding down her cheek. Breathing. Filling their lungs with air when she was incapable. A rock. Her rock.

His tranquility kept her sane. She could do this. She'd done worse. She'd been knocked over by her father's tortured body. She'd pulled him into her arms, held him until the cops got there and they'd taken a long while to come. That had been true agony. Waiting with his mutilated body in her arms nearly all night for the cops and the coroner to come.

Sufletul meu. He whispered the endearment into her mind. Just that. My soul. My air. The very air I breathe. She understood because he was wrapped around her. There in her heart. In her soul. Most of all, she could feel him in her mind, speaking to her, interpreting for her, sharing his life with her.

She had no idea how long the waves came, the convulsions or how powerful each wave was, because she endured. She gave herself to the pain. To him. To the new world she was entering of her own free will. She heard nothing but Maksim's voice, telling her of his life, of the world through the centuries he saw.

Swords. Horses. Battles. Beautiful places. The stars over-head and the moonlight in every stage. Forests. Cool mead-ows and blue ice caves. He gave her that, all in his velvet voice. His voice became her world and the only thing in it. The waves of agony twisted her body, picked her up and slammed her back into the welcoming earth, but she was so consumed by Maksim's voice, she barely was aware of what was happening to her.

He talked to her about what she meant to him. The ab-solute beauty of finding her—his unexpected gift—his miracle. He told her of searching for her down through the long, endless centuries, the black void when his memories of his home and his childhood, of his family, began to fade. He spoke of hunting friends and once, a family member, taking his duty and honor seriously.

Maksim talked to her of new worlds and how he no lon-ger could remember the beauty of seeing such things until she came into his world. The things he said to her about the way he felt were so beautiful she wanted to cry, but the tearing agony was too close, and she would have to acknowl-edge it if she did.

Some time later, Maksim held her in his arms, his lips whispering over her skin. "I can put you to sleep now, *lubi-rea mea*—my love. When you rise, you will rise as one of us."

She was exhausted. The pain was still there, but the hor-rible convulsions had stopped. She managed to lift her hand to caress his hard jaw. *Is Emeline safe?*

"Lojos gave her blood and she is asleep. He guards her."

Blaze gave herself permission to succumb to Maksim's control. He sent her to sleep and she went without a fight now that she knew her friend was safe.

MAKSIM woke as he always did, instant alertness, scanning the area above and below him. It was a little too early for

Blaze to rise. She needed more healing, so something else had interfered with his sleep.

I need a consult.

Tariq Asenguard. He wasn't alone. Maksim glanced down at the woman sleeping in his arms. She was beautiful. Pale skin, red hair. Lots of hair. He smoothed his hand over the mass. He'd put her in the ground with a messy topknot, and the thick mass was still trapped by the cord he'd wound there, but there seemed to be so much more of it.

He couldn't stop himself from rubbing his jaw along the soft, silky strands. He never, over the long centuries, ever really believed he would find her. The last few centuries had been bleak and never ending. A long, gray void. He accepted his life because Carpathian hunters endured. They lasted as long as possible. In the end all they had was honor, and that had to mean something. He had done his duty, but he never really believed he would find his reward. His gift. His own personal miracle.

Blaze amazed him; not once during her entire ordeal had she ever felt a hint of recrimination toward him. Not once. There was no fleeting thought that she hadn't made a good choice or she wished she could take it back. She hadn't made a sound. She hadn't looked at him with trepidation or anger. She clung to his every word and allowed him to transport her away from the agony of the conversion. It was agony. He felt it every step of the way in his own body. In his mind. His muscles were sore. His joints ached. Even now, after a day in the rejuvenating soil. He couldn't imagine how she'd feel when she awakened.

I will be right there. He couldn't go too far from her. She was vulnerable. Their enemies could find them in the ground, and she was in a deep sleep. Defenseless.

Maksim found himself smiling. His woman was far from defenseless. He nuzzled her thick topknot again, the silky strands catching in the shadow along his jaw, tying them together. He had never imagined himself with a warrior. In his mind, when he allowed himself to think about a lifemate, she was always shy and demure. In need of protection. He found himself smiling.

Blaze needed him, just not in the way he thought she would. He certainly needed her. Not just her beautiful body, but her soul—her warrior's soul. He admired her. Respected her. Believed in her. She had a protective streak as well as an independent streak. It would take her a little time to get used to having a partner. He would have to have patience when she forgot to consult with him, and he was certain that would happen often.

He waved his hand and opened the earth over them. The night sky was dark. No moon. No stars. Only roiling clouds. Black and angry. Churning. The wind blew hard, bringing the threat of rain with it. In the distance lightning forked. A few seconds later, thunder rolled. The weather was natural, not created by Carpathian or vampire. He liked storms. He always had, even as a boy. Floating out of the ground, he covered Blaze with a wave of his hand.

Maksim found himself reluctant to leave her, even for a brief meeting. Blaze was strong willed. If, in her sleep, she sensed him gone, or something wrong, she might wake. He didn't want her to wake beneath the earth, thinking she was buried alive. She would still have her human reactions in spite of her intellect and acceptance of the world she belonged in now.

Tariq waited for him inside his home, in the great room where the moon and stars glowed gold in the wood on the floor. The clouds opened as Maksim stepped into the room, the rain pounding on the roof. The wind slashed at the windows, driving drops of rain into the glass. Tree branches bent down toward the ground, and leaves created small eddies in the sky as they whirled and tumbled with the force of the gusts.

"Reginald Coonan is only one of several master vampires creating an empire below the city," Tariq greeted.

Maksim stopped moving, going completely still at the news. "Times keep changing," he murmured. "Shows we have got to keep up with them. Centuries ago, the vampire wouldn't tolerate another vampire in his territory."

"It was only this century the master vampire began collecting newly turned vampires to serve them," Tariq agreed.

"And now?" Maksim prompted.

"It seems the masters are conspiring together right here. The crime rate has quadrupled, but I never suspected it was because we were overrun with vampires. They are keeping a tight rein on their pawns," Tariq mused.

"You are certain of this information?" Maksim said. "There have been a few messy kills but only a few."

"We all thought Blaze's friend was targeted because she saw a vampire kill. But she said there were *two* vampires. We thought newly turned. But she saw them. Reginald and the other one. I recognized him from our homeland. That was one of the Malinov brothers, Vadim, I am certain. He has to be the one running the show. If they are not the only masters here in the city, even with Tomas, Mataias and Lojos, I am uncertain if we can clean out this nest."

Maksim's heart sank. The Malinov brothers were notorious in the Carpathian world. All five had deliberately turned on their own people, plotting over and over to kill Mikhail Dubrinsky, the prince of their people. Most vampires reached a point after centuries of darkness to reach for a feeling, a fleeting rush. Just as a junkie might reach for a drug, they kill for the high in the blood. The Malinov brothers deliberately made the choice, and they did it immediately. Together. They conspired and plotted before they sought to become the undead, and they continued to plot after.

"You are certain that was one of the Malinov brothers?"

Tariq nodded slowly. "It was Vadim for certain. Kirja was killed by Rafael De La Cruz. Mikhail killed Maxim. Zacarias De La Cruz killed Ruslan. I have no doubt if Sergey is alive, then he is close by. The Malinovs traveled together as a rule."

"Blaze shot him in the face. Vadim and his brothers were always physically beautiful and prided themselves on that." Maksim made it a statement, but the worry was there. Vadim wouldn't forget Blaze. He stiffened. "He did not kill the woman. Emeline. Blaze's friend. If he wanted her dead, he would have killed her instantly, but he tried to take her out of there. Reginald was a distraction, attacking Blaze, opening her veins so we would rush to her defense. The target was her friend."

Tariq shook his head. "You want the target to be her friend, but Reginald was taking Blaze out of the club. He opened her vein, but it was not enough to kill her right away. He knew she was strong. They wanted both women. The Hallahan brothers did not fight us, Maksim. When they came to Blaze's bar, they turned back when they saw us. It was not because they recognized what we were."

"They had orders," Maksim whispered. One fist clenched. "They wanted her alive. They were going to take her to the lair."

Tariq nodded. "Mataias followed Terry and Carrick. They went underground. It is a labyrinth down there. There is a command center somewhere, he is certain of it. They have electricity running and all the modern conveniences. He found a small area marked Research and when he entered, they had cells down there and are holding at least four prisoners there. He could not free them because there were too many pawns close, but he said we needed to get there fast."

"It will take planning. That is why Reginald was after the properties. They do not care about the businesses above them; they want what is beneath them. If they had already secured some of the properties in the past, and Vadim must have, they have been preparing for this for some time," Maksim mused.

"Vadim and his brothers were always smart and they were always plotting. Your lifemate is close to rising?"

Maksim nodded. "I need another night. I will wake her next rising and then we will go on the hunt. See if any other hunters are close enough to aid us."

"We will need to plan our attack carefully. Especially if they have prisoners they can use as hostages," Tariq said. "They will have the advantage down there. Mataias is trying to investigate enough that we can maneuver down there. Vadim and the other masters will have escape routes set up just in case."

Maksim sighed. "There's another thing, Tariq. When Xavier, the High Mage, was killed, two small pieces of him, shadow splinters, remained behind. Blaze fought the vampire's puppet, but when he was on fire, dragging himself toward her, she saw intelligence in his eyes. Malevolence. She described it as sheer evil. If one of the Malinov brothers managed to get a shadow splinter of Xavier and has it in him, he will not only have the cunning and intelligence of the Malinovs, but also that of Xavier."

There was a small silence as Tariq absorbed the information. "A master vampire could see through his puppet's eyes, Maksim," he finally reminded softly.

Maksim nodded, locking his gaze with Tariq's. "That is so, but the puppet was in excruciating pain. Agony. Burning. No vampire would risk getting caught in the dying throes of a puppet. This vampire did. Only a mage could do that and come out unscathed."

There was another long silence while the two hunters contemplated the nearly impossible task of going after a nest of master vampires. The impossible wouldn't stop either of them. They had faced worse odds over the long centuries and hopefully would again.

"We need to put out the call," Tariq agreed. "I've noticed the vampires seem to know when hunters move in. Since I made this area my home, the evidence of kills has become less and less."

"Yet there are many of the undead here," Maksim said.

Tariq nodded slowly. "I think they are becoming better at hanging on to their intellect. In the old days, once a vampire turned, he became cunning and savage, but his nature was so evil, the need for cruelty outweighed even safety."

"The Malinov brothers have changed that," Maksim said.

Tariq sighed. "I have no doubt it was them. Vadim is a genius. The problem was, he was always out for himself. He wanted power. He could have done so much for our people, but he believed we should rule the world. That humans should serve us."

"He has more patience than imaginable for a vampire," Maksim said. "To have acquired properties with the idea of using them a century later takes planning and patience."

Again there was a small silence. Vadim Malinov was infamous in the Carpathian world, every bit a legend as Lucian and Gabriel, the twin hunters. Vadim was a thinking man, even in his youth. He was a fierce fighter—the Malinov brothers on par with the De Le Cruz brothers when it came to their reputation in a battle.

"Maksim? What is going on beneath this city?"

Maksim shook his head. He had no idea. If that many vampires had gathered in one place, there should have been a bloodbath happening above ground. His head jerked up. "Above ground we are not seeing the crimes we should. But we have no idea what is happening below us. They could be taking their victims there."

"So we should be monitoring missing people as well. Homeless and prostitutes will be taken first. Anyone they know will not be reported missing right away," Tariq said. "They have infiltrated the police department."

Maksim nodded. "I examined as many as possible when I walked in there a couple of weeks ago and I smelled a few of them as 'dirty'—taking money from a crime boss. Vadim has to be that crime boss. He is acting human and building a human organization above ground to aid him. They do not know he is vampire. After witnessing what went on in that nightclub, I think he has police and officials through blackmail as well."

"The restraint it would take for him to pull something like this off is unbelievable."

"Gather as many hunters as possible. We will have to take this fight underground, and they will have the advantage," Maksim said.

"I will need at least two risings to prepare," Tariq said. "Mataias will have to go back in for information. We cannot go into a hornet's nest blind."

Maksim shook his head. Mataias would do it. Either of his brothers would as well, even though it was most likely a death sentence.

"So be it," he said quietly and grasped Tariq's forearms in the traditional manner of the Carpathian people. *"Arwa-arvo olen isäntä, ekäm*—honor keep you, my brother."

THIRTEEN

BLAZE WOKE TO the touch of fingers smoothing over her skin. Her lashes fluttered and she looked up to see the ceiling of the master bedroom in the house. The bed was a deep carved four-poster, very ornate and made of a dark, dense wood. The ceiling was high with a moon window directly over the bed. She could see the night sky and the small sliver of moon, a thin crescent valiantly trying to shine through the rolling clouds.

She breathed in, taking Maksim's scent deep into her lungs. At once hunger gnawed at her. Real. Terrible. She heard his heartbeat. Strong. Steady. His hands moved over her body, just a whisper. His touch light. Cravings grew. Her sex clenched. She felt damp heat gathering.

"Maksim," she whispered softly, her hand sliding into his wealth of hair. She loved his hair, all that soft thickness. Few men wore their hair long. Instead of making him look feminine, his hair seemed to accent his strong masculine features.

He lifted his head and his eyes met hers. Her breath

caught in her throat. A million butterflies took flight in her stomach. He was beautiful. Breathtaking. Her entire body reacted to his, going soft, pliant. Inviting. Her lips parted. Her tongue touched her lower lip in a small sweep. His eyes followed the gesture. Her breasts rose and fell, and his gaze lowered intimately.

"How do you feel?" he asked, his hand once again skimming her body. Sliding over the curves of her breast down to her hip bone.

She felt his touch like a brand. When she'd opened her eyes, she'd felt the coolness of the evening; now she was hot. Inside hot. Outside hot.

"Hungry," she answered honestly. Her voice didn't sound in the least like her voice. She sounded sultry. Tempting. An invitation. She ran her tongue along her teeth. She could already taste him in her mouth. "For your blood. For your cock. I think I'm addicted to both." She *craved* him. Needed. The need was dark and obsessive and more than a little terrifying, but she was honest with him.

He smiled against her breast, his tongue flicking at her nipple. His touch was light, yet she felt every stroke down her belly to her groin, like streaks of fire. Little darts that struck true, igniting something wild already smoldering inside of her. Those little caresses of his tongue sent a brutal ache spiraling through her.

"Maksim." She whispered his name. "I need . . ." She broke off, wanting to ravage him. Wanting to roll him over, straddle him and take everything she needed. Her hands tightened on his arms in preparation.

"I know what you need," he replied. "I just have to make certain you are alive and well. The conversion was brutal."

She felt him move in her mind. Filling her with warmth. His presence. She hadn't realized until that moment that she'd felt lonely. He was there with her. She knew him. Knew his needs. Knew what he wanted, yet until he was there, present in her mind, drifting into all those places that held sorrow and memories she couldn't face alone, she hadn't known exactly what she needed or why.

He saw the child whose mother drifted away. The father that was her everything because there was only the two of them. Emeline. What she meant. The sister she'd never had. The love they shared. The secrets that made them so different from every other girl around them. He took that. Those burdens. He lifted them and made them his as well. Shared.

She felt the rise of emotion. Pure and strong. He was a man's man. Strong, not just physically, but in every other way. He accepted her for what she'd been shaped into from practically the time of her birth.

"You were already more Carpathian than human," he said softly, "yet you were all human. A strong psychic, but not one drop of Carpathian blood in you. Your lineage is strong, Blaze, and you came through the conversion with almost no problem. You make me proud."

He kissed his way up and over the curve of her breast to her throat. Her heart fluttered at his words, and her belly did a slow somersault. He ignited a fire in her that would never be put out, but there was that emotion as well, the one she never expected to feel for any man.

His mouth was on her neck. She felt the scrape of his teeth. Her sex clenched. Dripped. Hungered. Her hands caught in his hair as he lifted his head, his gaze moving over her face. She knew he could read her easily. The need there. The absolute desire. She could read it on his face. The lines were cut deep. Lust. Love. Hunger.

His mouth took hers and the light touch was gone. His lips were hard and demanding. She opened her mouth and let him pour himself inside, the way his mind had poured into hers. He tasted delicious. Perfect. She wanted to kiss him forever. Over and over. Hot. Commanding. Maksim had a way of kissing that transported her mind away from her body so she was all about feeling. Pure feeling. She lost whatever connection she had with her brain and just let him take her over. Let desire pour into her. Desire and hunger.

His mouth lifted from hers so that his lips whispered down her chin. Her throat. Lower to the swell of her breast. She couldn't stay still. Already electricity seemed to arc over her skin everywhere his mouth touched. Her breath came in ragged, desperate gasps. Her breasts swelled. Ached. She wrapped her arms around his head, lifting her own head to watch as his teeth scraped back and forth, sending those little darts of fire straight through her bloodstream to her most feminine core.

With just that, tension was building inside her. Coiling tighter and tighter. Her hips moved restlessly. He shifted position, his thigh over hers. She felt his cock. Hard. Hot. Hungry. She swore she could count every heartbeat there as he pressed against her inner thigh. She wanted. He was just out of reach and no matter how much she squirmed, there was no way to impale herself on him. No way to relieve the building tension and get relief.

His tongue swiped over the swell of her breasts. Swirled. A groan escaped before she could stop it. She fisted his hair, tugging him closer—as if he could get any closer.

"Please, Maksim." The urgency in her was beyond her comprehension. She knew she needed him desperately, and he *had* to do something. Right now.

His teeth sank deep. The bite of pain sent another spasm through her sex and then the feeling was purely erotic. Ecstasy. The bite sent her over the edge, the tidal wave taking her, engulfing her fast. The orgasm went on and on as his mouth pulled strongly and she felt the overwhelming pleasure in his mind. He was as addicted as she was. She could almost taste herself. His cock was harder than ever and leaked small, precious beads against her thigh that made her mouth water with her own hunger.

One of his hands shaped her left breast as he took her blood, sliding beneath it to cup the soft weight in his palm.

His other hand slid lower. Just as her climax began to subside, his finger was there. Pressing in expertly.

Again, he demanded. *I need that again.*

He added another finger and then began to stroke and circle her hot little bud. Between his mouth and his hands working her body, he drove her up fast again. Taking her breath. Controlling her body. Her second orgasm swept over her so that she cried out, writhing beneath him, tightening her fists in his hair to anchor her. Already she was flying apart.

His tongue swept across the twin holes he'd made, and then his mouth covered the spot, suckling until she was marked. He kissed his way to her nipple and drew her breast into his mouth. That produced a streak of white-hot lightning sizzling through her body.

He rolled so that she sprawled on top, exactly where she wanted to be. She straddled him, pressing her hot, slick entrance over his hips as her hands ran up the defined muscles of his abdomen and chest. Hunger beat at her. Anticipation. His taste was there already, in her mouth, and she needed more.

She lapped at his skin, absorbing the way he felt with her tongue. She ran it over his muscles, tasting him. So strong. Physically beautiful. Her breath came in soft little pants and she couldn't stop herself from hurrying, although she wanted to explore. She just needed *so* much. There was no beating back the hunger. She actually felt the slide of her teeth, and her stomach rolled in a good way. It felt sexy. Erotic. Not at all as she expected it to feel. She leaned over him and he tugged the knot out of her hair, allowing it to tumble around her face and down her back, cascading over his skin as she pressed her mouth to the heavy muscle just above his heart.

That steady beat accelerated. His cock jerked. Kept beat. She swept her tongue across his skin. She didn't need his help when she thought she might. She wanted this. Just as she'd wanted to come into his world, she wanted to take what belonged to her without aid. Hers. He was hers. He always would be hers.

She found that strong pulse. Took it with a strong bite. Hers. He poured into her. His essence. Him. Maksim. Filling her in the way his mind filled hers. The exotic, masculine spice was amazing. An aphrodisiac that added to the growing hunger for him. Already, it was building and she shifted just a little, wanting him to fill her completely. Needing to be surrounded by him.

His hands moved over her back, down to her bottom, lifting her easily. She reached between them and found his gift, that strong, thick shaft, already pulsing with life. She squirmed, trying to impale herself, but he held her back.

Maksim.

Look at me.

She was busy. Her mouth took him into her. Her lungs breathed his air. Her mind accepted him into every dark corner so that he surrounded her. She lifted her lashes because he didn't move. She was strong willed, but she already recognized that Maksim had a hard, implacable edge to him and she wouldn't win if she came up against it. She lifted her lashes.

The look in his eyes burned through her. Ignited something wild and explosive in her. He looked exactly like what he was—a predator. He didn't bother to hide it, and she knew he was showing her what she was—and what she was to him.

His fingers dug deeper into the hard muscle of her hips. Holding her poised over him so she could feel the burning crown at her entrance. She could feel the intense heat and her body clutched emptily, desperate to be filled by him.

"This is not only because you are my lifemate. My miracle. A gift beyond all price to me. This is because I have fallen in love with you. Who you are. What you are. You need to know that."

She swept her tongue across the ruby red beads, instinctively closing the pinpricks and reached up to kiss him. He'd handed her the world. She felt the truth of his declaration spear through her straight to her soul. In accepting him, she knew she would never be alone and she would always have his loyalty and protection. She also knew he would accept her fully for who she was and not relegate her to the sidelines in a battle. More, she knew sex with him was off the charts. She hadn't expected—love.

Her mouth moved over his, her tongue sliding over his lips. He opened his mouth and let her tell him what that assertion meant to her. She'd never been particularly good at the woman thing. She hadn't been raised to be flirty or cute. She didn't know how to be. She hadn't been particularly attracted to anyone.

Maksim was different. Maksim was *everything*. He was all that she saw. Everything she needed or wanted. And he loved her. She kissed with everything she had and when he kissed her back, her body shuddered with pleasure, but it was her heart that turned over.

I love you, too, Maksim. You are my choice. Always. Because he was. She might not be able to say it aloud, but she could tell him telepathically and she knew that would be enough for him. He would know that she meant it, even before he'd tied them together, the moment she laid eyes on him—she'd known it was him or no one. She hadn't worked it out in her mind, but somewhere, in the back of her brain, the knowledge was there.

Maksim felt his heart swell. His cock did as well, which should have been impossible. He was already full and hard and pulsing with his need for her. He surged up as he pulled her down over him, impaling her, driving through scorching-hot, tight, silky folds. Her inner muscles gripped and squeezed, fighting his entrance, an exquisite torture that sent streaks of fire burning through both of them.

He rolled her under him, lifted her legs as he came up on his knees, not allowing a break in their connection as he pushed her legs over his shoulders. His fingers caught her hips again and he drove deep. Into paradise. She ignited as if he'd lit a match. He took her hard and rough, even though he felt soft and gentle inside. Even though she'd turned his insides into mush. Or maybe she'd just melted them.

He took her up fast, staring down into her face when she came for him. He loved that look—the burst of shock and surprise—and he always wanted to see it there. He moved in her, slamming deep, needing to be there. Surrounded by fire. By scorching silk. Squeezed, nearly strangled, yet coming as close to ecstasy as a man could get.

He watched her face, drinking her in, absorbing what she was feeling there in her mind. Taking her was such a gift, the way she gave him her body, her soul, and now her heart. She was amazing. Her body was amazing. He had it all and he knew it.

He took her up again, loving the ragged breathing, the dazed look in her eyes, the way her body went after his every time he pulled out. The shudder of pleasure each time he surged deep. He gave up everything but feeling, allowing her body to sweep him away until he had no control. Until he hammered into her, rough and hard and deep with every stroke.

"More," she breathed into his ear. *More,* she whispered into his mind.

He loved that, too. That she wanted him the same way he wanted her. He gave her more. He took more. He wrung two more orgasms out of her before he allowed himself the ultimate release, spilling into her, claiming her body for his own, triggering another hard quake in her.

He slowly lowered her legs to the mattress before collapsing over the top of her, burying his face in her neck. He loved the way she smelled now, with his scent all over her. He was too heavy for her, but he stayed where he was, pinning her soft body beneath his, his arms around her, locked inside of her, feeling every aftershock, every ripple. He began a slow glide. Gentle. Loving. Giving her that.

"I am going to roll us, but I want to stay inside you," he said against her pounding pulse. He wasn't ready to let her go yet. He was still hard. Impossible when he'd exploded with such force.

He tightened his arms around her and she circled him with her legs, keeping her body locked against his, just as reluctant to let him go. Maksim rolled so he was under her, Blaze on top, straddling him. Her breasts were pressed against his chest, her nipples hard little pinpoints, her breasts soft, her body pure heaven. He swept his hands down her back, shaping her, memorizing the feel of her. He loved her tucked-in waist and the way her hips flared out. Her skin was satin soft. Her bright red hair, tumbling around him like a fiery waterfall, falling on his chest and shoulders, so beautiful she robbed him of his ability to breathe.

Blaze pushed up slowly, sitting over his lap, her legs pressed on either side of him, her breasts swaying as he continued to glide gently in her. His hands went to her waist, holding her on him. He watched her. Her face. Her body. All his. He'd gone from an unrelenting gray void to this— the colors that would forever shape his life. The beauty she gave him.

"We have discovered that we are dealing with far more than we expected," he shared, watching her small white teeth bite down as she threw her head back. One hand stretched behind her to rest on his thigh. She looked more beautiful than ever.

Blaze made a small sound, as if she couldn't quite speak. Her moan was low and heated. He loved that she couldn't. That what he was doing to her was keeping her right on the edge.

"We are still mapping out the labyrinth beneath the city. The head vampire is extremely dangerous. He will have layers of protection and that means he has created an army both human and of the undead. We do not know what he is up to and we need to find out. Until we do, *sufletul meu*, I want you to stay hidden and very close to Emeline. She is in great danger. We think the vampires were trying to acquire both of you, but in particular, her. Vadim Malinov should have sent lesser vampires against us, but he sent one master and came himself as well. You do not *ever* expose your hand like that, put one of your most valuable pieces in harm's way along with exposing yourself to your enemies unless the end result is worth it."

He couldn't help himself. He was having a bit of trouble concentrating. Fire was beginning to streak from her scorching-hot core, right through his groin, up to his chest and down his thighs. She moved now, finding her own rhythm and riding him slow. The burn was back, hotter than ever and he found that slow, leisurely pace was beginning to do things to his control.

His hands tightened on her waist. "I am trying to tell you something important, Blaze," he bit out between his clenched teeth, because suddenly nothing seemed as important as the heat in his groin. That silken sheath gripping and milking. He was already as hard as a rock, harder even, a steel spike, wide and thick, surging upward to meet her downward spiral.

"Tell me later, honey," she encouraged.

His hands slid up her belly to her breasts. He used his hands and fingers, kneading and massaging, and then tugging and rolling. Each tug sent a wash of liquid heat over him, bathing his cock in hot honey. He caught at her body and brought her right breast to his mouth.

She cried out. Her breath left her lungs in a rush. Her body moved harder. Those inner muscles gripped him so tight he could barely breathe. His mouth was ravenous as he let her set the pace for as long as he could stand it.

"Faster, *dragostea mea*," he whispered, his voice husky with need. "Or I take over."

She didn't change the pace and he took over immediately, jerking her off of him. Pulling her up to her knees and pushing her head toward the mattress. He took her from behind, sliding deep. So hot. So good. Each time seemed like nothing could be better, but it was.

He lost himself in her just like every time before. She liked it any way he gave it to her, her hips pressing back every bit as hard as he drove into her. Her breath coming in little sobs. His name on her lips when he took her over the edge and kept going. This night was theirs.

He was a Carpathian hunter. He knew the danger they faced. He knew what having a lifemate was now. The beauty of it. The overwhelming emotion. This. The fire racing through him. The flames burning scorching hot.

He pounded deep, letting the fire take him—take them both. The rush came fast and unexpected as her climax shook her, sweeping him up in the tidal wave, rocking them both. He dropped his upper body over her back to nuzzle the nape of her neck. He liked the position, her curled on her knees under him, his cock buried as deep as possible.

"I do not know how you do it, Blaze, but every time you stun me with your beauty." He licked at the sweet spot just behind her ear, and then took her earlobe gently between his teeth, feeling her shudder in reaction, feeling the aftershocks rippling around him, squeezing him tighter.

"I don't think it's me," she said, and turned her face to the side to stare up at his face from the mattress.

Her lashes were long. They framed her large, beautiful eyes. He could stare into those green eyes forever. He pressed against her back to lean down and kiss the sweep of her high cheekbones. Her body was soft and yielding, but she was made of steel. He wanted to look at her face—those eyes—forever. He would take the memory of this moment, when he was locked deep inside of her, his body crouched over hers, his eyes on hers, into battle with him. If it was the last sight he ever saw, those long endless centuries had been worth it.

"I love you," she whispered. "Beyond that. You, Maksim. The man. Your honor and integrity is everything, but the way you touch me. The way you hold me. In my mind where I'm so broken. I feel as if piece by piece you've been gluing me back together again when I refused to even see I was so broken."

"You are grieving, Blaze, not broken," he corrected gently and nuzzled her nape again. He bit down on her shoulder, a biting caress. His tongue lapped at the faint marks. "You are made of steel, my warrior woman."

"I'm still broken inside, Maksim. Without you, I wouldn't still be alive and you know it. I was going to take the Hallahan brothers with me, but I didn't expect to live through that battle."

Blaze's voice was tight as she admitted to him what he already knew. She'd tried to tell him before. He was in her mind. She hadn't consciously made the decision, but still, it had been there.

"You provided an escape route for yourself on the roof, *dragostea mea*, so while it is possible you *expected* that you would not survive an all-out battle with four men, you still thought it possible you could live through it. Your traps were very extensive. I doubt any of the Hallahans would have lived through the night."

He slowly, reluctantly left her body and turned her into his arms, pulling her close to him. Her hair was everywhere. All that bright red. Her green eyes nearly glowed and her skin seemed translucent. There was a subtle change in her appearance. She'd always been beautiful, but something about the Carpathian blood enhanced the looks of the women.

She smiled up at him, clearly reading his mind. "Men,

too. You are gorgeous and I noticed your friends Tariq and Tomas are as well."

"You do not need to notice them," he pointed out, his hand smoothing back her hair and brushing it over her shoulder. He wrapped his palm around the nape of her neck, his fingers sliding along her cheek, his thumb brushing the corner of her mouth. "You have eyes only for me."

She laughed softly. "Women look at beautiful men just the way men notice beautiful women."

"We don't." He knew his voice was clipped. She'd been human, so perhaps that was something he had to get used to, but the thought of her noticing other men didn't sit well with him.

"You don't notice beautiful women? You didn't stare at Emeline?"

Keeping his gaze steady on hers, he shook his head. "No. I see the beauty in other women as well as creatures and even men, but it is impossible to be physically attracted to them, so there is little point in staring at them. Carpathian men do not judge beauty in the human way. We see that in our lifemates only."

Her eyebrow shot up. Her lips formed a perfect round O. Clearly he'd shocked her. "Really?"

"Really. We are attracted only to the woman who completes our soul. Of course, every species has anomalies, and we are no exception. There are a few born with a sickness that grows in them, and they reject their true lifemate. That rejection ultimately kills both. It is a sad situation. Every male with that sickness turns vampire. There has been no exception. One cannot endure without a lifemate, not for all time."

"That's both good and a little scary. Can't you become obsessed with your lifemate under those circumstances?"

"We are obsessed with our lifemates. We take their health and safety very seriously. You will not find many women going into a battle. Most men cannot accept the danger to their woman."

He saw the change in her face and he leaned in to brush his mouth against hers. "Apparently I am one of those men who find it sexy and appropriate for my warrior woman to battle at my side. You already have good skills, and the information you need to kill the vampire is in my mind, easily accessible to you. I would not want you to battle a vampire alone. Not. Ever. No matter how good you get."

He felt the shiver go through Blaze's body at his tone. He knew he sounded scary and dangerous and he meant to. He wouldn't like it. He wouldn't tolerate it. And he would definitely stop her should she ever be that unwise. She read that in his mind as well and she didn't like it much. She was independent and not someone who blindly followed the dictates of another—even her own lifemate.

"I am a male Carpathian, Blaze, and just as I am willing to compromise for you, you have to accept who and what I am and compromise as well. Still, I would want you to know how so you can protect yourself and our children."

She took a deep breath and nodded slowly. "I would prefer not to go up against one of them anyway. It was hard enough to try to kill those puppets. And I have to tell you, Maksim, when those eyes stared at me through the fire, it was the creepiest thing I've ever experienced."

He brushed another kiss over her mouth and trailed more down her chin before putting her aside. "I am going to have to go, Blaze. We need every man we have to gather information if we are going to wipe them out. Emeline will need protection. I will take you to her and the two of you can wait together. If they send someone to try to acquire your friend, you must call to me immediately. I will show you a few skills. Dressing. Cleaning. Even flying. I prefer you not use flying unless I am with you until you know what you are doing. Just wait it out until we get back and then, *sufletul meu*, we will form our battle plan together."

"Where are you going?"

"All of us are taking points around the city to try to

determine if there is another underground facility for them to escape to, and if they have established killing fields we do not know about."

She nodded, already reaching back to braid her hair. He nearly groaned when the action lifted her breasts invitingly. He needed these battles to be over so he could spend time worshipping his woman's body—a very long time.

FOURTEEN

BLAZE HUGGED EMELINE tight and then pulled back to sweep her gaze up and down Emeline's body, looking for signs of damage. Emeline looked pale and her startling blue eyes appeared even bigger than usual in her oval face. Her thick black hair shone with blue lights every time she turned her head. Like Blaze, she had it in an intricate braid, a fishbone falling to her waist. She really was beautiful, and Blaze couldn't imagine any man *not* falling under her spell in spite of what Maksim had said. He had to be the only man in the world who hadn't lusted after her in the club. "Tell me you're all right."

Emeline touched her mouth with shaking fingers. "Lojos gave me blood. He thinks I don't remember, but I do," she blurted out. "The taste of it . . ." She trailed off. "I thought it would be horrible. It should have been horrible." She looked around the room a little helplessly. "All those nightmares I have, they're coming true, Blaze. Including the blood."

They were in the apartment above the bar. Both had spent

a great deal of their childhood there in the living room, looking out the window at the streets below. There was a certain comfort in the familiar, and as if by mutual agreement, they both crossed the room to stare out the bank of large windows to the street below.

"Emmy, they had to give you blood to save your life."

Emeline nodded. "I know. I knew he would before he did it. This is all part of the nightmare." She curled her fingers into her palm. "I always knew it was real," she whispered. "So did you. We're part of this world no one else knows about. I don't know why, but we are." Her hand came up to stroke defensively at her vulnerable throat. "I think your father knew. That was why he began training you as early as possible. He tried with me. It just didn't take. I'm not equipped for violence."

"Emeline," Blaze whispered the name softly, hearing the guilt in her voice. "That's a good thing. And you're braver than anyone I know. You always have been."

"I told him." Emeline raised stricken eyes to Blaze. "Sean. I told him about the dreams. I told him they weren't just nightmares, that I was afraid they were precognition. I know things before they happen. I told him about the tunnels and the two of us running in them. It is horrible down there. The things we saw in our nightmares, honestly, Blaze, it is all real."

"*You* have precognition, not me," Blaze said with sudden insight. "I was with you every time I had the nightmares. You projected them into my subconscious."

"You're such an empath, Blaze. You and I were always connected, and what I felt, you did. When we were asleep, we stayed connected." She glanced at Blaze, once again meeting her eyes. "I knew all along if I came back this would happen. You with Maksim. Both of us in danger. I knew."

"Did you know about Dad?" Blaze asked, trying to keep her tone as gentle and as unaccusing as possible.

Emeline nodded, tears welling up in her eyes. "I warned

him. I told him to be careful when he was locking up. I drew pictures of the men he needed to be on the lookout for." She ducked her head. "He asked me not to say anything to you. I'm so sorry, Blaze, I should have told you anyway."

Blaze shook her head and turned her face back to the window. "Not if Dad asked you not to, Emmy. He didn't ask for much, and he had his reasons."

"He believed me."

"Of course he did. Dad always believed both of us. And in us." Blaze reached out and threaded her fingers through Emeline's. "It's the two of us now. And Maksim. We'll come out of this alive. You've got skills whether or not you like using them. Dad made certain of that. I do as well. Maksim and his friends will help us."

Emeline's fingers tightened around Blaze's. "I already know that in a couple of minutes, we're not going to have a choice, Blaze. We're going to have to leave this room and go down into those tunnels."

Blaze stepped back from the window immediately, tugging Emeline with her. "How do we change what you see? There has to be a way. Whatever you saw, we just won't go. We'll stay here until Maksim comes back."

In spite of the pull on her arm, Emeline didn't go with Blaze, her gaze remained on the street below. "I have to go, Blaze. You can call Maksim and tell him we don't have a choice, but whether or not you come, I have to go. If I could prevent this, I would."

There was no way Blaze would ever allow Emeline to go into those tunnels alone. "We don't even know where the entrance is."

"I had lots of time to talk to the other dancers in the club," Emeline said. "I was careful to pay attention to details, es-pccially when they talked about any of the Hallahans. Apparently they often go into a room in the back of the club and disappear for hours. A few times, someone has gone in looking for them and they were gone. Then, hours later, they reappear, coming out of that same room. There are probably dozens of entrances, but that has to be one, Blaze."

Blaze pressed a hand to her suddenly churning stomach.

What is it? Maksim was there instantly, pouring into her mind. *Tell me.*

I have a bad feeling. Emeline can see things that actually happen in the future. She sees us going down into the tunnels. Soon.

There was a small silence. She knew he was sharing the information with the other hunters.

She's for real, Maksim. She knows things. When she says something is going to happen, I'm fairly certain it will.

Wait for me. I am a distance from you. Do not go near those tunnels without us. We will be returning to you as soon as we can.

That didn't tell her anything. She clenched her teeth as Emeline suddenly stepped forward and pressed both hands against the glass. She heard her friend's swift intake of breath.

"That's how they do it," Emeline whispered. "Blaze, they take children. We have to go after them."

There was horror in her voice, and Blaze rushed back to the window. Below her, she could see what appeared to be a monster, a tall skeleton-like figure with bony fingers and glowing eyes wrapping his arms around two young girls. On the ground was a boy of about fifteen or sixteen, blood pouring from a head wound. Clearly he had tried to fight the vampire for the two children. One girl looked to be about fourteen, the other, maybe ten.

"There's another," Emeline barely breathed. "A toddler. I can't see her, but she's there, too." Already she was on the move, heading for the door.

Maksim. A vampire has children. He's taking them right now. Two girls. Emmy says a toddler as well. I'm sorry. I told you I wouldn't leave the apartment, but we can't let them have the girls without a fight.

The girls cried. Loud. The vampire hissed at them, dropped the youngest in order to strike the older one. She slumped over. He transferred her to his shoulder and reached down to grab the younger one when she tried to run to the boy on the ground.

"Emeline, wait for me. We need weapons."

We are on the way. Do not go into the tunnels without us. It is far too dangerous.

Blaze heard the sudden trepidation in his voice. He knew she wasn't going to wait. She *couldn't* wait. The vampire would use the girls, draining them dry—or worse.

I'm sorry, honey. I don't have a choice. Hurry, she replied.

"I'll follow them while you get the weapons," Emeline said, already yanking open the door.

"No. You wait for me. It will only be a minute and you need to be armed as well. You can't kill these things with your bare hands, Emmy."

Emeline turned back, her face a mask of anxiety. "He's got both girls. I don't see the toddler, but she's in my dream. She can't be more than two or three."

Blaze didn't hesitate; she gathered weapons and began stashing them in every conceivable loop in her belt, waist, shoulder holster and packs. She added as many of the explosives she still had from when she'd made them for her war with the Hallahans. Tossing a gun and a knife at Emmy, she added ammunition and then raced to follow Emeline down the stairs to the bar and then outside.

"The boy is still alive," Emeline said, hurrying across the street to crouch beside the teenager.

He sat up, one hand to his temple, trying in vain to stanch the flow of blood. "He took my sisters," the boy said. "A monster."

Emeline caught his arm and helped him stand. "We'll go after them, you get help. Call your parents and have them take you to a hospital."

"Don't have parents. My sisters only got me," the boy said. "I'm going with you."

Blaze was already rushing toward her motorcycle. Emeline could ride on the back. The boy was on his own. If they could move out fast, they'd leave him behind where he would be safe.

"I know where he's taking them. He already got the baby," the boy continued, raising his voice. "That's where we were going, to try to get her back, and he came out of nowhere. There's an entrance to an underground tunnel just under the dry cleaner's. We use the entrance for shelter when the streets get too cold."

Blaze skidded to a halt and turned back to the boy. He was pale and thin. His clothes were in tatters. If what he said was true, there was an entrance to the underground much closer than the club. "Show us."

"What's your name?" Emeline asked. "I'm Emmy and this is Blaze. I lived on the street for years, so don't be afraid," she added when he hesitated.

He eyed them both warily as he hurried down the street toward the dark dry cleaner's. "Danny. My name is Danny. These things have been coming after us for the last year. They killed my parents. If the state gets a hold of my sisters, they'll split us all up, so I'm keepin' us together." He said it defiantly.

"Do your sisters have any strange abilities? Something out of the ordinary?" Blaze asked, "Something you might call a psychic ability?"

Emeline flashed her a scared look, but she didn't say a word.

"Yes. Amelia can talk to animals. I know that sounds crazy but . . ."

"It doesn't sound crazy," Blaze prompted. "The others?"

"Liv and the baby, Bella, both can perform telekinesis. I'm not that talented, but I can see auras and things like that. Mom and Dad did, too," Danny admitted. Blood continued to pour from the cut on his temple between his fingers. It dripped down to his shoulders.

"Blood attracts them," Blaze said. "You have to get that under control. It would be better if you stayed up here."

Danny led the way through the narrow space between the two-story building housing the dry cleaner's and the brick building where the flower and bike shops had been. Both had been abandoned for over a year.

"Seriously, Danny," Blaze reiterated when the boy continued to ignore her and dropped down to crouch beside a metal grate near the ground of the building. "These things are difficult to kill. You don't even have a weapon, do you?"

Danny didn't even look at her. He pried open the door and crawled into the shaft headfirst, on his hands and knees. Emeline and Blaze exchanged a long look. Blaze followed him with Emeline close on her heels. Blaze understood him. She would have gone after Emeline no matter her age. Emeline would have come after her. That was family. That was the bond. That was love.

Hurry, Maksim, she whispered softly into her mind. *They have three girls and this wonderful boy is risking everything to find his sisters.*

You and Emeline are risking everything as well. Stay together. Remember, it will not be the undead that will come at you. First will be their humans and then their puppets. Maybe a lesser vampire. If we have not arrived, I will need to see through your eyes. Lojos gave Emeline blood. He can see through hers.

Blaze kept crawling through the narrow ventilation shaft, Emeline close on her heels. Danny clearly had come this way many times. There was no hesitation on his part at all. He moved with assurance in spite of the fact that the shaft was pitch dark. Blaze could see. Her night vision was extremely acute now, a by-product, she was certain, of the Carpathian blood running through her veins. Emeline didn't complain, either, so she had to be able to at least see Blaze.

The shaft narrowed and teed. Danny immediately was on his belly, using elbows and toes to thrust himself forward, following the shaft that led to the right and began a downward slant. There was definitely fresh air coming from somewhere. She couldn't imagine what these young children had coped with to drive them so far into the shaft to find out where it led. Emeline had been on the streets for years. She used the fire escapes and rooftops more than anything on the ground. She'd always said it gave her a sense of safety to be able to see anything coming her way.

Ahead of her, Danny tumbled out of the shaft onto cement flooring. Blaze followed, landing easily, looking around as she moved out of the way for Emeline. They were in a large tunnel. Very large. The ceiling curved above their head, and the hallway led in two directions. Sconces high up on the wall were lit, spilling light and shadow throughout the long, winding passageway.

"What's down here?" she asked Danny. No way would he bring his sisters to this level without some exploring first.

"The tunnels run under at least three city blocks," Danny said. Whispering. "We kept to the right and stayed just at the entrance so we could get back in the shaft as quickly as possible. Even the baby learned to be quiet down here."

Blaze shivered at the sudden note of tension in his voice. She already felt the difference, the moment Danny had turned down the shaft leading toward the left. The air emanating from the right side smelled clean and fresh. Coming from the left, there was a strange musky smell. Repulsive. Not strong, just enough to keep anyone from wanting to travel down that wide corridor.

"They can smell you," she told Danny. He needed to know, just in case they got the girls back and came out of it alive. She glanced at Emeline. "It's interesting that after all that time when they could have taken the girls down here, they waited to kidnap them until tonight. And right under the windows of the bar and apartment."

"I didn't think of that," Emeline said. "It's a trap then. They wanted us to come down here."

Blaze nodded slowly. *Maksim, they lured Emmy and me down here using the children. Danny and his sisters have come here many times over the last year. Why would they wait if they wanted them? How could they know Emeline would be with me tonight in my apartment?*

A scream filled the tunnels. High-pitched. Animalistic. One of the girls. Terrified. In agony. She had to grip both Danny and Emeline to prevent them from rushing headlong into certain trouble. Still, she had no choice. It was impossible to leave a child to the monsters. To allow the undead or their puppets to torture and feed off of them.

What they were doing was insane. Going straight into a hornet's nest and they were *waiting* for them. She knew that. She knew it in her brain and felt it in her gut. Still, the scream didn't let up. Now it was much more guttural. The throat shredded and raw.

I have to go, Maksim. I can't hear this and not go to her. I can only hope they don't want us dead. Get here soon. Hurry. Please hurry.

I could stop all three of you.

In spite of the implacable statement, she knew he wouldn't. She was well aware of him there in her mind, hearing what she heard. Knowing she would have to do this. He was afraid for her, but he wouldn't stop her because he knew and understood who she was. She couldn't live with herself if she didn't try.

I love you. She whispered the declaration to him softly. Intimately. Meaning it. Expecting to die, but hoping he would get there fast enough to save all of them.

If they waited and planned this, acquiring either you or Emeline or the both of you is their ultimate goal, Maksim stated.

Thankfully he didn't sound so far away as he had when she'd first contacted him. Still . . .

They could have killed you in the club, but they did not. If they get you, they will know you are my lifemate, but Emeline has not been claimed.

Blaze was horrified at the implication. *Can vampires have sex? Are you saying they are looking for a lifemate? That's the most disgusting thing I can think of. No woman would want to have sex with rotting flesh.*

They do not consider themselves rotting. Of course they can have sex, but to feel anything they would have to torture the woman and take her blood for the rush. To a vampire it might even be the ultimate high.

Blaze had begun to move slowly through the tunnel. The thought that Maksim could be right in his assessment of what the vampires wanted Emmy for turned her stomach, the imagery burned itself into her brain. She looked at Emeline. Emeline had a look of utter despair on her face. Her eyes were filled with sorrow. With trepidation. She knew something Blaze didn't.

"Emmy, you and Danny should stay here. I'll go ahead and try to get the girls. We can't all be in jeopardy. That would be foolish. Watch my back. You have a gun. I'll give one to Danny. Shoot the eyes and nose. That will at least blind them and hopefully make it so they can't smell you. Set them on fire if you can. Whatever you do, don't let them get their hands on you."

"I have to go," Emeline said softly. She pressed her lips together and then took a deep breath. "I can change things in my dreams, Blaze. I tried many different versions of this one, hoping to stop what I know is going to happen. If I don't go, those girls die. The baby first. I have to be there to get the baby while you're fighting off the guards. Danny has to be there as well to take the baby."

Get here fast, this is a disaster.

We are coming, Maksim assured.

It seemed like it had been hours since she'd first called to Maksim, but she knew it was only a matter of minutes.

It just seemed much longer. Blaze snapped her teeth together and set a much faster pace through the wide tunnel. The deeper they got into the maze of twists and turns, the more it felt as if eyes watched them. The more the stench grew. Small red eyes glowed at them as rats scurried to get out of their way.

Blaze had seen these tunnels before, and strangely, because she'd had the nightmare of running in them hundreds of times, she knew the way. She knew to turn left and then right. She knew when they neared the command center and the lights of the banks of computers and large screens would cast eerie green and blue lights across the ancient floors. She knew exactly where the room with dozens of cages was.

As they approached, she held up her hand to stop the other two from moving forward. This was her job. The prisoners were kept here. The ones used for food. The ones they experimented on. She took a deep breath, drew her knife and pushed inside. She'd gone over the scenario a hundred times. In her dreams she'd been killed over and over until she learned the exact sequence of events.

She saw the human first. A Hallahan. He was on his knees, a young girl on the floor, her clothes torn, her face swollen and bloody. This was Amelia, Danny's older sister. Blaze had never seen faces clearly, but she wasn't surprised to see a Hallahan assaulting a child. He looked up at her, shocked to find her there. She was on him in seconds, kicking him in the face, sending him flying off the girl.

"Into the hall," she hissed at the child, not looking at her. Carrick Hallahan grinned at her as he stood, wiping the blood from his mouth where her boot landed.

"My sisters . . ." the girl protested.

"Into the hall. Danny's there."

Amelia scrambled on her hands and knees, sobbing loudly. Too loudly. Blaze hoped Danny and Emeline would quiet her. Blaze whirled around, transferring the knife to her left hand while she gathered her throwing knives with her right. She threw them as she advanced quickly on Carrick. The knives went true, sinking into flesh from his belly to his throat. Four of them. He hadn't taken a single step toward her. He was still grinning macabrely at her. Her momentum took her past him and she kicked him hard in the back of the knee, taking him down, one hand reaching for his hair to yank his head back. Her knife bit deep into his throat and she shoved him away from her, already turning toward the door of the second room.

Another room for prisoners. Long tables covered in blood. Saws. Drills. Cages lining the room so the prisoners could see what would happen to them. He would be waiting above her. She couldn't be distracted by the room. She couldn't vomit at the stench of what she found there. She had to be prepared.

Blaze burst through the door, leaping into the air. She had forgotten she was fully Carpathian and her strength was enormous. Her ability to jump drove her straight to the ceiling, the knife unerringly finding the heart of the guard. Another human. Not a Hallahan, but she lost her knife when she'd pinned him so deep and she didn't take the time to yank it free. A through and through straight to the ceiling.

She couldn't look at the baby's face, swollen with tears. A smear of blood on her cheek as she lay in a cage beside a mutilated corpse. Blaze kept moving, straight across the room toward the other Hallahan brother. Terry Hallahan was ready for her, bringing up a gun. Behind her, she knew Emeline had entered the room. She couldn't look. She had her job and Emeline had her own. They had worked this scenario hundreds of times. Both knew what would happen; still, they couldn't leave the children there.

They had never known what drew them into the tunnels because they were already in it when their dream started. She kept her eyes glued to Terry, the last brother. He aimed at her kneecap.

"I killed them, you know," she said, her voice calm and

matter-of-fact. She kept walking toward him. "All three of them. I was the one who killed them."

His eyebrow shot up. The gun was forgotten for a split second while he tried to comprehend what she was saying.

She went in under the gun, sliding, taking out his legs in a scissor takedown, rolling so she was on top and he was pinned beneath her, the gun crushed between the floor and his chest. She leaned into him, her mouth to his ear, the knife from her boot in her fist.

"Your brothers. For my dad. It isn't a fair exchange, but then you all are scum." She drove the point of her knife deep into the base of his skull. And left it there. She only had one more knife and she drew it from where it lay between her shoulder blades.

Emeline was still crouched at the child's cage. She had to trust that Emmy could get her out. There was a man slumped in a cage, alert, his eyes on her. She felt compelled to approach that cage. In the dream she hadn't known why. It was a stupid thing to do when she needed every second to count, but now she realized he was Carpathian. A hunter. Ravaged. Drained of blood. Tortured. Maybe even mad.

Go, he whispered. *Leave me and save yourselves.*

It was an order. Arrogant just like the other hunters. She ignored him and crouched by the cage, because if he ordered her to leave, he wasn't insane. "You need blood," she whispered, her eyes, not on him, but on the door. The puppet would come next. Emeline and the baby had to be out of there by the time the puppet came. Emeline would be taken in the hall, but Danny would get the baby and Amelia out. That left Liv. It was up to her to get Liv.

She never knew what happened to Emeline after that. She would wake from the nightmare and Emmy would be huddled into a protective ball, her body shuddering, her fist jammed deep in her mouth and her eyes haunted. She always looked at Blaze with despair. With pain. With absolute terror.

Blaze always forced herself to wake after she shoved Liv into the hall so she could run to freedom. She forced herself awake because there was no way to win the battle beneath the ground. She died down there. Every time.

I cannot aid you. Leave this place. It is too dangerous. The other hunters are coming.

Leave me for them.

She couldn't. She'd left him several times and each time he'd died there in that cage, speared by a puppet cleaning up on his master's orders. She shot the lock as she'd done so many times in her dreams.

Can you make it out by yourself? I still have one more child to get.

He nodded. She wasn't certain of his fate. She couldn't stay. She didn't dare spare blood for him. She had to go into the next room where the puppet had Liv. Little Liv, the ten-year-old girl who shouldn't know there were monsters in the world. Little Liv, whose screams had brought them all running in an effort to try to save her from the fate she'd suffered over and over in Blaze's nightmares.

As she moved away from the cage and toward the door, she heard a whisper of movement. Of course. She should have known. Emeline came back. Emeline gave the caged Carpathian the blood to save his life. Brave Emmy who thought she was not a warrior. Who couldn't fight with guns and knives but fought back with sheer courage. She was already kneeling by the cage as Blaze went through the last door of the prison.

FIFTEEN

LIV WAS BEHIND the door, just as she was in the nightmare that had plagued both Emeline and Blaze for years. In the dark corner, the puppet crouched over her, devouring the child alive. Unlike in the nightmare, this time the little girl had a face and a name, but Blaze knew better than to look at the terrified little face as the puppet fed on her, tearing great chunks of flesh from her body with his rotten teeth. His fetid breath blasted through the room as Blaze entered. He raised his head as she burst through the door, those red, burning eyes focusing on her.

Blaze sliced a small, neat cut in her forearm to lure him from his victim. Flinging her arm over her head, she sent droplets of blood toward the puppet. He sniffed the air, dropped Liv and turned toward Blaze, stumbling to his feet with jerky motions. She was Carpathian, and he would want her blood above all else.

"Can you get up?" Blaze asked the child, keeping her gaze wholly on the monster shuffling toward her.

The child didn't answer. She didn't make a sound. Not

even to scream. Blaze backed away from the corner where the puppet had been feeding on the child, drawing the monster to her to give the child time to get to safety. There was movement. Still, Blaze counted her own heartbeats, breathing in and out, all the time her gaze glued to the monster she faced.

No gun, no knife, was going to end this puppet's existence. She had to kill it, though, in order to get out into the corridor to save Emeline. She'd never done it. Not one single time and she'd tried hundreds of times, playing out various scenarios in the nightmare. By the time she'd dispatched the monster, Emeline was already gone—taken by the vampires.

"You have to get up now," Blaze persisted, pouring steel into her tone. She couldn't sympathize. She couldn't so much as glance at the terrified child. She'd done that time and again, made that very mistake in the dreams and each time she had, everyone died. She knew better. So no sympathy. Pure steel. "Get up now and run to the tunnels. Danny's there. *Go. Right. Now.*"

The puppet was nearly on her. His face was distorted, almost as if the skin on one side had melted and his flesh was sloughing off. One eye hung half in and half out of the socket. His hair was ratted and fell in long, dank dreads. He had the child's blood smeared all over his mouth and chin. Up this close she could see flesh in his teeth. The smell and sight turned her stomach. Still, she had a job to do.

She moved the knife in a figure eight, her speed blurring, cutting arteries in his legs, arms and belly as she slid beneath him, coming up behind him. Before he could turn, she had his head jerked back and she cut him with the amazing strength of the Carpathians. It nearly took his head off.

Blood was everywhere, all over the room. She felt like she was drowning in it. She took two steps back and pulled the small bottle of accelerant from inside her jacket, flinging it over the puppet.

The door banged shut and she knew the child was gone.

Thank God. She already had enough trauma for ten children, let alone to see this. Blaze scratched the match and threw it on the top of the puppet's head. Instantly, the head was engulfed in flames. Blaze leapt back and hurried toward the door. She jerked it open, praying she was fast enough this time.

Something sharp and terrible stabbed into her ankle and she found herself on the floor, sliding straight toward the flames and that horrible, grisly, gruesome wreck of what has once been a human being. His fingernails were long thick talons, each sticking into her ankle. Deep, maybe a good three quarters of an inch. He dragged her back through the door toward his gaping mouth, a mouth that was surrounded by crackling flames. It was grotesque and insane. It made no sense that he could be on fire and still try to eat her alive.

Flames spread quickly over his body, but his eyes were on the cut on her forearm. Great thick strings of saliva hung from his wide-open mouth. Blaze refused to give in to the first reaction—to try to escape by flinging herself away from him. Instead, she went with the momentum of his strength. As he dragged her toward him, she hurled herself back at him, coming down across his wrist with the blade of her knife with every ounce of strength she had. She severed the wrist, kicked at his head right through the flames and scrambled backward.

Hard hands caught her under her armpits and yanked her through the door. It was the hunter—the one she'd rescued—the one Emeline had taken the time to give blood to.

"Emeline," she whispered, looking up at him.

He didn't answer. He set her aside and strode purposefully into the room with the burning puppet, ignoring her plea to leave her and save her friend. Blaze leapt to her feet and then collapsed when her ankle gave out. She glanced down and her stomach lurched. The hand was still embedded in her ankle. It took a few precious seconds for her to get the courage to rip the talons, one by one out of her flesh. Each time she tugged at one of the talons, her stomach rolled and bile filled her mouth.

She tossed the hand away from her, jumped to her feet in spite of the blood streaming from her ankle and ran back through the other two rooms to the tunnels. Like every single time in her dreams, Emeline was gone. This was where she woke herself up. There was no waking up from this. No do-over.

They have Emeline, Maksim. They took her deeper into the tunnels.

We are in the tunnels, draga mea. Every hunter we have available to us. Get out and let us take care of this.

She couldn't. She couldn't leave Emeline. The last of her family. She pushed down terror and followed her scent. Emeline always smelled like a combination of fresh magnolia and lily of the valley. Her scent was delicate and beautiful. Just like Emeline. She raced through the tunnels. Twice she shot a guard and kept going. Once she ran into a puppet, ripped herself out of his hands and continued. Behind her the hunter followed. Each time she shot a guard, he followed up, making certain of the kill. She glanced over her shoulder just as he plunged his hand into the puppet's chest and ripped out the heart.

She was very thankful she had rescued him and that Emeline had given him blood. He was thin and pale and clearly had been tortured for a very long time, but he didn't hesitate to guard a Carpathian woman. She turned the next corner and skidded to a halt. Emeline wasn't there, but there was no getting past the two vampires clearly waiting for her. Grinning maliciously. Knowing she was coming.

Maksim. She breathed his name. *Find Emmy. Please, please find Emmy.*

Look at them. I have to see them, Maksim ordered, his voice calm. *You have to concentrate on your fight, not on your friend. You know that.*

She pressed her lips together. Maksim didn't have a lot of give in him. There was no room for argument, nor was there time. She could only hope he was closer to Emeline than she was and that whoever had her kept her alive until the hunters could find her. She let out her breath slowly and kept her gaze glued to the two vampires. They separated and the one on the right crooked his finger at her.

"Come to me." The vampire to her right whispered the command.

She recognized the compulsion, but her brain didn't accept compulsion easily, and she remained where she was, shifting her stance, staying loose so she could move fast.

The moment he rushes you, and he will, run straight at him. Make a fist and use the combined momentum from your speed and his to drive your fist into his chest. Go for the heart. It will burn unlike anything you have ever felt. Ignore it and extract the heart. He will tear at you. You have to have patience and stay in position. The other will come at you, but get the heart. Try to keep the body of the undead you are fighting between you and the other at all times.

She didn't have time to digest what he said, or protest. She had come into this knowing she might have to fight a vampire. In any case, she knew the Carpathian hunter she'd rescued was somewhere very close. She saw the vampire's eyes and knew the moment he decided to rush her. She ran at him, at an angle, trying to do as Maksim had instructed, trying to put the other vampire on the other side of him. She slammed her fist into the chest wall, right over the heart, driving deep.

Pain blasted through her. Excruciating. Sheer agony. She kept driving forward, pushing pain to the back of her mind, although it wasn't working so well. The vampire screamed and ripped at her shoulder and neck with long, curled nails. He tried to lean into her to get at her with his teeth, but she kept circling, her hand buried deep in his chest.

Maksim moved in her mind, helping her to cut off the pain so she could continue. She heard movement and glanced over the vampire's shoulder. The other had moved toward her but he stopped abruptly. She knew instantly the other hunter had joined the fight. One moment the second vampire moved toward her, and then the hunter emerged between them.

Val Zhestokly. I thought him long dead. We all did. He is one of our ancient legends. Maksim breathed the name with utter respect. *No one knew what happened to him.*

She could have told him. He'd been in that dungeon a very long time. Years maybe. Enough time to drive him mad, but he'd endured like so many of the ancients did. She had no idea how. Her hand closed around the withered heart. She ignored the nails digging at her shoulder and began to withdraw her arm.

The sound was terrible. The feel of the withered organ pumping in her hand disgusted her. She needed to vomit. She didn't. She kept pulling the thing from the chest until she had it all the way out. She threw it as far from her as possible. Zhestokly dropped his hands on her shoulders and moved her gently aside.

She bent at the waist, gagging. Still looking. One vampire lay motionless, but his eyes were open and he stared intently at the blackened organ lying only feet from him. The undead she'd fought with lay in a corner where Zhestokly's powerful shove sent him flying. Flames arced in the air—and then leapt from the two hearts to the two bodies of the vampires.

She knew tears were running down her face, and she pressed her hand deep into her stomach. Zhestokly wrapped his arm around her waist. "You have to get out of here."

"They have Emeline," she whispered. "I wasn't fast enough."

"She gave me her blood. I can track her. You get to safety."

Blaze, get the children out. I am close to her. Zhestokly

will catch up. Mataias is on his way to help you guard the children.

Blaze looked into the ravaged face and beautiful but dead eyes of Val Zhestokly. She took another breath and slowly nodded. She had no real choice. She couldn't fight vampires, especially master vampires, and she knew Emeline had been taken to one.

Draga mea, go. Hurry. I am entering the lair now. I need to know you are safe.

I'm on my way, she assured Maksim. *Please be safe.*

Relief swept through Maksim as he entered the hidden lair of one of the master vampires. Immediately he realized this was Vadim's lair. It had been many centuries since he had encountered the Malinovs' particular brand of cruelty, but his lair said it all. There were several humans chained to the walls. Most were women, and all hung limply, in various stages of decay.

There was a woman on the floor by a bed with a shackle around her ankle. Clearly she had been pregnant and she had died recently—very recently. Vadim had killed her by cutting the baby from her. The baby lay on the bed, a twisted corpse that had to have been stillborn. He started to turn away, and something about the baby's features caught his attention. His breath caught in his throat as the truth hit him—confirming what he feared all along. Vadim was looking for a mate, and he thought he found her in Emeline.

He is trying to breed—to have children. That is why he wants Emeline. She proved to be a powerful psychic and he wants her to have his child. He sent the message to all the hunters.

The command center is for three things, Tariq said, obviously in the control room. *They are tracking Carpathian hunters, telling one another where we are, when there are signs of us in an area and to lie low or get out until we move on. They have the database of psychic women. And they are going after the women.*

Maksim stepped away from the dead woman and baby. No one imagined that a vampire could breed—or would consider it. The Malinov brothers were different—very different—and they were taking steps to incorporate humans into their war on the rest of the world. They were trying to own businesses and create the image of a crime lord family humans feared.

This cannot be their only base, Lojos added. *This is far too big an organization. They have moved their operations away from the Carpathian Mountains. Before they were focusing on killing the prince. Now, it seems, they are trying to build forces and incorporate into the human world. We didn't find evidence, but you know they have to have at least one more place of operation.*

Maksim was on the move, following the scent of Emeline's perfume. The lair had several exits, and Vadim had used one running beneath the city—a long, narrow tunnel with no torches to light the way. He knew Emeline had to be terrified.

Sergey is with Vadim, Val Zhestokly added. He was close behind Maksim, moving fast. *They are experimenting with children. Seeing how much blood they must give them in order to change the children to become like them. They mostly use humans to guard them, but sometimes a puppet finds their way into the prison and they devour the children. Vadim retaliates, but they lose one or sometimes several and have to replace them.*

Maksim kept his emotions away by reverting to the hunter he'd been for centuries. He couldn't think about those children or what they had gone through. There was nothing he could do about it. *Lojos and Tariq, circle around to the north side of the tunnels. Vadim has to come out somewhere with Emeline. He is heading in that direction. Split up and see if you can find other entrances to the north.*

Maksim streaked through the tunnel, shifting as he did so, becoming nothing but molecules, moving fast without form so that he could add more speed to his hunt. Emeline couldn't be alone with Vadim—not even for a moment. He would know they were after him. He would throw up obstacles to give himself time with her. He didn't want her dead—he wanted her to carry his child. He couldn't escape the tunnels with her, so he had to have time with her before the hunters found her.

Swearing in the ancient Carpathian language, he followed Emeline's elusive scent. This was Emeline—Blaze's friend. More, Blaze regarded her as family. A sister. All she had left until he had come into her life. Emeline had to be found.

Please, Maksim, Blaze whispered in his mind. *Please save her. Please bring her back to me.*

I will not let him have her, he promised. He shouldn't promise her. One couldn't predict the outcome of a battle with a master vampire, but he wouldn't stop until he got Emeline back. None of the hunters would.

He stopped moving abruptly because the scent changed. It went from delicate and afraid to sheer terror. More, the scent was mingled with that of Vadim. His powerful scent had permeated his lair and there was no dismissing that the master vampire was close.

Behind him, Zhestokly closed ranks, guarding his back as he carefully moved to the door of a chamber. The door was heavy and wooden. Very thick and ancient. He felt the safeguards instantly. He had no choice but to shift into his real form and begin to unweave the shields on the door. It was a slow, painstaking process. He couldn't make a mistake or he would have to start over, and Emeline didn't have that kind of time. Fortunately, Vadim was in a hurry and he couldn't have used a very difficult safeguard.

Emerging from the wall, Zhestokly whispered softly and shifted into his real form, facing the master vampire coming at them. Clearly he was the protection for Vadim.

He cannot run with her knowing he can get away. He will send everyone he has to slow us down, Maksim said. *He must have an escape route there in his second lair. You are weakened by long years of torture and short on blood. Take down his safeguards.*

Zhestokly didn't pretend he hadn't been weakened and that he was holding on by sheer willpower. He needed the rejuvenating soil that he'd been kept from. He needed the blood of the ancient Carpathians to help heal him and give him strength. He would take on a master vampire because it was his duty. He knew he had the skills and experience, but perhaps not the strength. He stepped up to the door, raising his arms, as Maksim whirled and rushed Reginald Coonan.

At the last moment Coonan disappeared to reappear behind Maksim, slashing at his throat with claws as he went by. Maksim had already dissolved, shimmered transparently, his back still to Coonan. Coonan took the bait and drove his fist hard through Maksim's back. His punch was so hard, so brutal, that when there was nothing there but air, he fell forward, stumbling with his own momentum.

Maksim was already in front of him, the illusion of himself disappearing as he slammed his own fist home, driving through muscle and tissue to reach for the withered heart. Coonan didn't wince, or scream. He simply leaned his head down toward Maksim's arm and bit through it with his serrated, pointed teeth. His teeth met through the thick muscle, and he jerked his head back to try to tear a chunk of flesh away. Maksim moved into him, hard, using his strength to drive Coonan's head back with the heel of his hand up into his nose, forcing Coonan to open his mouth.

With one hand still moving inside the chest cavity, seeking his prize, he kept punching with the other hand. Throat. Nose. Eyes. Back to throat. Over and over. Hard, chopping punches. So fast his fist blurred, but each punch knocked

Coonan's head back until the punches could include the mouth. He smashed at the teeth. Knocked them loose. Knocked them out. Sent them down the vampire's throat.

All the while Coonan ripped at Maksim with both hands, tearing strips of flesh from his ribs, but unable to get loose. As Maksim's fingers closed around the heart, Coonan realized he couldn't get away. He opened his mouth to scream. He was the first line of defense, but there were others. He needed to warn Vadim. He needed to call for aid. He'd been certain he could take the hunter, but Maksim had been too fast.

He screamed and howled, but nothing emerged from his throat. Not a single sound. Worse, each time he tried to swallow, his serrated teeth dug deeper into his throat and vocal cords as if they had a life of their own and were sawing at him viciously, cutting his insides to pieces. His throat, his esophagus, his intestines, everywhere inside his body as if the teeth had multiplied.

Coonan realized he'd become complacent when he hadn't fought hunters in over fifty years. He hadn't considered an ancient would find him. They were protected. Sergey and Vadim had all kinds of guards around them. He reached out, using the telepathic communication of his kind—the path of all Carpathians.

He is killing me. I need aid. Come to my aid! Even as he sent the message, he knew Vadim wouldn't release his other guards to allow him to live.

Vadim had a master plan, and he'd been working toward it for centuries. He found the woman he believed was strong enough to survive and keep his child alive. He wasn't going to risk it all for Reginald Coonan.

In any case the hall filled with Carpathian hunters. Ancients. He recognized some of them from his childhood, but there was no appealing to them. They had dead eyes. Emotionless robots that dispensed the prince's justice far and wide. He was caught and there was no escaping.

He felt his heart leave his body. *No. No.* He tried to moan. Even that didn't leak out into the hall, not even that despairing sound. There was nothing left of him, not with his own teeth devouring him from the inside out. Not with the hunter extracting his heart and tossing it like so much garbage onto the floor of the tunnel.

Humans are garbage. Fodder for us. We are superior to all of them. He tried to reason with them, stretching his hand toward his heart, willing it back into his body.

We can rule them. Take their riches. Their women. Feed on them. Make them serve us. See what we could be. Listen to Vadim and Sergey. They both share a splinter of Xavier and have his knowledge, his ability. Keep me alive. Join us. Join our cause and become great.

He repeated nearly word for word the mantra that had ensnared him. That he had come to believe in. If he could just convince them. His body swayed and his knees suddenly couldn't hold him. He smelled fire. Not just any fire, but white-hot, as if they had called down the lightning. That was impossible because they were beneath the ground, another layer of protection from the Carpathian hunters. Still, he smelled it. Saw the bright orange-red flames leaping from Maksim's fingertips to his heart on the ground.

Coonan lunged toward his heart, crawling on his belly, trying to cover the blackened organ with his body to prevent the flames from reaching it. He was far too late. The flames engulfed his heart just as he flung his body over it. The fire burned so hot, the organ disintegrated almost instantly and burned through Coonan's body at the same time so that orange-red tips danced across his back, bursting through the center of him macabrely.

The safeguards are gone. The room is filled with Vadim's pawns. I feel them. Some are gleeful, others know to feel fear, but they face us to give him time to escape, Zhestokly told the others.

Maksim knew his use of the telepathic path for all

Carpathians was deliberate—an announcement in the calm, measured way of the hunter. Vadim and his pawns would know the hunters were on them. Vadim would have to abandon the woman if he wanted to escape. Maksim finished incinerating the master vampire and turned with the others to the entrance.

They went in hard and fast, six of them. Maksim tried to stay close to Zhestokly. The ancient was weak, and Emeline's blood wasn't going to give him much strength. He'd been starved for years. It was a miracle and a testament to his honor that he had been able to keep himself from taking too much of her blood. He had stopped before he threatened her life or weakened her to the point of absolute vulnerability.

The chamber was large with a high ceiling. There were two arched doors with the same heavy wood. Maksim fought his way toward the door to his left, following Emeline's scent and Zhestokly, who had taken her blood and would know where she was. The Malinov brothers had recruited an army of lesser vampires. Many had no idea of how to fight experienced hunters. Maksim kept a firm grip on his emotions, pushing them deep so he could fight without feeling the kills of so many of his kind.

Malinov was recruiting from young males, convincing them they had a better chance of finding a lifemate with him than with Mikhail—prince of the Carpathian people. Some of the lesser vampires couldn't have been more than two hundred and fifty years old. They had no business turning. Nothing would drive them to that. Vadim and Sergey had to be very persuasive. They both had a splinter of the high mage Xavier in them. He was devious and cunning, but he also had a way of charming others, convincing them with his golden voice that he could rule the world and give to others what they deserved.

The slaughter was horrific. Bodies were strewn across the chamber floor. Maksim and Zhestokly fought through the lines to get to the door, and they made it with relative ease. Zhestokly went to work on the safeguards and Maksim fought off all attackers, to give the hunter the time to bring down the safeguards.

The undead appear to be nothing but cannon fodder, Lojos said. *There are at least three master vampires, and there have to be many others capable of fighting. Not children untried on the battlefield, yet none have come forth to fight us.*

They ran, Maksim said. *Vadim and Sergey have lost their brothers, and they retreated from Europe and South America, coming here to make their stand. They have learned to retreat and set up elsewhere. They probably have several lairs set up in other cities just like this one. There is no reason to stay and fight. They know they will die eventually facing us. So they throw their raw recruits at us to slow us down, giving them time to disappear.*

Maksim glanced down at the three bodies lying practically at his feet. The new recruits might be raw and inexperienced, but they were fanatical.

Safeguards are down, Zhestokly said.

Maksim went through the door first. Emeline was lying on the floor, her body wracked with sobs. Her face was swollen and bruised. Her clothes were torn and bloodied. She scrambled away from him when he approached her. He could see the evidence of Vadim's feeding on her neck. She had black blood smeared across her mouth where he'd forced her to feed.

He held up his hand. "Emeline, look at me. See me. Blaze sent me to get you. I will take you to safety."

The woman shook her head, pulled her knees up and wrapped her arms around them, rocking herself.

"Emeline." Maksim approached cautiously. "You know you cannot stay here."

"Don't," she whispered. "He made me unclean. You can't come near me. Blaze can never come near me."

"I will take you away from here," Maksim said. "Someplace safe."

"He said he would come for me. He will. I know he will."
Emeline kept her chin on her knees, raising stricken eyes to
Maksim. "He'll be able to see all of you through me. I can't
get near any of you."

The other hunters were there in the room. Silent. Watchful. Maksim waved his hand at them. "All of us will protect
you from him. Let me take you out of here."

Emeline took a deep breath, choked on a sob and nodded,
but she didn't move. Maksim walked to her cautiously, carefully, taking his time so as not to startle her or frighten her
any more than she already was. He didn't know all that
Vadim had done to her in the short amount of time he had
her, but now wasn't the time to ask. Vadim's scent was all
over her.

With torn clothes and evidence of a terrible struggle, he
could see that Vadim hadn't been able to control her with
his mind. That would frustrate and infuriate him because
he had so little time.

Maksim reached down, again keeping his movements
slow, holding out his hand to her. "Can you walk? Do you
need me to carry you?"

She swallowed hard. "You'll have to carry me. Can you
really protect me from him? Otherwise I can't go near Blaze
and I need her."

"We can protect you," he assured.

She nodded slowly, tears running down her face. "Then
please take me to Blaze. I need Blaze."

Maksim lifted her gently. A shudder ran through her
body and she held herself tight, withdrawn. She didn't look
at him, nor did she relax into him. The other hunters closed
ranks around her, showing her without words their intentions
to guard her. She closed her eyes and stayed very still, her
fingers curled into two tight fists.

SIXTEEN

"IT'S BEEN A week, Maksim," Blaze said unhappily, frowning at the door to the cabin on the Asenguard property. The house was more of a luxury guesthouse than a cabin, but it was made of logs, was two stories with a wraparound deck. "Emeline won't talk to me about what happened. She barely says anything at all."

Maksim reached for her hand, threaded his fingers through hers and drew her close, her front to his side, tucking her beneath his shoulder protectively. The moment Blaze woke each rising, before anything else, she checked her friend. The last thing she did before she went to sleep was reach out to her as well.

Blaze pressed her face against his chest, her fingers curling into his shirt. "I'm so worried about her. Emeline and the children. But it's Emmy I don't know how to reach."

Maksim looked up at the closed door of the cabin. Emeline was safe on the Asenguard property. Tariq had a sweet setup. He'd been there long enough to establish himself. His safeguards were strong, and when Maksim had joined in his efforts there to fit into the world and the century they lived in, he had added his protection to Tariq's property first and then, when he'd acquired the land bordering Tariq's, his own. Together they bought and slowly renovated a nightclub.

"Tariq has provided a good counselor for the children. They were living on the streets and now they have a good home. Tariq's boathouse is safe. I set up safeguards so the baby cannot possibly have an accident and fall into the lake. They understand that as long as they are on this property— or ours—we will protect them. Tariq is arranging for a teacher to educate them. They will have everything we can provide for them to be healthy and happy," Maksim assured her.

He began walking her away from the cabin. She loved Emeline and he couldn't reassure her that her Emmy was going to be all right. Only time would do that. Vadim could talk to her. Whisper to her. Try to draw her out into the open. None of them had the power to stop that. Eventually the master vampire would drive her mad if the Carpathians couldn't figure out a way to stop him. They could protect the air around and above the compound, but they couldn't stop a master vampire—one who had exchanged blood with his victim—from getting inside her head.

"I have no idea how to help her. I don't know if it did more than take her blood because she won't tell me." Knowing they were doing their best, but even that might not be good enough, Blaze asked, "Honey, what should I do?"

"You have to keep doing what you are doing, *draga mea*, keep going to her every day. She does not want to leave her house, that is fine. Just keep insisting she see you every single day. Tariq and I will keep trying to remove Vadim's blood from her system. We will take each day as it comes. That is all we can do for now."

Blaze sighed softly. "I'm so grateful I have you, Maksim. Thank you for getting her back for me."

"It was a team effort, Blaze. We had no idea Vadim and

Sergey Malinov were anywhere close, let alone in our city. Their operation is enormous. It could take years to ferret them all out and destroy them. This will not happen overnight, and Emeline will not heal overnight, either. The children were traumatized. She was as well."

"She knew what would happen to her and she still went into those tunnels," Blaze whispered. Her fist tightened in his shirt. She pressed closer to his warm, hard body. "I couldn't get out in time to stop them from taking her. Even being Carpathian, I couldn't do it."

"We prevented Vadim from taking her," Maksim pointed out. "She is here in the compound. We have Danny, Amelia, Liv and little Bella. Val Zhestokly is in the ground being healed. So is Tomas. The ancients gather each rising and supply him with blood. Mataias is searching neighboring cities for signs of another lair. We've sent word to Andre to come here to help us. We will take care of her."

"I didn't get to her in time," Blaze repeated.

"I think you did just fine, Blaze. We destroyed Reginald Coonan and all of the Hallahan brothers. You exposed all of us to a terrible threat, allowing us to do our jobs in the future. Emeline made her choice, and it was *her* choice. She has the respect and protection of half a dozen ancient hunters and hopefully more will come to aid us. She went into those tunnels to get those children out and she succeeded with your help. She took that chance and we got her out. At this point, Blaze, we have to call that a success."

Blaze nuzzled his chest. He was right. The vampires were gone, but she knew they wouldn't stay gone. All of them knew it. Vadim would be coming back at some point, when he determined he was strong enough to take on Emeline's protection, or, hopefully, when he decided Emmy wasn't worth his trouble and he moved on to a different plan.

"Tariq will have legal guardianship over the children in another few days. One of the Carpathian techs is making certain of that. No one will be able to dispute his claim.

Danny and Amelia are very happy to stay within our protection. They know what is at stake," Maksim said. "They are good kids and the girls have tested very high for psychic abilities. Vadim chose his victims carefully."

"He was tracking hunters," Blaze pointed out. "Warning other vampires to move out of an area if a hunter came into it. He's very sophisticated and has really incorporated the use of technology into his plans."

Maksim took a deep breath. "That was part of our downfall, Blaze. We studied the world around us, but we kept to ourselves. None of us believed that the vampires would be able to overcome their need for cruelty and selfishness in order to band together. Vadim recruits the very young. They do not want to wait for a lifemate. They see the ancients still do not have one and they want to take a shortcut. He exposed the weakness in our society and word has been sent to the prince. We need to correct our mistakes immediately."

He wrapped his arms around Blaze and took them both into the air, back toward their home. *I have need of you, sufletul meu,* he whispered into her mind.

Intimate. Sexy. Hungry. Predatory even. She shivered. She *loved* that—the way he poured himself into her, filled her mind with him. Filled her heart with him. She wanted him deep in her body, connecting them.

Blaze turned her face up to his. Ready for him. Always ready for him. The future was a little dark, but she was a warrior and she would stand with him to protect Emeline and the children. He would always make her world bright no matter what was happening around them.

I love you, Maksim. Always know that. I love you.

His face went soft, his eyes warm. His mouth curved into a smile. *I love you, Blaze.* His voice was tender, and when his mouth took hers, she ignited for him. Because he was her world now. She was his everything.

DEAD BY TWILIGHT

MAGGIE SHAYNE

PROLOGUE

Prom Night, 1955

I WAS IN the prom court. Princess, not queen, but I thought princess fit me better, anyway. Roseanne Parks got queen, and that was only because she'd given it up to most of the guys eligible to vote.

I'll never forget that night. It was the most magical night of my life, and as it turned out, the most horrible one too. And also, the last one.

The high school gym was draped in black and gold fabric. Spinning globes bathed the whole place in multicolored beams of light. Johnny and the Crusaders, gorgeous in their white tuxes, played "Last Kiss." Gosh, Johnny was dreamy with his jelly roll hair, jet black and gleaming. He was a local boy who'd made it big in the music biz. I heard he had a record deal. Nothing on the charts yet, but it was a huge score to have him come back to his alma mater with the band to play the senior prom.

And he noticed me, I know he did, when they announced

the prom court and called my name. My "prince" was Tommy Dillard. I didn't care much for Tommy, nor he for me as far as I knew. But he walked me to the front kind of gallantly. My dress was pink, and it had cost a fortune— almost a hundred dollars! It was the closest I could find to the one that had been on the cover of *Seventeen* magazine's September '54 issue. I'd had that cover on my bedroom wall ever since the start of my senior year. I couldn't believe my dad had actually sprung for it. But he'd said, "Chloe, my dear, you only have one senior prom. I want it to be one you'll remember forever."

Well, it was. But not for the reasons he thought.

He'd filmed most of the night on his pride and joy, a Revere 40 8-millimeter camera. He'd gotten it for Christmas from Mom, and I imagine it cost as much as my dress had. Maybe more. State of the art. He'd recorded everything from my date, Milton Cresswell, picking me up and awkwardly pinning on my oversized white corsage, terrified of touching my boob, to me pinning on Milty's boutonniere, to us walking out to his dad's flashy new convertible. It was a Thunderbird and the envy of most of the guys in school. Baby blue, with white interior and whitewall tires. I wouldn't have noticed if my dad hadn't made such a fuss.

I noticed everything about my dad. The way his glasses made his eyes look bigger, and the deep dimple in his chin that my mom was always touching with her forefinger, like it was irresistible.

They'd shown up later on at the school gym, with all the other parents and their cameras, so Dad could record the crowning of the Otselic Valley High School class of '55's royal court. And they were so proud of me that night. Mom cried. Dad grinned like the Cheshire cat.

They hugged me so hard before they left that night. And then they went, and stopped in the gym doorway to look back and wave at me.

I didn't know that was the last time I would ever see them alive. I didn't know that it was the last time I would set foot in my high school either. Or that my own life would end that same night too. The life I'd known, at least.

After the prom, Milton headed his dad's car up a dirt road for a little backyard Bingo and started pawing at my dress. I only managed to get out of it by telling him my dad knew exactly what time prom ended and was expecting me home, and that if he didn't get me there, I'd tell on him for trying to get fresh. But he was mad after that. Drove me home way too fast, stopped short, and made me hit my head on the dash. I got out of the car, pressing the heel of my hand to my forehead and hoping I wouldn't have a goose egg in the morning. And he took off before I could even close the door, burning rubber.

Some night. I tried to shake it off, and remember instead how magical it had been at the prom, standing up in front with the rest of the court, wearing my tiara. Never mind Milty. He was nothing but a creep. I turned toward my house, and as soon as I did, I knew something was wrong. The lights were all off. Even the outdoor one. Mom and Dad always waited up for me when I was on a date. I'd expected Dad to greet me at the front door with that darn camera of his still whirring.

I stood there on the sidewalk for a minute, looking at our pretty white house with its window boxes full of petunias, and its red front door. And something just washed over me. Something cold. My throat went dry, and I told myself I'd watched one too many scary movies. The wind picked up a little. I heard crickets, but not a sound from inside. Dad never missed *The Steve Allen Show*. Why wasn't the television blaring?

I should have turned around, right then, and gone . . . I don't know where. Down the block to the nearest neighbors, the Hamlins. But I don't know, something made me go to my dark front door instead. I remember how cold the doorknob felt in my hand, and how when I opened it, the darkness inside seemed like a living thing.

"Mom? Dad? Where are you?"

I smelled something . . . a little like my cousin Marnie's tap water, which Mom said had sulfur in it. My hands were shaking, but I found the light switch and turned it on.

Dad lay on the living room floor, staring at the ceiling. I took three steps closer before I realized he wasn't really staring at anything. He was white as a sheet. My heart seemed to stop beating, and my throat closed off so tight I couldn't scream. I bit my knuckle and moved closer, but then I saw Mom's feet, clad in her fuzzy slippers. The rest of her was blocked by the sofa, but I couldn't look. I just couldn't.

And then a cold hand clamped onto my shoulder, and a voice said, "You're mine now. And forever." I jerked away and opened my mouth to scream, but he grabbed me and yanked me to him, pulled my hair until my head tipped sideways, and then he did it. He bit me! Terror clawed at my brain so much I couldn't even think straight. It felt like my head was full of electricity, sparks flying everywhere all at once. Tears spilled over, spilling down my cheeks, down my face as I felt myself fading. Draining.

He was . . . he was a vampire. And he was killing me.

Only . . . he didn't.

I woke up. I don't know how much later. I was still in my house, lying in my bed. My pom-poms were hanging from my mirror along with my twenty-foot-long gum wrapper chain. For a second, I wondered if I'd dreamed the whole awful thing. I was still in my prom dress, and my tiara was on my nightstand. Maybe someone had spiked the punch. Maybe the whole thing was just a horrible nightmare. Maybe . . .

Then why did I feel so odd?

I sat up slowly in my bed, hearing the crickets outside, even though my window was closed. They didn't sound like they had before. It was like I could hear each individual chirper. And I could feel the touch of the crinoline against my skin in a way that made me want to take it off immediately. And I could smell . . . Oh, that wasn't sulfur at all, was it? It was blood. And it was on me. On my face!

I quickly swiped at my cheeks, my chin, and felt it there, sticky and drying, and in a panic, I dove out of my bed and leaned over my nightstand, staring into the mirror.

But I wasn't there. I wasn't there! I could see the wall behind me, my closed door, but not me. I waved my hand in front of the glass, but nothing. Nothing!

And then from right behind me, that voice. His voice. "You're like me now. Immortal. Ever young. You'll grow stronger with age. You are my mate, Chloe. I've chosen you, watched you grow up, waited for you. And now, at last, you're mine."

I blinked in shock, turning away from the mirror to see him standing right there and casting no reflection in the mirror. My hand rested on the nightstand, palm flat, like I was drawing strength from the wood. My fingertips touched my scissors, the ones I used to trim my bangs every third Saturday.

He looked to be about my age, and he wasn't pale, like my poor dear parents on the living room floor. His skin was nice and pink, and he had long dark hair and pale blue eyes, and my anger welled up inside me uncontrollably.

"I hate you," I whispered. "You killed my parents! I hate you, I hate you!" My hand closed around the scissors and I brought them around hard, with more force and more speed than I even knew I possessed. The blades sank deep into his neck, and his hand shot up for my weapon, but I drew back and sank in it again, and again, and again.

He howled and dropped to his knees, blood gushing from all the many, many holes I had made in him. I didn't know anything about vampires. I didn't know if he could die, I only knew I wasn't waiting around to find out.

I ran for the door.

"Wait!" he cried. "You know nothing. You won't survive!"

I didn't answer him, but I did turn back to grab my tiara from the nightstand, and then I bolted out into the hallway, down the stairs. My poor family still lay in the living room. It was still dark outside. Dad's camera was on the coffee table. I grabbed that too, and whispered a tearful good-bye to my parents as I dashed out the door. I took Dad's keys from the rack near the door, and took his oversized Country Squire out of the garage.

And then I drove away from my life, and from everything I had ever known.

The next day all the papers carried the news of the teenage prom queen (yes, they called me queen, not princess. I guess it made for better copy) who'd burned to death with her family. The house was nothing but a charred ruin. The fire had started in my bedroom, they said, but no cause had yet been determined, and the police were investigating because the family car had gone missing.

I figured that vampire must have gone up in smoke when the sun came up and shone through my bedroom window, slanting across my bed the way it always did, waking me up first thing in the morning.

I was glad he was gone.

They never did find the car.

ONE

Present Day

IT WAS MY night off. Otherwise, I'd have been driving a police cruiser up and down South Salina Street, watching for kids behaving badly. Very badly, what with their gangs and guns. They were not the greasers of days gone by, not anymore. They were brutal, the gangs of today.

Everything had changed since the night of my senior prom, so long ago. The entire world had changed. And so had I.

I'd been a vampire for far longer than I had been a mortal. And I'd learned how to survive as one mainly by trial and error. I knew enough to stay out of the sunlight. So when I felt the dawn pulling me under, much like the anesthesia had when I'd had my tonsils out at twelve, I found a sheltered place to rest. When the hunger got to be too much to bear, I found a blood drive and lifted a few pints to tide me over. And eventually, I figured out how to get by, and more importantly, how to seem like an ordinary human. I avoided other vampires. I hated them. I would always hate them for taking my life away from me. I wouldn't live as one. Not ever. I lived as a mortal, passing in a world that had only recently learned my kind existed, and who hated and feared vampires as much as I did myself.

But I did learn about my own kind. There was a particular bookstore not far from SU that specialized in occult and new age stuff. I liked to go there at night and buy books about my kind. I'd done so a few times, always buying several other books as well, so I wouldn't tip off the sloe-eyed, caramel-skinned woman who ran the place—owned it maybe—who was always looking at me like she sensed something different about me.

Anyway, I wasn't on gang patrol tonight. Working the night shift on the city's police department suited me and fit my schedule. But like I said, it was my night off. I was doing my off-duty work. Watching, from a distance, the goth girl in the bar who was all but wearing a neon "Vampire" sign around her neck. I was pretty sure she was a killer; being female, I figured I was safe. Her victims were men. At least, the three that had been found so far had been.

It was a state police case. I was a city cop. But I wasn't going to sit still and let some vampire go around murdering innocent people. I couldn't.

She wore a black bustier that pushed her busty bust almost to her chin. Bloodred lips and nails. Long skirt that I thought had probably been a slip or something before she'd shredded it to look a little stupider. She wore a black velvet choker around her neck with a big red stone front and center that was probably supposed to emulate a ruby. It wasn't a real ruby. If she could afford a real ruby that size, she wouldn't have had to self-shred a slip. She'd have bought a *real* vampire skirt. Maybe a castoff costume from a Terence Fisher flick on eBay or something.

She'd dyed her long hair black, and her skin was pale as porcelain. She held court in the darkest corner of the bar, with the candle on the table pushed as far away from her as possible, as if she feared the flame.

I'd have just blown the thing out. She, however, would rather blow the guys currently ogling her, as she demonstrated by the ice cube she was holding in those red-shellacked claws and tonguing in a way that should not be done in public. I'm as hip as anyone, but for crying out loud.

Okay, I'm not hip. I aspire to be hip. I pretend to be hip. I go around in my faded jeans and my biker boots and my brown leather jacket. But the last time I saw the sun I was wearing bobby socks and a poodle skirt. It's tough being cool when you come from the age of innocence.

A few of the crazy chick's admirers had worked up the nerve to go over to her since I'd been sitting at the bar, pretending to nurse a drink. A Bloody Mary. I may be a nerd, but I do have a sense of humor. They'd tried out a line or two, only to be put down and sent scurrying away. She was fussy.

Very fussy. She had to choose just the right guy, based on I don't know what. His blood type or maybe the size of the bulge in his jeans. But she *would* choose one. I was pretty sure of that. And then she was going to take him to some secluded spot in the great outdoors, screw his brains out, drain his blood, and leave his empty husk for some unsuspecting jogger or kid to stumble over in the morning.

I was pretty sure of this, because two unsuspecting joggers and a group of fourth-grade kids had stumbled upon three such husks so far this month. Goth-vamp-girl had been the last person seen with each of them.

No one knew that but me. Yet. I was hoping to take care of this little problem on my own before it got any worse.

There was a guy at the end of the bar who'd been watching her almost as intently as I had. I'd been watching him watch her, and thinking it would be a crying shame if he became her next victim, because he was kind of dreamy. Thick brown hair in that messy, tousled style that made it look like it had been combed with an egg beater. You know the one I mean. Long, unruly hair had grown on me over the years. And his looked as if he'd been pushing his hands through it in pure frustration. Maybe he had, what do I know? He had big expressive eyes. Brown, brown, brown eyes. And a dimple, right in the middle of his chin, that made my heart knot up in my chest, and my fingers ache to touch it. And he smelled good.

Yes, I could smell him from my end of the bar. He smelled like delicious human male and Old Spice. Nothing new. Good old-fashioned Old Spice.

I could not smell her, or feel her essence either. She was farther away from me. I was careful not to get close enough for her to sense my presence. My reading had taught me that a vampire could feel another one pretty easily, and usually from farther away than I was from my target at the moment, but I had become really good at hiding what I was from everyone, mortal and immortal alike. I had read everything written about mentally shielding myself, and I was good at it. I could walk past vampires in the night and they wouldn't even pick up on me. I had done that. Not on purpose, but I had.

I was doing what they used to call "passing," back in my day. Living in the mortal world, passing as a mortal being, working the graveyard shift to cover my odd sleeping patterns, and using a combination of foundation and regular meals to keep my skin tone up to snuff. She had no clue I was near.

He did, though. He'd glanced my way once or twice, in a way that made me wonder if he'd ditch his admiration of her to try to hit on me instead. The notion made my skin tingle, which was weird. I didn't normally let the sight of a handsome male distract me from a case.

But something about him . . .

I forced myself to focus on the job at hand. Catching a serial killer. Stopping a rogue vampiress from continuing her little game of Black Widow.

Damn, he was sexy, though.

I tore my eyes off Vampirella to steal a look at him again, only to see him finish his drink, smack the tumbler onto the bar's gleaming top, and get up to go over to her.

Ah, hell. He was either going to end up dead and blood-less, or I was going to blow my cover and rescue him. Because she might be fussy, but she'd have to be dead—not Undead, but *dead* dead—to turn this one away.

She looked him up and down as he approached her table, and I saw the little lift of her eyebrows, and the way her tongue darted out to lick her lips. He was dead meat. Hell.

I heaved a sigh for the fate of mankind, which would certainly be wiped out by stupidity sooner or later if males couldn't stop thinking with the organs designed for repro-duction. Then I grabbed my oversized bag that matched my leather jacket, slung it over my shoulder, and threw a ten-spot on the counter to cover my tab.

I went out the door only seconds behind them, but slowly, keeping to the shadows, moving with that silent stealth that had become second nature to me, and the vampiric speed that still made my head spin. You ever get that funny blur in your peripheral vision like something moved, but when you look, there's nothing there? That was probably one of us, flashing by too fast for you to catch more than just that blurry suggestion of motion.

I didn't have to use that speed just then, but it came in handy a second later when she got into the passenger side of a black Audi TT that had me rethinking my earlier as-sessment of her tax bracket.

He got behind the wheel. He didn't have to adjust the seat. Okay, his car, then. That made more sense. And then they took off, and I had to focus my energy into a burst of speed to keep up with them.

He drove like there was testosterone in his gas tank. It was all I could do to keep pace, but I did, and by the time they stopped at Lookout Point—okay, it was just an unmarked pull-off alongside the Parkway—I was actually tiring. Me. And my hair probably looked like Medusa's.

I ducked behind a tree as the car doors opened, and she took him by the hand and, laughing in a sultry tone, tugged him through the scrub brush and litter lot, over the railroad tracks, and out of sight.

The man had to be a complete idiot.

I followed them, maintaining both my distance and my invisible shield. It had its detriments, staying shielded to avoid detection by another vamp. I couldn't read her thoughts. I couldn't read his either. I'd have to open myself up to do that, and that wasn't gonna happen.

I pushed away from my tree, rapidly gathered my insanely tangled hair into a little fawn-colored scrunchie I'd had in my purse, and took off again at a pace only a little faster than theirs, just to catch up.

By the time I did, she was tugging him into a massive mausoleum that resembled a miniature castle, and I realized she'd taken a back way into Oakwood Cemetery.

Oakwood was massive, a hundred and sixty acres, a century and a half old. It was beautiful, and creepy as hell, even to me. I hadn't spent a lot of time there. Hanging out with the dead wasn't my thing. I don't really think too many vampires spend a lot of time in graveyards, as a matter of fact.

On the other hand, I'm not aware of too many vampires.

Hell, they were out of my sight, inside the crypt. There were towering pillars, all engraved with vines and blossoms. The lettering was almost too ornate to read, but I thought it said Collins, and wondered if Barnabas was home. Maybe not funny. I thought so, though. The stone was fox brown, and there were real vines competing with the engraved ones, creeping over the thing. Its door was open. She'd left it open.

I didn't need a flashlight. Not me, what with my preternatural vision. But I was getting way too close for her not to sense me. Still, what choice did I have? There'd be another dead guy before morning if I didn't step in.

Pitch dark, and dry and musty smelling, this crypt. I stepped through the door, and looked into the darkness.

There they were, on a bier, he, lying on his back and she, straddling him and holding his arms over his head. I was completely hidden, but baffled as to why she didn't sense me there. I mean, I was close now. Only a few feet away from her. Maybe my shielding technique was even better than I thought.

I stood there a moment, watching, feeling like a perv. Her handbag was on the floor, so I slipped my hand inside. Then I heard fabric ripping and focused on them again. She'd torn his shirt open and was kissing his chest, nipping him here and there. I didn't see or smell any blood, and hoped I wouldn't. If my eyes lit up all red and bloodlusty, the jig would be up for sure.

Damn, he had a nice chest, though. I mean, what I could see of it beyond her.

And then he said, "Ow!" and I knew I couldn't wait any longer. I dropped my shields, and spoke to her, and her alone, mentally.

Get off him, bitch.

She kept right on nipping and biting him, moving toward his neck now. That seemed to make him nervous—so maybe he had a brain, after all. He grabbed her shoulders, and rolled her over, so he was straddling her now.

"Oh, you shouldn't have done that," she said, and then there was a snapping sound, a couple of bright flashes, a rush of pain exploding from him. He flew off her, landing on his back on the cement floor, amid twigs and leaves and I didn't want to think about what else. She jumped up and leaned over him, something in her hand.

I sprang, grabbed her by the hair, and whipped her around behind me, tossing her right out the door. She was only airborne for a second, and he was grimacing with his eyes closed tight, so I didn't think he saw. Didn't wait around to find out, either, but strode out of the crypt and, standing on the top step, looked down at her as she scrambled backward, sniveling. "What . . . what . . . what . . . ?"

I bared my fangs and hissed at her. "That's what."

She scrambled to her feet and ran, and I let her, because shoot, I couldn't have hurt her, anyway. She was no vampire. She was just an ordinary mortal playing blood drinker to get her kicks.

I turned and walked back inside to check on the idiot, my mind wide open now. He was getting up off the floor, staring down at the item she'd dropped, which I now saw was a Taser. Then he looked up at me, and I flashed my badge and said, "It's all right. You're safe. I'm a cop."

"It's not all right," he said. "I was already safe, and you just blew my case." He flipped a badge from his own pocket. He was state. I was city. That explained why I didn't know him. But I was picking up a lot more about him now that I'd let down my defenses. He was one of The Chosen. He had the Belladonna Antigen. So had I, as a human. So had every vampire. You couldn't turn someone unless they had it. If you tried, you'd just kill them, or turn them into some mindless zombie slave, or so I'd read.

"That vampire is a killer, and I was about to arrest her," he said, furious with me.

"Oh, you were *arresting* her. Huh. You know, I don't think that's how it's done," I replied. And then I added, "And for the record, she was no vampire."

TWO

"SO THE VAMPIRE got away?" Lieutenant Harris, the former college basketball star turned cop, asked. His big eyes seemed to be bugging out of his head a little bit, and he was so tall I felt like one of Dorothy's munchkins in his presence. "Because of her?" he went on, looking my way.

"Hey, don't talk about me like I'm not here," I said. I glanced at the clock on the wall behind his desk. Four thirty. I had about ninety minutes till dawn, and I was feeling like Scary-Cinderella. "I was working the same case."

"We checked," Harris said. "No one else was looking into this particular vampire."

"I was looking into her. And she was no vampire."

"Why do you keep saying that?" The handsome hunk in the chair beside me looked me up and down. I was still standing. "How can you possibly know that?" he asked.

I shrugged. "Experience. She's not a vampire."

"Well, we may never know, now that you've scared her off. We don't even have an ID on her. I asked around the bar before I ever approached. No one there knows so much as her name."

"I know her name." I dipped into my pocket, pulled out the goth chick's driver's license, and held it up.

"How the hell did you—"

"Slipped it out of her bag while she was licking your sternum in the Collins crypt." He reached for it, but I pulled my hand out of his reach. "Uh-uh, no way. I'm gonna bust her myself."

Lieutenant Harris looked from one of us to the other. "I'm not following. Shepherd, who the hell is she?"

"Again, Lieutenant, I'm right here. Stop talking *about* me and try talking *to* me." I'd loved watching women evolve into equality with their male counterparts, and it was a trait I wholly embraced.

Harris pressed his palms to his desk and rose up onto his feet. He had to lean way forward to meet my eyes. His head was as bald and shiny as a malted milk ball. "Who the hell are you?" he asked.

"Chloe Madison. I'm with Syracuse PD."

He reached for his phone.

"What are you doing?"

"I'm calling Chief Rivers to verify your story. He's a friend of mine."

"Not for long, you go waking him up at four in the morning." I pulled out my badge, showed it to him.

He looked at it, but didn't take it from me. His hand lowered away from the desk phone, though. Then he looked past my badge at me. "You're out of uniform, Officer."

I sighed. "Technically, I'm off duty."

"Aha! I knew it!" said the hunk.

"Go suck an egg, Detective Shepherd."

"It's investigator, not detective, and Daniels, not Shepherd."

"He just called you Shepherd," I accused.

"Shepherd Daniels." He looked me in the eye when he

said it, and I got that tingle again. It wasn't entirely due to his hunkiness. My kind were always drawn to his. We can detect the Belladonna Antigen in those few mortals who have it, more clearly than I was still detecting his Old Spice. We can't hurt The Chosen. We're compelled to protect them instead, which is probably why I'd followed him to save him from a predator. Even with my shields in place, I'd felt that instinct.

"We're gonna need that ID, Officer Madison," Lieutenant Harris said. "Our case is official, and yours isn't."

I shrugged. "It'll be official as soon as I let Frank know I've ID'd our serial killer vampire impersonator." Which I was *not* going to do. The goth chick wannabe vamp was still the last person seen with a series of dead men who'd clearly been the victims of a vampire. I had to try to talk to her, see if I could puzzle out what she was doing, and with whom she was doing it. And I was way more qualified to do it than either of the men in the office.

I got to my feet, wanting to get clear of these two before they tried to take the ID and forced me to put them both on the floor and blow my cover for real. And also before the sun came up and turned me into Dustbuster bait. I headed for the door.

"You're not going anywhere," shouted the cop who had a last name for a first name.

"Let her be," his lieutenant told him.

I was at the office door, but I shot a look over my shoulder. Seriously? He was just going to let me walk out?

"I'll work this out with Chief Rivers," the lieutenant said, pausing for a glance at his watch. "In a couple of hours when he gets up. Go ahead, Madison. Get home and get some sleep. You're looking a little pale."

"Not as pale as your boy here would've been if Vampirella was what we thought she was," I said.

Shepherd rolled his eyes.

I batted my lashes and said, "You're welcome."

"We'll be in touch, Madison."

"I can hardly wait, Lieutenant. Wish I could say it's been a pleasure."

I headed out the door, and then all my bravado deserted me. I'd been barely holding my own in there. And now I didn't know what the hell to do. My kind were supposed to protect The Chosen.

So what did we do when one of them turned out to be a cop on the trail of a serial killer who was more than a match for him? He'd get himself killed if I let him have this case.

And I was sorely afraid my chief was going to make me hand it over.

Wouldn't that be a bite in the backside?

I made it back to my apartment with twenty minutes to spare, threw a bag of O neg into a bowl of very hot water to take the chill off it, walked into the living room, and flicked on the projector. It was already set up, and aimed at a sheet I'd tacked to the wall in lieu of an actual screen. I'd been feeling nostalgic lately. Thinking about Dad a lot.

Shep had that same chin dimple. Maybe that was what drew me to him.

I let the machine and the beverage warm up while I changed into comfy jammies. My tiara hung on the night-stand next to the bed. They were just like the nightstand and bed I'd had in my room sixty years ago, except the mirror was missing. I didn't like mirrors. They were reminders of the life I'd lost that night. Who knew what I might have become? I might have had a family, a little white house with flower boxes, a kid of my own.

I picked up the tiara and plunked it crookedly on my head. Then I scuffed back out, poured a big glass full of the stuff of life, sat myself down in my reclining chair and hit the button to start the film.

As the black-and-white images flickered over the screen,

my heart broke open and the grief I would never be rid of flooded out of me. This whole case, some vampire going around murdering innocent people just like my parents, seemed to have brought it all back to me. I'd changed that night. I'd changed from an innocent prom princess into a vigilante. I'd killed the creature who had murdered my mom and dad and stolen my life from me. I would kill this one too, because I'd changed a whole lot more over the past sixty years. Not physically. But in every other way, I'd changed. I was stronger now. And I wondered, as I had before, if maybe this was my calling. Maybe this was why I existed in this life of endless night. Maybe everything that had happened that night happened solely to create a vampire killer like me.

BY the time my eyes popped open at sundown, my little cell phone had about a dozen voice mails on it from my chief Rivers and that Lieutenant Harris from the state police. Probably demanding I turn over the license.

My outgoing message was very clear. "I will be absolutely unreachable until after seven p.m." (I updated the time with the changing seasons.) And God knew, I did not want to call right back. I wanted to take a long, hot shower, drink a hot mug of sustenance, and scroll through my newsfeed. But like a dummy, I picked up the phone and dialed Chief Rivers's cell.

"It's about freaking time, Madison."

"Hey, you know my days are spoken for. You knew it before you hired me."

"I didn't know you left the planet, though. You're harder to get hold of than a summer breeze."

"You got hold of me. And I'm sorry I screwed up the BCI's case last night, but I honestly thought I was preventing a murder."

"Lieutenant Harris says you took evidence without a warrant."

"She dropped it out of her purse. On public property."

"In a crypt. A privately owned crypt."

"During the commission of a crime."

"Trying to jump a cop's bones is no crime, Madison."

"How about indecent exposure, lewd conduct, sex in public. And hey, trespassing in and defiling a privately owned crypt."

He breathed slow. I didn't need to read his mind to guess he was also counting, but there was no way he made it all the way to ten. "I need you to come in. Pronto. Harris wants a meeting."

"Where?"

"His office. I understand you already know where that is."

"Yep. I'll meet you there. Can I have . . ." I looked at the clock. "An hour?"

"Half an hour."

"It's a twenty-minute drive!"

"And the clock is ticking. Move it, Madison."

Ah, hell. There was nothing I hated more than starting off my night by having to rush.

I hit the shower, thanking my stars for my fine straight hair. I'd hated it in my teen years when wavy and curly were in, and dead straight was not. Dead straight. That's kind of funny. By the time the sixties rolled around and girls were straightening their curls with their moms' flat irons, it no longer mattered so much.

I lathered, rinsed and didn't repeat, pulled a comb through, and gathered it into a ponytail, where it would dry in no time. Then I dove into clothes, chugged my morning refreshment, took that extra minute to rinse the mug in case of I don't know what. A fire. A break-in. You didn't want a bloody coffee mug in your sink when strangers were around. I brushed my teeth last of all.

All told, I was out of my apartment in fifteen minutes, and pulling into Troop A's barracks in another seventeen.

Two minutes late. If you're within five, you're on time. That was my motto.

I hurried inside, bursting through the lieutenant's office door, and slowing my pace only halfway through. Kind of catching myself, slowing down, pasting an unconcerned expression over my rushed and harried one.

"Are you freaking kidding me?" Shepherd Daniels asked, jumping to his feet as I walked in. He'd looked at me first, then at his boss.

"Apparently, I missed something. What's got the hothead boiling over, Lieutenant?"

Lieutenant Harris almost smiled. He might have thought he'd hidden it, but I saw that little quirk of the lips, and it settled my roiling nerves a little. "You," he said, pointing a forefinger at Shepherd. "Sit down and be quiet."

Reluctantly, and with a sigh that seemed to suggest he was being horribly abused, Shepherd sat.

I slid a look at Chief Rivers, sitting in the other chair in front of the lieutenant's desk. He nodded reassuringly at me, but didn't get up to offer me his seat. Not that I'd have taken it if he had.

"Officer Madison, the State Police Bureau of Criminal Investigations is forming a Vampire Crimes Unit that will be headed up by Senior Investigator Daniels."

"*Senior* investigator?" I glanced sideways at the hunk. He looked like he'd just bitten a lemon. "Congrats on the promotion, Shep. Shouldn't you be, I don't know, smiling or something?"

"Do *not* call me Shep."

I smiled, because I knew that's what I would call him anytime I ever had reason to say his name ever again.

"We want you on the team, Madison," the lieutenant said, startling me right to my fangs. "You'd come in at the rank of investigator, and that's a significant bump in pay from what you're getting at SPD. You'd report directly to Senior

Investigator Daniels. VCU will work exclusively on crimes perpetrated by and crimes perpetrated against vampires."

"Wow." I looked from Lieutenant Harris to Shep, who was still scowling, and then to Chief Rivers, who looked for all the world like a proud father.

"You've got my blessing on this, Madison, though I hate like hell to lose you."

"Wow," I said again.

"So?" That was Shep. "You want the job or not?"

"Well, jeez, can't I take a day to think it over?"

"I'm afraid not, Madison," Lieutenant Harris said. "It's time sensitive. We need your answer now."

I blinked, looking at Shep and Shep alone. "Why am I being offered this?"

He looked at his lieutenant for help, but Harris shook his head slowly. "Go ahead, tell her, just like I told you."

Oh, he really didn't want to do that, I could see it. But he sighed, and started ticking off reasons on his fingers. Nice fingers, I noticed. Long, elegant, with clean short nails that were so immaculate I wondered if he was fond of professional manicures, and decided probably not.

"You're already accustomed to working graveyard," he began.

"Accustomed to it? She thrives on it," Chief Rivers put in.

"You managed to tail us to the crypt, walk inside, and get the suspect's ID, all without me so much as noticing."

"That kind of stealth is crucial when dealing with the Undead," my chief added.

"You claim to know she's not a vampire, but rather posing as one. And if it turns out you're right about that—"

"I'm right about that."

"How can you be so sure?"

I shrugged. "I just am. It's a thing with me. I can always tell." I shrugged again and left it at that. I'd really wanted to handle this case on my own, but I didn't have a clue how

I could refuse their offer, much less refuse to hand over my evidence, without throwing up a million and one red flags. Better to play nice, be cooperative, go with the flow. It was how I'd kept what I was secret up to now. I sighed, shot Rivers a look. He gave me an encouraging nod.

"Okay. I'm in," I said. "Who else is on the uh . . . VCU, you're calling it?"

"There's no one else. It's just the two of us," Shep said.

Lieutenant Harris said, "We don't have enough vampire crimes to justify more than that. If and when we do, you'll get more help. Any other questions?"

"Yeah," I said. "Could we maybe come up with a better name? I mean, VCU is kind of boring, don't you think? What about Vamp Squad, or Night Stalkers or something?"

Shep scowled at me, so I guessed the answer was no. "All right, question two. When do I start?"

"How does right now work for you?" the lieutenant asked.

I lifted my brows. Shep was getting to his feet, head low. "Come on, partner. We've got a suspect to question."

"I took the liberty," Chief Rivers said, picking up a big shopping bag from the floor on the far side of his chair, and handing it to me. It contained all the stuff from my old desk.

"You were that sure I'd take the job?"

"You'd be crazy not to," he said. "Stay in touch, Madison. You need anything, you call me. Promise?"

"Sure, boss. You bet."

He lowered his head awkwardly, then came in for a hug that I hadn't been expecting. I guess he liked me more than I knew. He shoved the bag at me, then headed out the door.

"You got that evidence with you, Madison?" the lieutenant asked.

"Yeah, I brought it."

He nodded, came around the desk with a badge in a leather holder, and handed it to me. "We'll do the formalities later. Your ID will be ready by the time your shift is over. There's a temp in here for now. I want you to book that suspect's license into evidence and before you head home in the a.m., I'll need a report outlining how you legally obtained it."

"Yes, sir." I took the wallet, opened it, and looked at the New York State Police BCI badge.

Lieutenant Harris thrust out a baseball-mitt-sized hand. "Welcome to BCI, Investigator Madison."

I shook, making my grip firm, but not firm enough to break any bones. "Thank you, Lieutenant."

"Now get outta here. And grab a jacket or something. Your hands are like ice."

In my rush, I hadn't heated up my cuppa this morning. Mistakes like that were not okay. I was a vampire. I was also, holy crap, the first (okay, second) cop hired for the brand-new Vamp Squad. It was almost laughable. It also, the way I saw things, made it even more important for me to maintain my cover as an ordinary mortal with cold hands, a warm heart, nocturnal tendencies, and a naturally ivory complexion. Right?

Besides, I had to take the job. I had to make sure whoever was out there killing good-looking men didn't get my new partner. Boss. Whatever. Working right by his side seemed to me the best imaginable way to do that.

THREE

I DIDN'T END up booking the driver's license into evidence. Instead, I photocopied both sides of it while trying to remember just how clearly an ordinary mortal female would see in a pitch-dark graveyard on a dark, moonless night. I hadn't had mortal eyesight in sixty years, and I hadn't spent much time in graveyards when I had.

If this vamp wannabe, Martha Jane Billingsworth, recognized me from last night, my cover would be blown.

I was riding in an unmarked Dodge Charger with Shep, who had insisted on driving, the chauvinist, and turning the license over and over in my hand. "According to this, she's twenty-three. Did she look twenty-three to you? You got a much closer look at her than I did."

He shrugged. "Give or take. Doesn't mean she's not a vampire. She could be a recent convert."

"It wouldn't matter," I said. "It's not like they age. And what do you mean by *convert*? It's not a religion you just decide to join."

"Not a religion. Definitely a choice."

"Sometimes it is. Not always." I shrugged. "But I mean, even when it is a choice, it's a choice between dying before you hit your forties or living forever."

"*I'd* never choose it."

"That's easy to say if it's not an option for you," I said, because I wondered if he knew that it was. He had to know, right? He was a cop. He would have to know his own blood type. Hell, they probably kept a few pints of BD positive on ice for him, just in case. The Chosen tended to bleed profusely when cut. And transfusions were hard to come by. Still, I was curious, so I pushed a little more. "You have to have the right blood type to become one of them, you know. And it's a rare one."

He nodded, like he already knew that.

"Bella Norte Platelets or something," I said, still pushing.

"The Belladonna Antigen," he corrected. Okay, he knew that much. Did he know he had it?

"That's it. So do you?"

"Do I what?"

"Do you have it? Is your declaration that you'd never choose to be a vampire based on having the actual means to make that decision, or are you just blowing smoke?"

He shot me a look. "Would *you* choose it?" he asked, instead of answering my question.

I shrugged. "I don't know." And that was the truth. I hadn't been *given* a choice. "I mean, eternal youth, superpowers, immortality . . . what's the downside?"

"Never seeing daylight again. Never enjoying a burger. Turning into a monster."

"*Wow.*"

He sent me a look, because my reaction had sort of burst out of me without my permission. "What, you don't think they're monsters?"

"Yeah. I mean, I always have thought so. But hearing you say it makes me wonder if I'm as bigoted as you sounded just then. Monsters, huh?"

"The same way a full-grown lion or a grizzly bear running loose up and down Erie Boulevard could be called a monster. They're predators. Their very survival depends on them killing us."

"That's an . . . interesting perspective."

"You disagree." He shook his head, leaning back in the driver's seat, which had pushed back as far as it would go to accommodate his long legs. His arm was stretched out in front of him, one hand resting on the top of the steering wheel. He seemed relaxed to the point of lazy. "They've partnered me up with a bleeding heart liberal."

I said, "Did you ever give blood to save other humans, Shep?"

"Of course I have. And don't call me Shep."

"So how is that different? If a human needs your blood to survive, you'll give it. If a vampire needs the very same thing for the very same reason, they're a monster. How does that make any sense?"

"The human," he said, "wouldn't kill me to get it."

I opened my mouth to argue further, but changed my mind. I didn't want to make him my enemy or tip him off. Besides, he was voicing exactly the opinions I'd always had about my own kind.

And yet, I was a vampire. And I didn't feel I was a monster. I certainly didn't prey on humans and I'd never kill anyone to get their blood.

"So why do you hate them so much? Vampires maul you as a child? Eat your puppy or your goldfish or something?"

His lip twitched and I knew he was trying hard not to smile. "Nothing that cut and dried. I just don't like being bumped down from the top of the food chain."

"Ah."

"I don't think it's possible for vampires and humans to coexist. One is going to wipe out the other. They're stronger than us. They're immortal. If they decided they wanted to, they could probably outnumber us in pretty short order. It takes a human nine months to produce another human, and twenty years to raise one. They can have another fully functioning adult-model bloodsucker in, what, a minute and a half?" He shook his head.

"A couple of hours," I said.

"They could take over."

"They don't even have civil rights."

"They will, though. They'll get the vote. They'll get to run. They'll take over."

I shrugged. "And they'd do . . . what exactly? Exterminate their own food supply? Despoil the planet with pollution? Wage war all over the world? Oh, wait, that's already being done."

"You just wait and see." He nodded toward the windshield. "That's her building up there."

"Lots of glass, for a vampire."

"Yeah, yeah." He found a parking spot. I had resisted the urge to dig around inside his head, you know, read his thoughts and find out more. I was itching to do that, but it was bad form. A huge invasion of privacy. But I thought there was more to his dislike of vampires than he was saying. Maybe working with me would prove to him that our two worlds *could* exist together. Or at least that a human like him and a vampire like me could. Maybe being my partner was going to help us both evolve into better, more enlightened people.

And maybe monkeys were going to fly out of my butt.

He parked by a meter, in front of the building, got out of the car, and didn't put in a quarter.

I dug one out of my jeans pocket and popped it in. Hearing the click and whir of the device, he stopped his perusal of the building and turned my way. "What're you, a Girl Scout?"

"Was once."

He frowned at me, but quickly shook it off. "What's her license say about her apartment number?"

"Three-F. Top floor."

He nodded and went to the front entrance. You needed a keycard to open it, so he hit Martha Jane aka Vampirella's buzzer. And then he hit it again, and again.

While we stood there bathed in the glow of the outside lights, the click clack of heels came along the sidewalk and I turned to see a gorgeous blonde heading our way, head down, eyes on her cell phone. She came up the steps without even looking, then stopped when she saw my boots, which were not as amazing as hers. Her head came up, and she looked at me briefly, then slid her big round eyes toward Shep. Her whole demeanor changed. Her lips smiled, and her eyes softened. Her heartbeat sped up too. Okay, I wasn't *trying* to listen, but you can't help some things.

"You need to get in?" she asked.

"Yeah. It's official." He flashed his badge, and her pulse went even faster. Cops were apparently on her list of turn-ons.

"Always happy to help the police," she said, and whipped out her keycard, using it to unlock the door. Then he opened it, and held it for her. "Oooh," she purred. "An officer *and* a gentleman."

"Senior investigator," I corrected.

He sent me a look that said I was kind of clueless.

"So why are you here? Anything juicy?" she asked, lowering her voice a bit.

"Got a report of some building code violations," he said. "Boring as hell."

She didn't believe him. I could tell by a mishmash of impressions, without even having to invade her brain. Her eyes narrowed just slightly, her gaze sharpened, her lips pressed a little more tightly. Yeah, she was curious. And interested. In both my partner and in our reason for being there.

He was still holding the door. I said, "You want to move it along, ma'am? We've got six more buildings to check out after this one."

"Oh, sure. Sorry." She hurried inside, glancing over her shoulder at us as she walked toward the elevators. We stood there and let her go. She was too curious, wanted to see whose apartment we were heading for. It wasn't something she needed to know. Those were my reasons for hanging back. I suspected Shep just wanted to watch her butt while she walked away.

He waited until the elevator doors closed on her, then headed for the stairs, and we went up. The third floor came fast, and he wasn't even winded. I noticed that because I was paying attention. I was paying attention because I knew that people who had the Belladonna Antigen usually started to weaken in their midthirties, and usually bought the farm before they hit forty. I pegged his age at around thirty, and was glad to see no signs of the inevitable end. Well, inevitable unless you came over to the dark side, so to speak.

We went right up to her door, and Shep knocked. Then he knocked again, a little harder. "Miz Billingsworth," he called. I noticed his voice was a little deeper than when he spoke conversationally. Probably subconscious. Probably didn't even know he was doing it. It sounded intimidating, strong. And sexy.

No answer.

Then something hit me and I blurted, "I smell blood!" then tried to suck the words back in, but too late. They were out there.

"You . . . what, now?" He looked down at me with one eyebrow cocked up higher than the other. And that was sexy too.

"I have a . . . highly developed olfactory function, and I smell blood," I said. "I know it's weird. I'm a weird person. But it helps more than you would think in police work and I—"

"Are you sure about this, Madison?"

"I am," I said. "And that's probable cause."

He nodded, tried the door. It wasn't locked. He opened

it slow, and the smell hit me even harder. God, had she murdered another one already?

"Miz Billingsworth?" Shep said again, "Martha?"

We stepped inside and the smell got stronger. He had his gun out, doing the cop thing, checking around every doorway before stepping through. I went along with it, but thought it was a waste of time. The scent of death was even stronger than that of blood. And I knew where it was coming from too, but decided it would be better to just let him figure it out for himself. I'd already given away more than I should.

So we checked the kitchen and bedroom of the tiny apartment before we finally got to the bathroom. Its door was closed, but the smell was coming from behind it. The feeling too. Death had an energy to it that I couldn't name. Or maybe it was an absence of energy that made it so obvious to me when the reaper had come to call.

Shep opened the bathroom door.

She lay in the bathtub, eyes wide open but filmy, a gaping red gash across her throat, soaked in her own blood. Her own *very fresh* blood.

FOUR

I TURNED FAST, putting my back to the bathroom, and stepped to the side to put a wall between me and the bathroom mirror that was shining Shep's reflection back at me, but not my own.

Mistaking my reaction, he came to me, sliding a hand over my back and curling it around my shoulder. Warm, that hand, and it sent tingles all the way to my toes. "I know. You never get used to it."

"No, you don't," I said. But my voice was deep and raspy, and I knew my eyes were glowing red. The fresh blood had flipped that predator switch inside me, brought the bloodlust to life in me so powerfully that just his touch on my shoulder was erotic, despite my leather jacket and the blouse underneath it. So it wasn't entirely my fault that I turned and buried myself against his chest, pressing my face into his shirt, inhaling his scent and closing my illuminated eyes in hunger and longing.

"It's all right, kid. Come on, now, we've got to call this in, get forensics in here, comb the place for evidence—"

I moved my face a little, and wound up with it nestled in the crook of his neck. His pulse thumped steadily, quickly too. Oh, yeah. His blood was rushing just beneath the skin, a river of ecstasy just waiting. I could sink my teeth into him right now, take just a sip, show him how it could feel to be imbibed by a vampire. And then I could keep on sipping while we ripped each other's clothes off and . . .

"Chloe," he said.

I grabbed hold of myself, backed up off him, put my back to him again. "Call it in, then. I need some air." And I headed out the apartment door as fast as I could manage without giving myself away.

I jogged down the stairs and out the front doors, then lifted my face to the cool night air and let it kiss me, let it soothe me.

God, that was close! What would he have thought of me if I'd lost it in there, thrown him down on the floor, and mounted him while a dead woman lay a few feet away? What kind of human woman got turned on at the scene of a murder? A kinky one, right? An uncaring, screwed-up sicko. A serial killer, maybe. A monster—just like he thought I was. Or would think so, if he knew.

I wasn't that. I'd died a virgin. I'd been shy, uncomfortable in my own skin, self-conscious, and sure saving myself for marriage was the decent thing to do.

That changed when you became what I was. The bloodlust was so closely and intimately related to sexual desire that the two entwined, became inseparable. When you felt one, you felt the other. When you fed from the living, it was orgasmic. And if you were having sex at the same time, your head would probably explode.

I can only guess, since I'd never done it. I'd fed from the living only twice; both times it was a criminal, and both times I'd let him live, willed him to forget. But I'd read things in those books I'd bought at that odd little bookstore on Westcott Street.

Dammit, I needed to eat, sate this bloodlust, and get back to looking relatively human again. I glanced behind me, but Shep was still inside. I had, I figured, fifteen minutes before the forensics teams arrived, and I looked up and down the sidewalk and spotted a bar a few doors down. Bars were the best hunting grounds, so I headed that way, my black boots tapping the sidewalk all the way to the end of the block where the bar stood right on the corner. I didn't know its name. I didn't care. I stood outside the entrance, opened my mind, and let the rush of human thoughts come flooding in. So many of them, so much noise, all at once. When I'd been a newborn, that had overwhelmed me. But with time and practice, you can master anything. Anything, really, it's true. So I let the flood come, latching onto a voice, a thought, a feeling, an emotion here and there. Letting go of the useless ones, sifting, sorting, searching.

And then I found the one. Male, horny, drunk as hell, looking to cheat on his wife . . . again. I kept my attention on that one, like turning the lens on a camera, focusing in on him and him alone. All the background noise faded to nothing, and I sent my will to him with a whole lot of oomph behind it. *Get up and come outside.*

It wasn't really much of a challenge. I didn't even have to tell him twice. I felt him feeling me, responding to me, sliding off his stool, staggering toward the exit. I looked around, found a secluded corner, all shadowy and dark, the view blocked by a tree struggling to survive in the circular opening allotted it amid all the concrete. It was suffocating on automobile exhaust and cigarette smoke. But it was giving me a perfect spot. I went to the tree and waited, calling mentally to my victim until he stumbled right into the shadows, right into my arms.

I held him to me and smelled the beer he'd been drinking and the cigarettes he'd been smoking. He didn't ask questions or argue or anything at all. Of course, I had him in a bit of a thrall, but not a very powerful one. I dropped down to my knees, and he dropped trou so fast you'd have thought his pants were on fire. Pig. I leaned closer, found the femoral artery, and sank my teeth into his inner thigh about halfway between the knee and groin, all the while tightening my grip on his mind a bit more so he wouldn't scream or try to pull away. I drank deeply, about a pint, and then I withdrew.

He was all dreamy eyed and smiling when I stood up again. Yeah, giving was as good as getting where blood was concerned. It could be, anyway. He stood there all dopey, drunk and feeling good, and I fished the little plastic tube out of my purse, pulled it apart, and took a cotton swab out of it. Its end was soaked in my special blend of Avitene and epinephrine. It's what cutmen use on boxers between rounds, and it's not easy to come by. Then again, I didn't need it very often. A little would go a long way for me. I dabbed the damp cotton swab over the tiny wounds I'd made in his thigh, and watched to make sure the bleeding would stop.

It did. It always did.

Pull up your pants.

He obeyed my mind's command, almost falling over, but getting it done. I used my fingernail to rip a small tear in the fabric, right over where the wounds were, to let the sun get at them.

Now curl up right here and go to sleep. You're not to wake again until you feel the heat of the morning sun on your leg. You got drunk, stumbled out here, and passed out. I don't exist. You never saw me. There was no woman. Say it.

"There wash no'ummin."

Close enough.

His eyes were closing before he even got himself all the way onto the ground, but he curled up and was fast asleep within seconds. The minute sunlight touched the wounds of a vampire, those wounds healed themselves. There would be no evidence he'd been my snack food tonight.

All of this took no more than ten minutes. Then I was

dabbing my mouth very carefully, and heading back to poor dead Martha's apartment building.

On the way, I glanced upward, feeling eyes on me. But when I looked at the windows, there was no one there.

"SHE wasn't a vampire after all," Shep said as we stood in the living room, trying to stay out of the way while the geek squad processed the scene. He was looking at me expectantly. "You can say 'I told you so' now."

"You just said it for me. So how do you know she was human? Check for fangs or something while I was gone?"

He cracked a smile. "How'd you know?"

Because it's the first thing you mortals think of when you hear the word vampire. Out loud I just said, "Lucky guess."

"You look better. Got some color in your face now, anyway."

Yeah, and a breath mint in my mouth to hide the reason why. "I don't work too many homicides. Not used to seeing dead people." *Just Undead people.* I almost grinned at my own internal joke.

He was wearing latex gloves and moving around the living room, thumbing through books, opening drawers. I hadn't donned gloves myself, and opted to just stick close and look over his shoulder. No point in both of us disturbing evidence. Not that he was. He was careful. Meticulous, even. He looked at every item on every shelf and stand, opened every drawer. No telephone stand or desk. No computer, but there was one of those giant-sized cell phones lying on the coffee table. Its screen was black, but it was on. I knew it was on because I could hear the buzz of electricity moving through the device as clearly as you hear a dial tone when you pick up a landline.

He couldn't touch the screen with his latex gloves, and I couldn't with my bare hands and risk covering up the prints that had to be blanketing the thing. I figured he'd bag it, but he surprised me, pulling a stylus out of the pocket of his white shirt. He'd had a jacket on at the beginning of the night. Casual, but still a suit. He looked killer in it. He looked like a man to be reckoned with. And hot.

And hotter now with the jacket gone, and the white shirt-sleeves rolled up to his elbows, showing the taut skin and dark hair of his forearms. The tie was still on but tugged loose, the button underneath it undone.

He whistled then, soft and low, and I realized I was watching him instead of the paperback-sized phone. I shifted my focus, and saw him flipping from website page to website page, all of them porn. The kinky kind, folks all trussed up in leather, with blindfolds and ball gags.

I told myself to look away and couldn't. He just kept moving that stylus, pausing every now and then on some really hard-core stuff.

"So we know what she was into, dominance and submission. Bondage and discipline," he said.

"And we know which end of the paddle she liked by her recent behavior, and the fact that she tasered you when you tried to take charge of the . . . uh . . . the uh . . ."

"Yeah. Got it, Madison."

I had lowered my head but I looked up at him, trying hard not to smile.

He was trying hard not to smile back, but we both did it, anyway.

"Look at her texts," I said. "That's gonna be where all the action is. Her generation doesn't talk on the phone or write emails. They speak in shorthand with their thumbs."

He was still looking at me, but the smile died slowly. "Her generation, huh?"

Shoot.

"'Cause I would've thought you were part of her generation. Just how old are you, Madison?"

"Old enough to remember when that was considered a

really rude question to ask a lady. And also, a lot older than I look."

He held my eyes for a second, so I nodded at the phone. "Will you open the darn messages?"

"I'll open the darn messages."

And he did, and then he held the phone toward me.

The most recent conversation was pretty one sided, and consisted of eight texts from "Jackie G," whose avatar was a pair of front-facing and profile-view mug shots of James Cagney, side by side.

Hey, MJ.

MJ? U there?

WTF? Answer me.

Please?

Bitch.

Sorry. MJ?

U OK?

Screw it. Coming ovr.

"So do you think he came over?" I asked.

Shep didn't look at me. He was still looking at the phone, staring at the text like it was gonna change shape and spell out a clue or something.

"What makes you say he?" he asked me back.

"James Cagney." I shrugged. "He's a guy."

"You think people always use their own gender?"

"Would you use a female profile picture?" I asked him.

"I don't have a profile picture."

That made me smile.

He looked at me for a second too long. Then he went back to the phone, continued skimming poor Martha's messages and emails and apps. Then he pulled out his own phone, and started dialing a number.

It rang a few times—he hadn't put it on speaker, but I could hear like a bat—before someone picked up, and when they did, it was a male voice and sounded sleepy and irritated. "If this is a sales call—"

"It's a police call," Shep said. "Is this . . . " He glanced at the big phone on the table. "Jackie G?"

"Jackie Geraldo, yeah. What's this about, man?"

"Mr. Geraldo, do you know Martha Jane Billings—"

"I knew it. Something happened to her. Dammit, I knew it. Is she dead? Just tell me, is she dead?"

"Yeah. She's dead, I'm sorry."

Shep looked at me, eyebrows raised. I nodded, agreeing that this guy was interesting. After giving Mister G a minute, he spoke again. "I read your texts on her phone. You said you were coming over."

"I did come over. I pounded on the door like ten minutes, man. She didn't answer." The guy paused there, and a gust of air came out of him. "I should'a busted the damn door, shouldn't I? I knew I shouldn't just leave. *Dam*mit."

"What time were you here, friend?" Shep's voice had gentled. Aw, my partner had a heart. What do you know.

"About an hour ago."

He nodded. "I don't think it would'a done you any good, kicking in the door. She's been gone longer than that."

There was a loud sniff.

"I'm uh, I'm gonna need to talk to you, friend. I'd like you to come into my office, tell me everything you know, so I can—"

"Evything I *know*," Jackie G said. "You tellin' me somebody *killed* her?"

"We don't know anything for sure. Will you come in, talk to me?"

"I can come over there, talk to you right now."

"No, I'm leaving."

"I'm four blocks up. I'll be there in a minute."

He rang off. Shep lifted his brows and shrugged. "Hell, I guess we're having company." Then he turned toward the bathroom. "Guys, cover her up, can you? We've got a friend on his way over."

FIVE

JACKIE G WOULD have finaled in a Pee-wee Herman lookalike contest. Mug-shot Pee-wee, not Playhouse Pee-wee. He was not what I'd expected. He had a body that whispered "bully bait" and a voice that said "street thug."

He came in, looking around nervously but trying to act like he wasn't.

"She's in the bathroom," I told him. "They've covered her up. We'll be taking her out of here soon."

"I'm sorry for your loss, Jack," Shep said. "Can I call you Jack?"

Jackie G looked up at him and nodded in two jerky motions. "My mamma called me Jack."

"It's a good name," said Shep, who I thought probably couldn't bring himself to call the man Jackie. "So how did you know her, Jack?"

"We were . . . friends."

"You were friends. Were you the kind of friends who share a bed?"

"Not like that." He lowered his head and his eyes. "We just liked to play sometimes."

"Sex games. Bondage and shit, right?" Shep said.

The other man nodded. "She liked to pretend like she was a vampire." He lifted up his head, and I gasped in spite of myself. His neck was covered in bruises and cuts. You couldn't call them hickeys. He'd been assaulted, for cripes' sake.

"Jeezuz," Shep muttered. "You let her do that to you?"

He smiled, dipping his head lower. "I like it."

"You like it." He gave his head a little shake. "Well, pal, whatever turns you on, I guess. Does she . . . play these kinds of games with anyone else you know of?"

"Well, yeah. I mean, at the club."

"At the club."

He looked up then, his eyes wide. "I don't think I'm supposed to talk about that."

Shep looked at me. I could see he was a little amused by the guy. I shrugged and said, "If you're not supposed to talk about it, and you do anyway, you'll probably get some pretty interesting punishment, don't you think?" And I wiggled my eyebrows up and down.

Shep let loose a gust of what I knew was laughter, but he tried to make it into a choking sound instead, pounding his chest for authenticity.

Yeah, he was starting to like me. But hey, what's not to like?

"Tell us about the club, Jack," Shep said.

He looked at Shep, shook his head left, then right.

I reached out and took hold of his chin, digging my fingernails in and turning him to face me. Then I got up real close to his face and I said, "You tell me about that club right now, Jackie G."

"Yes, ma'am!" His eyes widened, and his nostrils flared.

I shoved his chest, knocking him into a chair. "Talk."

I glanced back at Shep. His eyes were huge, but approving. And then Jackie G started talking.

* * *

IT took most of the night to finish processing the apartment. Everything was booked into evidence, and from there the smartphone and clothing were going to the lab for processing. We have to oversee all of it, preserve the chain of evidence and all that. And then there was paperwork. Mountains of it.

I sat across from Shep in an empty conference room we'd turned into Vamp Squad Central (VCU to everyone but me). He was on one side of the long table, and I was on the other. There was a corkboard on one wall, where he'd tacked up crime scene photos. I had deliberately sat on the side facing away from it. I didn't like looking at dead people, and I didn't need another rush of bloodlust coming on. It would be tough to cover, being alone in a room with him.

"I hate filling out paperwork when we should be checking out the club Jackie G told us about," I said.

Shep said, "That's the first thing on our agenda next shift. This one's almost over."

I looked up at the clock and rolled my eyes. It was late. Or early, depending on how you looked at it. I needed to finish this stack and beat the dawn back to my lair, aka perfectly ordinary apartment . . . you know, aside from the windowless closet with the trapdoor in its floor, where I slept.

"Besides, who'd be at an S and M club at four in the morning?" he went on.

I took a deep breath. "I'd kill for a cup of coffee," I said.

He got up just as quick as if he wasn't at the end of an endless shift. "I'll get you one. Cream and sugar?"

"Sure." I didn't care. It wasn't like I was going to drink it.

He looked at me oddly, and then left the room to get it for me. Sweet of him. As soon as the door closed, I zipped through the stack of paperwork, scribbling so fast my pen got hot. By the time he came back, I was pulling on my jacket and hiking my purse up onto my shoulder.

He held out the cup. I took it. "Thanks a bunch. I'm all done. Heading out before I fall asleep on my feet."

I watched his brows push against each other and battled the urge to smooth my forefinger over that spot in between them, where everything was all puckered up.

"You're finished?"

"Yeah. I'd stay and help you with yours but I have to get home." *Or I'll be toast.*

"It's fine. Go on." He tipped his head to one side. "Nice job today, Madison."

"Thanks. You too, Shep."

"Don't call me Shep."

I smiled and left.

I made it home with time to spare, looked around my spartan apartment and thought it needed to look more lived in. The prop food in the fridge was all well past its expiration date. My real food supply was in a mini-fridge that was built into the wall, padlocked shut, and hidden behind a hinged painting like a freaking billionaire's wall safe. There was a layer of dust on most of the mismatched dishes I'd stacked in the cupboards just for show. I used a coffee mug and the microwave once in a great while, though I liked my blood heated naturally a lot better. Nuking it altered it somehow.

I used it then, though, 'cause time was short. So I filled myself up, and yet somehow, still felt an odd emptiness. A weird hunger. Very much like the craving for blood, but with a slightly different angle to it.

And then I recognized what it was I was actually craving. Sex.

With Shep.

Being around him for hours on end had lit up some fuses in me that hadn't been lit in a while. And as long as it had been for me, I figured there was a powder keg waiting at the other end of them.

Darn.

The sun tugged at me, meaning there was no time for

watching home movies of my childhood. That was probably a good thing. So I did my evening routine. Brushed my teeth, changed into comfy pajamas, messed up my bed like I did every night, and then walked into the giant closet that had been my apartment's biggest attraction. I closed the door and locked it behind me. Didn't turn on a light. I didn't need one. My mattress on the floor was swathed in downy comforters, soft as a swan's nest. I snuggled in nice and warm, closed my eyes, and saw Shep right in front of them. My partner. The guy who hated vampires.

And had no clue that I was one.

I woke at sundown, stretched, and smiled, looking forward to my next shift in a way I never had when I'd been working for Chief Rivers. Yeah, there was some pretty powerful chemistry happening between me and Shep, no denying it. It probably wouldn't end well if I followed where it was leading.

At the very least, my cover would be blown. And I'd have to leave central New York and start over someplace far away. New name, new job, new life. I liked the current one too much to risk all that. So I'd better cool my jets where he was concerned.

That decided, I headed for the shower, snatching up my phone on the way and then stopping at the notifications on the screen. He'd called. Ten times. All within the past hour.

Sighing, wondering if I was ever going to get a leisurely evening routine again, I called him back while warming up my breakfast.

"What's up?"

"What the hell, Madison? Did you think I'd be calling if it wasn't important?"

"Are you aware you're sort of yelling at me?"

"Why didn't you answer your phone?"

"I turn my phone off when my shift ends. It's just how I

operate. Always has been. You don't like it, fire me and I'll go back to my old job. I'm not gonna argue. It's not up for debate."

"That's ludicrous. We're on the trail of a serial killer."

"I know. We got anything new? I'm assuming we must or you wouldn't have been wearing out my voice mail."

He sighed. I was exasperating him and it made me smile. Then he said, "There's another one."

I frowned. "Another body?"

"Yes. Another body. I'm at the scene now. That falling-down hotel off Carrier Circle. You know the one?"

"Yeah." In my day it had been thriving.

"Get here, will you?"

"Quick as humanly possible." I could do it as quick as vampishly possible, but that would be a giveaway. So I took another record-breaking shower, keeping my hair out of it this time, and jumped into my car. Then I broke land-speed records (well, you know, as much as you can in an original VW Beetle) getting there. I braked to a stop beside three cruisers and Shep's Audi—his personal car. He must've come directly here from home. They were all parked in front of a falling-down building that used to be a motel, with rusted and busted chain-link fence all around it, and weeds and beer bottles littering up the place. A party spot, maybe. The building was brick, but wouldn't stand up to any huffing and puffing. Most of the windows were broken out, glass hung in shards in the black, gaping holes.

I could see people gathered around one side, so I headed that way, climbing over the fence in a spot where it was lying mostly on its side. Three more steps and I smelled it. Death. And something else.

There had been a vampire here. A real one, not a goth chick with a vampire fetish.

I put myself on full alert, which meant not shielding myself. I'd tried that route, and another human had been killed. Time to be blatant about it. Let the killer sense my presence. Maybe it would give him (or her) pause. Vampires didn't take well to their own kind murdering the innocent, much less leaving bloodless corpses lying around to be discovered by human law enforcement. It was bad for all of them—us—especially in the supercharged fear-driven climate that was suddenly the norm. Vampires tended to police their own, or so I'd read. So he would probably be expecting one to show up.

"Madison!" Shep called. "In here."

I looked toward his voice, but it was beyond the cops milling around a big opening in the bricks that was, apparently, our entryway. Then I made my way to him, and it was easy as hell. It was like he gave off some kind of homing beacon that I could follow. I mean, I could home in on pretty much anyone, unless they were shielding. But with him I didn't even have to try.

I picked my way over broken boards and stray bricks and other litter, deeper into the darkness of the building. He was near the body, and in another few steps I was too, right beside him, looking down at the poor unfortunate fellow.

He was rail thin and stark naked. I could count his ribs, and his belly was concave. Had an Ichabod Crane sort of look to him, protruding Adam's apple, long horselike face, big, curving nose. He was white as a sheet. There wasn't a mark on him—none that Shep could see, at least. I could still make out the telltale pink spots on his neck, just above his jugular. I glanced toward the nearest broken window, knowing the sun must've touched the wounds and made them vanish.

"He's been here awhile," I said.

"Since sometime before dawn. Around four a.m. is the initial guess."

I frowned. "But Martha was already dead."

"Yeah. Maybe we should check the morgue, make sure she didn't get up and run off."

"She wasn't a vampire, Shep."

"Maybe she became one, after she died."

I shook my head. "That's not how it works."

He touched my chin, dragging my gaze to his. I'd been staring at the dead guy hard, like I expected him to start talking and tell me who had done this to him.

"You okay?" Shep was searching my face, my eyes, like he gave a damn. "I remember the last one shook you up a little."

His palm was on my cheek, and it was . . . intimate. And the way he was looking at me . . .

"I'm good," I said. "No blood this time. It's cleaner. Definitely a vampire, though."

"And you can tell that just by looking?"

"Can't you?" Had I slipped again? Sometimes things are so obvious to me, and have been for so long, that I forget ordinary mortals can't see them. I swallowed hard, tried to point out the obvious. "He's chalk white. And look at the parts of him making contact with the floor. You see any lividity? There's no blood left in the poor guy to pool there."

He looked at the body, then at me again. "Good stuff, Chloe." Chloe. Not Madison. Was he starting to like me? "But where are the marks?" He hunkered down, looking the guy over head to toe, using a gloved hand to move him a little. I presumed that meant the photos had already been taken.

"The marks would've faded as soon as the sun hit them," I said, and I pointed at the window. "If he's been here all day, it would have slanted in on him at some point."

He frowned, nodded. I thought maybe he hadn't known that little tidbit.

"We got an ID on him," he said. "Theodore 'Ted' Hartwell. But more interestingly—" He took my upper arm in his hand, and led me back to where the group were standing around outside. The forensics guys were packing up their kits, and Lieutenant Harris had arrived, as had the meat wagon. A body bag and a gurney were trundled out of the back, and I thought they wouldn't need much muscle. A bloodless corpse was surprisingly lightweight. Shep picked up an evidence bag, held it in front of my face.

It held a glossy black matchbook with vivid, bloodred lips, two white fangs, and a droplet of scarlet blood. I took the bag from him, turned it around. The name of the place they'd come from was on the reverse.

"Vampire Fetish Club," I whispered. "That's the place Jackie G told us about. You found this on the victim?" I asked.

"No. Found it on the floor three feet away from him."

"So it could've been dropped by the killer."

He nodded.

"We have got to get into that club," I said.

"Yeah, but not as cops."

I looked up at him slow. My eyes met his and widened. "You mean . . . we pose as . . . ?"

"I'll be the sexy vampire and you can be my mortal slave girl," he said. "And I can pressure Jackie G to get us in."

My throat was so dry that when I spoke again it sounded like I'd swallowed a frog. "When?"

"Tonight," he said. "No time to lose. Whoever this is, they've killed two nights in a row. We can't let tonight make three."

Oh, hell. Still, I nodded. But then I said, "I'm gonna be the sexy vampire, though. So far it's been female phony vamps involved in this. So, um, you get to be my slave boy for the evening. Got it?"

He nodded slowly, and there was something a little bit excited in his eyes.

SIX

TED HARTWELL HAD been seen leaving a bar with a girl by the name of Kara Stacks. But Kara had apparently skipped town. Her place was empty, her car missing, and all her dominatrix gear had been left behind. I borrowed a few pieces that still had the tags on, because I wouldn't have touched the rest without soaking it in bleach first. No, I can't catch mortal illnesses. But I can still get thoroughly grossed out.

Kara was not a vampire. I knew it by the scent in her place. Human, through and through. No vampire had been there. And since her neighbors had seen her by day as well as night, it was obvious to Shep as well.

There was a vampire behind all of this. Apparently, he was using dominant women with vampire fantasies to bring him his victims. That was my theory. I'd felt the presence of a malevolent vampire where we'd found Hartwell. So I was sure of it, but I had nothing to base that theory on that I could share with Shep.

We got the rundown on the club from Jackie G. He didn't

want to help us, but when Shep started getting all macho cop on him, I took pity and sent a little mental nudge. He couldn't refuse me. It wasn't so much that he was weak willed as it was that he liked being told what to do. Being given no choice. I told him to help us and so he did.

And now I sort of wished I hadn't. I was standing with Shep outside a dark strip club with tacky neon silhouettes of nude women in various lewd poses. And that was on the outside.

Shep wore a leather vest with no shirt under it, skintight black jeans, and biker boots with large silver buckles that matched the one on his belt.

And I wore a black trench coat, its sash knotted as tight as I could knot it.

"You're gonna have to take it off sooner or later," he said. "I know you don't like it, and I agree you're being objectified, but it's a job. It's a case, Chloe. I promise not to get out of line."

I closed my eyes slow, but picked at the knot. When it came free, I glanced up and down the street, then reluctantly opened the coat.

He stared. He *really* stared. I mean, it was like he was trying to get his eyes to meet mine again and literally couldn't. I hadn't been able to look in the mirror, of course, so I couldn't get the full view of what I looked like. I wore a black leather bustier with red satin trim and a leather skirt so short my butt cheeks felt a breeze when I moved. The boots were knee-high with spike heels so tall I could barely walk in them. I was wearing vivid red press-on nails and matching lipstick, and I had a cheesy vampire cloak under my coat, all bunched up and uncomfortable. All I had to do was shake it loose and flip up the tall, pointy collar.

"Well, you . . . certainly look . . . convincing."

"Gee, thanks."

"You'd better take my Taser," he said, pulling it out of somewhere and handing it to me.

"You think I'm going to need to use it?" I asked, and I couldn't keep the alarm from my voice.

"Yeah." He cleared his throat. "Possibly on me." His gaze dipped downward again. "Damn, woman."

I grinned. Couldn't help it. "Let's do this, shall we?" I pulled my coat closed, and nodded at him to open the door, getting into character.

He obeyed, holding it open, and keeping his eyes downcast. At least, they appeared downcast. But I knew he was scanning the club, anyway. Wall-to-wall people, mostly middle-aged, overweight males. Most of them a couple of sheets to the wind. All of them ogling the women on the stage, who wore thong panties and were on platforms, rubbing themselves on stripper poles.

A hostess met us halfway across the floor, cleavage up to her chin. "Table for two?"

"No, thanks," I said, and I showed her the card Jackie G had given us. It bore the same logo as the matchbook we'd found at crime scene number two.

"Oh." She looked at me, looked at Shep, frowned a little, but didn't say more.

I didn't think she was buying that he was my submissive. I tried to stand a little straighter, look a little more dominant. "Eyes on the floor until I say otherwise," I told him. And I smacked his butt for good measure.

He jumped in surprise, and I could tell he was biting his lip to keep from smiling at my efforts.

We followed the hostess through the place, passing way too close to the stage, so the jiggling boobs and nearly naked backsides were only feet away from us. Ick.

There was a door in the back, which she tapped on, and when it opened, she stood aside for us to pass. The guy holding it open wore a full leather mask with a zipper over the mouth. God, the crap that turned some people on.

He bowed to us, and stood aside so we could walk down a curving staircase into a basement full of debauchery.

There was a floor show, a three-ring circus of people abusing other people. In the center, a nude woman knelt in the midst of a circle of men who were all wearing ruffled shirts and phony fangs. She was giving oral sex to one of them. The men were fully clothed, except for the obvious. One of them slapped her backside with this fringy whiplike thing, and she quickly left the one she was with to scurry to him. Then another one smacked her and she moved again. It was like a game. To their left, there was a man kneeling on the floor, licking and sucking his mistress's toes while taking another man from behind. The mistress wore a leather bikini, boots that came to midthigh, and a black velvet cloak with red satin lining. And phony fangs. On the far right side, a woman was captive in a set of old-fashioned-looking stocks, her head through one hole, hands through two others. She was awkwardly bent over, forming a right angle almost, and anyone who walked past could do what-ever they liked to her. Anyone dressed as one of the vampire dominants, that is. And they were. Sometimes several of them at once.

I didn't think it was probably much different from any other BDSM club, except for the fact that all the dominants were pretending to be vampires.

"Best take off the coat, Chloe," Shep whispered. "You stick out like a sore thumb. And smack me or something, will you?"

I slid off my coat, and held it out to him. Shep took it, keeping his head respectfully lowered, and followed where I led like a loyal servant. I made a winding path through the place, my senses open, because I was searching for a killer, after all. The place smelled of sandalwood, patchouli, and sex. The drinks were all bloodred, but not real blood. I'd have smelled that a mile away. The masters varied in the vampirish accoutrements. Some wore cloaks, some cravats, most wore false fangs, and a few had filed their incisors to sharp points, the idiots.

What I didn't feel was distress. Everyone in the place was thoroughly turned on, including the ones being paddled, spanked, whipped, and ravaged. No one was pleading for mercy or crying in pain. Every *smack* was followed by a palpable rush of pleasure.

I spotted a table in a corner and headed for it, sliding into the rich red velvet upholstered seat, glancing back at Shep, and pointing at the floor. He knelt, keeping his head down, but his eyes sneaked a look at mine.

"All the other slaves are on the floor," I whispered.

"It's fine. All the other slaves are also . . . doing something," he whispered back.

I looked around the room again, and my throat went dry. "What do you suggest I have you *do*?" I snapped, almost too loud.

He shrugged one shoulder, and I saw his eyes slide to our left, where a male slave knelt in front of his mistress, eagerly lapping at her breasts while she pulled his hair.

"How about that?"

"How about you scurry over to that slave with the cocktail tray and bring me back a drink?"

I could see the twinkle in his eyes, but I didn't think anyone else could. It was dark. In fact once I could drag my eyes off the *entertainment*, I saw that the place was really just a repurposed basement. The walls were cinder blocks, painted a deep purplish red, like blood in need of oxygenation. There were three chandeliers, holding dozens of lighted candles, suspended from the ceiling by chains, and lots of red velvet curtains where there could be no windows. The only other light in the room was a red strobe that flashed randomly.

As soon as Shep hurried off to obey, a dominatrix in tight leather shorts, which wouldn't have been flattering on a skinny woman, came to my table and slid into the seat across from me.

"You're new here. Maybe you don't know the rules."

I lifted my eyebrows. She was an ordinary mortal and I was wide open, trying to read her. I didn't pick up on any murderous intentions, but a lot of hostility all wrapped up in sexual excitement.

"Rules?" I asked, looking around. "I thought it was pretty much anything goes."

"Anything goes. But nothing doesn't."

I frowned and felt the breeze as her words flew right over my head.

"You can't just watch. This is not a spectator sport. At least, not here."

"Oh." I got it. I wasn't joining in the orgy, and that made those who were nervous. "I just got here," I said, and I made my tone a little snarky. "You care if I have a drink first?"

Shep returned with my drink, set it on the table, and returned to his spot on the floor at my feet like an obedient pup, keeping his head down and his entire demeanor submissive. It was so opposite who he really was that I found myself kind of grimacing inwardly. I guess I'd learned something about myself, then, hadn't I? I liked him strong and bossy better than weak and obedient.

"You, slave, take off your mistress's boots. Move!" the woman said, her voice stern, but none too loud.

And that's when I felt the presence. A mind so sharp and powerful that it stood out amid the cacophony of mortal thoughts like a laser beam among 25-watt bulbs. I slammed my mind closed, my eyes at the same time, as if that could help to hide me from him. Quickly, my shields went up. But it might have already been too late.

Shep's hand was on the zipper of my boot, gently tugging it down while our hostess, or whoever the bossy bitch was, watched eagerly. I couldn't read her thoughts now, but I could guess at them. She was going to make him put on a show for her viewing pleasure. Well, not on my watch, she wasn't. I had to show dominance here. Especially if the vampire I'd just sensed was our killer. Because that was what he liked.

I put my hand on the top of Shep's head and said firmly, "No." I didn't shout. I didn't have to.

Shep stopped, and I got to my feet, met the woman's eyes and said, "He serves me, and me alone." Then I looked away from her, beyond her, searching for anyone who could've been the vampire I had sensed here. He might have just come in, or he might have been here all along, and only just lowered his shields. Either way, I'd picked up more than just his energy and power and age. He was old. Very old, and that meant very strong. Stronger than me. I'd also picked up the red haze of his bloodlust, raging. He was hunting tonight.

The woman was responding to me, but I was ignoring her now, hearing but not listening. "This is my domain, newcomer. Whatever I say here, goes. I am mistress even of the masters and mistresses who come here. I command them all."

Not the one I just felt, I thought. *No one commands him.*

He was watching us now. I felt him.

"No one commands my slave but me!" I snapped, facing her. She was taller. I needed her to back down. To be cowed, so I opened my mind a mere crack, just enough to send my will. *Obey me.*

Shep squeezed my calf, where his hand still rested, and I bit my lip. He was right. We were undercover. But I couldn't give in. I sensed it. The vampire was watching us. If my theory was correct, he wanted a full-fledged dominatrix. His first one had died, and his second had fled. He needed a third, and I had to fit the bill.

The mistress in front of me backed up a step. And I knew I had won. Then, I looked at Shep, sat slowly, and said, "Continue."

He gripped the zipper of my boot again, with his teeth this time, which seemed to please the woman immensely. She smiled as he tugged the zipper down, and then he slipped the boot from my foot. I had stockings on, black ones.

"Now worship me as a slave should worship his mistress. Show me your devotion."

He bent to my foot, pressing his lips to the top of it, kissing each individual toe, and then moving around to the ankle. Bolts of lightning struck everywhere he put his mouth, and shot up my leg. He kissed and nipped a slow, sexy path over my shin, opening his mouth to gobble up the back of my calf, and moving slowly, steadily higher. When he used his tongue to tickle the hollow behind my knee, I gasped out loud and the lightning bolt set fire to my soul and a full-blown inferno erupted inside me. He kissed a path around then, to my inner thigh, and I almost exploded in pleasure.

I put both hands on his shoulders and pushed him away. "Enough."

He backed off and I knew he was feeling my reaction. He had to be.

Smiling now, the dominatrix nodded, satisfied with what she no doubt considered my capitulation, I thought, and finally walked away in search of more exciting pursuits. Shep dared to look up at me, but I closed my eyes, knowing the red glow of lust was shining from them.

"Are you okay?" he asked.

"There's a vampire in here. He was watching."

If distracting him was my intention, it worked like a charm. He stiffened, and quickly looked around the room. "Where?"

"I don't know."

"You didn't see him?"

"No, I . . . felt him."

"You felt him," he repeated, softly, but I heard the doubt all the same. And it was a relief, to be honest, to have the real Shep talking to me, and not the make-believe submissive.

"We should get out of here," I said. "We've either convinced him or we haven't. It gets dangerous from here."

"But I was just starting to enjoy myself." I opened my eyes, shot him a look, and he jumped and muttered, "Jesus."

Shit. The eyes. I forgot. Quickly shielding my eyes with one hand, I said, "Ow! That strobe light just about blinded me."

Then I peered at him from behind my hand as I got to my feet and started across the room, leaving him to follow, and wondering if he bought it. He'd seen the red glow in my eyes, I was sure of it. And I'd better darn well have it under control before he looked at me again, outside, in the dark.

We got to the staircase, and he took my coat from the male slave who came running with it the second we approached. Shep put it over my shoulders, and I turned as I was sliding my arms into it and felt eyes on me. Not human eyes.

And then I saw him across the room, talking to the alpha female I'd challenged. He had pale blue eyes that reminded me of the vamp who'd killed my parents, but that was where the resemblance ended. He was bald, pale, emaciated, had disturbingly red lips, and he was staring at me. He smiled slightly when I met his eyes. My mind was closed up tight, and so was his, but I knew a vampire when I saw one.

And I figured he probably did too.

Lifting a bony finger, he pointed it my way and leaned close to whisper something into the mistress's ear. I gripped Shep by the arm and sped up the stairs, out through the door, and then tugged him across the crowded dance floor.

"What is it?" Shep asked as we wound our way out.

"Didn't you see him? That guy who was staring at us as we left?"

"Someone was staring at us?"

"God, you couldn't *feel* that?"

"Um, no. But you can. You can *feel* when people are looking at you and can *sense* when a vampire is in a room.

And you can smell blood, let's not forget that. You have . . . heightened olfactory function."

He was asking me to explain myself, sort of. But I didn't. I couldn't, really. So I just kept walking, hurrying, toward the door. I felt pursued, but wasn't certain if the vampire was following or not.

We reached the far side of the crowded club, and I looked back, saw the doorway to the dungeon opening slowly, and didn't wait to see who would appear on the other side. "Come on, will you?" I ran, still gripping his arm, unwilling to run ahead of him and leave him behind to fend for himself against a rogue vampire. Might as well leave him alone to fight a hungry lion.

Finally we were at the exit, and I all but dragged him through the doors, then broke into a run. He didn't argue or resist at all, just kept pace until we reached his car, and he got behind the wheel. He sent me a look, but I was still looking behind us.

"You're really shaken up, aren't y—"

"Go!" I shouted. The vampire had stepped out of the club onto the sidewalk and was looking up and down to see where we'd gone. "Will you go already!"

He frowned, glancing at me, and then behind us at the Nosferatu, and that's what he looked like. Then he nodded, started the car, and pulled carefully and calmly away from the curb.

I saw the vampire look our way, saw him seeing us, the car, the plate number. Hell. He would know. He would be able to find us. Find Shep. And yes, that was the plan. That was what we'd hoped. To make contact. To root out a killer. But I hadn't thought far enough ahead, had I?

I couldn't leave Shep alone again. Not at night, anyway. Or he might end up being the next victim.

SEVEN

"HEY," SHEP SAID. Then he reached across the car and tapped my shoulder, because I was still twisted in the seat and watching behind us. "I think you can relax now."

I couldn't. He would follow, I knew he would. Either from a distance, or he'd get a line on Shep's brain waves and track us down that way. He'd seen me. He knew what I was. A human could look at a vamp and not know, unless we wanted him to. But a vampire could see the details that a human would miss. The way the paleness of the skin wasn't just on the surface, but all the way through. And how fine and small our pores become over time, until our skin is as smooth and flawless as a figure in a wax museum. Our eyes are different, our pupils larger, our irises more vivid. Our hair is stronger, and more lustrous because of it. Everything about us is different. More. Just more.

Frankly, it baffles me that mortals can't identify us on sight. But then, I've been a vampire for sixty years. It's easy to forget what it felt like to be a human. I imagine in a hundred years, it'll be even easier.

"You're really scared, aren't you?" he asked.

I looked into his eyes. He really couldn't see me at all. So I nodded. "Yeah. Pretty scared."

"It's amazing how you spotted him. Are you sure he was a vampire?"

"I'm sure."

"You're good at this. You should be the one in charge of the Vamp Squad, not me."

He'd called it the Vamp Squad. That was what I called it, and up to now he'd grimaced or rolled his eyes every time.

Shep tilted his head, glancing my way periodically as he drove. "How did you get to be this . . . tuned in to them?"

I shook my head. "I don't . . . want to talk about that."

He frowned, but then nodded. "Okay." He took a right, and I finally realized where we were.

"We can't go back to the station," I said. "If he finds out we're cops, we're dead."

Shep said, "We're not being followed. I can spot a tail a mile away."

"He can follow us from ten miles away, Shep. And he is. Trust me on this. If we want to keep our cover intact, we need to do what he would expect us to do."

Shep said, "What he'd expect us to do . . . if we were legitimate perverts, you mean?"

"Yeah." I wasn't thinking, I was feeling. Gradually inching my mind open, bit by bit, almost afraid to expose myself, but knowing he already knew I was his kind. He already knew I was with Shep. I wasn't hiding anything from him except that I was a cop, and I knew how to direct my thoughts to avoid him discovering that. If he probed my mind too deeply, I'd feel him and close myself off again. "Don't think about what we're really doing. Be fully in the role Shep, or he'll probe your mind and find the truth."

"Don't worry. I'm completely distracted."

I shot him a look, but then glanced behind us again.

"I didn't think this through. Yes we want him to approach

me, try to get me to bring him the next victim. But we don't want that victim to be you."

"Don't worry. I can handle myself."

I looked at him again. Gorgeous. Confident. And very turned on.

"So if we have to do what he'd expect us to do," he said, "then that means we have to go back to my place and have wild sex all night, right?"

I blinked like a doe in headlights. "What?"

"You said we should do what he would expect us to do if we were in that club because we belonged there. That's what we would do. Shit, that whole place was just one big kinky round of foreplay."

I stared at him wide eyed.

"Not to mention you in that outfit. And kissing on your leg back there, which was, I've got to tell you, not a chore. Not a chore at all."

"Shep, this is a *case*."

"Yeah, and you were squirming in your chair. Don't deny it."

I shrugged. "You had your head between my legs."

"And you liked it."

"So did you."

"Damn straight I did." He shifted in his seat a little, and I didn't have to wonder why. Then he took a left, which was not the way to the station. "I'll tell you what I didn't like, though," he went on.

"Pretending to be submissive," I said.

He sent me a quick look. "Was it obvious?"

"That you wanted to tell Mistress Ratched to stick her riding crop where the sun don't shine?"

"I would have, if I wasn't afraid she'd oblige me."

I laughed. He was succeeding in lightening my mood, drawing my focus off the killer whose attention we had managed to gain. "I didn't like you all obedient, either, to be honest. Too opposite your natural inclinations."

"I gotta tell you, Chloe, my natural inclination was to throw you over my shoulder, carry you to the nearest dark corner, and do what came . . . naturally."

I was getting hot and steamy again, and if he kept talking like that my eyes would show it.

"Where are we going, Shep?"

"Back to my place. Got any objections?"

I held his gaze for a long moment, my insides tightening, heating. Then I closed my eyes, and said, "Not a one." Bad idea, I thought. Very Bad Idea.

HE opened the front door of a modern house, a tall, but narrow, stained-wood wonder with an asymmetrical, one-sided roof and a ton of windows. It was outside the city but not far, with a large yard, all bordered in towering, seventy-year-old pines, so it seemed like the neighbors didn't exist. As he ushered me inside, I noted plush carpet, oversized sofa, love seat, and chairs that seemed like they'd hug you when you sank into them, paintings of autumn foliage and wildlife on the walls, and him, closing the door behind us, then facing me. Two inches between his face and mine. Less between our bodies. He stared into my eyes, his hands closed on my waist, tugged a little, and I was flush against him. Hip to hip, chest to chest.

"I . . . I need to tell you something," I said.

"Tell me later." He kissed me then. Kissed me like it was the last time he'd ever kiss anyone, and I lost the ability to think, much less talk.

I slid my arms around his neck and kissed him back. It was delicious, the way he kissed me. First, softly, his tongue dipping, sampling my taste. And then more. Deeply, hungrily. Like I was a drug and he was an addict. His hands were on my backside, eagerly shoving the leather micro miniskirt higher, and holding me tight to him, leaving me no room to doubt what was about to happen here between us. Briefly, my mind tried to whisper a warning, but my body was already on board a speeding train to heaven. I arched against him, pressed closer, kissed deeper, and we stumbled across his house, that way, banging into walls and furniture until we finally reached the stairs. And then he grabbed the backs of my thighs and pulled my legs up and around him. I hooked my ankles at the small of his back. If we'd been naked, he'd have been inside me. But our clothes prevented that. His did, anyway. My panties wouldn't have posed much of a barrier.

He carried me up the stairs that way, down a hall and through a door, and then we were collapsing onto a huge, unmade bed, him landing on top of me, snug in the saddle of my welcoming thighs. Then he slid lower, kissing his way down my body until he reached my boots, and he unzipped them, peeled them off, one and then the other, kissing and tonguing every inch of calf he exposed. He tossed the boots aside, and they thudded softly into the deep carpet. Then he was kissing his way higher, again, to my knees, around behind them, making my entire body sing with need and hunger and longing.

I felt the bloodlust come alive in me in a way it had never done. I trembled, I tingled, I moaned. I wanted him, all of him, as he kissed a path up my inner thighs, and then higher. When I felt his breath through my panties, his mouth, his tongue, I thought my head would explode. And when he pulled that scant barrier aside, I knew it would. Every touch, every movement, every hot sigh pushed me higher, and when I screamed aloud in anguished pleasure, he climbed higher, up my body, one hand moving down to struggle with his jeans as the orgasm ripped through me. My eyes were closed tight, my head turned to one side and then the other as wave after wave of pleasure possessed me. He pressed a palm to the side of my face to hold it still, covered my mouth with his to capture my cries. And then he slid inside me while I was still in the grip of ecstasy, and he drove deep. My eyes flew open wide, to find him staring right into them.

And his widened, and he jumped off me, out of the bed. "Jesus, Madison, you're . . . you're *one* of them!"

I was trembling, hungering, and yes, my eyes were glowing with the power of the bloodlust. I felt it, knew it. And yet his reaction was rapidly cooling my heat. I pulled the skirt down to cover myself, sat up in the bed, trying to straighten the corsetlike top. "I . . . I was going to tell you before we . . . but then things just . . ."

Daring to lift my gaze to his, I saw just what I'd feared I would. Fear. Anger. Maybe even disgust.

"How could you let me—why didn't you tell me? You know how I feel about them."

"I guess I thought working with me would show you how wrong and bigoted you were about them. Us."

"Right."

I slid out of the bed, painfully aware there would be no more kissing tonight. No more fondling. No more sex. And the disappointment was excruciating, but not quite as much as my disappointment in his attitude.

"You should go," he said.

"I can't go. We got the attention of a killer, Shep. I can't just go and leave you."

"Then I'll go and leave you." He'd skinned off the clothes during our wrestling match, and he was putting more on now. Boxer briefs, a pair of jeans, a black T-shirt that fit like a second skin.

"Shep, don't. Can't we . . . Shouldn't we at least talk about this?"

"You've been deceiving me from day one. Hell, Chloe, you're the first cop hired for the VCU, and you're one of them? And you didn't think that was something I should know?"

He grabbed his coat, his keys.

"I thought I could do some good," I said, but it lacked conviction. I sounded as miserable as I felt. And I knew why. The feelings that were growing in me for this jerk went beyond desire. Beyond bloodlust. And beyond the natural bond between a vampire and one of The Chosen. Why it had taken me until now to realize it, I don't know.

He shook his head, turned, and left the room.

I scrambled out of the bed, grabbing my boots on the way, and ran down the stairs after him. He was near the door, but I put on a little speed and got in front of him, startling him so much he almost jumped out of his skin. Then he seemed to gather himself, closing his eyes briefly. "Don't. I'm leaving. I need to . . . think."

"If you tell anyone, I'll lose my job, Shep."

He met my eyes, shook his head. "You can go back to your old one."

"Chief Rivers doesn't know either. No one does. I've been a cop for five years, and no one has ever known."

He just stared at me. I finally lowered my head, defeated. "You don't have to leave. I will." I picked up my coat from where it lay on the floor, and didn't remember how it had gotten there. I wasn't going far. I'd stay outside, watch the place, make sure he was safe. I'd get the rogue, and then I'd leave town. Start over somewhere new.

"Good-bye, Shep." And I walked out, closed the door behind me, and didn't look back.

EIGHT

I WALKED DOWN the sidewalk to the road, kind of surprised my tough, edgy, unfortunately ignorant cop partner lived in such a cool place. It had been designed by an artist, clearly.

Maybe he'd come around. It had to have been a shock to see my eyes glowing red like that at him from the darkness. And his mind had been all warped by the heat of passion. Maybe once he'd had some time to process this, he would realize what a complete jerk he was being.

I should've told him. I really should've told him.

I hadn't been outside more than ten minutes before I felt the presence. It startled every other thought from my mind, and I quickly opened my senses, going on high alert.

The vampire stepped out from behind a maple tree between Shep's place and the road, and I looked him up and down and remembered him from the club. Bone thin, almost skeletal, and pale, sickly pale. He hadn't fed overnight. I hadn't had a sip since breakfast myself, and the love games with Shep had left me hungering in a way I had never hungered before.

The vampire looked me over just as thoroughly. And then he nodded. "You will do as I say, and you will live."

I lifted my eyebrows and tried to get back into character. "If you didn't notice last night, I was on the upper end of the leash. I don't take orders, I give them."

"You play at being dominant. Like all of them do. But you would never truly hurt your slave. You use safe words. Your whips are more like ticklers, and your chains have soft fur linings. I do not play. I dominate. And you will surrender and do as I say, or I will simply kill you."

My cover was intact, then. He didn't know what I really was.

"Oh, but I do," he said softly, reading my thoughts even though I'd been shielding them. "You're a vampire. Just as I am. At least that part of your sex game is real."

I lowered my head and my eyes quickly, directing my thoughts away from anything he might not yet know about me, by focusing on how hungry I was. How close the dawn was. How far I had to go to reach shelter. Which route I would take. Whether I'd have time to warm up a mugful before I went to my rest.

"I'm a vampire, yes," I said. "So are you. So what?"

He shrugged. "Dominating mortals who think themselves dominant has been a fascinating experiment for me. Pushing them to do things they wouldn't do. Watching them relish it as they feel true mastery over another soul for the first time." He smiled slowly, revealing the tips of his fangs. "It will be even more delicious bending you to my will. To watch you awaken to the truth of your own nature."

"My nature?"

"As a predator," he said. "Here's what you're going to do for me, love. Tomorrow night, you will find me a victim. A man. A strong man, but mortal. One who secretly desires to be submissive, one who fantasizes about having sex with a vampire mistress. You will lure him to me. I will tell you where. You will fuck him while I watch from the shadows.

You will drink from him, rendering him terrified as he, at last, realizes what you truly are. And then you will step aside, and surrender him to me. You will kneel and watch me take him and drain him of his blood and his life."

I lowered my head, shook it slowly. "I'm not a predator. I don't kill. And I won't help you take an innocent life."

"Then I'll assuage my hunger on your lover. I've already taken him from his home. Or had you not realized that yet?"

"Shep?" I spun around and raced back up the sidewalk, through the front door I'd exited. I crashed through his little house, speeding through the first floor before heading to the second, and into Shep's bedroom, then the bathroom. But he wasn't there. "Shep! Shep, where the hell are you?"

The only answer came from the voice inside my head. *He's with me, darling. And he will remain with me until tomorrow night. Get me a victim by midnight or he will do nicely as a substitute.*

I fell to my knees, lowering my head. *I'll do exactly what you want me to. Please don't hurt him.*

Keep your word, and I will keep mine.

And then he was gone. I felt him withdraw from my head, from the area, like a lightbulb when you flick the switch off. Gone.

I searched for clues to where the bastard had taken Shep, and didn't find any. I'd been out in front for maybe ten minutes before he'd shown up. He must've gone in through the back door, and he must've kept himself completely shielded from detection. But he'd left no clue. Still, I looked until I was out of time, then crawled underneath Shep's big bed as I felt the approach of the sunrise.

By the time I woke again, I was so hungry I could hardly think straight. Shep's phone was ringing like mad, and mine started ringing shortly thereafter. The lieutenant checking in. He knew we were going undercover last night, and it was understood that we might not be able to stay in constant touch. But he must be getting worried. We were supposed to check in when we could.

If he sent someone to Shep's home—hell, someone was knocking on the front door.

I crawled out from under the bed and smoothed my hair. I was pale. Needed to feed. And my supply of sustenance, not to mention my makeup, was at my place, not his. I grabbed one of Shep's T-shirts from the drawer, pulled it on over my black and red bustier, and figured it was better than nothing. And longer than my skirt.

"Shepherd, open up or I'm coming in."

Hell, that was Lieutenant Harris himself. What the hell should I do? The notion of scurrying out the back way seemed preferable, but then I saw him on the other side of a window, hands cupped, looking in at me. "Let me in, Madison. Now."

Nodding, I swung the door open. He came inside, his eyes sweeping the place. "Where the hell is Shepherd?"

I swallowed hard, and decided Shep would probably want me to come clean. Not entirely clean, of course, but as clean as I could. "He was abducted by the serial killer. I was out cold, only just came around."

He swore, then asked, "Drugged you, did he?"

"I don't know. Maybe." I pushed my hair away from my face, then let it fall again, remembering how white my skin must be. "He wants me to get him another victim. Lure some guy from a bar to some yet to be named location and hand him over."

He rubbed his chin, nodding slowly. "So this is what he's been doing all along. When he thought we were onto his lackey, he killed her and found another. That one left town, probably in terror. So now he needs another."

"Exactly."

"Why wouldn't he just kill Shepherd? If a male vic is all he wants—"

"He gets off on controlling people who think they're the ones in control. Dominating the doms. Making them help him kill. Get it?"

"Sick bastard."

"He doesn't know we're—" I bit my lip, looking around the room. But it was barely sundown. Surely, I wasn't being watched yet. Still, I shielded my mind like never before and whispered in spite of myself. "I have to go along with it, so we can get Shep back alive."

"That's exactly what we're going to do."

"We?"

The lieutenant nodded. "Yeah. We. I'm gonna be the victim." He shook his head. "Go home and get cleaned up, will you? You look like a stiff breeze would blow you over."

"Yeah, okay, LT. Just you get out of here first, and keep your face hidden and your thoughts focused on a movie or a song. Yeah, get a song stuck in your head and get out of here."

"And where do I meet you?"

"Tony's Pub at nine. Okay?"

He nodded, looked at his watch, and then he left. He'd hold off on bringing in a crew to go over Shep's place for evidence. At least until our nine o'clock date. I didn't have much time. I was going to have to act fast. As I watched the lieutenant's car round a corner out of sight, I went outside myself, about to pour on the vampiric speed and race for home. But a small hybrid car was coming slowly up the street, so I walked along the sidewalk, waiting for it to pass. Only it didn't.

It pulled up beside me. Its window rolled slowly down, and a woman said, "I can help you. Get in."

I looked up fast, startled to see a familiar face behind the wheel. The dark-eyed woman from that odd little bookstore on Westcott. I stared at her, felt her. She knew what I was, held my eyes. "You look like you could use a drink. And I have what you need. Come with me." She pushed open the passenger door. "Get in. He could be back here any second."

It startled me that she said that. Like she knew what was going on. And maybe she did, maybe she really could help me somehow. At that point, I was desperate enough to try anything. I got in.

BACK at the bookstore, she led me through a door in the back, and then beyond a set of beaded curtains, into a room that was so attractive I wished I could stay there. Leather chairs, rich and old. Shelves and shelves lined in books. I could smell the paper and ink and binding. God I loved that smell. The woodwork was stained dark, as were the built-in book-cases, which had wide posts at either end with elaborate owls tooled into the wood on either side. Like the guardians of wisdom, I thought.

She closed the door and said, "It's safe to talk here. We copped the technology that your persecutors have used against your kind in the past. No one can hear you or read your thoughts through these walls."

My brows shot upward. "We?" I asked.

"The Sisterhood of Athena," she said softly. "We've been around almost as long as you have."

"Then why haven't I heard of you?" I asked.

She made a face, one brow lifting higher than the other. "You don't exactly socialize with your own kind. And there's nothing in the history books about us. We're a secret society. We observe you, but don't interfere unless it's absolutely necessary to protect the preternatural order."

"Preternatural order," I repeated. "Like . . . the natural order, only . . ."

"Only the parts of it most humans think of as . . . super-natural." She shrugged. "I can't tell you more than that. Why don't you fill me in on your . . . situation."

I looked around the room, wondering if I could trust her

but sensing that I could. Her mind was mostly open to mine, with some shadowy corridors blocked off. That a human could even know how to do that was stunning to me. She walked away from me, fussed around at a bar that looked to have come from the middle ages. I heard glasses clinking.

"I've been working with the police to stop a rogue."

She turned quickly, a glass of scarlet joy in one hand. "The one who's been killing men these past six months."

"Yes. But he kidnapped my partner."

"Senior Investigator Shepherd?" she asked, offering me a glass brimming with exactly what I needed.

I jumped to my feet, not taking it, my eyes widening, maybe even glowing a little in alarm and hunger. The scent of the beverage was already tormenting me.

"Just take it and sit down. I told you, we observe. Naturally we took note of it when a vampire posing as a human cop was hired onto our area's first Vampire Crimes Unit." She pushed the glass into my hand, and my fingers tightened around it. "Drink that so you can think straight, will you?"

I sat down, watching her mind work. I drank. The power of the blood set my veins on fire, a rush that's hard to describe if you've never felt it. Like warm energy filling every cell in my body. My hunger eased, but she came back with a decanter, and filled my glass all over again.

"You'll have your hands full, Chloe."

"You know who he is?" I asked, stunned, and realizing too that I hadn't told her my name.

"No. No one does, but trust me when I tell you that others of your kind are aware of his activities, and eager to bring a stop to them. It's his boldest move yet, trying to force one of his own to assist him in his killing of the innocent."

"He doesn't know we're cops."

"That's good, at least. What is your plan?"

"My lieutenant wants to play the victim."

"That's probably not the best idea. Let me take his place. I'm good. You'll be safer."

"It's supposed to be a male," I told her, wondering just what this group was she belonged to.

"Then I'll send you a male."

"He'll read him. He'll know."

"We know how to block. Maybe better than you do, Chloe."

I looked at her for a long moment.

She only smiled. I tried to read her thoughts, and she smiled even wider, her eyes inviting me to give it my best shot. And I did. But there was nothing. Not a barricade to her mind, which to me was the same as a sign reading "I am hiding something from you!" No, this was just a black hole. Emptiness. Like there was nothing there. Nothing, that is, except her name. Sabine. She let me know only what she wanted me to know, and nothing more. How did she *do* that?

"I'm not sure there's time to stop the lieutenant," I told her. "He's supposed to meet me tonight at nine at Tony's Pub. From there, I'm supposed to lure him somewhere else. The rogue said he'd contact me to tell me where."

She nodded slowly. "Don't go to Tony's Pub. Go to the one just around the corner. The Underground. Sit at the stool on the very far end of the bar. I'll meet you there in . . ." She looked at her watch. "A half hour. In the meantime, I'll get word to some of your kind. I have a few friends among you."

I lowered my head at the thought of other vampires.

She said, "You hate them for what was done to you, yes?"

I admitted it with a slight nod. "I was forced into an existence I never wanted. One I wouldn't have chosen."

"I wonder if that's really true, though."

"I think I would know better than you," I said, defensive. I wanted Shep back, not analysis.

She shrugged. "Ask yourself, then, if you truly prefer death to the life you have, why haven't you walked into the sunrise by now?"

I blinked, because it was a good question. "Maybe I'm a coward."

"I don't think so. Either way, unless you intend to die, you might as well live. Let go of what was, and try embracing what is. I think you'll find it makes for a much more pleasant experience." She nodded at my glass. "Drink up and go. I'll find you some clothes and makeup. It's getting late."

NINE

THE BAR KNOWN as The Underground wasn't crowded yet, but it was beginning to fill up as people came in off the street. Not one by one, but several at a time. It was ten before nine. I'd spent twenty minutes in the restroom.

I made my way to the bar, and saw a young black man sitting on the stool I was supposed to take. He was lean and lithe, wore an oversized knit hat that had extra room on top so that it leaned to one side. Brown leather jacket. Black leather gloves, butter soft and ultrathin.

I approached him from behind, cleared my throat. "Excuse me, um . . . would you mind if I—"

He turned, the barstool spinning easily around, looked right into my eyes. His were deep brown, thickly lashed, easily the prettiest eyes I'd ever seen. Feminine eyes. I frowned. And then he said, "You Chloe?"

And that's when it hit me. He was a she. "Sabine?" I asked.

She nodded and slid off the stool. The jeans were baggy, and she wore a pair of Columbia boots, unlaced with the tongues out. She put a hand on my shoulder, and nodded toward the back of the bar. "We should have a drink first. Make it look good in case he's watching," she said.

I nodded and walked along.

"Laugh or flirt or something, girl. You're s'posed to be luring me into your clutches, aren't you?"

"Sorry, I've never tried to trap a vampire before."

"Yeah, well, relax. All we've gotta do is get him out in the open." She stopped at a small table, and pulled out my chair, like she was an attentive date. I took it, and she moved opposite to take her own. "Your relatives will do the rest."

"My relatives?"

She nodded, leaned closer. "Vamps."

My heart skipped a little in my chest. "They're coming, then?"

"Yeah. They've been hunting this one for a while. He's slippery. Heads up, here comes the waitress."

We ordered drinks. I didn't drink mine, of course. Sabine slugged hers back in no time flat and was nursing another when I heard him in my head again. The rogue.

Have you found me a victim, or will I have to take your lover?

I'm with him now. He's very drunk. It will be easy.

Not too easy, I hope. Bring him to the Collins crypt at Oakwood Cemetery. To find it you—

I know where it is.

Silence. Had I blown it? I lowered my head, and added, *It's near where my mother is buried. I see it every time I visit her grave. One of the most elaborate crypts on the grounds. Hard not to notice.*

He hadn't shown up yet that night when I'd scared off his lackey and rescued Shep from her clutches. He hadn't seen any of that or he'd have recognized us long before now. I prayed I was right about that, while I awaited a reply. And finally, it came.

All right. Come, then. I'll be waiting.

Is Shep all right?
Fine. And he'll stay that way as long as you obey me. No tricks, understand?
I understand.
Good.

SABINE and I made our way among the tombstones of Oakwood, the same place where all of this had begun for me. The grave markers stood like soldiers, some of the older ones tilting drunkenly, but most were erect and straight. There were slender rectangles, rounded tops, thick squares of gleaming granite, obelisks, crosses, and crypts in every size and shape, all standing still amid swirling ribbons of mist. The fog moved, twisting and writhing among the headstones like a living thing. Here and there, a towering tree, ancient, older than the cemetery, most of them. Maples, their leaves moving softly, like whispers on the wind and here and there, one that rustled a reminder that autumn was arriving, creeping in as inevitably as death. To a mortal, anyway.

Not to me. I could live as long as I wanted. I was a seventy-seven-year-old woman in the body of a seventeen-year-old. That was not a bad thing, I supposed. I had claimed I wouldn't have chosen this life, but the truth was, if I hadn't been turned, I'd have died in my thirties just as anyone with the Belladonna Antigen would do. And what if I hadn't been one of The Chosen? What if I'd been a normal human being with a normal life span? I would be turning eighty in a few years, give or take. I wouldn't be a cop. And I certainly wouldn't be having nights like the one I'd just spent with Shep. Which, I had to admit, had been pretty spectacular, even if it had been cut short.

I was starting to wonder if Sabine had a point.

We came to the crypt, looming like a tiny gothic house of stone, there in the night. Its door stood open.

Don't go in, the rogue vampire said mentally. *Take him right there on the steps, so I can watch you.*

Sabine met my eyes, and I had no question she had heard him as well. Impossible! What kind of mortal was she?

She grabbed my hand and ran ahead like an eager lover. "Let's go inside!"

I ran behind her, knowing exactly what she was doing. The rogue had too much cover outside. He could be hiding anywhere. We had to draw him out into the open. And yet, I wondered if it would do any good. Because I was scanning the area continuously and I could not sense any other presence besides his. She was wrong. There were no other vampires coming. We were going to have to take him ourselves. Lieutenant Harris wasn't going to show up to help us either. He was probably still waiting for me at Tony's Pub.

Still, I ran behind Sabine until we got inside the crypt. She jumped right up onto the empty stone bier, and I climbed onto it as well. She lay back, and I straddled her, held her wrists to the stone above her head, my back toward the entrance, and I waited. Her eyes were glued to the doorway behind me, wide and watchful.

I knew when he was there, because I felt his presence like a chill of ice down my spine, and her gaze flicked back to mine. "Baby, you kinky," she said in a falsely deep voice.

Bite him, now! But don't take too much. Just a sip, just enough to reveal what you are and terrify him.

Suddenly, Sabine rolled right out from beneath me, landing on the floor in a ready crouch. "She don't scare me, rogue. How about you give it a try?" She yanked off the hat, and her lustrous curls fell all around her. Then she gave a running leap, and connected with his chin before he could even dodge out of the way. The element of surprise beat out vampiric speed and reflexes. I'd have never bet on that happening.

I sprang up as the two of them sailed out of the crypt,

and pulled my sidearm. But the rogue flung Sabine off him, turned to me, and gripped my jacket's lapels in one hand, lifting me right off my feet. He took my gun from me with his free hand, crushed it and dropped it to the ground.

I hung there with my feet treading air. "Put me down, you murdering bastard!"

"You just cost your lover his life, fledgling."

I had no choice. I had to be what I truly was, even though I felt Shep's eyes on me from somewhere nearby. I felt his frustration, as he struggled to get free of his bonds.

From deep inside my chest, I emitted a long, low growl, then I brought both feet up between us, kicked against the rogue's chest to push off, and backflipped before landing on the ground again. I bared my fangs, and charged him, my eyes blazing, but not with lust this time. With fury.

I hit him hard, my head and shoulders plowing into his belly and carrying him twenty feet, before we hit a gravestone that broke in half under our force. He landed on his back on the ground, then he sprang up and came at me again.

Sabine charged from the side, and she was good. Amazingly good, but she was mortal. She leaped, delivered a series of rapid-fire kicks to his head. He caught her by the ankle before she could touch ground again, and flung her thirty feet. I was about to land a blow to his throat by then, but he caught my fist in one hand, stopping me. Then he cupped a hand behind my head, and yanked me close.

"I'm going to drink you, fledgling! Vampire blood is the best kind, you know."

I heard Shep scream "No!" as he came charging out of the darkness, knotted rope still dangling from his wrists. He leaped onto the rogue's back, and punched him in the jaw so hard I swore I heard his fangs break off. The killer shook himself, dropped me, and grabbing Shep's arms, flipped him over his own head and onto the ground, hard.

"How did you get loose?" the vampire roared. "Fine, I'll

kill you first, while your girlfriend watches." He bent over, picked Shep up by his shirt, leaned closer, then stopped.

"Put him down, rogue."

The voice was powerful. Vampiric, no question, and female.

Then, as the rogue looked around him in panic, vampires seemed to materialize out of the mists. They appeared from behind markers and crypts and trees, completely surrounding him. Beautiful, they were. Hair like satin in every shade, and porcelain skin and piercing, powerful eyes.

Shep scrambled backward, getting to his feet and coming to stand beside me, as if he'd protect me from them. Sabine came to my other side, limping. I smelled blood and feared for her safety.

One of the vampires was more stunning than all the rest. Tall and lean with raven hair halfway down the long dress she wore. I glimpsed the huge black panther at her side and bit back a yelp.

As the rogue stood there, ten feet from us and surrounded now by other vampires, his wild eyes darted from one of them to the next. She walked up to him, and he gazed at her, clearly terrified. "R-R-Rhiannon?"

"I was in the neighborhood. You do know, of course, that it's forbidden to kill innocents, much less try to harm one of The Chosen." She lifted a slender hand, gave a nod, and several powerful vampires surged forward.

The rogue bolted, but there were too many of them. I watched, horrified, as they mobbed him a few headstones away, like a pack of wolves in a feeding frenzy. They covered him, taking him to the ground, draining him. Taking his blood, and his power, for their own.

I stood there, shaking and wide eyed, and then Shep slid an arm around me, pulling me close to him as if he would protect me from a similar fate.

Rhiannon smiled at him. "Admirable, mortal. But I don't intend to harm her. And I can't harm you. You're both perfectly safe." And then she held out a hand to me. White as chalk, with bloodred daggers for nails. "Nicely done, for a fledgling. We've been after that one for quite some time."

I took the hand she offered, unsure if she wanted me to shake it or kiss it, so I settled for a squeeze and then let it go.

Beside me, Sabine nodded to Rhiannon almost as if she'd met her before.

"You have our gratitude, Sabine. Now go. There is vampire business to attend to here."

Sabine glanced my way. "I can call Tony's Pub, let your boss know it's all over."

"Thanks. Tell him we'll call him later."

With a nod, she took off at a limping jog, not seeming the least bit nervous about the dozens of vampires that had been feeding on one of their own only moments ago.

I looked around, and whispered, "They . . . they killed him, didn't they?"

Rhiannon nodded, her elegant hand lazily stroking the panther's head. "We do not tolerate vampires who take innocent lives. We police ourselves, you might say. Which is why having one of our own working for the police is something that has been of great interest to us. We've been watching you, Chloe Madison."

I lowered my head, looked at Shep, who was just taking this all in, but ready. I didn't doubt he'd try to fight them all if necessary. And I was blown away by how brave that was.

"It won't be an issue anymore. I was passing as a mortal. They'll never keep me on the force now that they know—"

"The only one who knows is me," Shep said. I looked at him. He stared back at me, and there was something in his eyes, and emanating from his mind, and maybe from his heart, that I wanted to explore.

Rhiannon cleared her throat, drawing both our gazes back to her. "Do you mind? We are fugitives. We have eluding and escaping to get back to."

"Sorry," I said. "Sorry."

Rhiannon nodded. "I want you to tell your lieutenant what happened here tonight—that we came and that we dealt with the rogue in our own way. My Roland believes that we need representation in the halls of authority if we ever hope to live in peace with mankind. Tonight's events seem to support his opinion. Your service on the police force, Chloe, and particularly in this newly formed Vampire Crimes Unit will put his theory to the test. When and how you reveal your true nature is up to you. And, apparently," she added with a look at Shep, "to you as well. But in the meantime, we will be watching. Good luck, fledgling."

Then she turned and vanished in a burst of vampiric speed. I only knew which way she'd gone because of the huge cat bounding after her and vanishing into the mists.

My knees had already dissolved and had only been holding me up by some force of willpower. They gave out then, and I sank toward the ground, but Shep caught me and held me up, close to his side. "You can collapse after we get out of here, okay? This place gives me the creeps."

I looked up at him. "I'm sorry I didn't tell you sooner, Shep. The first day we met, you told me you hated vampires and didn't believe we could coexist."

"That I did. Apparently, I was wrong on both counts."

I blinked, waiting for him to continue.

"I don't hate vampires. I mean, I don't hate you, and you're one. Right?"

I nodded slowly.

"And then there's the little fact that a herd of vampires just saved my ass. I can't really hate them after that, can I?"

I shook my head.

"And apparently we can coexist. I mean, we coexisted the hell out of each other last night, didn't we? Well, you know, almost."

My eyebrows rose and I searched his eyes and saw a teasing light in them. He put his hands on my shoulders, drew a deep breath that expanded his amazing chest, and then nodded. "I'm falling for you, Chloe. You know that, don't you?"

I shook my head from side to side and wondered when my ability to speak was planning to return.

"Well, it's true. And I'm gonna keep your secret for as long as you want me to. And when it does come out—and it will, you have to know that sooner or later, it will—I'll be on your side fighting for you. Because I want you on my team. And I want you in my life. Understand?"

"Wow."

Finally I could talk, and all I could say was wow? I straightened my spine, and tried again. "I want that too. All of it. And when your time comes, and you have to decide whether to die young or become what I am—"

"Let's take it one step at a time, okay, Chloe? I've come a long way in the past few days. Let me catch my breath."

I lifted a hand to his cheek, tipped his head downward, and reaching up, kissed him deep and slow. When our lips parted, I whispered, "I have no intention of letting you catch your breath, Shep."

"Good." He swept me into his arms, and carried me through the cemetery toward the road, kissing me every three steps, and making the journey take longer than it needed to. "My place or yours?" he asked.

"Whichever is closer," I told him.

I realized right then that I would choose this existence over anything I'd seen so far. Including the one I'd left behind on prom night sixty years ago. I would choose this life, this job, this man, every single time. Because this, I thought, was where I belonged.

I was immortal, ever young, more powerful with every sunset. And as of that very minute, I intended to fully embrace my true nature. I was, and am, miraculously, amazingly, perfectly . . .

Vampire.

CIMARRON SPIRIT

LORI HERTER

*To Maggie Shayne and Christine Feehan,
who expanded romantic vampire fiction after me
and brought the genre to new heights. It's an
honor to take part in this anthology with you.*

ONE

"I THINK YOU should marry me." Looking across the dinner table at her, Brent said this with the same glimmer of fun in his eyes that appeared whenever he was about to tell an amusing story.

Annie Carmichael smiled with bafflement as she pushed back her overgrown brown bangs. Where was this coming from? He'd invited her to dinner at the Kai, an expensive restaurant near Phoenix featuring Native American–inspired décor and cuisine. They were celebrating the fact that Brent's lawyer won their court case.

"We're like two peas in a pod," he added.

Annie had found that he loved colloquial clichés. "We do get along nicely," she agreed as waiters in black shirts and tuxedo jackets removed their plates. They'd both enjoyed elk loin with risotto.

Studying his expression, Annie still couldn't tell if Brent Logan was kidding or what. Having known him for almost five months, appreciating dinners he'd treated her to at fine restaurants, and several delicious meals prepared by his

cook, Inez, at his ranch, Annie found him charmingly un-
predictable. Brent was forty-eight, a widower raising a head-
strong teenage daughter. She didn't think he'd joke about
marriage. Yet, it was hard to take him seriously. He wasn't
saying he loved her. Maybe a macho rancher was uncomfortable expressing feelings? He'd never suggested they start a
physical relationship either. Though Annie was thirty-five,
long divorced, and no youthful innocent, she was consider-
ably younger than he. Was that what held him back?

Brent leaned forward, pushing his empty wineglass out
of the way. "I really think you should marry me," he persisted. The smile creases that fanned out from his blue eyes
deepened, as did the appealing vertical lines in his cheeks.
A lock of his graying brown hair fell over his forehead. He
was quite handsome, had a rustic western drawl, and he
knew how to spin a rope and capture a steer. Annie had seen
Brent do this one day when she was visiting his ranch. She
suspected he was showing off, but she had to admit, she was
impressed by his skill.

He reached across the white tablecloth and took her hand.
"Annie, I was smitten the first time I laid eyes on you, when
you came to my door to ask permission to excavate. For
many decades my father said no to eager archaeologists
itching to dig that ruin. After he died I followed his example.
But you won me over just like that." He snapped his fingers.

Annie smiled and decided to chalk up the lighthearted
marriage proposal as part of his homespun flattery.

"You've been very kind, fighting this long court battle
so I could start work on the cliff dwelling," she said. "Now
that he's lost his lawsuit, I hope Rafael de la Vega won't look
for some other way to prevent me. His attorney must have
tried every delay in the books. You've said you've never met
de la Vega, though his land borders yours. Did your father
know him?"

"Not at all. At the courthouse last week, I learned that
de la Vega's own lawyer hasn't met him in person. Few have.

Long ago he sent a terse letter to my dad claiming that the cliff dwelling was on his property. Warned us to stay away. We Logans never bothered to contest his claim—that is, until a pretty professor named Annie came knocking. The ruin *is* on my land. I don't see why de la Vega objects. That rough canyon is useless for any other purpose."

Brent paused as a waiter brought coffee. "Rafael must be an aged codger by now. He's always been considered a cimarron by old-timers."

"A cimarron?" Annie took the dessert menu the waiter handed her.

"It's a timeworn cowboy term. Refers to an animal or a human who runs alone and has little to do with others of his kind. Like a lone wolf," Brent explained. "Which reminds me, there is a wolf in the area that's often seen near that canyon. Kills several head of my cattle every year. Strange critter doesn't eat much, just drains a lot of blood. So far, my men haven't been able to shoot it. Local Indians, Inez tells me, believe it's a protective 'wolf spirit' that can't be killed."

"Do you have to kill it?" Annie asked, troubled. "Can't it be captured and taken to some other area, away from cattle?"

Brent's dark eyebrows drew together. "Don't tell me you're part of the save-the-wolves crowd."

His attitude took her aback. She shrugged. "I love animals."

"You just finished eating elk," he pointed out.

She pressed her lips together and bowed her head. "Point taken. I'm trying to eat a more vegetarian diet." She leaned back. "So what were you saying about Inez's belief that it's a wolf spirit?"

His expression softened. "I've seen the animal through binoculars. The sun was setting, so the light wasn't good, but it looked like an ordinary black wolf. Tried to snap a photo, but the critter didn't show up in the picture. I love

Inez, bless her heart. She's half Pueblo Indian, I think I told you. Hard to believe she's turning sixty-five soon. I've known her all my life, but I can't buy her superstitions. I'll give you a gun to take to the dig."

Annie's back straightened. "No, please. I don't like guns. Wouldn't know how to use one."

"I'll show you. If you're going to be out there all on your own, as you insist, then you need a gun. No arguments."

His firm attitude made her uneasy. She'd told him it would take several weeks to study the ruin and plan the excavation before she brought students out to help with the fieldwork. She'd arranged a semester sabbatical leave from the University of Arizona, where she taught. To have an untouched ruin all to herself was an archaeologist's dream, and she loved the opportunity to be alone out there. The idea of toting a gun didn't suit her, but she knew Brent meant well and appreciated the way he worried about her safety.

"So," Brent said in a lighter tone, "we've gotten off the subject at hand. I asked if you'd marry me."

Annie looked up from her dessert menu and blinked. "You're serious?"

"Better believe it."

She took a bantering tone. "Well, you haven't gotten down on one knee, declared your undying love and pulled out a diamond ring."

"You want me to?" Brent set his napkin on the table, preparing to get up.

She laughed. "Not here in a five-star restaurant."

"What better place?" he said.

She set her hand on his jacket sleeve to restrain him. "You've taken me completely by surprise. I'm honored by your proposal, but I'll need time to think."

Brent grinned and relaxed in his chair. "So there's hope? About that diamond, when you say yes, I'll take you to the best jewelry store in Scottsdale and you can pick out the finest rock of your choice."

"Oh, my God," she muttered under her breath.

"Too much, too soon?" he asked.

Annie's mind was spinning. "Well . . . "

"Take your time, sweetheart. Oh, and by the way, I want you to stay at the ranch while you're working on the dig. It's a long commute from Phoenix."

"I was going to rent a trailer—"

"No way. There's an unused bedroom, decorated all pretty, next to the room that belongs to Inez. It's in the opposite wing of the house from my room and my daughter's. So it'll all be on the up-and-up. Have to set a good example for Zoe. She's only sixteen and I caught her sexting the other day."

"Oh, no."

"Yeah," he said with exasperation. "She needs a mom. I don't know how to handle her, except to yell, take her phone away and ground her. Caught her smoking a few months ago, and she threw it in my face that I like a good cigar now and then. Had to give away my stash from Cuba to a friend. Though I'd love to have it otherwise, Annie, I can't invite you to my bed till after we're married." He chuckled. "Inez can be your chaperone."

Annie nodded with an amused expression, her smile hiding her relief. She'd never met a man who could move so fast and so slow at the same time. Much as she enjoyed Brent's company, she realized she wasn't quite ready to start a full-fledged relationship.

Or marry him, for that matter.

TWO

SEVERAL DAYS LATER, as the autumn sun grew low in the sky, Annie worked alone at the cliff dwelling. She'd spent the morning taking photographs of the ruin, located on a deep ledge beneath an overhang, on the side of a steep sandstone cliff. Thirty feet below lay a braided riverbed bordered by a stand of cottonwood trees at the bottom of the canyon. Compared to other ancient Anasazi dwellings, this was a small one. Not nearly as dazzling as the large, picturesque villages that drew tourists to Cliff Palace in Mesa Verde, or the Betatakin and Keet Seel ruins in Navajo National Monument.

This site had once housed a small community, perhaps no more than three or four families in the thirteenth century. Annie discerned the remains of eight small, square rooms filled with rubble from collapsed ceilings and walls. Some of the rooms would have been lived in, others used for storage. At the edge of the dwellings she saw the round shape of what looked like a very well-preserved kiva, a ceremonial chamber partly below ground level and covered with a roof made from wood topped with flat slabs of sandstone. This one looked remarkably still intact. Annie wondered how it remained preserved, when the roofs of the other structures had caved in over the centuries. This little community had most likely been abandoned around 1300, when all the Anasazi villages in the Four Corners area were forsaken, possibly due to decades of drought.

Annie had used up her afternoon taking measurements and making diagrams and notations in her field notebook. The day had been warm, though the rock overhang twenty-five feet above gave some cool shade as the sun moved westward. Sitting on what was left of a wall, she looked up from her notes to realize that it was getting close to sundown. She'd forgotten that days were growing shorter as winter approached. Better pack up while there was still enough light. She had a rough climb to get back to her Chevy pickup, left on the mesa above.

She'd gotten down to the ruin by way of a side gulley in the canyon a quarter of a mile upstream, which allowed her to hike along a natural path that was gradual enough to reach the level of the ledge without a ladder. From there she could walk along the narrow ledge to where it widened into the broad, open cave where the ancient village had been built.

As she stood and hoisted her backpack over her shoulder to leave, Annie enjoyed the thought that perhaps the path she'd devised was the same way the ancient Pueblo people had gone to and from their home. All at once, she heard a noise. A scratching beat, like a dog trotting across dry ground. She looked around, and at the spot where the ledge began to narrow at the far end of the ruin, she saw him. A black wolf, standing still, staring at her with golden eyes.

She stopped breathing. He was a big animal. Thick, coarse fur. Intelligent gaze. Maybe if she didn't move, the wolf would decide she was harmless and go away.

He lowered his head, eyes seeming to narrow, as he

sprinted toward her. He halted about five feet from where she stood. The beast growled and bared its teeth, exposing long incisors. Annie's backpack slid from her shoulder as panic threatened to overtake her. Moving slowly, she bent to unzip the pack with shaking fingers and pulled out the revolver Brent had loaned her. Remembering the lesson he'd given her only yesterday, she cocked the gun and pointed it at the wolf.

"G-go away. I don't want to hurt you." Annie hoped the animal would somehow understand.

The wolf edged closer, eyes flashing as he growled even more viciously.

She tilted the gun toward the sky and fired a warning shot. The recoil from the gun made her lose her balance and she fell to the ground.

The wolf appeared unperturbed. Instead of running away, he slid backward on his haunches, ready to pounce. Annie squeezed the trigger again in a spasm of fear and blinked as the shot rang out. Her ears felt deafened.

The wolf collapsed as blood spurted from his chest, a vivid red streak flowing onto his black coat. Had she shot him in the heart? The animal lay still, and she believed he was dying. Filled with remorse for killing such a magnificent creature, she set the gun on the ground, went to him and stroked the dense, springy fur over his rib cage.

"I'm so sorry," she whispered, tears filling her eyes. "You should have just gone away. I wouldn't have hurt you."

She sat with the wolf for a few minutes while he seemed to breathe his last shallow breaths, hoping to comfort the animal as it died.

But then something strange happened. The wound on the wolf's chest began to not only stop bleeding, but close up and disappear. Annie wondered if she was hallucinating. And then the wolf raised its head, slowly sat up on its haunches and stared at her with hypnotic eyes that seemed to glow in the setting sun.

Frightened again, Annie grabbed the revolver and scrambled to her feet. She began walking backward, away from the wolf, pointing the gun.

"There are more bullets. Don't make me shoot you again."

The wolf rose on all four feet and began to move toward her, but slowly this time and without a single growl. Annie continued to back away. Suddenly, faster than she thought any creature could move, he whooshed past her. She turned, finding the wolf behind her, stopping her from taking another step backward. And then she realized she was only a few feet from the edge of the cliff. The wolf stared at her with alert, intense eyes, and she instantly understood that he had prevented her from unknowingly falling off the precipice.

Annie lowered her gun, mystified. The wolf was protecting her. But why, after she'd shot it?

As quickly as he had moved to save her, the wolf turned, jumped down the steep cliff, landed in the shallow water of the stream below and disappeared into the cottonwoods.

Annie sank to the ground, her legs weak. She took long breaths and tried to calm herself. But the sky grew darker and she knew she had to leave. Gathering her things, including the gun, she hiked up to her truck on the mesa above.

Maybe she shouldn't tell Brent what had happened. He'd probably order one or two of his ranch hands to stand guard, and she didn't want that.

Brent had said that local Indians thought this particular wolf was a protective spirit. Annie could understand why. Her encounter with the creature almost seemed like a mystical experience, as if the wolf hadn't been quite real. But the blood he'd shed had been real—she'd smelled it. And then his wound had healed as if by magic.

Magic? Annie laughed at herself. No, better not tell Brent any of this.

* * *

HE watched through the cottonwood trees as the trespassing woman hiked out of the ruin and disappeared over the rim of the mesa. Alone again, Rafael closed his eyes, concentrated, and in a whirling instant changed from wolf form into his human self. That is, as human as he could ever be anymore. Transmogrifying was the only part of his vampire existence he enjoyed. To run free with the extra power four legs provided, to not feel guilt when he fed as a wolf, to be outdoors in waxing or waning sunlight because the thickness of his fur protected him from rays that would destroy him in human form—all these abilities made him cherish his wolf self.

Naked, he bounded on two bare feet up the steep slope to the ruin with no trouble. Vampire agility allowed him to move in ways no mortal human could. He strode directly to the kiva. Fortunately the woman hadn't tried to open it, or she would have found him resting there. A vampire's sleep, heavy and lethargic, during those hours when he had to hide from the sun, either beneath the earth or in a coffin. While she was preoccupied taking notes as the sun sank, he'd changed to wolf form and silently left the kiva, then trotted to the edge of the ruin where she first saw him. How long would it be before this intruding archaeologist discovered his favorite resting place? Next week? Maybe tomorrow.

But she was beautiful, sweet and kind. She'd actually felt sorrow at wounding a snarling beast.

Rafael gazed into the nocturnal dark from the roof of the kiva. His relationships with mortal women never ended well. Though he felt forever lonely, he ought to keep his distance for her sake. Yet this adorable interloper wasn't keeping hers. She'd soon discover what was in the kiva. And Rafael wasn't about to change his habits or abandon his favorite place of rest over the last several centuries.

If a desirable woman invaded his world, was that his fault? He'd grown weary of feeling guilt. He was what he was.

THREE

STILL SHAKEN, ANNIE arrived at the Logan ranch house, parked her truck, and entered through the back door, since her jeans and hiking boots were full of dust. She passed by the spacious kitchen, where Inez stood sautéing something that smelled delicious at the expensive-looking cooktop set in the middle of a shiny granite counter over white enameled cabinets.

Annie stopped at the open kitchen door. "Do I have time to clean up before dinner?"

Inez turned and smiled, her long gray hair hanging in a single thick braid down her back. She wore a chambray cotton blouse over a long broomstick skirt and sneakers. "Glad you're home. Dinner will be done in a half hour. That enough time?"

"Sure, thanks. Whatever you're cooking is making me hungry."

"Spanish rice with onion and bell pepper. A recipe on Pinterest. Is your work going well?" Inez eyed her as she stirred with a wooden spoon. "You look a little dazed."

"I am." Annie wondered if she could confide in her. Brent had said Inez had beliefs about the wolf spirit. Annie took off her dirty hiking shoes and crossed the terra-cotta-tiled kitchen floor. When she got near enough to Inez to speak in a low voice, she asked, "Have you ever been to the cliff dwelling?"

Inez hesitated as she added some spices to the pan she was stirring. "When I was young, I used to go there. The ancestors of the Pueblo Indians, my mother's people, built the dwelling. I would go there to feel close to those who came before, going back many generations. I felt at peace there."

Annie loved what Inez told her. "It is a peaceful place. So quiet that when a crow flew past, I could hear its wings flapping. Do you still go there?"

"No. It's . . . too steep at my age."

"Come with me sometime. I'll help you down the cliff."

"No." Inez's tone grew a bit sharp.

"Okay." Annie hesitated, wondering why Inez's manner had changed so abruptly. Yet she felt compelled to gently probe further. "If I tell you something, would you promise not to say anything to Brent or Zoe?"

Inez stirred more slowly, then turned her wisdom-worn brown eyes to Annie, who sensed the older woman's reluctance.

"I would not tell Brent or Zoe," Inez said softly as she set the spoon on the countertop. "Something happened at the ruin?"

Annie told her about the black wolf. "He saved me from backing off the cliff. After I'd shot him. I don't know how he recovered from such a grievous wound."

Inez lowered her gaze, bowed her head, and said nothing. A still sadness seemed to come over her.

Annie didn't know what to make of Inez's reaction. "I'm sorry if I'm bringing up something you'd prefer not to talk about, but Brent said you believe there's a protective wolf spirit in this area. Do you think that's the wolf I encountered?"

Inez brought her fingertips to her mouth, her knuckles enlarged with arthritis. After a moment, she lowered her hand and gazed at Annie with troubled eyes. "I feared for you going to that ruin. But it's not my place to stop you."

"Because the wolf prowls there?"

"He is no ordinary wolf." Inez raised her voice a bit, emphasizing each word. "Be careful. I would tell you to give up excavating the ruin. I know it's your work and you see it as a great opportunity. But it would be best if you never go back there."

"Well . . . why? Did you encounter the wolf at the ruin? Is that why you won't go back?"

Inez seemed about to reply, but stopped herself. She picked up the wooden spoon, then paused before stirring. "Are you religious?"

The question took Annie by surprise. "Um, no, not really." She thought of her mother and father who were in their forties when she was born. They'd both passed away in the last several years. "My parents weren't. I've only ever been to a church for friends' weddings."

Inez nodded in a thoughtful way. "My father was Mexican and Catholic, so I was brought up to be devout. Maybe life is easier for you. No worries about your immortal soul."

Annie grew baffled by Inez's wandering train of thought. "I'm sorry I asked about the wolf. I'm afraid I've upset you."

Inez set down the spoon again and took both Annie's hands in hers with a firm hold. "We all must deal with whatever enters our life in our own way. Be on guard, Annie. Leave the ruin well before dusk. Brent and Zoe will never hear about our conversation from me."

Annie hesitantly thanked Inez and left the kitchen, feeling rather unnerved. She went to her room, decorated in a southwestern style with a patchwork quilt on the bed, a colorful striped Indian blanket hung on the wall, and cactus plants arranged in Mexican pottery by the window. She took a quick shower and changed out of her jeans into a denim skirt, yellow sleeveless blouse and loafers. As she hurried to dinner, Inez's words still occupied her mind, leaving her confused.

When she walked into the large dining room with its rustic wood-beamed ceiling, she found Brent and Zoe already sitting at the big oak table. Brent rose and pulled out a chair for her.

"Sorry I'm a little late." Annie took her seat.

"You were gone all day," Brent said as he sat down. "Must have gotten a lot accomplished."

Annie told him about the many photos and notes she'd taken. "The hours just flew by, I was enjoying my work so much. An Anasazi ruin all to myself!"

"I'd be bored as hell," Zoe said, her short blond hair with its fuchsia streak gelled into pointed tips that stood away from her head. "It's hot out there, too."

"Zoe—" Brent chided.

"I wore a light T-shirt." Annie kept her tone easy. "It's cool in the shade of the rock overhang. Have you been out there, Zoe?"

"Sure, when I was a kid. Bunch of dry old rocks. Why would Indians have lived there?"

Inez came in, pushing a cart with serving dishes laden with food. "The ancient ones didn't know about air-conditioning," she told Zoe in an arch tone as she set dinner on the table.

"Looks wonderful, Inez," Brent said. "How about sitting down and joining us? Help welcome Annie as our houseguest."

"Thank you, but I have work in the kitchen," Inez replied in a gracious tone and wheeled the cart out of the dining room.

Brent shook his head. "She never wants to sit with us. Only at holidays when we invite all the ranch hands."

"Where does she eat?" Annie asked.

"In the kitchen by herself, I think. After she's served the employees who live on the property. She sure knows how to prepare good food." Brent turned to Zoe. "Something you ought to learn, young lady."

Brent's statement bothered Annie. Does every girl have to learn to cook? She hoped he also advised his daughter to explore career choices.

Zoe was serving herself some of the Spanish rice and looked at her father, sarcasm in her blue eyes. "Why? Mom never cooked."

"Because she married me and we already had Inez. How can you be sure you'll marry a man who can afford hired help?"

"I've got Mom's looks," Zoe said with confidence, tugging on her knit top with its deep V-neck. "And I have her flashy style. I can even imitate her Swedish accent. She caught you. Why wouldn't I attract some rich guy, too?"

Annie listened to their conversation with quiet curiosity. Brent never talked much about his wife, Inger, except to say she'd died three years ago in a car crash. She'd been on a shopping trip with friends in Scottsdale, he'd said. She'd had too many martinis over lunch, and was driving under the influence, which caused her to run off the road and into a building. That was all Annie knew. She hadn't heard that Inger was from Sweden. There were framed photos of Inger and Zoe on a wall that led to Zoe's room. Annie had chanced to see them and noted that Inger had indeed been quite a beauty. Zoe was growing into a beauty, too, if one looked beyond her spiky hair, heavy eye makeup and surly manner.

Brent appeared to be pondering Zoe's assertions as he forked a slice of roast pork onto his plate. "You think I married your mother only for her looks and charming accent?"

"No, you were head over heels," Zoe blithely replied. "Mom said you were. But it went sour, and she started drinking. And now you're nosing around Professor Annie with her ponytail and drab clothes"—she pointed to Annie with her fork—"looking for someone to grow old with."

"Zoe!" Brent raised his voice. "You apologize to Annie. Right now!"

"That's okay," Annie said in a soft voice, feeling increasingly awkward and uneasy.

"No, it's not okay," Brent insisted. He turned to Zoe again. "If you don't apologize this minute, you're going to your room. Annie is our guest. Treat her with respect."

Zoe rolled her eyes. "Sorry."

"A little louder and with sincerity," Brent told her.

Zoe wet her lips. "I'm sorry," she said in a more polite tone, though she did not make eye contact with Annie, looking at her glass of lemonade instead.

Not used to dealing with any teenager under college age, Annie wasn't sure how to handle the situation. "I accept your apology."

"Okay," Brent said. "Let's talk about something else."

Zoe did not hesitate. "At school today, Emma told me she's planning to have a Halloween party. Can I go? Or will I be grounded forever with no phone?"

"Halloween's a month away," Brent replied. "We'll see if you can behave yourself between now and then."

Zoe rolled her eyes again.

Annie recalled Brent saying he'd caught Zoe sexting. The possibility of becoming a stepmother to Zoe began to weigh on Annie's mind. The girl would be a handful. And Zoe was already balking at the idea that Brent might marry her. Annie couldn't help but ponder the girl's assertion that her father had married Inger for love, but now was looking for someone to grow old with.

As a teen, Annie had been an incurable romantic, dreaming of adventure, of one day finding her soul mate. But she'd long passed the point where she was hoping for any great love affair anymore. She'd thought she had that in grad school when she'd fallen in love with Steve, a geology student. They married young, and their separate careers quickly drew them apart. It was a friendly divorce, but Annie didn't want another failed marriage.

As she'd entered her thirties, she'd given up on her old romantic notions in favor of a mature and practical approach to life. Would saying "I do" to a steady, solid rancher with a sense of humor, who wanted someone to grow old with, be such a bad idea? Maybe compatibility was a better basis for wedlock than passionate love. Brent seemed to have learned that. Though he once loved Inger, he didn't appear to mourn her loss. Why had their marriage gone sour?

As Zoe continued to press her case for the Halloween party, Annie pondered her life and her future. What *did* she want? A home and family, perhaps even a child of her own? Years seemed to be passing quickly, and she wasn't getting any younger. Or should she continue to focus on her career? Archaeological excavations satisfied her youthful longing for adventure. Here at the ranch, she might have both family and career.

The Logan cliff dwelling could take years to excavate. And if she became Mrs. Logan, she'd be part owner of the site. This thought was a bit too appealing to contemplate. Feeling guilty about mixing her priorities, she quickly reminded herself that she'd be marrying Brent, not the Anasazi ruin.

FOUR

THE NEXT AFTERNOON at the cliff dwelling, Annie had every intention of leaving well before sunset. But she'd discovered some potsherds in a room where she'd been removing fallen debris. She'd gotten engrossed in determining whether the pieces of pottery, with their black-on-white geometric design, were from the Basketmaker or the Developmental Pueblo period.

Sitting on an old blanket on the ground, she was using her brush to remove dirt from a potsherd when all at once she felt something sniff behind her. Instantly she turned and found herself face-to-face with the black wolf, his snout only inches from her nose. She dropped the potsherd and backed away as best she could, only about a foot. Why hadn't she heard the animal coming, as she had the day before?

The wolf sat down on its haunches and they stared at one another for a long while, measuring each other, testing intentions. The creature made no sound. His ears stood straight up from the top of his head, two black, furry triangles. He almost looked like a big dog you'd like to pet. But his slanted yellow eyes delved hers with mesmerizing acuity. She hadn't had a chance to tell if the animal was male or female, but she somehow sensed a very male presence.

"Hello, again." She tried to keep her voice and body from trembling.

The wolf turned its head, looking away, which puzzled Annie. And then he rose up on all fours and walked around her. She shifted her position to watch him go behind one of the ruin's ancient sandstone brick walls. Soon he came out, carrying something in his mouth. He approached her and quietly dropped the flat, gray object in front of her, like a gift.

"Oh, my gosh." She recognized it was a sandal woven of yucca fibers, in quite good condition considering it had most likely been made and worn over seven hundred years ago. She picked it up carefully and examined the close weaving and the fiber straps attached. Gazing up at the wolf, who stood watching her in silence, she said, "Thank you."

Inexplicably, he turned, sprinted across the floor of the cave and jumped off the cliff edge. Annie dropped the sandal, pulled her binoculars out of her backpack and got up to see where the wolf went.

She focused on a moving object on the other side of the stream below. It was growing dark but she was quite sure the shadowy figure she saw in her binoculars was the wolf moving slowly.

And then the scene through her lenses went misty. She lowered the binoculars and with her naked eyes saw that there was in fact a cloud of dust or vapor where the wolf had been. Out of the cloud, into the blackness beneath the cottonwood trees, she saw something swiftly jump. She caught only a fleeting glimpse, but the figure that bounded out looked like it moved on two feet, not four.

Like a human.

What had she seen? A chill swept down her spine. Was she hallucinating again, as she had when she thought she saw the wolf's wound heal?

You're being silly, she scolded herself with a sharp exhale. It was too dark in that shadowed valley to see anything properly. The cloud must have been dust the wolf kicked up.

Nothing abnormal to get spooked about.

Annie returned to the spot where she'd been working and slipped her binoculars into her backpack. She carefully wrapped up the sandal and some of the potsherds in plastic she'd brought along, placed them in her pack, too, and hiked up to her truck as the sunset colored the distant clouds in salmon hues.

BEFORE dinner, at a decorative oak side table beneath the draped dining room windows, Annie laid out the sandal and potsherds for Brent to see. She didn't mention the wolf.

"I'm so excited. These potsherds look like they're from the Developmental Pueblo period, the most highly evolved era of the Anasazi."

Brent placed his arm around her shoulders and gave her a warm squeeze. "Good for you, Annie."

Annie relaxed in his embrace. He kissed her on the cheek, and then on the mouth, as he had on their dates over the last few months. She felt very comfortable with Brent and began to wish their relationship could be more physical.

"Ewww. Ick," Zoe said as she walked in and saw them. She wore a black miniskirt, a close-fitting black top and tall boots.

Annie recalled that when she was sixteen, it was hard for her to imagine her parents being romantic. Though in Zoe's case, perhaps it was more likely that the girl just didn't like seeing her dad embracing Annie in particular.

"Look what she found at the cliff dwelling." Brent stepped aside so Zoe could see the sandal and potsherds.

Zoe gazed at the items, crinkling her nose. "Like, that's a shoe?"

"Sandals provided some protection against the rough

rocks," Annie said. "Sandstone gets really hot under the sun, too. There are different weaving patterns the Anasazi used to make these. This one is particularly nice because of its tight weave."

Brent glanced at Zoe in a bemused way. "Must have been the height of fashion back then."

Zoe made a guttural sound of contempt. "Yeah, right."

Inez came in, placing a pitcher of water on the dinner table, where plates, napkins and silverware had already been set. Annie motioned her to come and look.

Inez peered at the artifacts with profound interest, almost reverence. "One of my ancestors may have worn that." She picked up the sandal and examined it. "Beautiful. Where did you find it?"

Annie hesitated. "Behind a wall."

Inez studied her. "Not the kiva."

"No. I haven't gotten to that yet."

Inez set the sandal down again in a deliberate way. "I'm sure there's much to explore without opening up the kiva. A kiva is sacred."

"They were built for religious ceremonies," Annie acknowledged. She grew concerned, wondering if Inez felt excavating it would be a desecration. Then again, Inez was a devout Catholic. But perhaps she still wanted her ancestors' beliefs respected.

As Inez left for the kitchen, Annie looked at Brent.

"Like I've said, she's superstitious," he said quietly. "You organize your work however you see fit." He hugged Annie against his chest, and she smiled.

Zoe looked on with deadpan annoyance. "Seriously. Get a room."

FIVE

THE NEXT EVENING, as the sky darkened at sunset, Annie used her flashlight to finish writing her field notes as she sat on the blanket she kept at the ruin. She'd found the small hidden storage room where the wolf had picked up the sandal. It turned out to be a treasure trove of unbroken pottery, baskets, cooking pots, a mano and metate used to grind corn, and even a small stash of ancient grain. She'd photographed everything and was making meticulous notes. Though it was growing dark, she was no longer worried about the wolf. She didn't fear him anymore.

When she heard a slight noise behind her, she assumed it was the wolf. But as she turned to see, she found a man standing there, looking down at her.

Wearing jeans and a white shirt, the man had an angular face, unruly black hair and dark eyes. His muscular build looked formidable. When she quickly stood to face him, she grew conscious of the fact that he was several inches taller than she. Who was he? One of Brent's men? Had he come because he'd heard she worked here alone? She thought of the gun inside her backpack and edged toward where it lay on the ground nearby.

"Hello?" she said in a strong voice. She still had the flashlight in her hand and shone it on his face. "Who are you?"

He shifted his weight from one booted foot to the other. The brightness of her flashlight seemed to bother him. He squinted in a way that made him look sinister.

"I am Rafael de la Vega." His voice was low with an aggressive edge as he pronounced his name with an authentic Spanish accent.

Annie stood in shocked silence for a moment. *Rafael de la Vega?* He was supposed to be an old codger, according to Brent. This man looked about thirty, thirty-two at most. Why was he here? To shoo her out of the cliff dwelling he'd claimed was his?

"Did you have to sneak up on me?" she asked, a little angry now. "I'm Annie Carmichael, an archaeologist. Brent Logan gave me permission to excavate this ruin. Brent owns this property and the survey he had done proves it."

"So my lawyer informed me." Rafael took the flashlight out of her hand in one swift move. "This hurts my eyes." He turned it to shine in her face. "Do you like it?"

Annie lifted her hand to block the blinding glare.

He switched the light off. "The moon is almost full tonight. We can see." He handed her the flashlight.

She blinked, getting her vision back. "Why are you here?"

He studied her for a long moment, his black eyes glistening. "To see who this archaeologist is who is invading a place I consider my own."

"Well, it's not yours."

"Historic ownership papers must have been altered," he insisted. "I specifically claimed rights to this place."

"*You* did? You're too young."

He bowed his head. "Never mind. The court has ruled in your favor. How long will you be here?"

"Many months," she asserted. "Years. I'll be bringing students to help me excavate."

His eyes flashed sharply. "No!" He stepped closer. "That is not acceptable."

The hostility he exuded made her take a step back. "You don't have any say in the matter."

Rafael tilted his head to one side, looking slightly amused now, studying her with a curious mixture of annoyance and warmth. "I *can* have my wishes respected," he said in a softer tone. "You have no idea. You are in grave danger here."

Annie kept her stance. "Are you threatening me?"

"Warning you."

"Of what?"

He stared at her with a penetrating gaze that seemed to go to the core of her being. In the moonlight his eyes revealed every shift of thought in his mind, but she could not decipher what those thoughts were. Then his eyes shone, powered by some inner energy.

"You are very beautiful." His voice was just above a whisper. "I would not wish you harm. Your intentions are pure, I see that. You have a sweet soul. Please. Go and don't come back."

Annie felt totally baffled by his words and mesmerized by his gaze. She could not look away. "I . . . I can't go. It's my work, my career. Brent gave me permission, even went to court for me."

The inner light in Rafael's eyes faded. "Are you his woman?"

She drew her brows together. He certainly had an archaic concept of relationships. "You mean, are Brent and I . . . ? We're . . . dating. I wouldn't say I was 'his woman.' I'm my own woman."

"You're staying at his ranch."

"How do you know that?"

He shrugged. "Word travels."

"I have a room to myself, next to Inez's room. What business is it of yours?"

After a hesitation, he asked, "How is Inez?"

The question took Annie by surprise. "She's fine. You know her?"

"I used to. So you are still a free woman?"

Annie stumbled over how to answer. "Brent asked me to marry him. I'm thinking it over. Any more prying questions?"

Rafael's face had taken on a brooding aspect. "I'm sorry if I'm inquisitive. You are invading my favorite place. I want to know about you."

"I don't know a thing about you," she countered. "Where do you live? You have a ranch house?"

"Yes."

"A wife and family?"

"No."

She had to laugh at his terse replies. "I guess you don't like anyone interrogating *you*."

He ignored her statement. "It's time you left, or Logan will wonder. We don't need him coming here to search." He moved past her, picked up her backpack and slid his arms through the straps so it hung from his broad shoulders. "Use your flashlight. I'll help you up the slope."

She wanted to protest, but by now it had gotten too dark to properly see the rough pathway up to the mesa. And she supposed he had to climb up the slope, too.

As they walked to where the ledge narrowed, she asked, "How did you get down here so quietly? I didn't hear you."

He was leading the way and turned his head. "You were preoccupied writing."

"You're as quiet as the wolf who comes here. Do you know about him?"

Rafael stopped. "Indians call him a wolf spirit. They revere and fear him. So should you. His powers are real."

Annie sniffed. "You're just trying to scare me. He brought me a sandal, like a puppy dog. I'm not afraid of him."

Rafael's jaw tightened at her assertion. He motioned that she should take the lead, and they began to ascend the steep slope. She shone her flashlight on the ground in front of her. Silence closed in on them. All Annie could hear was their trudging footsteps, and it made her uneasy.

"Brent says a black wolf is unusual in these parts," she said, just to break the silence. "I knew this was once the habitat of the Mexican gray wolf, but there are so few left, maybe other wolves are edging in."

"Yes," he said on an exhale.

"You sure can be monosyllabic," she muttered.

"That's a word I don't know."

She turned to ask, "Is Spanish your first language?"

"Yes."

"You're from Mexico?"

"No."

Annie faced forward again, annoyed with his terse answers. All at once she lost her footing on a loose rock. He caught her under her arms and kept her from falling. With ease he lifted her to her feet until she regained her balance.

But he didn't quite let go. His arm slid around her rib cage and pressed her back against his chest.

She lowered her eyes, absorbing his masculine strength. Why wasn't she objecting? He'd told her she was beautiful, and now he made her feel desirable. This was getting dangerous . . .

She pushed out of his encircling arm. "Thank you. I'm all right now."

They continued up to the mesa top without further word. When they reached her truck, she noticed there was no other vehicle in view.

"How did you get here?" she asked.

"I often walk at night. Go, before Logan misses you." As he shrugged out of the backpack and placed it in the wagon of her pick-up truck, an acquisitive gleam appeared in his gaze. He looked at her with steady, unblinking eyes. "Don't marry him."

She laughed at his audacity. "Why not?"

With no warning, he caught her up in his arms and kissed her on the mouth in such a fervent, feverish way her knees grew weak.

When he drew away, he smiled slightly, and she noticed for the first time his white teeth, the points of his incisors. She also couldn't help but see how handsome he was, his black hair wavy with blue highlights shining under the moon, his square jaw, his eyes keen with longing.

She clung to him, recovering, catching her breath. "Y-you shouldn't do that."

"But you are your own woman. You don't belong to anyone yet." His hand slid slowly up to her neck, and he pressed his thumb against her carotid artery so that she could feel her own pulse. "Your heart is beating fast. Blood is rushing through your body with desire. You feel alive. Can Logan fulfill your secret yearning?"

And then he let her go. Feeling dizzy, she leaned against her white pickup. She opened the door and got behind the steering wheel. Before she could close the door, Rafael took hold of it. "Have I frightened you?"

"No," she declared, working hard to keep her wits about her. But in truth she certainly was disconcerted, if not frightened by the ease with which he took liberties. "Don't think you can ever do that again."

"Then stay away from the ruin." He said this in a gruff voice and shut the door.

With shaking fingers she found the key in her jeans pocket and started the ignition. As she drove away, she looked in her rearview mirror, but could not see Rafael. Nor could she find him in either side mirror. How odd. She twisted in the seat to look out the truck's back window. She could see Rafael standing where she'd been parked, watching her go. Facing forward again, she increased her speed as her truck bounced over the rough grasses of the flat mesa until she reached the dirt road that would take her to the Logan ranch.

ANNIE rushed in the back entrance of the ranch house. Inez came to the kitchen door as Annie hurried toward her room.

"We've been worried," Inez said.

Brent came down the short hall from the dining room. "Why are you out this long after dark?" he asked. "I was afraid something happened."

"No . . . sorry. I-I found a wonderful stash of artifacts and got carried away making notes." She took her field notebook out of her backpack and showed them the pages she'd written. "See? You're right, though. It was hard getting up the slope in the dark. Good thing I had my flashlight," she babbled, still disconcerted.

She didn't want to say she'd seen Rafael there, or Brent might cause trouble. Especially if she somehow let it slip that Rafael had kissed her.

Brent glanced at her notes and handed the book back. "Okay, young lady, but don't let this happen again. I don't like you being alone out there even during the day."

"I know," she replied. "Am I late for dinner?"

Inez smiled. "Almost. I can keep the food hot and serve in fifteen minutes. Okay?"

"Thanks." She rushed to her room and showered quickly, then dressed in a fresh pair of tan pants and a checked shirt.

As Annie, Brent and Zoe ate dinner, she noticed Brent keeping his eyes on her.

Finally, he said, "You look flushed, Annie. Feeling okay?"

"I do?" She had to admit to herself that she still felt the heat of Rafael's kiss, and the shock of his making such a bold advance less than a half hour after meeting her. "It was a hot day," she replied, thinking fast. "Summer seems to be hanging on, doesn't it?"

"Take a canteen with you?" Brent asked.

"Of course. I'm fine. Maybe overexcited at the wonderful artifacts I found. Even a pot of corn kernels several hundred years old." She chattered on about her finds, and Brent seemed to relax as he listened. Zoe, meanwhile, ate in silence, looking bored.

By the time Inez cleared the dinner dishes, Annie felt exhausted from the events of her day. Having to improvise conversation to keep Brent from suspecting that anything unusual had happened further frayed her nerves.

"Inez outdid herself tonight with such an array of Mexican dishes. I should help her clean up in the kitchen." Annie said this in a bright tone as she rose from the table.

Brent rose, too, and smiled as he said to Zoe, "See how thoughtful Annie is? You might consider helping Inez now and then."

Zoe noisily sucked up the last of her lemonade through a straw. "Isn't that what you pay Inez for?"

"She's got arthritis and could use some help," Brent said.

"What about homework?" Zoe countered. "Can't do it if I'm stuck scraping dishes."

Annie quietly left the room, happy to escape the rest of the argument. Besides, it had occurred to her that though she couldn't tell Brent everything, she did have something to tell Inez.

After a few minutes of small talk, Annie glanced at Inez as they were placing dishes in the dishwasher.

"Please don't say anything to Brent, but Rafael de la Vega came to the ruin."

Inez's eyes grew wide. The dish she was holding slipped from her hands and clattered onto the lower rack of the dishwasher.

Annie grabbed the plate and set it upright. "It didn't break." She looked at Inez, whose brown complexion had suddenly grown ashen. "Are you okay?"

"You saw him?" Inez said in a hushed voice.

"Yes. He's a rather odd person. Full of mixed signals. But he said he knew you. And he asked how you were."

Apparently feeling faint, Inez sat down on a chair at the small cherrywood table near the café-curtained window. Annie hurried to her and placed a hand on her shoulder.

"What's wrong? Shall I get you some water?"

Inez shook her head. She looked up at Annie with harrowed eyes. "He asked about me?"

Annie nodded. "I told him you were fine."

Inez's brown eyes filled with tears. "I never imagined he still thinks of me," she murmured.

"When did you know him?"

"Long ago . . . " Inez blotted her eyes with the lower edge of her flowered apron.

"So . . . he must have been a child. You took care of him?"

Inez looked up, confused. "A child?"

"He looks like he's about thirty, so if you knew him long ago . . ."

Raising her gnarled hands to her face, Inez rubbed her eyes, then slowly lowered her hands. "Yes, I . . . took care of him for a time." Her tone had grown cryptic.

Annie sat on the other wooden chair at the square table. "Brent said no one had seen Rafael in many years, that he must be very old. But he's probably younger than me."

Inez did not reply and looked away as if collecting her thoughts.

"Could he be a grandson with the same name?"

Inez kept her eyes lowered. "Of course, that's it."

"And Brent doesn't know? With the court case, you'd think he'd have heard that old Rafael's ranch had been inherited by the young Rafael."

Inez nervously wrung her hands. "It would be better not

to ask questions, Annie." She swallowed. "What else did Rafael say?"

"He didn't like my being there. Told me to go away. And then the next minute he . . . well, he said I was beautiful." Annie sensed she'd better keep the kiss to herself.

As if struck by a sudden pain, Inez's eyes shut tightly. "Oh, Annie. Don't go back."

Feeling an anxious chill while observing Inez's reaction, Annie wrapped her arms around her waist. "But I have to. I asked for a sabbatical so I could explore the cliff dwelling. I told Rafael he can't prevent me, and he knows he has no legal standing."

Inez struck the tabletop with her closed fist. "He *can* stop you." Her voice was growing hoarse with emotion.

Annie remembered Rafael making the same assertion. "How?"

Inez didn't reply for a long moment while she carefully straightened her apron over her long skirt. Finally she said in a calmer, softer tone, "There are things in this world we don't understand. I will pray for you, Annie."

Though Annie wanted to ask more questions, she sensed Inez would say nothing more. She got up and finished loading the dishwasher while Inez remained at the table, silent and deep in her own thoughts.

SIX

THOUGH UNSETTLED AND disconcerted by the events of the previous day, and despite warnings from Rafael and Inez, Annie went back to the cliff dwelling. There in the peaceful stillness and the sunshine, she forgot her doubts as she worked.

By late afternoon, she had done a thorough preliminary examination of all the rooms, taken photos and copious notes. Some had too much fallen debris from their damaged roofs to properly investigate. She'd need help from students to move heavy stones and remainders of wood beams. That left the unopened, apparently still-intact kiva to explore. Inez's belief that it should not be excavated weighed on her mind. She didn't like to disrespect Inez's wishes.

Annie stood staring at the round structure, about twenty feet in diameter, rising only a foot above ground. It was covered by flat, closely fitted sandstone rocks that formed a smooth surface. If this kiva was typical, the roof slabs would be resting on wood beams held up by six to eight masonry pilasters. The pilasters would be sitting on top of a stone bench that circled the floor. Kivas always had a fire pit and a built-in air vent.

Annie stepped on top of the structure tentatively, in case the wood beams underneath had deteriorated. The roof seemed quite firm under her feet. Women may have sat on top here, grinding corn in ancient days, but the inside of the ceremonial chamber was most likely reserved for men. She rather enjoyed the notion of invading a place designated for men only.

While she liked and respected Inez, Annie couldn't let her interfere with her work. Many Anasazi kivas had been opened by archaeologists. The preserved and reinforced kivas in Mesa Verde were trampled upon by tourists every day. Annie decided she had no good reason to leave this one untouched.

She walked to the spot in the middle of the circle where a thinner slab of sandstone covered what she suspected would be the opening. From there men would have climbed down into the structure using a ladder fashioned of wood. Annie doubted any such ladder would still exist intact.

Stooping and calling up her muscle strength, she pulled the slab aside. It moved easily and cleanly, to her surprise. She'd expected it to be somewhat cemented in place by time and weathering. On her hands and knees now, she peered into the darkness below. Astonished, she saw a wood ladder set below the entrance hole, its upper end resting against a crossbeam.

Eager to see the inside of the subterranean room, Annie got up to find her flashlight. She hurried back and shone the light down the length of the ladder, which seemed to be seven or eight feet long. She could make out the fire pit in the middle of the floor below, but from her vantage point couldn't see much else. Carefully testing the ladder's strength, she stepped onto the highest rung, then slowly climbed downward.

When she reached the smooth sandstone floor, she slowly

turned her flashlight along the walls, noting the typical pilasters and stone bench. And then the beam of her light came upon some shining metal objects that looked like antique armor.

The sight she saw next made her cry out with shock. Near the armor lay the body of a man. Not an ancient skeleton. A man, dressed in jeans and a shirt. As the bright glow of her flashlight crossed his face, he winced and turned his head away.

Oh, my God, he's alive! Annie crept toward him, keeping light on his face. And then she recognized him.

"Rafael," she exclaimed. "Are you okay? Why are you here?" Seeing he was still averting his face, she pointed her flashlight away from him, set it on the ground, but did not turn it off. "What's wrong?"

He rolled his head toward her, slowly and apparently with some effort. His eyes were filled with shock and sorrow. When he caught sight of the opening at the top of the ladder, admitting daylight, horror filled his gaze.

"Close it!" he told her, his voice barely a whisper.

"But . . . why?" Seeing the agony in his countenance, Annie hurried to the ladder, climbed it and shifted the sandstone slab to cover the opening.

She came back down and sat next to him on the ground. In the dim remaining light, she saw that he was resting on a thick blanket. No pillow. He seemed more relaxed now, his eyes almost closed. In fact he seemed to be in a deep slumber from which he couldn't quite awake.

"Have you taken some drug?" she asked.

He barely shook his head, but she recognized he was saying no.

"Is there something I can do for you? Are you sick?"

Again he signaled no in the same silent way.

She sat next to him for several minutes, thinking it wasn't right to leave him there, but not knowing what to do. The metal objects caught her eye again. One piece looked like body armor that would fit over a man's chest. The other was a helmet. She knew she'd seen pictures somewhere, sometime, of helmets that looked just like this one but she was too rattled to remember.

Gazing about her, she noted that the kiva seemed to have been swept clean and was in excellent condition. The walls still had earthen plaster covering them.

She looked at Rafael again. His half-closed eyes seemed to be trying to focus on her.

"How about if I get you some water? I'll bring down my canteen." She began to rise, but he caught her hand in his, weakly.

"You want me to stay? You aren't dying, are you?" she asked with apprehension. "My cell phone doesn't get reception out here, or I'd call 911."

He squeezed her hand. "Not dying," he whispered. "Already dead."

"Don't say that. Are you delirious?" She ran her free hand over his forehead, wondering if he had a fever. His skin was cool.

He shook his head again, but his eyes had gradually opened fully and he appeared more alert. "Only a while longer," he said. "When the sun goes behind the cliff."

"What then?" she asked.

"I will rise again. Wait with me."

"Okay." Completely perplexed, she sat in silence, his hand holding hers, for several long minutes. Thank goodness her flashlight had fresh batteries. With the entrance closed, they would be in total darkness without it.

Eventually, he slowly sat up, still keeping hold of her hand. "You're better?" she asked.

"When sunset approaches, I begin to regain strength."

"Why? You have some kind of reaction to sunlight?"

His eyes filled with empathy for her, as if anticipating

her reaction. "Full rays from the sun would destroy me, Annie. I am a vampire."

Annie drew her brows together as she pulled her hand away. "A vampire! Don't be silly. Are you trying to scare me again?"

He studied her face. "No, not really."

"Vampires don't exist. Why are you saying such a thing?"

"Five hundred years ago, I would have dismissed it as folklore, too."

"Five hundred . . . Y-you're making this up! I don't understand you at all." Angry now, she reached for the flashlight and began to rise to her feet.

Rafael took hold of her wrist with a strong hand and prevented her from leaving. "Hear me out."

She tried to twist out of his grip. "Let me go!"

"I will let you go if you promise to stay and listen to what I have to tell you."

Pressing her lips together in belligerent acquiescence, Annie sat on the floor again, putting as much distance between them as the length of her arm allowed.

He let go and took the flashlight from her, setting it on the ground so that it shone away from him.

He paused a moment, eyes gravely lowered, apparently collecting his thoughts. "In 1540," he began, "I joined Coronado's army to search for the legendary Seven Cities of Gold. In May of that year, on our horses and wearing our armor, we entered what is now Arizona."

Annie glanced again at the metal armor. Instantly she realized the pointed and curved visor of the helmet was indeed just like those she'd seen in artists' depictions of Spanish conquistadors. She began to feel like the darkened, curved walls about her were starting to spin. This was all impossible. Was she having another hallucination?

He reached out and touched her cheek. "You're not going to pass out, are you? I can't call 911 either. Be strong. Everything is all right."

"Am I in some kind of nightmare?" she asked, wondering about her sanity.

"No." He playfully tugged on her earlobe. "See? I'm really here. You're really here. I'm simply telling you my story. All is well."

"But it's not. This is crazy."

He shut his eyes, seeming to call upon his patience. "Be calm. Listen. Our army moved northward over rough terrain. On the night of my thirtieth birthday, I went to sleep, camped out in the open. Before midnight, I found myself savagely attacked at the neck by a wolf. I died. My comrades buried me in the desert, leaving me my armor as a tribute, for I was well liked. This is what I assume, because later, I don't know how long, I awoke in a shallow grave. I clawed my way out of the desert sand. They had made a cross of wood for me and moved on. It was night and I was all alone. My first thought was that I had somehow survived the fierce attack and they didn't know they'd buried me alive. My savage wounds had healed."

Rafael looked at Annie with a profound gaze. "But soon I craved blood. I felt dehumanized. I didn't understand yet what had happened to me, but over time I realized I had been turned into a vampire."

Annie didn't know what to make of all this. She tried common sense. "How could a wolf do that?"

"I believe it was a manifestation," he replied. "A supernatural creature, not a real animal. You see, back in Spain, a gypsy woman had put a curse on me."

Annie rubbed her forehead and pushed back her bangs. "Your story is getting more and more unbelievable. Are you sure you aren't on drugs or something?"

"Annie, just because you don't believe in the supernatural doesn't mean it doesn't exist. Now that you have invaded my world, you must expand your mind to accept that world."

"Okay," she said, humoring him. "Why would this gypsy put a curse on you?"

Rafael shifted to sit cross-legged on the blanket, facing her. "I was born the second son of a wealthy man in Salamanca. This meant my older brother would inherit my father's land and fortune. I was expected to live a gentleman's life while penniless due to the laws of inheritance. In that era, it was considered degrading for a Spanish gentleman to work. So I stayed in my parents' house, attended university and lived a privileged but idle life. Being youthful and restless, I amused myself with women. A tempestuous young gypsy girl caught my eye. I enjoyed her boldness, and she eagerly began an affair with me. She knew I was from a wealthy family and presumed I had money. Soon she expected me to marry her."

He paused, tilted his head and seemed angry with himself. "She was completely unsuitable, of course. I should have known she'd be trouble. Even if I had wanted her as a wife, my family would have never accepted a gypsy. When I told her she and I would never wed, she threw a fit, called me foul names. The next day her mother, a formidable woman, came to me. She warned me that she had laid a very bad curse on me. If I did not marry her daughter by my thirtieth birthday, I would become one of the living dead."

Rafael lifted his shoulders. "I laughed. Had no thought such a thing could happen. The next year I left Spain for the New World to share in the spoils of conquest rumored to be had there. Perhaps even acquire an estate of my own. Many of the conquistadors were second sons, like me, with similar hopes. Only my hopes were destroyed by a curse potent enough to fulfill itself across a vast ocean. And that is how I became a vampire." He grew quiet. "Though I have managed to acquire an estate through the passing centuries, and money is not a problem, I would give it all up to be a mortal human again." He gazed at Annie, obviously waiting for her reaction.

But Annie wasn't sure how to react. His story seemed completely far-fetched, yet he told it so matter-of-factly. His demeanor seemed genuine. And there behind him lay the conquistador armor.

"Is that why you're so reclusive?" she asked, going along with his story, for the moment anyway. "No one has seen you in many years. Not even your lawyer."

"If I'm to go on and on as I am," he replied, "I've learned, as the world grows more populated and modern, that it's easier not to deal with people. They always wonder why I don't age, why I'm only seen at night."

"Then . . . why are you confiding in me?"

He leaned toward her. "Because you discovered me. Because you are kind and gentle. You challenge me and I feel alive. I have new hope that my cruel destiny might change. Perhaps God is forgiving and has sent you to ease my loneliness."

Annie's eyes widened at his notion that she might ease his loneliness. "Wait a minute. How do you know I'm so kind and gentle?"

"When you shot me, you wept and comforted me."

"When I shot you?"

He exhaled. "Annie, as a vampire, I can shape-shift into a wolf. I am the wolf you shot. The wolf who brought you the sandal." With a smile, he added, "The wolf you called a puppy dog."

Annie began to feel faint again.

"You need fresh air. It's dark enough for me now. If I stay at the back of the cave, the fading sun's rays won't reach me." Rafael rose, picked up the flashlight and helped her to her feet. He climbed the ladder and pushed aside the flat piece of sandstone, then reached back to steady her as she stepped up each rung.

Quickly he strode to the back of the cave, and Annie followed.

He turned to face her. "You'll have to leave soon, or Logan will wonder."

She nodded. "He doesn't like me to be here after dark."

Rafael's expression changed. A dark glint sharpened his gaze. "And you do what he says? I thought you were your own woman."

"I am. But I can't stop him from worrying about me."

Rafael nodded grimly. "Logan wants to marry you. Then you will have to choose," he told her with unequivocal bluntness. "Him or me."

"W-what?"

"I won't tolerate a rival. And I can't risk you confiding in him that you discovered Rafael de la Vega is one of the living dead."

"I wouldn't. Brent wouldn't believe me anyway."

"Understand, Annie, I need to protect my secret. There is only one way I can be sure of you."

She didn't like the aggressive look in his eyes. "How?"

"I must put you under my power," he told her, his voice soft now and ominous. "I'll taste your blood and then you will be bound to me. You will willingly die for me rather than reveal anything that would put me in danger."

"No!" She backed away from him in horror, but he took hold of her shoulders.

His eyes shone with emotion. "I don't want to. I've seen how my bite takes away a woman's free will."

"You've done that to others?"

"I've had relationships over the centuries. To be sure a woman would not betray me, I would put her under my power. She'd become like a slave to me. When I'd call her with my mind, she'd come to me in the night, unable to resist."

"What happened to these women?"

"They grew old. Died. One woman wanted to become like me, and I turned her, thinking I would have a companion for eternity. I drank from her, then let her drink my blood. But once she acquired a vampire's power, she left me. That was perhaps fifty years ago. I don't know if she continues to exist. I stopped caring."

Annie felt her stomach tighten into a spasm of revulsion. "And you want me to be the next in this long line of women?"

His brows turned upward at their inner corners, causing creases in his forehead. "No, Annie. If I had a choice, I would not. You are very special. With you, I feel like a human being again instead of a creature of the night who shape-shifts and craves blood. I love your spirit and your defiance, despite your fear. And I can see you do indeed fear me. You should. And yet you argue with me as if I were still that young man in Salamanca I used to be."

"Rafael, what is it you want from me?"

"I want you to be mine."

"But—"

He pulled her against him and kissed her with insistent passion. His lips moved over hers with an urgent fervor, while he slid his hand to her buttocks and pressed her against his body. She could feel his erection. Why wasn't she repulsed? Her conscious mind told her to push him away, but her body melted into his and she grew limp in his embrace.

Rafael drew back, allowing her to catch her breath. "You see how it can be between us." He brought his hand up to caress her breast under her bra and T-shirt, making her wince with pleasure. "Even without taking your blood, you desire me as if I had." He grinned. "I like this. You and me, as equals."

Annie barely knew what he was saying, for his thumb was teasing her nipple, sending hot sparks of need through her body.

He lifted both hands to her shoulders again and gave her a shake. "I am going to trust you not to betray me. Give up Logan. Be mine."

She looked at him through glazed eyes. "How can I make such a decision?" Her voice came out a whisper.

"I will give you time." He glanced over the valley. "The sun has set. I'll take you up to your truck." Turning, he pulled her arms over his shoulders and lifted her onto his back, piggyback-style. Startled, she held on tight as he swiftly ran across the ledge to the path that led up to the mesa. He raced faster up the rugged slope, with no misstep, than any normal man could.

When they reached her truck, he set her down. "Go, and say nothing to anyone at the ranch."

Annie nodded. "I won't say a thing."

He kissed her again with swift, aching passion. "Think of me until tomorrow."

As she drove away in her truck, she looked for him in the rearview mirror and could not see him. According to folklore, this was further proof that he was what he said he was.

A vampire.

An icy chill came over her, her mind seemed to go wild for a moment, and she almost lost control of the truck as she drove over bumpy terrain. She slowed down and turned onto the dirt road to the ranch. The ranch, where everything would be normal and civilized.

She should never go back to the ruin. Wouldn't that be the wise and logical thing to do?

SEVEN

ANNIE AVOIDED ANY private conversation with Inez when she walked into the Logan ranch house. She sat at the dinner table, trying to look composed and at ease, though she was neither.

"Sorry I'm late."

Brent seemed only a bit concerned. "Not as late as yesterday. You're improving."

Zoe eyed her. "You look jumpy." The girl said this in the same flat tone as she might state that grass is green.

Annie grew self-conscious and made an effort to appear languid as she ate her food.

"You look just fine to me," Brent reassured her. "Any new discoveries?"

Yes, a really unsettling one. "More potsherds," she improvised in a nonchalant manner. She decided changing the subject would be a good idea. "How was your day? Did your men get the broken fences mended that you talked about the other evening?"

"That's done. They found another dead cow, attacked by that wolf."

Annie choked on the piece of asparagus she was chewing.

As she coughed, Brent rose and pushed her water glass closer. "Need a slap on the back?"

She swallowed and shook her head. "I'm okay," she managed to say.

He sat down again. "Critter can jump any fence and avoid any trap we set."

Annie blotted her tearing eyes with her napkin. "Are other ranchers in the area losing cattle, too?"

"Met several neighboring ranchers at a charity luncheon yesterday, and they had no such complaints. Of course, my closest neighbor, de la Vega, never appears anywhere, so I don't know about him. He raises horses."

Annie blinked. "He does?"

"Yup. The Appaloosa breed. Makes good money, I imagine. They're excellent jumpers in competitive events. I run into his foreman now and then. Quiet fellow. Never says much, but when I ask how's business, he usually gives me a ready thumbs-up."

"You have horses, too," Annie said. "Do you raise them?"

"Ours are just for the men to do their cowboy stuff," Zoe said, pushing her asparagus to the edge of her plate. "You know, round up the cattle."

"We have a few colts born each year," Brent said. "But they're workhorses."

"Why don't we raise fancy breeds?" Zoe asked. "A horse from our ranch might be in the Olympics then."

Brent began to give his daughter some reasons. Annie stopped listening, her mind full of other thoughts. Rafael raised Appaloosas. How incredible. Despite his claim of being a vampire, he had a purpose, a place in the world. Yet he seemed to feel so alienated. She found herself wanting to know more about him.

Nevertheless, the logical thing to do was to avoid Rafael.

But how could she give up her work? The solution, of course, was to leave the ruin well before sundown. That's what she must do, she promised herself, and absolutely without fail. Or Rafael might overwhelm her—a thought that made her pulse race.

After dinner, Zoe balked at being sent to her room to finish her homework. Brent reminded her of the Halloween party she'd be allowed to attend if she continued her good behavior.

"Your strategy seems to be working," Annie said to Brent as they sat alone in the comfortable living room. The flat-screen TV was tuned to a popular sitcom.

He slipped his arm around her as they sat together on the tan leather sofa. "Zoe needs boundaries. I think you're a positive influence on her. She's not talking back so much."

"Me? What have I done?"

"You're a good role model. You work hard, and you don't wear a ton of makeup and put streaks in your hair. You're providing a wholesome feminine image for her."

Annie felt complimented. And yet, secretly she knew that allowing a vampire to fondle her was not the most wholesome thing. This thought only reminded her of the sensual reaction that had seared through her body when Rafael kissed and caressed her. What would he be like if—?

"All the more reason you and I should tie the knot," Brent said, interrupting her wayward thoughts.

Annie swallowed and quickly brought her mind back to the present. "You think so?"

She turned to face him. Brent pulled her close to kiss her. Already feeling semi-aroused reliving her experience of only a few hours ago with Rafael, Annie did not object. In fact, she kissed Brent back. He responded by bringing his hand up to the nape of her neck, beneath her long ponytail, and kissed her more warmly.

Brent's kiss was sweet, but not the same. It drew no torrid physical reaction inside her. She took his hand and placed it near her breast. He responded by squeezing her flesh gently, while breaking the kiss to murmur, "So you do like me."

"Wow! Guess I'm interrupting," Zoe chortled.

Brent immediately took his hands off Annie. "What about homework?"

"Done. Came down to watch TV with you." She smiled slyly. "Unless you need privacy to go at it on the couch?"

"No!" Brent said, his face coloring.

Zoe plopped down on the carpet, and Annie had to admit she was glad for the interruption.

As she turned her eyes to the TV, Annie's thoughts grew conflicted. She enjoyed being here with them, feeling she was indeed becoming part of the family. Having been on her own for so long, this comforted and pleased her. Brent was a good father, a solid citizen and a handsome man.

But Brent's embrace was nothing like Rafael's. This realization shook her to the core, bringing back the memory of her youthful dreams of soul-fulfilling passion and finding the love of her life. Dreams she'd thought she'd outgrown years ago.

EIGHT

AS SHE WORKED at the cliff dwelling the next day, Annie vowed she would keep track of the time and leave well before sunset. But she found herself glancing at the kiva hour after hour, wondering if Rafael was inside in the darkness, lying on the blanket by his armor, in a deep lethargy. *Don't look. Don't look!* she repeatedly told herself. And she didn't.

Before four p.m., about the time she should leave, she noticed the sky darkening too soon. Black clouds had rolled in and she heard a thunderclap in the distance. She began to pack up her things, hoping to climb back up to her truck before it started to rain. Desert storms could be violent and cause flash floods.

As she shoved her notebook into her backpack, the dense low clouds were illuminated by a flash of lightning. Then more thunder, closer this time. All at once it began to pour. Annie moved to the very back of the cliff cave to avoid getting wet.

She wondered how long the storm would last. Should she try to make it up to the mesa now?

Her eyes widened as she saw the cover stone of the kiva slide to one side. And then out popped the wolf. He trotted over to her, carrying something in his mouth. When he reached the rear of the cave, where she stood near her backpack, he dropped what appeared to be a roll of blue denim. He glanced at her, then looked out at the rain. Black clouds above had made everything very dim.

Moving away from her a bit, the wolf stood still, closed his eyes and suddenly became engulfed in a thick mist. For a moment she couldn't see him. And then as the mist faded, Rafael appeared. Annie was so astonished, she didn't notice at first that he was completely naked. He bent to grab the denim jeans he'd carried with him as a wolf, turned his back to her and pulled them on. She caught a glimpse of his firm, well-formed backside. He had no shirt, and she held her breath as she took in his broad shoulders, muscular arms and narrow hips.

He turned to face her. His bare, hairless chest looked like a chiseled work of art.

"How are you aboveground?" she asked. "The sun hasn't set."

"When black clouds block the sun, my strength returns. If I shape-shift, my thick wolf fur is enough protection when the sun's rays are weak. In a storm, in the darkest part of the cave, I've found I'm safe even in human form." He stepped closer and took hold of her hands. "But it is a risk. I needed to see you again, and I feared you would avoid me. This storm is a blessing, giving me a chance to have more time with you."

Annie didn't know what to say. Nature had literally rained on her plan. Now she was here alone with him again. And he was so desirable . . .

"Good," she said, taking on a masterful tone, hoping to keep control of herself and the situation. "I have some questions for you."

He tucked in his chin. "Indeed. Then get your blanket so we can be comfortable while we talk."

The old wool blanket lay folded on top of a low brick wall where she often sat to make notes or eat her bagged lunch. The wall was in the middle of the ruin, a spot that was not so dark as the very back of the cave. The reason, no doubt, that he asked her to get it.

Annie retrieved the blanket. He took it from her, partly unfolded it, and spread it on the ground. They sat down next to one another, facing the downpour outside the cave. She sat cross-legged while he stretched his long legs in front of him, one bare foot crossed over the other at the ankle.

"Brent said—"

"I don't want to hear about Logan."

"But I need to ask you. Do you kill cattle when you're the wolf?"

Rafael bowed his head. "It's the way I feed. Vampires need blood. You may have heard."

"Yes, but I don't know what's real and what's just made up on TV shows and movies. I didn't know a vampire could change into a wolf."

"I didn't either. Accidentally discovered the ability," he said in a dour tone. "At my ranch, on long nights when I'm not out howling at the moon, I've read books about vampires. The ability to change into a wolf, or a bat, is recorded as vampire behavior going back centuries in eastern Europe."

"Same as a werewolf?"

He shook his head. "Never met one, but from what I've read, a werewolf is a man who can be out in the sun and live a normal life. It's only when the moon is full that he temporarily and unwillingly changes into a wolf, or a man-wolf combination. I can change into a wolf whenever I want. And change back just as easily."

"Where do you get the books?" she asked. "You're such a recluse."

"Decades ago, I'd go to bookstores that were open at night. Now I just buy them online."

Her head went back in surprise. "You have a computer?"

"Of course. Best thing a vampire can have. I wouldn't need to leave my ranch house at all."

"How did you learn to use a computer?"

"Taught myself. There are those books for dummies."

This struck Annie as so incongruous and funny, she laughed out loud.

Rafael watched her reaction and smiled. "I love to be with you and see you happy."

She pushed her bangs out of her face, telling herself she shouldn't be so at ease with him. And then he reached in back of her and pulled off the scrunchie that held her ponytail together. Her long hair fell over her shoulders.

He ran his hand through her dark tresses. "Why do you tie your hair back? It's so beautiful."

"It would be in my way. I've had a ponytail for years." She grew irritated. "You're changing the subject."

"In my mind, you are the only subject," he said softly.

"I heard you raise Appaloosa horses," she said, purposely pushing her hair back over her shoulders.

"I do. They win prizes. People from all over the world buy them."

"And you have a ranch foreman?"

"I employ several men who run the ranch for me. And an excellent horse trainer."

She swallowed, fearful of how he would answer her next question. "And . . . do you t-take their blood so that they won't betray you?"

"There's no need."

"You said you've done that to women. You threatened to do it to me so I wouldn't tell."

Rafael drew in a breath and sighed, as though a bit bored.

"Men's minds are simple. I can control them without initiating them. I can even make them forget, if they've seen something they shouldn't."

"You mean like hypnosis?"

"That's a word mortals use, but I suppose it's similar. My mind control came after I changed into a vampire. I don't understand it, but I found I could do it. Comes in handy."

"So why do you bite women?" she asked, feeling uneasy.

He smiled and she saw his eyes taking in the features of her face.

"Women are complicated. If I try to get into their heads, I only grow confused by all the thoughts springing this way and that. I can control men, but not women. Unless I take their blood—then they are under my power, almost completely. The bond that results is convenient. But not satisfying. I feel guilty about taking away part of a woman's free will."

Annie took this in, growing mystified. She wondered exactly what his intentions were toward her.

She looked out at the sheets of rain pouring over the canyon. "Why do you keep coming back to the kiva when you have your own ranch to pass the daylight hours?"

"Two reasons. After the curse took effect, I wandered for months, looking for places to avoid the sun, often digging a temporary grave to hide myself under the earth. Eventually I found this place. Back then, no one ever came here. The kiva protected me from the sun. It became my home for hundreds of years. As settlers came, I made money playing poker—my ability to read men's minds enabled me to win. I made a claim to this land almost a century ago and eventually had the ranch built a few miles from here. This cliff dwelling was included in my claim. Somehow the old boundaries got altered or misread. But because this was my first safe haven, I cherish it."

Annie listened with interest. "What's the second reason?"

"You're here. At first I wanted to scare you off. But my

wolf self didn't frighten you. And then I fell in love with you."

"In love . . . ?" She could barely catch her breath at his words.

"I'm lonely. I'd given up hope. And then you invaded my world, my senses. Very quickly I understood that you are my true soul mate. The woman I've waited centuries for."

Annie took in deep breaths, feeling both exhilarated and frightened by his declaration. She looked up to discover him watching the rise and fall of her chest.

With painful longing in his eyes, he reached for her. She wanted to object, but didn't. Her body longed to be in his arms. He pulled her against him and kissed her fervently. She couldn't help herself—she responded in a feverish, wanton way. His hand slid under her T-shirt and he pulled it off over her head. He pushed her bra off her shoulders and down to her waist. With shaking fingers, she undid the clasp and let it fall.

"You are so beautiful," he murmured, caressing her breasts with his big, masculine hands.

She closed her eyes, tears beginning at the tenderness of his touch. And then she found herself being pressed backward onto the blanket as he gently settled himself over her. He kissed her again and she slid her arms around his back, writhing in pleasure, desire making her moist.

He drew back a bit to unfasten her jeans. After a half second of wondering if she was making a foolhardy mistake, she knew only that she wanted to experience him. Quickly she pulled off the rest of her clothes. She lay beneath him, breathing hard as she parted her thighs. He rested his weight on one arm while he unzipped his jeans, releasing his strong erection. She gasped as he entered her, the length of his member sliding smoothly into her. He began slow, long, rhythmic thrusts, causing such voluptuous sensations in her body that she lay back in a sweet delirium.

She heard the continuing rain, felt the darkness around

her as if softly shrouded in a dream fog while he took his time ravishing her. His chest rocked against her breasts as her legs crossed over his lower back, so that he penetrated her even more deeply. The sensations he evoked made her moan with anticipation.

The sky thundered again, bringing a pounding shower. Lightning suddenly struck as nature's storm coincided with the climax of ecstasy in her body. She clung to Rafael as wave after wave of electricity shattered through her. Dizzying lights flashed across her closed eyes, and she lay back spent and profoundly satisfied, breathing erratically in the damp air.

"Are you all right?" he asked, brushing her hair away from her face.

She weakly nodded yes, but she knew she would never be the same again.

In her life, she'd slept with Steve and a few others, and she'd enjoyed physical relationships. But this was different. Rafael had overpowered her with his lovemaking, and she wanted to worship him for the blissful heights he'd taken her to.

This was sex at an unimaginable, sublime level. How could she ever be satisfied with any ordinary man after knowing Rafael?

RAFAEL cradled her limp, naked body in his arms. "You're sure you're all right?" he asked with concern. He'd been thrilled at the ardent, sensual way she'd responded, bringing his own pleasure to a new plateau. But now she seemed near to fainting, and he worried he'd forgotten his vampire strength and been too forceful with her delicate mortal body. He wanted her so, he couldn't help himself.

She seemed to gather her wits and sat up, leaning against him, her head on his shoulder. "Rafael," she said in a breathy whisper, "I'm more than all right. Just need to recover."

The rain began to let up as the storm passed. His instincts told him the sun had set.

He stroked her soft hair. "My love, it's time to go, before they miss you. Get dressed. I'll take you up to your truck."

She lifted her head. "Oh, you're right. It's so dark. Where are—?"

Rafael reached to grab her jeans and T-shirt and handed them to her. As she dressed, he got up and found her back-pack.

"How can you see?" she asked, dressed now and feeling the floor of the cave for her shoes.

He set the backpack next to her and placed her shoes beneath her hands. "I call up my wolf vision, and I can see in the dark."

While she put on her shoes, he searched her pack and found her flashlight. He switched on its light and gave it to her. She picked up the pack and they walked to the edge of the ruin. Rafael then carried her swiftly up to the top of the mesa, piggyback as he had before. The rain-soaked path posed no problem for him to navigate.

After placing the pack in her truck, she stood facing him, her hair wet from the light rain still falling. Moonlight had broken through the clouds above, bringing glistening high-lights to her adoring but troubled eyes.

"I won't tell anyone," she promised him. "But what do we do, now that we've . . . ?"

"We go on making love," he said.

"But the sun sets earlier and earlier. They'll surely ask me why I stay after dark."

"Leave quietly during the night and come to my ranch. We can spend hours together."

Annie seemed to think this over. "And then sneak back to the ranch before everyone wakes up." She nodded. "That may work. But when will I sleep?"

"Go to bed early," he said.

"But they'll wonder why. Ask if I'm sick." She gazed at

him. "I won't be able to come to you every night. Maybe once a week?"

He looked down at her wet T-shirt clinging to her sweet curves. He pushed the shirt up to bare her breasts and caressed her. Immediately she closed her eyes and her face softened in sensual bliss.

"Is once a week enough?" he asked.

"No," she whispered.

Rafael smiled at her ready reply. He hadn't taken her blood, and yet she behaved as if she were indeed under his power. Maybe it meant she loved him.

He slid his arms around her back, pulled her so close that he felt her breasts warm his chest, and kissed her.

"Go," he said. "Drive away before we can't stop ourselves."

She pulled down the T-shirt to cover herself and got into the truck. Before he closed the door, he gave her directions to his ranch.

WHEN Annie walked through the back door to hurry and change for dinner, she almost bumped into Inez.

"Sorry," Annie said. "Guess I'm late again."

"I was going to look for you. It's raining and Brent asked if you'd returned." As she spoke, Inez's gaze wandered over Annie's loose hair and wet T-shirt.

Annie realized she wasn't wearing her bra. It must have gotten left at the ruin. She glanced down and could see her nipples showing through the soggy cotton shirt. Her mind raced for some explanation.

"It got kind of hot at the ruin, before the storm hit. I . . . took off some clothes. No one there to see, so why not?" she chattered.

Inez studied her with worried eyes. "And your hair? It's covering your neck. Isn't it cooler to tie it back as you usually do?"

"I was running to the truck in the downpour, and the scrunchie fell off." Annie felt guilty inventing one fib after another. She valued truthfulness and usually never lied about anything.

Inez nodded, her expression grim. "Dinner will be in twenty minutes. I'll tell Brent you've returned." Under her breath she added, "Safely, I hope."

NINE

THE NEXT DAY, Annie had second thoughts about continuing her secret affair with Rafael. Though she'd made no commitment, she felt like she was cheating on Brent, a good man who wanted to marry her. And she was having sex with a vampire. She'd never thought vampires were real, until she met Rafael. He was one of the undead—she should be repulsed. But he'd given her the most thrilling moments of her life, exquisite orgasms far beyond the bounds of what she'd thought possible. How was she to resist such a transcending experience?

Annie thought about all this as she worked at the ruin, and found she couldn't concentrate. She wasn't getting much done. In midafternoon, she finally succumbed to the temptation of opening the kiva. Taking her flashlight, she slid the thin slab of sandstone aside, climbed a few steps down the ladder and slid it shut again. Turning the beam of her flashlight downward, she could see Rafael's reclining form on the thick blanket. She went to him and knelt beside him, careful not to point the light onto his face. He looked so handsome, and so vulnerable. She set her hand on his chest, wondering how someone as powerful and overwhelming as he could lie there helplessly, hiding from the sun.

His eyes opened lethargically. His mouth formed a slight smile of recognition.

"I'll come to you tonight," she said, her heart beating with profound feelings for him.

The hint of a glow formed in his eyes.

Surprised at the depth of her own emotion, she leaned over him and kissed him near his mouth. His eyes closed in a serene expression. She got to her feet, climbed the ladder and stepped out into the sunlight, quickly sliding the rock in place to cover the opening. Feeling the sun on her face, she sat on top of the kiva and pondered what it must be like to have not seen a sunny day for hundreds of years. Tears filled her eyes, and she wept for Rafael.

PACING the blue-and-white-tiled floor in the entry hall of his Spanish-style ranch house, Rafael wondered when Annie would arrive. He'd thought she might come at midnight, and it was past two o'clock. Had she fallen sound asleep? Maybe she'd changed her mind.

Anxious, he opened the big oak door and stepped outside. Just as he did, he saw headlights in the distance. They drew closer and closer until he saw Annie's white truck at the end of his long gravel driveway.

He rushed to meet her. As she stepped down from the truck he picked her up beneath her arms and slowly twirled her around.

"I was afraid you wouldn't come."

"Brent was up late watching TV. I was afraid he'd see or hear me. I waited until he went to bed and had time to fall sound asleep."

"No one saw you?"

"I don't think so," she said as he let her down. "I parked on the far side of the house and didn't turn on my headlights until I was well away from the ranch."

"I'm so glad you're here." He gathered her into his arms and kissed her. She readily responded.

"I can only stay a couple of hours." She said this with breathless excitement. "Inez gets up very early."

Rafael enjoyed the erotic feel of her soft breasts against his chest. "Then we must not waste time." He picked her up, one arm beneath her knees, the other under her back, and carried her into his house.

He took her to the bedroom, furnished and decorated for appearances so that his home would look normal to those few visitors who came and to his ranch workers who might stop in to discuss business in the evening.

"A big bed," Annie said as he set her down on the quilted spread. She looked puzzled, gazing at the floor-to-ceiling drapery. "Do you sleep here?"

"No. My coffin is in a secret room at the back of the house. That's where I rest most days. I have other places, too, besides the kiva, so I can travel some distance when I need to. I even have a house in Phoenix."

Her beautiful face grew sad. "I wish you didn't have to live this way, without sunlight, without anyone close."

He stroked her hair, which she'd left down, falling over her shoulders. "You're here. I'm not lonely now."

Pressing her back into the pillows, he unbuttoned her blouse. She wore no bra and her nipples were already peaking with desire. She moaned softly as he kissed and caressed her body. Breathing hard, she unfastened her jeans and let him tug them off along with her panties. He unzipped his jeans, moved over her as she parted her legs, and entered her in an impatient rush. He wanted to be gentle, but he needed her so. She gasped in surprise and pleasure, slipping her arms around him, her small hands squeezing his buttocks.

He maintained his erection, slowing his thrusts so as not to overwhelm her, and soon they were wrapped in a vibrant rhythm that allowed him to feel fully alive and free while satiating his lonely desires. He loved taking his time, allowing her to reach her own heights of pleasure, until she grew restless with anticipation. Her body arched and she cried out as she reached several strong orgasms he could feel inside her body. Letting himself go, he moaned as his member throbbed in powerful, satisfying bursts.

He smiled as she lay back, looking at him in delirious joy, her arms limp around him, catching her breath.

Tears formed in her eyes. "Being with you is beyond anything."

"You are so special to me. I didn't want you to invade my world, but now I can't imagine existing without you."

He kissed her again, sweetly at first, but soon desire returned. Her eyes grew big as she felt him swell inside her.

"Again?" she whispered.

"And again and again, if you wish."

She smiled and closed her eyes in renewed pleasure as he slowly brought them back into a sumptuous erotic rhythm. With Annie as his, Rafael believed he could find happiness in his future years of endless existence. He wanted her forever. Would she be willing? Clearly she reveled in the voluptuous satisfaction his superior stamina provided her. But could he convince her to leave Logan's ranch and her normal human life to be with him, a vampire?

Rafael knew very well that he could take her blood and then manipulate her mind so that she couldn't help but choose him. But it would break his heart to do this to Annie. He loved her too much. He wanted her to choose him of her own free will, because—he hoped—she loved him.

He also knew there was another option. He could turn her into an immortal like himself. But would she stay?

As she sensually writhed in his arms and cried out with

joyous release, he could believe she would willingly be his forever.

But afterward, as he watched her drive back to Logan's ranch, he wondered if his dream would remain only that. An unfulfilled fantasy leaving him bereft for eternity.

TEN

THREE WEEKS WENT by, and Annie was feeling exhausted. She craved her hours with Rafael and had been sneaking off to see him every other night or so. Their ardent lovemaking fulfilled her as nothing else ever could, but left her physically spent. Her sleep pattern had become mixed up, and she wasn't getting enough rest. She often took naps at the ruin instead of working.

As Annie drove back to the Logan ranch as fast as she could, because dawn was breaking, she hoped Inez would still be asleep. After their hours of ecstasy in bed, Rafael had taken her for a moonlit horseback ride. He'd gone to his stables and brought out two of his beautiful, dappled Appaloosa horses, and they'd spent a splendid hour under the stars, riding over his land. She'd stayed with him much later than usual, and now had to race home.

She parked her truck at what had become her usual spot away from the house and unlocked the back door as quietly as she could. Conveniently, Brent had offered to give her a key, wanting her to feel that his house was hers, too.

As she tiptoed down the hall to her room, she glanced into the kitchen as she passed by. Standing at the sink, Inez turned and saw her.

A great sadness came over Inez's face. "Annie, Annie. I know you've been sneaking off at night. You're going to be with him, aren't you?"

Annie stepped into the kitchen, sensing she could hide nothing from Inez anymore. The wise Indian woman seemed to already know her secret. But how? She closed the kitchen door and walked up to Inez.

"You mean . . . ?"

Inez nodded. "You've become Rafael's mistress."

Annie's head went back. The word *mistress* made her relationship with him sound tawdry. She cared deeply for Rafael. "How did you know?"

"I wasn't sure at first," Inez said. She gently pushed aside the collar of Annie's shirt. "You have no marks on your neck. But you seem so tired, lacking sleep. Sneaking off in the middle of the night. There's a faraway look in your eyes. The signs are all there."

"W-why would you look for marks . . . ?" Annie paused and, in the overhead kitchen lights, she noticed that Inez had two small scars, one above the other, on the side of her throat near the carotid artery. "Oh, my God . . . ."

Inez's hand rose to her neck, apparently to hide the scars, but then she lowered her hand and pointed to them. "Yes. I was his lover, his mistress, for over thirty years."

Annie leaned against the sink, feeling weak. "He took your blood?"

"When I was young and first got a job here—my aunt used to be the Logan cook and she asked Brent's father to hire me—I'd go to the ruin on my day off. As I told you, I felt happy there, close to my mother's ancestors." Inez paused and swallowed. "But one afternoon I stayed too late. As it grew dark, the black wolf appeared. I was frightened, but he didn't hurt me. He seemed curious. You must understand that I was nineteen and quite pretty then. Before my eyes, the wolf shape-shifted into a man."

"Rafael," Annie murmured. "Did he . . . ?"

"Seduce me?" Inez nodded. "Or perhaps I let myself be seduced. I was a virgin and eager to know what sex was all about. Rafael was so handsome in a hypnotic way, that I let him lie with me, despite my religious teaching that I should save myself for marriage."

Annie felt sorry for Inez, understanding how easily Rafael could make her forget her scruples. "If you gave yourself willingly, why did he take your blood?"

"He feared I would tell someone, reveal his secret. I promised him I wouldn't, but I was very young and maybe he didn't trust me to keep quiet. While I was still in his arms, I felt his teeth sink into me. The moon was in the sky and it seemed to turn red as he drank from me. I almost passed out." A tear streamed down Inez's cheek. "Yet he was gentle and kind as he massaged my shoulders and brought me back. After that, I was under his spell."

"What was that like?" Annie stopped breathing, waiting for Inez's answer.

Inez wiped away the tear. "He entered my mind and made it impossible for me to even say his name. So I couldn't betray him. I would hear his voice in my head, in the night, and I would go on horseback to be with him." She sighed deeply. "It was an unholy adoration, but I loved him."

Annie took in a deep, harrowed breath, shocked at Inez's revelation. "And it lasted thirty years? How did it end?"

Inez wet her lips and attempted to smile. "I grew older. He did not. I worried more and more about my immortal soul."

Annie's shoulders sank. "I see."

"I even went to confession and told the priest that I was having sexual relations with a vampire." Inez tilted her head with amusement. "He told me I must be watching too many horror movies."

Annie tightly shut her eyes at the irony of Inez's story.

"The priest didn't believe me, but I knew what I was doing was a mortal sin. Rafael understood. He'd been a Catholic, too. And so he allowed me to end our relationship. He told me he would block the bond we had and no longer enter my mind." New tears sprang to Inez's eyes. "He's been true to his word. Our bond has died. All I have left are the scars on my neck. For years I wore a bandana to cover them. But my skin has grown wrinkled, and no one would notice the bite marks anymore. Except you."

Annie held open her arms and the two women embraced, as new questions entered her mind.

"Did you worry about getting pregnant?" Annie asked, wondering about herself. She wasn't on the pill and used no other protection when she was with Rafael.

"I did worry at first," Inez said. "But in all those years it never happened. Maybe one of the undead can't father a child. Or maybe I was infertile. I don't know."

Annie hesitated before asking, "Did you ever marry, Inez?"

Inez shook her head. "Who could ever be what Rafael was to me?"

Annie felt devastated, understanding perfectly. With a sense of foreboding rising inside her chest, she wondered what this meant for her.

"If I'd never met him," Inez continued, "I probably would have married someone, had children and grandchildren. A full life. Yet I can't regret my years with Rafael."

"How did you cope, after separating from him?"

"It was very difficult. My life seemed so empty. But over time, habit replaces happiness." Inez nodded with conviction as she said this. "I had my work here. Brent, and his parents before him, always treated me like family. I feel at peace with God now. I'm content."

Annie stood speechless for a long moment, tired, her mind in a whirl, feeling faint and swaying a bit on her feet.

"Go rest," Inez advised her. "It's Saturday. Stay home. Say you're fighting off a cold."

Annie nodded. "Okay."

"Give your mind and body some respite. I remember how Rafael could overtake my sanity. Poor thing, you can think of nothing but him, can you?"

"No, I can't," Annie admitted, tears welling in her eyes.

"You must decide," Inez told her. "Do you want to live in his night world? Or our world. Our world may seem ordinary, but sunshine gives us life. He lives on blood, in eternal darkness."

"He's so lonely," Annie whispered. "He needs me. He loves me."

Inez grew quiet, great sad tears filling her eyes. "I wish he could be cured of his affliction. I once brought him to an Indian shaman to see if he had a sacred ritual that might make Rafael mortal again. The shaman said he did, but warned that he might not survive the cure. I got frightened that Rafael would perish. He didn't go through with it." She looked at Annie. "Do you love him?"

Annie drew a shuddering breath. "I'm afraid I do. It's more than just the profound sex. It's the way we talk and understand each other. I'm so happy when I'm with him."

"You have that close affinity, and he hasn't taken your blood," Inez marveled, wiping her eyes. "He must love you, to place so much trust in you. He's risking himself for you."

"Oh, Inez. What should I do? I want him, but I want my life, too. And Brent wants to marry me. You're right, I can't go on like this."

"Get some sleep." Inez's voice was motherly. "I need to start breakfast."

"Thank you, Inez. You're the only person who understands."

Annie went to her room, got into bed and closed her eyes, her mind in a murky, ominous whirl of confusion. Eventually she fell asleep.

* * *

ANNIE woke up around noon. She showered and threw on some jeans and a sweater. Feeling stronger, but still weighed down by her dilemma, she left her room. No one was in the kitchen. She entered the dining room.

She found Inez serving lunch to Brent and Zoe.

Inez smiled. "I'll get you a place setting."

Brent got up to greet her. "Feeling better? Heard you might be down with a cold."

"Yes, better," Annie said. She took the chair Brent pulled out for her.

Inez set a plate and cup and saucer in front of her. As they talked about the chilly fall weather, Zoe sighed with impatience.

"So can we go shopping for my Halloween costume?" she asked, interrupting.

"Can't you just get a white sheet and go as a ghost?" Brent said.

"Are you serious? Everyone at the party will have a cool costume. Emma said she bought hers at a store in Scottsdale that has awesome stuff."

"What do you want to go as?" Annie asked, trying to participate in the conversation, though her mind was elsewhere.

"Catwoman. Or maybe Wonder Woman."

"Sounds expensive. And I suppose you'll only wear it once," Brent said. He turned to Annie. "Want to come with us? I could use some feminine help on this one."

After lunch Brent took Zoe and Annie to the costume shop in Scottsdale, an hour-and-a-half drive. Among the many clothing racks, Zoe quickly spotted a Wonder Woman suit, a gold-belted leotard with a push-up red top.

"That skimpy thing?" Brent said. "No way you're wearing that, Zoe."

"But Dad—"

"I think maybe Catwoman is more covered up," Annie told Brent.

It took Zoe only two minutes to find a Catwoman costume. Brent looked doubtfully at the shapeless length of stretchy black material, but he agreed to let Zoe try it on in the fitting room.

Annie's heart sank when Zoe came out in the skintight costume. She was all covered up, but every curve showed. And Zoe had impressive curves.

"You can't go around in that!" Brent exclaimed.

"But I look sassy and slinky. This is just what I wanted," Zoe argued from behind the cat face mask with ears.

"Way *too* slinky," Brent said. "Will there be boys at this party?"

"Well, yeah!"

"That settles it. No Catwoman for you. I'm thinking you shouldn't go at all."

Zoe looked horrified. "Dad!" she wailed.

An idea popped into Annie's head. "Zoe, how about if you went as Katniss from *The Hunger Games*?" She glanced at Brent. "Katniss wears cargo pants and a hooded jacket. Clothes Zoe could wear anytime."

"I don't want to wear ordinary old pants and a jacket," Zoe protested.

"Katniss looked pretty darn good wearing that in the movies," Annie said. "And she's a strong, resourceful female. She outwits others who want to kill her. She saves people. Guys are in love with her. Her intelligence and prowess with a bow and arrow set her apart. Wouldn't you rather look like a real girl who's skillful and smart instead of like a cartoon character?"

Zoe's mouth was open, as if to object, but no words were coming out.

Annie turned to Brent. "It would complete her costume if she had a bow."

He raised his eyebrows. "No problem. My old bow and

arrow set is up in the attic. You've seen it, Zoe. Your grand-father gave it to me when I was a teenager."

Zoe's eyes widened. "I could carry it over my shoulder."

"That would be very cool," Annie said. "Have a trendy jacket that's cinched at the waist. You'll look awesome."

Zoe squinted. "Can I get a new jacket?"

"Sure," Brent said, looking relieved. "We'll drive to the mall next."

Beaming, Zoe went up to Annie and hugged her. "Thanks!"

Taken by surprise, Annie hugged her back, feeling warmed and affirmed. Maybe she and Zoe could get along after all.

"Hey, I'm the one who's buying the jacket," Brent said, amused.

As Zoe hugged her dad, Annie looked on, feeling buoyant and pleased, like she was filling the missing part of their little family.

Her thoughts were disrupted when a boy of eleven or twelve rushed by, on his way to show his parents the costume he was trying on. He'd put on a black cape with a high collar and red satin lining.

"All I need is fangs and white face paint," the kid said with excitement. "I'll look like a real vampire!"

Annie felt sick. To this boy, a vampire was similar to a cartoon character. And Rafael, though real, was not part of the natural world. The juxtaposition of the two worlds she was caught between came into clear focus. She was enjoying what had turned into a comfortable, productive afternoon with Brent and Zoe. If she married Brent, she would be part of their family. She might be like an older sister to Zoe, if not a stepmom. She could have a home at the Logan ranch, continue her career and have a good life.

What kind of life would she have with Rafael? Under his power, Inez had been prevented from making the right decision. Annie told herself she must do what Inez had been unable to—leave Rafael before it was too late, before her life was more than half over.

As they walked out of the store, Brent slipped his arm around Annie's shoulders while Zoe went ahead of them to the parking lot.

"You were brilliant handling Zoe," Brent said. "She and I both need you in our lives. When are you going to say yes and marry me?"

Annie felt as if she were in an elevator that was going up too fast, leaving her stomach feeling weightless and her head light. Nevertheless, she'd made up her mind. She'd convinced herself it was the right decision.

"Yes. I'll marry you."

ELEVEN

THE NEXT WEEK sped by too fast. On Monday Brent took Annie to a jewelry store. She picked out a modest diamond in a simple setting. Brent seemed amused and told her she needn't be thrifty. He put the ring she'd chosen aside and asked the jeweler to size another ring he'd spotted, a two-carat diamond surrounded by small diamonds that sparkled like crazy. Annie wore it but felt self-conscious, like she was flaunting expensive tastes she didn't have.

Annie said she preferred a small wedding. Brent agreed. The less plans to be made, the sooner the wedding could take place, he said, and suggested they have the ceremony at the ranch. A friend who was a judge could marry them. This sounded good to Annie.

"You'll need to find a wedding dress," Brent said over dinner on Tuesday evening.

"There are beautiful bridal shops in town," Zoe told Annie. "Can I come along?"

Annie poked food around her plate. "If we're just having

a small wedding, can't I wear a nice suit? I was married before, you know. I shouldn't wear white anyway."

"Why not?" Zoe asked. "We were at a wedding last year where the bride wore a long white lace dress and veil. The whole works. And it was her third marriage."

"I agree with Zoe," Brent said.

"That's a first," Zoe muttered.

"Aren't we just inviting family and friends?" Annie asked. "Why spend all that money on an expensive dress?"

"I'll buy your dress. There'll be at least a hundred guests. Not a huge wedding," he assured her. "We need to set a date."

One hundred sounded huge to Annie. "January, after the holidays?"

Brent laughed. "I'm not waiting till January. How about the weekend before Thanksgiving?"

Annie stared at him. "That's not enough time. Especially if you want me in a bridal gown that has to be ordered and fitted. And a hundred invitations sent out. Flowers ordered, too, I suppose."

"Hmm." Brent seemed to ponder this. "Okay, you can wear what you want, and maybe we'll cut the guests to fifty. We can email the invitations. That'll be quick."

"Email them?" Annie said. "What's the hurry?"

Brent grinned. "I've got plans! We're going to Tahiti on our honeymoon."

"We are?" Tahiti sounded lovely, but couldn't he have consulted her?

"There's a cruise that had an opening, and I grabbed it. So we have to have the wedding before we leave at the end of November. Fits great into my schedule and we'll be home in time for Christmas."

As she slowly nodded, Annie thought this through. "So that uses up all my sabbatical. I won't be as far along in my work at the ruin as I'd planned." Though she wondered how comfortable she'd be at the ruin, knowing Rafael might be resting in the kiva. "I start teaching classes again in January."

Brent shook his head. "You won't be teaching."

Zoe glanced at her dad and quirked her mouth. "Uh-oh."

"What do you mean?" Annie asked.

"You won't need to work. I'll be supporting you."

"But I want to work. It's my career. I have plans, too."

"And make that hour-and-a-half commute to your university every day?"

"I can schedule my classes for one or two days a week."

Brent still did not seem to approve. "We'll talk about it later."

"Dad," Zoe said, her tone sounding rather adult now, "don't make the same mistake twice. We don't want Annie turning to booze."

He looked at her sharply. "What an impudent thing to say!"

"It's only the truth," Zoe said under her breath.

"Keep quiet and eat your dinner," he ordered. "You're a kid. What do you know about marriage or your mother's problems?"

"A lot," Zoe said. "I saw it all. And I'm not stupid." She lifted her chin. "Gonna send me to my room?"

"Are you going to behave?"

Her young eyes increasingly stubborn, Zoe looked across the table at Annie. "He wouldn't let Mom continue with her career. She'd been a set designer for a theater in Phoenix. She was a talented artist. After she had me—five months after their wedding—all Dad would let her do is help plan fund-raisers for Dad's charities. She hated it. Started drinking. Everything went downhill." Tears filled Zoe's eyes as she turned to face her father. "Mom confided in me. She didn't feel like she could talk to you. I know how unhappy she was. So don't repeat the same mistakes with Annie." She brushed away a tear. "I'll go to my room now. No need to holler."

Zoe left, her dinner half finished. Annie felt completely blindsided. Brent said nothing for a long while, staring at his plate.

"I did make mistakes," Brent admitted. He gazed at Annie. "If you want to continue teaching, go ahead. I'd prefer if you were gone only a few days a week. Only because I don't like you making that long drive. And"—he made a hapless grin—"I like having you around. You do have a nice little ruin right here to work on."

Annie tried to smile. She liked seeing that Brent could acknowledge his past mistakes. But would he be able to change? She was beginning to notice he had some old-fashioned ideas about marriage and women. Still, he was trying and she appreciated that.

As far as her work at the ruin, Annie found that difficult to contemplate. Even if she left well before sunset, the kiva would be a temptation. If she opened it to catch a glimpse of Rafael, would she be able to resist the memory of being with him?

Rafael. She needed to tell him she was going to marry Brent. She had to explain her decision to have a normal life. Would he understand? Or would he seize control in a different way than Brent ever could?

That thought caused a sensual lull to fall over her. Part of her secretly longed for Rafael to overpower her by taking her blood, so that she would no longer be responsible for her wayward desires. She could continue to be Rafael's lover and the burden of making a rational decision would be removed.

But she'd be cheating on Brent. It was one thing to give herself to Rafael when she'd made no commitment to Brent. Now, with an engagement ring on her finger, it simply wasn't right to see Rafael anymore. And she shouldn't *want* to be with anyone but her husband-to-be.

Would Rafael accept her decision? He'd let Inez go. Annie had only known Rafael for several weeks and they had no blood bond. Yet she felt as if she'd known him for a lifetime. Breaking off with Rafael was going to be terribly painful. Devastating. But it had to be done.

OUTSIDE in the dark, in the shrubbery beneath one of the dining room windows, Rafael in wolf form silently crouched, listening. With his highly sensitive ears, he could hear the conversation inside.

His head hung low, ears cocked back. So Annie was planning to marry Logan. No wonder he hadn't seen her for several days. If he'd taken her blood, she would never have said yes to Brent.

He raised his head and sat back on his haunches. There was time. He could still drink from her. He could turn her and make her his vampire bride. Annie couldn't possibly love Logan the way she loved him.

Forget scruples about her free will. Snatching her away was his only option now.

TWELVE

LATE THAT SAME night, Rafael sat in the front room of his ranch house, angry and brooding. All at once he saw distant headlights through the window. He glanced at the clock on the fireplace mantel. Two a.m., the time Annie usually came to him.

He rose from his chair and paced, his senses acute with anxiety. Knowing his own powers, he had the hope and confidence that Annie would indeed be his. And yet, a foreboding of tragedy gnawed at him. Why? He mustn't let any sense of human fairness get the better of him. He was a vampire, forced to live a lonely, inhuman existence. Only Annie could ease his pain. He would have what he wanted!

Rafael glanced out the window and saw Annie's truck pull up. He went out his front door to meet her as she got out of the vehicle. Her eyes carried a sad, stricken look as her gaze met his under the desert moon. He knew she'd come to say good-bye.

Tears were already in her eyes as she whispered, "Rafael . . ."

"You've decided to marry Logan."

"How did you know?"

He hated to admit he'd eavesdropped. "Word gets around. Why do you want to be with him?"

She sniffed and wiped away a tear. "It's not that I prefer him to you. But I want a normal life, and I can have that with him. I talked to Inez. Saw the . . . the marks on her neck. She told me everything."

Rafael straightened as his shoulders sank. "I see."

"I know you let her go, but she gave you decades of her life. She never married, has no family. I don't want that to happen to me."

Rafael felt guilt-stricken despite himself. Why did she have to bring up Inez?

"I have to part from you," Annie went on, "before I'm so in love with you that I can't live without you. I don't love Brent the same way, but I think I can have a good life with him. A life in the daylight, with no sneaking off in the night, into the darkness, to be with a secret lover whose very nature I'm forbidden to reveal."

Rafael stepped close and pulled her against him.

"No, don't kiss me," she begged. "We have to say good-bye."

He raised his hand to her neck, pressing his thumb into the pulse of her carotid artery, as he'd done the evening she'd met him.

"There's another way I can kiss you. I can make you mine." He lowered his head, his lips near her throat.

"No . . . " she said. But it was a weak protest.

She breathed in gasps, her body trembling in his arms. He could feel her willpower melting and it gave him joy.

"Do it," she urged, her weight sinking against him as she seemed to grow faint. "Make me yours."

Rafael pulled her closer, his sharp incisors grazing the tender skin of her delicate neck. Her artery throbbed and he could smell her blood. Desire and thirst filled his body.

He needed her. He longed to taste her blood, make her obedient to his will. Make her *his* bride. He wanted his beloved soul mate for eternity.

But his conscience made him draw back. Annie *was* his soul mate. His beloved. He'd vowed he wouldn't compromise her free will. He loved Annie too much and wanted her to be happy. Could she ever be truly happy with him? He'd cared about Inez and knew she had misgivings, yet she could not resist the blood bond he'd forced on her. How could he commit such a sin, and a sin it was, on the one woman he loved above all others? If he did, it would prove he had no soul left.

Rafael stepped back and let her go. Annie swayed on her feet, but he resisted taking hold of her shoulders to steady her. If they had to part, then he'd better not risk touching her again.

"Go," he told her. "Forget me. Live your life. Be happy."

Annie raised her hands to her face, her fingers trembling. She looked into his eyes for a long moment. "Good-bye, Rafael," she said in a soft, harrowed voice. "I love you."

She hurried into her truck and drove away.

Rafael watched her go, knowing that, for once, he'd done the right thing. But how could he go on without Annie? He sank to the ground as a tear streamed down his cheek. Why not just stay here till dawn and meet the sun?

THIRTEEN

"ARE THE FLOWERS ordered?" Brent asked Annie as she sat at the dining room table, looking over the guest list. She'd talked him out of emailing the wedding invitations, and he'd phoned friends and relatives to personally invite them.

"Flowers?" Her mind felt foggy. "Weren't you going to do that?"

"Me?" Brent seemed impatient. "What do I know about flowers? That's a woman's job."

Their wedding day was less than a week away.

"Okay, I'll do it," she said tiredly.

"Your dress is all set?"

"All set. I bought a cream-colored silk suit in Phoenix yesterday. It's in my room."

He nodded halfheartedly. "Still wish you were going to wear a wedding gown. What about your hair?"

Annie looked up. "My hair?"

"You're sticking with a ponytail?"

She made an effort to smile. "I'll wear it down."

"You should have a hair stylist come out that morning. Put some curls in it or something."

"My hair is naturally straight," she told him, annoyed. "Getting it to stay curled would require a ton of hairspray. You're not marrying a glamour girl, you know."

He shrugged. "Okay, but lots of people will be meeting you for the first time."

Mostly *his* friends. "So? Why can't I just look like me? I'm not Inger."

Brent's eyebrows drew together. "That was uncalled for. Why are you so out of sorts?"

"Why are you trying to make me over?" Annie drew in a breath, calling up her patience. "I'm sorry. Having to put together this wedding so fast is making me nervous. I don't have much experience planning events. Haven't been sleeping well."

Annie also couldn't keep from thinking about Rafael. She'd escaped the ranch house for a few hours two days ago and gone out to the ruin. She'd looked in the kiva, just wanting to see Rafael's face one last time. But the kiva was empty. Even though she'd left him for good, of her own volition, she'd felt forsaken, looking at the thick blanket where he used to lie. His conquistador armor still shone in the beam of her flashlight, making her remember the startling moment she'd discovered him resting there. How he'd weakly held her hand to make her stay. The memory made her feel lonely now. Which was silly. She was about to get married.

"You do look tired. Call a doctor for some sleeping pills," Brent said. He placed a hand on her shoulder. "You need to get yourself together for the wedding, young lady. Not to mention the honeymoon," he added with a wink.

Annie nodded in agreement, but her heart sank. This wasn't how a bride should feel. It was all she could do to keep herself from bursting into tears in front of her husband-to-be.

* * *

ANNIE awoke at four a.m. on the morning of her wedding day, after a few hours of fitful sleep. She hadn't taken any sleeping pills the night before, because they made her feel dopey and she wanted to be alert for the ceremony and socializing with guests.

She lay awake in bed, filled with doubts about whether she really wanted to be married. Her life as a single woman had been good. She shooed off those uncertain thoughts, telling herself that once the wedding was over, she'd settle into a new life here as a wife and stepmom.

But she'd have to learn to put her foot down with Brent. He'd become more and more authoritative, sometimes speaking to her in the same parental way he talked to Zoe.

Annie closed her eyes, hoping to catch a few more hours of sleep. A distant sound outside her window drew her attention. What was it? Hoofbeats, she realized. It sounded like a horse, galloping closer and closer.

Her pulse accelerating, she got out of bed and went to the window, gathering up her long, pale blue nightgown so as not to trip. She rolled up the shade. Outside, in the dim light of the back door's night lamp, she spotted a horse and rider. She could see by the dappling on the horse's rump it was an Appaloosa. As the rider swiftly alighted, he turned his face toward her.

Rafael. She knew he saw her through the glass. He rushed to the window, his eyes glistening with urgent emotion.

Annie unlocked the window and Rafael opened it fully. Cool night air from outside washed over her. It felt like freedom.

"Why are you here?" she asked breathlessly, disconcerted with happiness to see him.

"To take you away with me." He searched her eyes.

"But . . . "

"Do you love me?" he asked.

"Yes."

"Then don't marry Logan. Be with me!"

Annie swallowed. Various answers and reasons swirled in her mind. She knew she wanted a normal life. But seeing Rafael again, she knew she wanted him more.

As she hesitated, Rafael noisily pushed aside the pots of cactus plants on the windowsill and climbed in. He caught her in his arms.

"I can't exist without you," he said. "You are the only one who can make me feel whole."

As Annie leaned against him, thrilled to be so close to him once more, there was a knock at her door. Before she could answer, Inez peeked in. When Inez saw Rafael, she swung the door open, her mouth gaping in astonishment.

Rafael looked at her with surprise. "Inez," he said softly.

"You've come to claim Annie," she said in a fateful tone, hugging her robe around her.

"Yes," he said. "I love her."

"You must," Inez agreed. "You haven't taken her blood. If she goes, it's by her own choice." She looked at Annie. "What will you do?"

"I want Rafael. But it's the wrong decision, isn't it?" she asked, desperate and unsure. "I thought I wanted an ordinary life, to marry and be part of a family. What you don't have, Inez."

Rafael bowed his head. "I'm sorry," he told Inez. "What I did to you was wrong."

Inez stepped closer. "I forgave you long ago." She turned to Annie. "Follow your heart. Can you truly make a good life with Brent, when you know Rafael exists, loving and needing you?"

Inez's question put everything into perspective. Annie's muddled mind cleared.

"No." Annie laughed with relief as tears slid down her cheeks. She hugged Rafael with joy. "I want you and only you. No matter what."

Rafael's dark eyes shone with elation. He reached to take Inez's hand and squeezed it. "Thank you." He looked at Annie. "We need to go. Dawn is coming."

Annie nodded, but said, "I should leave Brent a note, so he won't think I went missing and call the police."

She hurried to her desk and tore a blank page out of her field notebook. *I'm sorry, Brent, I can't go through with the wedding. I wish you well. Good-bye,* she scribbled.

The moment she put the pencil down, Rafael swept her up into his arms and carried her out the bedroom door. Inez opened the back door of the house to let them outside.

"I'll drive your truck over and bring your things before Brent wakes up," Inez told her.

Rafael set Annie on her feet, mounted his Appaloosa, then stretched downward, extending his hand. When she took hold, he easily pulled her up to sit in front of him, encircled in his arms.

Annie looked to Inez, who was waiting by the door. "Thank you, Inez. You've been so kind. I'll miss you."

With a smile, Inez replied, "I'll visit you when I can."

Annie and Rafael thanked her again. He turned his horse and headed away from the ranch at a gallop. When the ranch house had disappeared in the distance behind them, Rafael slowed the horse's pace.

With his arms about her, bathed in starlight, Annie had no second thoughts. What her future would be, she wasn't sure. But she felt she was escaping into an adventure, with Rafael as her guide, her soul mate, her lover.

He tugged on the reins to make his horse stop. "Annie, there is a way you and I might have a normal life. An Indian shaman believes he has an ancient ritual that may cure me. Make me mortal again. I've been wary of it, afraid I might perish in the process. But if you wish, I'll take that risk so we can live our lives together as mortals. I want you to be happy, whatever it takes." He gazed into her eyes. "Would you like that?"

Annie pondered this and sighed. She slid her hand under his shirt, feeling the smooth skin over his strong collarbone, anticipating the rapturous fulfillment only he could provide.

"Maybe someday," she said with a little smile. "Not yet."

LOVE

ROMANCE
NOVELS?

For news on all your favorite romance authors, sneak peeks into the newest releases, book giveaways, and much more—

"Like" Love Always on Facebook!

 LoveAlwaysBooks